To my husband for his encouragement and unwavering enthusiasm. To my daughter for her inspiration and unbridled support. And to my son who never ceases to amaze me.

Southern Discomfort

Copyright © 2011 by Stella Benson

All rights reserved. No part of this book may be used or reproduced by any means, graphic, electronic, or mechanical, including photocopying, recording, taping or by any information storage retrieval system without the written permission of the publisher except in the case of brief quotations embodied in critical articles and reviews.

Southern Discomfort is a work of fiction. All incidents and dialogue and all characters are solely the product of the author's imagination and are not to be construed as real. Situations, incidents, and dialogues are entirely fictional and are not intended to depict actual people, events or occurrences. Any references to real people or real places are used fictitiously and any resemblance to actual events, places or persons is completely coincidental.

Bennett books may be ordered through booksellers or by contacting:

Bennett Media and Marketing
1603 Capitol Ave., Suite 310 A233
Cheyenne, WY 82001
www.thebennettmediaandmarketing.com
Phone: 1-307-202-9292

Because of the dynamic nature of the Internet, any web addresses or links contained in this book may have changed since publication and may no longer be valid. The views expressed in this work are solely those of the author and do not necessarily reflect the views of the publisher, and the publisher hereby disclaims any responsibility for them.

Any people depicted in stock imagery provided by Shutterstock are models, and such images are being used for illustrative purposes only.

Certain stock imagery © Shutterstock

ISBN: 978-1-957114-83-5 (Hardbound)
ISBN: 978-1-957114-84-2 (Paperback)
ISBN: 978-1-957114-85-9 (eBook)

Printed in the United States of America

Bennett Media rev. date: 06/28/2022

Southern Discomfort

STELLA BENSON

Quote

"… and wrong reasoning sometimes lands poor mortals in right conclusions; starting a long way off the true point, and proceeding by loops and zigzags, we now and then arrive just where we ought to be."

George Eliot
1872

STELLA BENSON

About The Book

She was beautiful, talented, cultured, refined and well educated. Nothing in her flawless upbringing had been overlooked or left to chance. As a sophisticated, young San Francisco socialite and recent graduate of the oldest and most prestigious all girls boarding school in the Maryland hunt country she was an accomplished equestrian who, at a very young age had reached distinction as well as National recognition. She was determined and dedicated to her chosen sport. And her passion to ride consumed every aspect of her life. Nothing could de-rail her plans for success until she met Nat.

Unlike anyone she had ever known; he was undisciplined and arrogant with a volatile temper and a tangled Southern accent nearly incomprehensible to her ear. Though handsome, charismatic and charming when it suited him, his charm hid a darker side of insecurity and ignorance. He was the product of a small, rural town, ripe with suspicion and steeped in a tradition of intolerance and prejudice.

Both had roots firmly established somewhere else, and each had been shaped by their own culture. The differences, so easily cast aside, would come to define each of them in their own way.

Neither one ever intended for their relationship to go so far but their passion for each other quickly overcame the differences between them until betrayal and deceit slowly seeped in to poison and possibly destroy one of them. It is said "opposites attract" but for how long, to what end and at what cost?

Can passion be controlled by reason? And, why is it, when a relationship isn't what we thought it would be or should be that we suddenly become reflective and feel the need to go back and analyze each and every day in an attempt to pinpoint where it went wrong. – if indeed, it has gone wrong. I go over and over as many conversations as I can remember; all the words we said to each other, the good as well as all those that cannot be taken back. I try to unravel the lies and speculate at the sheer size of the web that together we unknowingly spun and its sheer complexity in an attempt to understand why it exists at all and how it developed in the first place. I feel caught in a web so delicately spun; the treads of lies and the depth of deception wrapped so carefully around the truth that I can feel myself slowly suffocating. I am overwhelmed by the lies; the secrets hidden within secrets and finally I realize that I have somehow, unwittingly become a part of it all. I can't remember how it started and I have no idea where it will end. But, end it must.

Sitting here quietly on a bale of hay, feeling the prickle through my breeches, my paddock boot's ankle deep in fresh, cedar shavings. I am forced to take advantage of this opportunity to be alone, in my world, and consider all that has happened in the last few weeks. I need to restore a sense of order in my life, if I can. That is why I'm here alone in this corner; my corner. I have far too many unanswered questions whirling around in my head. I admit I am not blameless but it's also possible he's not entirely without fault. Perhaps it's immaturity on both our parts or maybe we're too selfish; too absorbed in our own lives that there is nothing left to give to each to each other.

She had been given every advantage. He had not. A San Francisco Socialite questions her relationship with a young man from the rural, deep South.

Southern Discomfort

Stella Benson

Chapter One

Why is it, when we are in love, we are incapable of thinking clearly and rationally about ourselves, the one we love, and the relationship as a whole? Are we so caught up in our own emotions and expectations that all our good sense simply slips away so slowly that we fail to notice? Is our ability to be objective gone forever or is it possible to somehow reclaim it? Is it too much to strive for, or at the very least, hope to reconcile what our hearts feel and our heads say? Can passion be controlled by reason? And, why is it, when a relationship isn't what we thought it would be or should be that we suddenly become reflective and feel a need to go back and analyze each and every day in an attempt to pinpoint where it went wrong – if indeed, it has gone wrong. I go over and over as many conversations as I can remember; all the words we said to each other, the good as well as all those that cannot be taken back. I try to unravel the lies and speculate at the sheer size of the web that together we unknowingly spun and its sheer complexity in an attempt to understand why it exists at all and how it developed in the first place. I feel caught in a web so delicately spun; the threads of lies and the depth of deception wrapped so carefully around the truth that I can feel myself slowly suffocating. I am overwhelmed by the lies; the secrets hidden within secrets and finally the realization that I have somehow, unwittingly become a part of it all. I can't remember how it started and I have no idea where it will end. But, end it must. I analyze the extent of the deceit and wonder if it is the reason why all trust seems to have mysteriously evaporated into thin air. Is every journey we take into the past full of delusions and questions that have no answers; just distorted false images? Can our perception of the past be that grossly misinterpreted by our hearts? Questions, questions and more questions. I find this entire exercise of self-examination exhausting. No sooner do I answer one question than another one presents itself for inquiry. They appear to be endless. The answers are few and far between, well beyond my grasp much less my understanding. They never seem to match up like socks or mittens and they seldom find a satisfactory mate. The questions seem destined to remain mismatched even though I try in vain to convince myself that the answers are out there somewhere. I have to continue the search for those answers, regardless of the thoughts circling around in my head in no particular order. There are always one or two left rattling around - unanswered. Those that remain continue to gnaw away at my mind, slipping from my grasp and indefinable. They are too elusive and I find their constant presence annoying. Hindsight is rarely productive unless you intend to learn from your mistakes. For me, the problem seems to be in identifying those mistakes and then deciding whether or not I care to learn the lessons they may or may not suggest. I could simply ignore them to be considered another day or possibly not at all but I am running out of time. I continue to go over the last six years of our lives together. The years play continuously; an endless loop in my head while I hopelessly struggle to make some sense of the past. The questions continue to ricochet like billiard balls in my mind, moving too fast to grasp. And the corresponding answers are nowhere in sight. I desperately want to close my eyes, if only for a minute and not have to think about thinking. I need to dissect each and every frame of that loop in an attempt to comprehend what went wrong and why. When and where did the tear in our relationship occur? Is it irreparable or can the damage be salvaged? I admit I am not blameless but it's also possible he's not entirely without fault. Perhaps its immaturity on both our parts or maybe we're both too selfish; too absorbed in our own lives that there is nothing left to give to each other. No understanding, no compassion and even less mutual desire to compromise. There is no surplus. I try to recall any fond memory of just the two of us; together, alone with no one else present and nothing comes readily to mind. Nothing memorable leaps to memory. How is that possible? If that's the case, what then am I so desperately holding onto? Certainly not the lack of sketchy, hard to pin down memories. I have to find a way to put a stop to this now, before it goes any further. This is far from a level playing field; the footing is too uneven and there are too many obstacles and unknowns. I'm so very tired of all the lies and the deceit. I can no longer, in good conscience delude myself and continue down this path.

That is why I'm here, alone in this corner; my corner. I have far too many unanswered questions whirling endlessly around in my head. So many questions and too few answers. It's as though we have both spent so much time coloring outside the lines that the original image is no longer clear to either one of us. We have lost sight of the boundaries.

Sitting quietly on a bale of hay, feeling the prickle through my breeches, my paddock boot's ankle deep in fresh cedar shavings, I am forced to take advantage of this opportunity to be alone, in my world, and carefully consider all that has happened in the last few weeks. I need to restore a sense of order to my life, if I can. It has all been too unsettling and I'm feeling overwhelmed at this point, which isn't all that unusual for me. Lately I seem to be in a constant state of confusion, which lends itself to a continual troubled state of mind. Nothing seems to make any sense any more in what until now; I believed to be my highly organized life. I can feel my life slipping out of my reach and crumbling before my eyes and I am at a loss as to how to slow its progress or stop it altogether. These heavy, four wooden walls are as familiar to me as my own room and just as comforting. I hope they hold the answers I am so desperately searching for. As I run my hand across the nearest board, I can feel its strength and not surprising, it's smooth to the touch, having survived years of contact and warm bodies brushing against it. Though beaten, battered, bruised and chewed over time, these walls have withstood countless numbers of residents, each seeking the same security and refuge that now brings me to this place. This place where I belong. My name, Jory Berg Alexander, beautifully engraved on an aging brass plague, hanging precariously on the stall door, designating it as mine.

Every horse here has their on story to tell; their own history and individual though varied destinies. A few have gone on to become recognized champions; many were reliable schooling horses, faithfully plodding along with young beginners. Others have been gratefully donated by parents whose children have either outgrown them, lost interest altogether or could no longer afford the staggering expenses associated with owning a horse. One or two have been gracefully retired from service and now have the luxury of quietly passing their remaining years and what little time they have left with as much dignity as their old age will allow. Every one of them lovingly cared for and not one of them neglected or abuse. I know every wrinkle, every bump and bruise and every twitch; every wet nose and every sideways cock of their heads.

Chapter Two

On a hot summer day, with the sun pounding down relentlessly on the roof of the barn, the heat can rise to a suffocating level. With both heavy, wooden doors wide open at each end of the massive barn, very little of a cooling breeze can ever find its way down the length of the central corridor. Flies and bothersome little black gnats accumulate on the sticky, yellow strips hanging from the beams in the rafters while pairs of ears flick continually and tails swish in vain, hoping to stir enough air for a brief few moments of relief. Even the scrawny barn cats evacuate the barn before the heat rises to hide under wilting bushes thick with dust or to sleep in the shade under the corrugated, metal water tanks, dripping with condensation. Everyone waits impatiently for the sun to finally slip behind the western hills and disappear for another day, bringing with it the cool of the evening. Dry dust and flaky chaff settles heavily on every available surface with little or no air to move it from one place to another while the ceiling fans above hum and drone rhythmically, ruffling what little air there is. The thick dust motts and chaff float aimlessly in the stagnant air making it difficult to breathe. I can feel the dust in the back of my throat and worry that it is silently accumulating in my lungs, while small piles settle in the soft round curves of the horse's nostrils and ears. The horses shift miserably from one leg to the other in their stalls; their breathing purposely slow and labored. The steam visibly rises off their flanks as they try to doze away the heat of the day, exerting as little energy as possible. Occasionally they will lift their heads to gaze down the long aisle, hoping their owners or a client will feel the heat too and fail to appear to ride or for a lesson, leaving them all in relative peace. With little or no exertion on their part, they, like the rest of us, wait for the setting sun and pray for a cooling breeze. The air is stagnant and heavy and the stench of sweating bodies and manure permeates everything and everyone as all activity winds to a standstill - all waiting for the chill of the evening and relief from the persistent heat.

It is now barely the middle of August, the worst of the summer heat is finally behind us but the horses have become spoiled; lazy with inactivity and reluctant to move any more than is necessary. Many of my younger clients, usually underfoot for the long days of summer, carelessly chase each other through the barn as though it was their own private playground. Soon they will return to school and their riding lessons will be rescheduled to the weekends only. Their mothers, finally freed from the demands of the summer holiday, will resume their own lessons where they left off at the beginning of the summer. Many of them are what we, as trainers, refer to a "posers or wannabees." Reluctantly they have succumbed to the social pressure in this community to participate in something that appears to be vaguely athletic. Riding has suddenly become fashionable – de rigueur – the thing to do – or at least give the impression that you do. They are, for the most part, terrified and deathly afraid of horses and it shows the minute they show up for their first lesson. Try as they might, they can't hide their fear or intimidation. Most of them have never in their lives spent any time anywhere near a horse. They all fear a presumed danger from both ends, as well they should. At least they have that much sense! Intuitively sensing that fear, the horses, in their boredom cannot resist the temptation to take unfair advantage of each one and send them scattering back to wherever they came from, leaving them in peace. For those who persevere, the resulting recipe for disaster makes my job, as a trainer, that much more difficult as I struggle, hopelessly, to calm the horses and reassure the nervous clients.

Most of these women, overdressed in what they perceive to be the trendiest equestrian fashion don't particularly care for the animals or this environment.

They arrive initially in Ralph Lauren and then, feeling the pressure from their peers, move on to Gucci and finally Hermes. Most of the trainers can spot them the minute they pull into the barn parking lot, revving the engines of their small, expensive foreign cars. There would appear to be a predictable progression in their choice of wardrobe and accessories before they even mount a horse. Custom made saddles materialize as do custom fitted Italian Francotucci tall dress riding boots. If they paid any attention at all, they could not fail to notice that tall dress boots are worn only in competition and seldom, if ever, on a daily basis.

Hermes scarves are tucked into silk shirts around bejeweled necks or casually tied around carefully coiffed ponytails bobbing under their black velvet riding helmets. Not surprisingly, it's all about the bragging rights, the clothes and the accessories. Not the horses. They seldom listen to my instructions. They appear to know better than I. Easily frustrated with their own lack of progress, they can't seem to understand why I won't allow them to fly over a 3 foot jump after just two or three hard fought lessons. For the most part, they prefer to slowly walk around and around the arena, secretly glancing at themselves in the large mirror mounted at one end of the ring. The idea of actually jumping over a fence is a terrifying prospect that most of them dream of, but in reality they cannot see themselves as successful with any degree of grace much less dignity. It is painfully obvious to the trainers and to some extent the horses, that these women would much rather prefer to be seen lunching at the local Pub or Grille or attending a charity event in San Francisco – anywhere other than a dirty, smelly barn on a hot day. As long as they continue to pay for their lessons and present themselves at the appointed hour, it is not for me to question their motives. It is my job as an experienced trainer to tolerate their presence. They are a frustrating and tiresome bunch and very much accustomed to getting their own way.

Many of these novices quickly arrange a private fitting for a custom made, butter soft leather saddle that requires both the rider and the horse to stand perfectly still for the hour's long, arduous measurements taken by an equally well dressed corporate executive, tip-toeing through piles of manure and puddles of urine to obtain the exact measurements of both. Sooner, rather than later and to no one's surprise, especially mine, most of them give up on their weekly lessons for a myriad of vague reasons and take an altogether different approach to the sport. Rather than put in the time, energy and patience to learn to ride for themselves, they simply convince their husbands to purchase or import sleek, young and usually very green animals of unquestionable lineage that are expensive to purchase in the first place and even more expense to maintain. Having given up on the sport themselves, they now hire me to train, exercise and show their horses for them which I am more than happy to do. As owners, they have the luxury of experiencing the pride of ownership, the satisfaction of watching their horses perform and their horses progress - as long as they are not actually required to sit on the horses back themselves. The one aspect of horse ownership they fear the most. They proudly brag about their horses accomplishments to their friends; the points earned, the ribbons won or cups awarded without ever having to appear at the barn much less break a sweat. I in turn, have access to these pedigreed animals and the opportunity to ride and train horses normally beyond my reach but not my experience. All in all, it's a mutually beneficial arrangement for everyone concerned - one that I appreciate and accept.

With winter, the unwieldy, heavy barn doors are firmly closed, each stall securely shuttered yet the cold still permeates the old, weathered siding finding its way through every crack and crevice. Thin layers of ice crystals form overnight on each stalls water trough creating a constant source of amusement to the younger horses who, unaccustomed to ice, are fascinated by it's presence. But it is a nuisance to the older, wiser horses as well as the grooms who are required to break through the ice the first thing every morning. The center concrete aisle quickly glazes over with a fine layer of glassy frost, causing both horse and rider to move carefully and with extreme caution or risk falling on the slippery surface. Every horse is blanketed in heavy wool; their legs carefully wrapped to keep their muscles warm. Now, they watch and wait anxiously for their owners or a client to appear. Rhythmically stomping the floor in anticipation, or striking out at the walls; nostrils flaring, blowing steam and eyes rolling looking anxiously at me, knowing full well that if no one appears, I will be the one to free them from their confinement. After days of inactivity their bodies cry out for exercise, regardless of the cold and yet because of the cold.

There is never an accumulation of snow on the ground to consider in Northern California. The temperature often drops below freezing causing the deep ruts, the potholes and the puddles created last fall from continual hoof traffic to freeze, forming an uneven, dangerous footing in the outdoor rings and trails. The obstacles and the hazards they present can be treacherous to navigate for even the most experienced rider. Both horse and rider have to be completely aware of exactly where each hoof may or may not land. It can be an exhaustive exercise requiring your full attention because horse's legs have been known to break over less. The farm tractor, dragging an enormous web of heavy chain behind it is incapable of grading a relatively smooth, workable surface until the Spring rains soften the ground sufficiently for it to be effective.

With the first spring rain and thaw, these same ruts quickly fill with water and overnight the rings become a quagmire of mushy slush that produces an even more dangerous surface than that of frost or ice. The sheer weight of the horse and rider combined can cause hooves to sink deeper and deeper into the mud, creating a suction effect that puts further strain on their leg muscles. Shoes can be sucked off, overall balance is upset and both horse and rider can easily topple or slip into the mud. Riders and horses alike are caked with mud; clinging, wet and pervasive, while the grooms work overtime to hose out the stalls and rinse off each and every horse several times a day. As soon as the rings dry out, the atmosphere in the barn takes on a new life and clients arrive with a renewed sense of enthusiasm. The seasonal hazards of riding are all but forgotten and the clients are free to ride unencumbered without risk. There remains, however, one unlikely peril lurking out there that can go unnoticed by many who are "up" on schooling horses or are too inexperienced to anticipate the long term danger staring them in the face.

New shoots of green grass and wild hay pop up overnight around the edges of the barn and cover the adjoining pastures on the other side of the fences. The intoxicating smell of new grass and fresh hay can be too great a temptation for a horse; overwhelming the senses to the point that many will charge through a fence of attempt to go over it in order to eat their fill and gorge themselves. Too much too soon can bring on a severe case of colic and there is no greater danger to a horse than the unexpected onset of colic. The colic will invariably lead to an expensive call to the vet who will issue a well deserved lecture about your own stupidity, your obvious inexperience or your inability to control your horse; exposing it unnecessarily to untold harm. Colic routinely requires prolonged professional care, an even longer period of convalescence, forced stall rest and absolutely no exercise as the horse recuperates – all of which could have been avoided had the rider recognized the danger.

By far, the best time to ride is the autumn. The countryside is breathtaking as the leaves change colour and crunch under hooves; the eucalyptus trees surrounding the ring give off that sickeningly sweet odor vaguely reminiscent of cat urine. The fall as we know it in Northern California pales in comparison to the vibrant burst of colours that occur in New England but one puny maple tree, with total disregard for its environment, defies the odds to survive. It's fragile, narrow trunk and five spindly limbs delicately outstretched, search for the sun under a canopy of shade provided by the redwood trees surrounding it. Using every ounce of its energy to grow in spite of the adversity it faces and burn bright red in all its glory, undaunted by its limitations. Everyone at the barn sympathized with that little tree, as we watched it grow over the years and applauded its effort and gradual success. It was not unlike most of us, stubborn and determined to obtain a measure of achievement and hopefully, recognition. That sorry, little tree was an inspiration that we all recognized for its effort.

The air is cool; apple-crisp cool, not yet cold and the sun gradually warms your back. Neither horse nor rider is too cold or too hot; the conditions are ideal. The riding rings are not frozen or sloppy with mud but in good working order and easily maintained to provide an even, hazard free footing. The grass has turned brown, no longer a temptation and the neighboring hay has been cut. The only possible obstacle now is the occasional falling pine cone. All foreseeable harm has been considered and eliminated and both horse and rider are free to get down to the business at hand, take pleasure in each others company and savor the smells and colours of fall for as long as it lasts.

The atmosphere of the barn triggers so many memories for me; the years of wins and losses, the ribbons and trophies won, the endless hours of disciplined, often excruciating exercises as well as the numerous falls and competitive disappointments. The constant repetition that will, one day, hopefully, lead to perfection. Everyone here knows who I am so my presence at this late hour will go unnoticed by the other owners and clients, coming and going. The horses are indifferent to my presence though naturally curious. The barn manager is an old friend as are the other trainers, grooms; vets and farriers, even the men from the local Feed & Seed who deliver fresh hay and shavings are indifferent to my presence.. All pass by with nothing more than a simple nod of recognition – a few with a look of concern. Even the men who arrive daily to haul away the piles of manure and waste seem to sense my need to be alone. To anyone passing, I am the picture of my usual calm. Outwardly that would appear to be the case but inside I am in a state of pandemonium, my head reeling with so many unanswered questions.

Pigeons flutter noisily in and out of the wooden ceiling rafters; their incessant cooing annoying and at the same time, comforting and familiar. Hopefully they will stop soon to roost in the eaves and beams overhead, pairing up, side by side for the night. I wonder if they mate for life? I wonder too, if I will mate for life? A solitary, old owl, who years ago took up permanent residency high above the beams of the barn, hoots his displeasure; disturbed by my presence at this late hour. Like a rooster at dawn, he will hoot continually throughout the night.

This then is my life – the one I chose, when I was not yet three years old. The rhythm of the barn, the natural ebb and flow of the seasons, the horses, the sounds and the smells, all contribute to who I am and my passion to ride. The seasons will pass; the horses will come and go as will their owners and clients but this is where I belong and this is where I will stay. My job as a trainer will keep me here for as long as I want to stay. But if not this barn, then another and another, if need be, until the a stable of my own.

Chapter Three

I glance down anxiously at my cell phone, carefully laid on the bale of hay beside me only to realize there are no recent messages. Nothing new there. I don't really know what I was expecting. There haven't been any calls or texts; and nothing has been forwarded to either my voice mail or my email account all day. The phone is fully charged, the ring tone set to its maximum, and all possible in-coming calls have been blocked except the one I am waiting for. I have checked my phone every fifteen minutes for the last several hours. Starring at it won't make it ring any sooner and I can't stare at it any longer. I wish I had the nerve to throw it across the stall, stuff it between two bales of hay or turn it off altogether. Odie hates my phone. To him it is nothing more than a noisy diversion; something that draws my attention away from him. But I can't miss this call, if and when it comes. It may very well alter the course of my life. I am tired of waiting and tired of the suspense that comes with waiting. The primary question swirling around in my head, amongst all the others, is whether or not I really want my life to change so dramatically. Why should I give up everything I have come to love? And, more importantly, what is causing me to hesitate? What exactly is holding me back?

In my heart, I am thoroughly committed, ready to follow through. My head, on the other hand is saying, "Not so fast." What assurances do I have that this is the right thing for me to do? Are there really any guarantees in a relationship or in life for that matter? Sometimes I believe I have spent so much of my life surrounded by and working with animals that I have a tendency to rely too heavily upon my own instincts, ignoring my heart as well as my head. Right now, those instincts are telling me to stop, stand still and consider every aspect and every alternative. But, if I just stood still would anything change? Or would everything remain the same?

I look across the stall to the corner opposite to where I am sitting and watch Odie patiently devouring a cube of alfalfa. A rare treat from his regular ration of oats but we are both exhausted and he more than deserves a special meal. He is visibly weary and I am mentally worn out. He has been brushed, curried and combed, his hooves carefully scraped clean and a thin fly sheet is draped over his long back. Having finished his alfalfa, and slowly coming to the realization that there doesn't appear to be another in his future, he turns to look at me for the first time since my arrival. I have to smile at his expression - his emotions so clearly apparent on his face. I have learned to watch closely and I know what to look for. There is nothing duplicitous in his look. With his ears perked, he gazes at me for a few minutes with a questioning look as if to ask, "What is it this time?" Immediately his expression shifts to acceptance and finally resignation. In his liquid, brown eyes, I am once again safely ensconced in my usual corner sharing his stall. As far as he's concerned that's normal behavior for me. He's used to my presence but I can sense his concern and curiosity.

When I was much younger, I would often fall asleep in this corner, snuggled warmly under one of his coarse, scratchy blankets, smelling of damp wool exhausted by the endless, daily chores required of any horse owner no matter how young. I was then and probably still am, and will always be, what is often referred to as "a barn rat."

Odie has always been fully aware of all four of his hooves, unlike younger horses who have not yet come to the realization that they do indeed have four feet. When they are very young, all four feet have a tendency to spread out in four different directions, usually at the same time, until they learn to collect themselves and get their feet under them in some kind of working order. Odie was always careful not to step on me; sensitive to my presence even though appeared to be just a lump in the corner. He would never hurt me, quite the opposite. For as long as we have known each other, his mission in life as he sees it, is to be my protector. He is a 1500 pound mass of moving, potential danger to anyone who dares threaten me or come too close. He does however; seem to take great pleasure in poking and prodding me relentlessly with his warm muzzle, blowing his heated breath in my face, trying to elicit a reaction and loudly nickering whenever I slept. I'm sure he thought I was hiding from him and this was a game we'd play. He was convinced that somewhere under that lump of a blanket that hid me was an apple or a bag of carrots. His role was to ferret both out. He wouldn't give up or stop gently nudging me until I was fully awake and acknowledging his persistence, hopefully with an apple to offer. If I giggled or laughed he knew he had won and I had lost yet another go-around.

He has been mine and I have been his, for over twelve years and we more or less grew up together. He knows all my secrets and I know his. As my only true confident, I trust him completely and without question. Just as he trusts me. Over the years, I have confided to him everything that was going on in my life no matter how large or small; bad grades, dumb boys, and my more often than not my obnoxious little brother. He even listened to a detailed description of my first prom dress, and still, he has never judged me. He listens patiently, nods his head in agreement or paws at the ground with impatience. Like most animals, he responds to the tone of my voice, not the actual words. It isn't what I say, the words themselves have no meaning to him, but rather how I say them. The tone and inflection of my voice are a direct indication of my emotions; whether anger, anxiety, frustration or fear – he can read them all.

I have learned over the years that he is particularly sensitive to my tears. My crying, for whatever reason, visibly upsets him. Confused by such a show of emotion, he will slowly lower his head, and place his broad brow gently against my chest and stand, quietly, not moving as he leans into me, nearly pushing me over with his weight. It's the closest thing to a hug he can manage. Just as I can anticipate his moods through his body language so too can he predict mine. If I am the least bit nervous going into the ring, so is he. If I remain calm, so will he. If I see a snake or a ground squirrel in the grass and give out a blood-curdling yell, or react in any way out of the ordinary, he'll rear up and I'll find myself in the next county before we both regain our composure. With his limited vision, he doesn't see what I see but he reacts to what I see. Like any animal, his first instinct is to flee and it usually doesn't matter where. He wants to put a safe distance between us and whatever danger I have perceived to be lurking out there. If something unknown threatens me and he can feel me react, his initial, almost immediate response is to shield me from what he interrupts as the potential danger, whatever it may be and defend us both. I learned early on that what I felt, he felt. I had to be fully in control of myself and acutely aware of our surroundings every minute I spent on his back if I expected to control him and have him respond to my direction. We were now, after years of working together, completely in-tune with each other but it has taken a great of patience and understanding on both our parts to reach this level of compatibility. It's a wonderfully tenuous bond based entirely on unquestionable trust, one that we share, unconditionally. I am proud of how far we've come together and how much we have accomplished but we still have a long road ahead of us. At least for now we are a team, finely honed and in complete harmony.

Odie is half Arabian and half Dutch Warm Blood, a dark dappled grey that will slowly, over time, become lighter and lighter as he ages, until he is nearly white. The Arabian half of his breed contributes to his energy level, high intelligence, a gentle disposition, physical endurance and an unusual capacity for patience. At 16.1 hands, he is well suited to the demands and discipline of dressage. He is not a jumper nor will he ever be. He made up his mind about jumping years ago and stubbornly refuses to jump over anything even a four inch cavaletti in the sand. It's much easier in his mind to simply go around any obstacle that presents itself. He steadfastly refuses to jump regardless of the height or the lack of it. His front legs lock in a rigid brace, his knees stiffen, his hind hooves dig in, and with eyeballs rolling and ears flat, he won't budge for all the carrots or apples in the world. Dressage however, is his forte. I am convinced he knows the required dressage test patterns far better than I do; moving gracefully, deliberately and with precision through the difficult and exacting patterns. He often appears to lose patience with me if I make a mistake; pawing and puffing, swinging his head from side to side to make sure I am aware if his displeasure and blaming me if we don't perform well. It has to be my fault, not his, not ours together; just mine. Of the two of us, I'm the fallible human who is unsure of what I'm doing. He did what he is required to do; what I asked him to do and if we don't place well in a competition, it is obviously my fault, and my misdirection that is to blame not his response. He doesn't tolerate fools! He knows exactly what he is doing. He's just trying to figure out if I know what I'm doing. To him, I can be quite puzzling at times.

The Warm Blood half contributes to his size and over-all conformation. He is well muscled and powerful with a proud, almost arrogant carriage – all genetically ingrained. His breed is well recognized for its agility and natural athleticism as well as a willingness to perform – especially in a dressage ring. The truth is, he's a show off who wallows in all the attention, knowing we are being closely observed; the focus of the judge's full attention while we are in the ring. Together, we have been unbeatable. Both he and I are now nationally ranked in the Top 10 in the United States – a standing which took us years of hard work and patience to achieve and one we will both have to struggle to maintain.

As in any sport, there will always be someone much younger than I, someone more eager, hungrier and more determined to knock me off my current pedestal; out-perform me if they can, and better my scores. It's been one battle after another; one I've had to fight every day of my life for years in order to stay on top. It's been a non-stop fight and a constant skirmish not to lose the ground we have both fought so hard to win, gain and hold. More importantly, riding is the only sport in which men and women compete equally. It has nothing what so ever to do with a rider's physical strength but rather their ability to subtly and successfully communicate their wants and needs to an animal. It's a matter of confidence and body language. With the possible exception of dog-sled racing, it is the only competitive sport that combines and yet defines the relationship of man and an animal; working together toward a common goal. It is the perfect example of the power of unconditional love and trust that can exist between both.

I'd like to believe, I am not attributing human emotions or characteristics onto an animal, for my own purposes or gratification. My ego is not such that it would tolerate that degree of disrespect. Animals function purely on instinct, unlike humans who seem to have lost that ability and feel compelled to think, rethink and analyze every feeling, thought and impulse. Animals never question. Their instincts are pure and unaltered by the thought process. There are no shades of gray. Love exists or it doesn't. There is mutual trust or there isn't. It's that simple and there is no in-between. They don't half trust or nearly love. It can be a very tenuous bond, rather like the fine thread of a spider web, easily broken or ripped from the overall structure, rendering the whole irreparable and damaged beyond repair. As in any relationship, it takes years of painstaking effort to create and establish such a bond. It cannot be accomplished overnight because animals cannot be fooled or lulled into a false sense of security. The do not recognize lies or deceit because within their realm of understanding, neither exists. They have no insecurities to pass onto another for repair or compensation. Ask a horse that as been abused, regardless of the circumstances, to walk, trot or cantor and no matter who you are or the extent of your experience, you will inevitably be met with resistance. A determined resistance that you will never overcome. Conversely, ask a horse who has been well treated and respected to do the same and the results are surprisingly gratifying. Their innate desire for approval exists for no other reason than to please. The end result is the power of trust and unconditional love. It isn't in their nature to lie or deceive. They are exactly what they are. All they require is your respect. They have no desire or thought to change who or what you are and do not expect that you, in turn, will attempt to change who they are. It is possible for the two of you to peacefully coexist for the mutual benefit of both – albeit, carefully, slowly and respectfully.

Why can't I have this kind of relationship with a man? One that starts out as a friendship and grows into a lifelong love based entirely on trust. One of mutual respect and understanding; without all the lies, deceit or games that are so subtle and so skillfully applied that they come dangerously close to abuse. Why do most men always insist upon changing me, making me into something I am not or pushing me into a mold of their own design for their own purposes? Why am I never allowed to be the person I am? Why is that never enough? Where is unconditional love without boundaries? When things start to go wrong, we invariably feel the need for self-analysis in a selfish attempt to understand why and where it went wrong in the first place, usually with disastrous results.

Directly across the barn aisle stands Sundae; glaring and huffing and puffing at me, obviously jealous that I am here spending time with Odie and not in her stall with her. Her displeasure comes in the form of kicking her stall walls, throwing her head from side to side, attacking her water trough as though it is the resident enemy and in general, doing whatever she can to sway my attention toward her and away from Odie. Her name suits her well; she looks as though some unforeseen hand has squirted Hershey's chocolate sauce randomly all over what should have been a pure white coat.

My mother and I purchased her when she was only a week old, believing we saw in her the potential to one day become an outstanding hunter/jumper. To look at her now, I have to wonder – what were we thinking at the time? Her future as a jumper seems unlikely, though I am hopeful. At first she was a puny, wobbly weanling, and then a leggy yearling that her breeder assured us had every possibility of one day becoming a first class jumper. She has the same bloodlines as Odie, the same Dame and Sire but the unusual color combination was completely unexpected. As a black and white paint, she resembles an Indian War pony rather than a reflection of her prestigious pedigree. Now, at three, she is all skinny legs and knobby knees, barely able to support her own weight. Her head is vastly out of proportion to the rest of her body, giving her a strange, almost alien appearance.

She has a reputation within the barn as a klutz, a clown; routinely stumbling over her own feet, falling to her knees, then looking around stunned and embarrassed to see if anyone has noticed or dares to laugh out loud. Her skinned knees never seem to heal no matter what I do or how often I treat them with salve or wraps. Her hocks are rubbed raw, her ears seldom move in the same direction at the same time and she is fascinated by her own tail; not at all sure that it is attached to her and if so, for what possible purpose? At this stage, she resembles an aluminum folding chaise lounge that could collapse at any minute with very little provocation. She's unstable and unsure of herself; never quite aware of where all her feet are at any given time.

The most important person in the life, success and longevity of any horse owner is, quite simply, a trusting farrier. An old, wizened little man who is your blacksmith and responsible for shoeing your horse. Without his knowledge of equine anatomy you and your horse are doomed to failure. A good farrier; an old-school blacksmith, who knows the gait as well as the body weight of your horse, his movement and overall development can make or break you. He knows, from years of experience, the physiology and the nerves that traverse a horse's leg, culminating in its hoof. A badly placed nail, pounded in with total disregard or by someone inexperienced can render a possible champion lame and in pain within a few short weeks. You can be left with nothing more than a very large, expensive lawn ornament; out of commission and competition, in pain and barely able to walk let alone compete at any level. You can very easily destroy an animal all in the name of economy or ignorance. Nothing is worth that.

Sundae like any other three year old filly is filled with the exuberance and the impatience of youth. Her world is full of wonder waiting to be explored and she will take every possible opportunity to do just that if she is left unattended. Everything in the barn is new and exciting and if we all are not very diligent and watch her every waking moment, everything will eventually find its way into her mouth. Horses don't have a gag reflex which makes it physically impossible for them to vomit. Like human toddlers, they have to be constantly monitored against the possibility of ingesting anything that could cause them to choke. It's the primary reason any decent barn is diligently kept picked up and spotless. It can happen in the blink of an eye and so unexpectedly the results, more often than not, are fatal. Empty, crinkly, potato chip bags and plastic water bottles are her favorites. She lives to kick empty soda cans down the aisle – anything that makes a lot of noise captivates her imagination – the louder, the better. Out of frustration and running out of ideas, I once gave her an old soccer ball that held her interest for about ten minutes before she casually bit through it and tossed it aside looking for the next piece of mischief. To her, as with any youngster, noise equals attention and attention is more often than not followed by carrots or apples – her ultimate objective. She'll do anything to appease her insatiable need for attention. At least she has figured out cause and effect so there is hope for her future development. There is a brain lurking around in there somewhere. She is gangly, extremely spoiled and has absolutely no idea as yet, that she is a horse. I don't know what she thinks she is but a horse is probably not on her list.

Everyday brings the possibility of a new adventure, just as it is to those of us who have to keep track of her. There are so many different smells in the barn, so much activity; garbage cans readily available to be easily kicked over, spilling over with all sorts of interesting things to explore. There are gates to be opened, fences to wiggle under and all the older horses to harass. We never know what she'll do next or what she'll find and it drives the grooms to distraction trying not only to anticipate her next exploit but to merely keep up with her. The owl and the pigeons overhead are unreachable but that doesn't stop her from trying to pursue them. The trucks seen coming and going are of particular interest because she doesn't know what they hold and if she's lucky, someone will be forgetful and casually leave a full crate of carrots unattended just within her reach. Needless to say, she has yet to settle into the rhythm and the routine of the barn and so far doesn't give much indication of trying. She's a handful and a continual challenge to me personally and to everyone and everything within her reach but I am fairly confident that one day, she'll come together. Sooner or later, she'll get all four feet firmly beneath her and hopefully learn to jump over something. She has the necessary bloodlines, the build is coming as she grows and the potential to be a stunning competitor is in there somewhere. There is promise in her; I can see it - but where? For now, one day at a time.

She is still uncomfortable with the weight of a saddle on her back, let alone a person, even one fitted out in body armor and padding, anticipating a toss. A halter buckled on her face will send her spinning in circles in an attempt to shake or scrape it off. I am in for the long haul with her but as difficult as she may be, I am looking forward to the challenge; no matter how long it takes to reach some degree of understanding. I'm hoping we can achieve the same sort of working relationship that Odie and I share. She just needs time to mature and grow beyond her adolescence and into herself. There is a very fragile line between breaking her to a saddle and breaking her spirit. Her spirit is what defines her. I'd like to think that was true of people too. If I raise my voice to scold her she immediately sinks into a full blown pout, lowers her head in shame and will reluctantly allow herself to be lead back to her stall. Once there, she will head for the far corner and stand there with her face to the wall, like a four year old child condemned to a ten minute time-out. It doesn't take long for her to forget what she did or why she is standing there, gazing at nothing but the wall and within minutes, with a coquettish toss of her head, she's out of the corner and planning her next adventure. She has already competed in several shows and won a few classes for two year olds and under; winning, I'm sure, for her striking appearance, not particularly her ground manners. The judge's love her for her mischievous spirit and there is no question that, given her overall appearance, she definitely stands out in a crowded arena. She cannot yet be defined by any stretch of the imagination as a graceful, "noble steed." For the time being, she is an overall embarrassment to her breed and an awkward, clumsy, klutz. But… she is my klutz.

Right now, sitting with Odie, I don't have the energy or the patience to acknowledge her appeals for my attention much less try to appease her. She'll settle down soon enough. I'm too tired to look for the answers to my own questions and I have a feeling I'm running out of time. Its late here and three hours later on the East Coast. I'm exhausted; my mind and my body screaming for the rest that I know won't come to me any time soon. In all likelihood, he won't call tonight. Maybe that's a good thing; it will give me more time. Or maybe it's just another skillful attempt at manipulation; another game that I'm unfamiliar with. I don't know the rules to this game anymore than I knew the rules to all the others. Why this long, drawn out suspense? Is this building up to something? I don't know and it seems I won't know until he calls with an explanation. It's late; I know I should consider leaving the barn and heading back to my apartment or just keep driving down the coast to my parent's home in Carmel-by-the-Sea. Or I could just stay here in the barn with Odie. How am I going to explain all that has recently occurred to my parents when I can't begin to explain it to myself? None of it makes any sense and I have no idea where to begin.

For the last three weeks, I've felt as though I am on a Ferris wheel with someone else at the controls. It has come to an abrupt stop for some reason with me swinging, back and forth in the gondola at the very top, alone. The view is breathtaking and the world seems to go on forever with no distinctive horizon; spread out at my feet, mine for the taking. Then that sudden, unexpected start and with a lurch that sends your stomach flying up into your heart, you feel a tingle of fear, as you begin a slow descent. As you pass the bottom you begin to feel that chug, chug, chug of the heavy mechanism as you rise up the other side to the top once again. And on and on it goes until you decide its time to get off. A little less than three weeks ago I was on top of my world, or so I thought. Then a week ago, he called to ask, "fur some time ta think" Could we mutually agree not to communicate with each other in any form for a full week and consider "whar we was aheadin?"

It occurred to me briefly that six years into this relationship or any relationship for that matter, that that was not a healthy request. Any fears or insecurities I may or may not be harboring suddenly came bubbling to the surface. Initially I shared his opinion, and readily agreed; believing I too could benefit and use the time to look carefully at our relationship. As I listened to the tone of his voice, it didn't appear I had much choice in the matter. Under any other circumstances and coming from anyone other than him, that request alone would have and should have raised an alarm in my mind. If it did, I failed to notice or recognize it for what it really was. So much has happened so fast. I was overwhelmed and there was so much to consider if we continue as we have been for so many years. I was under the impression that where we were "headed" had already been mutually agreed upon. I may not have a ring on my finger but I do have a promise. Or do I? It was that one question, more so than any others that had set my head spinning with more questions than answers. Is a promise made in bed still a promise or does it require the light of day to give it validity? That and perhaps I would do well to consider the source. How many other promises, over the years has he broken? Far too many too count. Was this particular promise really any different from all the others?

This week seemed to have no end and it was only now, sitting here in Odie's stall that it suddenly occurred to me that I haven't done the thinking I promised myself I would do. He'd given me time to consider but I hadn't used it. I'd actually done everything I could do to avoid it, until now. I have that familiar, aching feeling in the pit of my stomach as I slowly descend the down slide, waiting all too eagerly to be pulled back up to the top. That was our last conversation, ten days ago and three days longer than agreed. But still I wait. I can't help but wonder at myself. How did I get to this point in my life where I wait for a man, any man? When did I become one of those women who waits? Men usually wait for me. Yet, here I sit on my bale of hay – waiting, quietly lost in the chaos of my own mind.

Chapter Four

I am tall, reasonably thin and athletic and, on the upside, my bottom has been pounded flat by years of continual posting. The result of countless hours and just as many years bumping up and down against a flat, hard saddle. I feel as though I was born on a horse and have spent very waking moment on one's back. There was a gentler time, not so long ago, when a young woman was judged not only by the consistency of her embroidery stitches but by the turn of her ankle and the scars on her inner calves from a saddle.

To those doing the judging, those scars were a clear indication that the lady under scrutiny by any prospective beau or his family, could properly sit a horse and had spent an inordinate amount of time in the saddle. Anyone who has ever ridden knows there is a considerably more to riding than just maintaining your balance and holding on for dear life while the horse appears to do all the work. It is physically challenging; requiring every muscle in your body and mentally demanding; requiring all of your concentration and unwavering focus. There has to be an unspoken, subtle communication between horse and rider. I have already suffered a broken arm; several cracked ribs, a few fractured teeth and nearly a broken jaw when a neighbor's horse that I was hired to exercise while they were in Europe, reared up unexpectedly and kicked me squarely in the face. As a result, I have a deep, dark pink, four inch scar under my chin that no amount of make-up can disguise - an example of what can happen when you get lazy or slightly overconfident about your own ability. All things considered I am extremely lucky that that is the full extent of my injuries so far.

I was born a strawberry blond with a mass of fine, pale, unruly, cork-screw curls that couldn't be tamed much less contained by the strongest elastic or scrunchie. When I turned thirteen, I decided it was time for a change so I cautiously approached my mother one afternoon as she sat at her desk.

With one hand on my hip and one foot anxiously tapping the floor I boldly announced. "I want to get a tattoo."

Without even looking up from her desk, she calmly said, "What exactly did you have in mind? Do you intend to go with a lot of colour or will you limit yourself to black and white? Don't bother to give it much consideration because it doesn't really matter. It is not going to happen!" She replied.

"I thought just the black outline of a horses head in the middle of my back. Something simple yet elegant. Not too large. Everybody I know has a tattoo. But no one will have one like mine" I replied in an excited tone.

"Well, you thought wrong! Tattoos are permanent! They never go-away. Imagine how elegant that would be peeking out of a strapless wedding gown some day. Or do you see yourself arguing a case in a courtroom with an exposed tattoo? That alone blows the hell out of your credibility and takes my breath away just thinking about it!"

This conversation was not going the way I had hoped. Maybe this wasn't the right time to approach her. With my mother, timing was everything. I didn't see this as open rebellion on my part or teenage angst; considering the world of teenage angst had not yet been recognized much less diagnosed. Determined to press on and gain control of this conversation, I said.

"Then I want to pierce one eyebrow." I insisted.

"No." she replied calmly.

"Then I want to pierce my tongue."

"That will never happen as long as I draw breath." She replied.

"O.K. then I'm going to have my navel pierced. And if I can't do that maybe I'll just run away!"

"You ran away once before when you were nine – remember? You got as far as the end of the driveway and then wondered back home when it got dark! If you're going to run away over this, at least have a more feasible plan in mind before you go and by all means, please leave me a forwarding address where you can be reached in case of an emergency. If you want to get a tattoo you are free to do so the day after you turn 21 – not before. I don't approve of tattoos and I have no intention of paying for one or jeopardizing your health because of one. There is a reason why they are called 'tramp stamps!' Jory, what is wrong with you today? Do you have a burr under your saddle? Why this sudden need for a change? You're beautiful just as you are. If you were meant to be punched full of holes and inked up you would have been born that way. Not to mention the inherent risk of infection and possibly hepatitis – neither of which I care to deal with right now nor do you. You can discuss this with me or with your father – your prerogative. But I can tell you, your father will have serious concerns about the sterilization process involved and will, undoubtedly agree with me on this. The answer is still a resounding, no! To all of the above." she said.

"I want to change something about me because I'm boring – I'm a boring, normal person. I replied. There's absolutely nothing unusual or interesting about me."

"You're anything but boring; and you're very interesting just as you are. For goodness sake – you're an accomplished equestrian, one of the youngest nationally ranked in this country. Isn't that cool enough for you? You're competing against most of the trainers in this area including your own. Not too many teenagers can say that! Is there anything else on your mind because your current body language is saying otherwise? Come in and sit down and tell me what's going on."

I knew I was loosing this go-around, reluctantly, I plopped down in a soft, pastel print chair, swinging my legs impatiently across the arm and said, "Well, then I want to dye my hair."

"Why on earth do you want to do that? What color did you have in mind?" She asked.

"Black!" I said.

She just stared at me for a long minute and then calmly said, "Are you out of your mind? Where do you get these ideas? Has your subscription to Horse and Hound expired.?"

Ignoring her question, I replied, "I want the blackest black I can find. Coal black, the color of the tar they spread on the highway."

"I'm afraid to ask but, why black." She said.

"I think it would go well with my eyes." I replied somewhat nonchalantly.

"You're just bored. Why aren't you down at the barn today, riding? Go read a book. Goodness knows we have a house full of them. But just for the sake of argument, suppose, just suppose, I help you dye our hair and you don't like the end result, what then? Have you thought about that?"

"I will like the results, I promise, you'll see. It will really make me stand out. It'll be great. I've given this a lot of thought" I said, suddenly excited.

"Oh – it will definitely make you stand out. We can do this only if you agree to one condition," She replied.

I thought, here it comes; there's always a condition attached or a promise involved somewhere when dealing with my mother. It was always a give and take; a back and forth that I, more often than not, lost. She could and usually did outmaneuver me at every turn.

Resigned to the inevitable condition, I said, "What's the condition? She had finally agreed, reluctantly to something. It wasn't my first choice but it was a start. It had been a struggle to come this far but dealing with my mother was never easy – timing was everything.

"The condition is, that we use a temporary rinse that is guaranteed to wash out if you are unhappy with it the results. Something that will eventually return your hair to your natural color. Think about it and make absolutely sure this is what you want to do? If you still want to go through with it, we'll go to the pharmacy tomorrow and see what we can find. Agreed?" She said. Convinced that between now and tomorrow, I would reconsider.

The next morning, true to her word, we drove to our local pharmacy where I quickly picked out the blackest black hair rinse I could find while she read every label, box and insert she could get her hands on. After what seemed like hours of research on her part, that included a lengthy conversation with the pharmacist, we decided on a deep black that was 100% guaranteed to wash out after five shampoos or your money back. It was perfect!

"Are you sure you want to go through with this? I just can't imagine you with hair this color. You're far too fair for black hair especially one this black. I don't understand why you are so determined to do this. What's wrong with your natural color?" She said.

"I want a change. I want something different and striking! Just wait. You'll see. I'll be a knock-out." I replied.

"Oh, you'll be a knock-out, all right. No question about that. Your father won't recognize you and you will probably scare the wits out of Odie the next time you show up at the barn! He won't recognize you either!" She said.

When we got home, she gathered as many old, worn, tattered towels she could find and cut a hole in a white garbage bag to pull over my head. My father happened to come around the corner at just that moment and asked, "What's going on? What are you two up to now?"

"We're about to dye her hair black." My mother answered.

"Why? He asked. What's wrong with her natural colour? "And why black?"

"Because it appears to be the least offensive option we have." My mother replied.

I looked at my father and said, "Daddy if you can't be supportive, then just go away until we're finished."

"Are you kidding? I wouldn't miss this for the world." He said.

Armed with the kitchen timer, and my head in the sink, we followed the instructions to the letter. Finally, after 20 minutes and several rinses, we were finished and I ran upstairs to see the results for myself, anxiously anticipating my immediate transformation to knock-out status. I let out a scream that I'm sure every neighbor within a 5 mile radius heard loud and clear. My reflection was terrifying! I looked like death warmed over, my eyes radiating out of my face like two piss holes in the snow. I started to cry, hysterically, while running back downstairs to the kitchen.

"Mother, change it back, change it RIGHT NOW!" I pleaded.

"Calm down! I have to admit it is surprising and a little bit shocking. You're just not used to seeing yourself look like that. It's actually not all that bad. It definitely makes your eyes appear to be bluer. According to the instructions on the box, it should gradually wash out and you'll be back to normal after a few shampoos." She said.

"Daddy! I screamed, do something! Call the 1-800 HELP customer service number on the box and ask them how to get it out."

"I've been on hold for the last 10 minutes." He said quietly. My father was an only child, as a result, many of the things women did and the reasons they did them were a complete mystery to him. Having not had a sister growing up, he was uncomfortable and often confused by female hysterics, often questioning their reasoning.

"I don't think there is much we can do or undo at this point. We talked about this and this is what you wanted. You were so sure. Now that you have what you wanted, you have to live with it at least for the time being, or until it rinses out. There is a lesson here someplace. This is what I believe is commonly referred to as a teaching moment. You're just going to have to get used to it until it fades or rinses out. Besides, Halloween is only a few weeks away – it's perfect!" My mother added.

My father gave my mother one of those knowing looks and said, "Well, that went well! What are the chances of you getting your money back for this? So much for their money back guarantee!"

On Monday afternoon, my school called to inform my parents that they had a policy regarding "unnatural hair colour" and I was definitely a blatant breach of that policy. Would my parents please restore my hair to the blond I was the previous Friday, as soon as possible. Halloween was only a week or so away, and they had visions of every student in school doing something similar to their hair, causing a large scale situation they hoped to avoid – initiated of course, by me. My mother went to great lengths to explain the circumstances but they continued to call every Monday for nearly a month until my mother finally informed them the only viable alternative would be to shave my head. Fearing would cause a widespread, if not virulent fashion trend among the middle school populace, they finally ceased to harass her with calls and I continued to scrub my head frantically at least twice a day. The last thing the school wanted was an open rebellion or a student body comprised of little shaved heads or a myriad of unnatural colours! By this time, I had more than exceeded my five shampoos and I was nowhere near my original color! To make my humiliation complete, my little brother insisted on calling me, "Morticia."

Thirteen years and several hundred shampoos later, my hair is a thick, dark brown brunette; a thick mass of curls that still refuses to be restrained. Over the years, a few well placed highlights and lowlights and regular professional salon cuts seem to have softened the black color and I have grown used to it. What choice did I have? Unfortunately, I will never again be a blond. Looking back,

I learned the hard way that we all make mistakes and misguided decisions no matter how well thought out. It was indeed a teaching moment. Big or small something as simple as changing your hair colour carries repercussions. Many decisions can be reversed, others, sometimes corrected or undone but in the end we have to live with the consequences. This decision was mine and mine alone.

My parents, of course, knew exactly what was going to happen as well as my reaction but chose to take advantage of the opportunity to teach me the importance of my decisions. I can't blame them; they had done and said everything possible to discourage me. I just didn't want to listen.

My eyes are wide-set and an alarming, electric blue, now even more so in contrast to my dark hair and they have a tendency to change color depending upon the light. According to my mother, they are the exact color of a hockey rink once the Zamboni has finished sweeping back and forth, cleaning the ice. Complete strangers have often told me the combination of very dark brunette hair; a fair complexion and ice blue eyes can initially be alarming and often intimidating. Apparently, I take some getting used to. My once desperate desire to stand out and be unusual seems to have matured into an unsolicited air of mystery.

Chapter Five

My mother was born and raised in Minnesota. The home of Charles Lindbergh, F. Scott Fitzgerald, Paul Bunyan and Frostbite Falls. After college in New York City and living and studying in Paris for over a year, she returned to the States and was immediately hired as a flight attendant for an international carrier. She traveled all over the world and lived for months at a time in several different countries on temporary assignment. She finally settled in California shortly after meeting my father while he was in medical school in Washington DC. As she so often says, "She was Northern born and raised" with typical Midwestern sensibilities and deeply rooted in Scandinavian tradition and heritage.

When my brother and I were small, and bored, and looking for some mischief, usually on a rainy day, we learned very quickly that if we could sufficiently provoke my mother, she would very often forget herself and launch into a non-stop tirade of loud, unintelligible Swedish. Arms flaying, her voice rising to a volume designed to be deliberately offensive, she'd let fly with what we could only assume was a stream of obscenities directed at both of us. At first we were stunned, not at all prepared for what was to come, and though we never understood a word she said we thought watching her was far more fun than watching television. Further enraged at our apparent lack of understanding, she would crank it up. We would fall down, roaring with laughter while my father did his best to discourage us, though he usually laughed along with us. It didn't take her long to realize we had provoked her on purpose, just to watch her performance. Frustrated, she'd give up, and laugh with us, forgetting what we had done to set her off in the first place.

Growing up, she had a large, extended family of aunts, uncles and cousins, who had, for the most part, moved away from Minnesota over the years and spread out to other parts of the country. They would periodically appear for a visit during the hot, humid, mosquito ridden Midwestern summers, purposely avoiding the bone-chilling winters. They were all anxious to spend a week or two of their stay on or near a lake. Coming from other parts of the country, the time spent on a lake was a novelty and a life experience not to be missed.

My father, an only child, grew up in San Francisco with a large widely dispersed family too. Like my mother, he seldom saw any of his relatives until they felt the need to experience San Francisco. When they were newly married and discussed the subject of children and family, my mother dreamed of a large family in a big, old, restored farmhouse somewhere in the country on several acres with no less than four boys who would run wild and do all the things that boys usually do. She envisioned a huge, rambling home that had been added onto over the years by successive generations without any definite plan or obvious thought to design. A house with high ceilings and large scale rooms filled with natural light from numerous, crooked windows, painted over so many times over the years that they may or may not open.

A home reflecting generations of character and history. Wide, dark, well worn, plank floors and stairs that would creak; loosened from years of trampling feet pounding up and down. Old, natural stone fireplaces in every room and surrounded by a wrap around porch and large baskets dripping with flowers hanging from every cross beam. Most importantly, a warm, rustic, farm kitchen that would be the heart of the family and the center of activity. She longed for screened sleeping porches off of each bedroom and a dining room that could seat at least twelve people. A house full of antique furniture, flea market finds and meaningful treasures brought home from various trips that held special meaning. Her grandmother's handmade quilts casually, yet deliberately lining window seats overflowing with plump print pillows and books stacked and tumbling everywhere.

A house of slamming doors; bursting with the noise and the presence of rambunctious boys constantly in motion and getting into all sorts of innocent trouble, all squabbling over who would be first to lick the spoon. She envisioned piles of dirty, smelly sports equipment stacked in every corner; hockey sticks to climb over, tennis rackets gathered in a basket and baseball bats blocking every doorway. Loose soccer balls, tennis balls, footballs and baseballs rolling around, uncontained without any direction or purpose. Everything in a continual state of disarray with several large dogs adding to the confusion and perhaps a cat or two just to keep life interesting.

A house of very carefully calculated untidiness in the midst of order; exuding a sense of highly organized chaos. And, most importantly, a sprawling garden; fenced at least eight feet high to discourage the deer and the base carefully lined with chicken wire so that the persistent moles, voles and gophers –" the enemy below" - didn't attack from the bottom up, destroying the roots of her struggling vegetables and roses.

She proudly imagined herself at the helm of all this confusion and she alone would be in control; the matriarch of a mini dynasty of men. Boys are allowed to get into trouble, play silly pranks and let off steam; that behavior was expected, accepted and more or less condoned. That's what they were supposed to do – that's how they learned. Girl's not so much! Raising a girl would require her to take a different approach altogether, the responsibility seemed greater; her confidence in her own ability as a parent stretched to the limit. Girls presented a challenge she wasn't sure she was prepared to face and required a set of skills she wasn't at all sure she possessed. She wasn't sure she could be as successful raising a girl in today's world. Boys were simply easier in the long run.

Boys would be less demanding, requiring supervision, of course, but as long as they were loved, kept reasonably clean and well fed that's all they required. Their lives were effortless and their futures, for the most part, secure as long as they were prepared. She would teach them right from wrong, educate them to the best of her ability, give them every opportunity to find their way and then simply let them loose on the rest of the world. She would see to it they would learn to ski, skate and swim.

My father would be responsible for teaching them everything boys need to know; the basics, as well as cars, wine, cigars, fly fishing and hunting. They would know how to properly break down and clean a shot gun and good bourbon from bad. All the things young men should know that would be crucial to their development and outlook; both physically and mentally in order to become functioning and contributing members of our society. She, on the other hand, would see to it that they all had impeccable manners; recognized a fish fork when they saw it, knew enough to order salmon not sall-mon and that potatoes were never to be referred to as ' taters or tomatoes as 'maters. Proper etiquette was an indication of the man and in her mind, and there was never an excuse for bad manners. Above all, she would see to it that they respected women as equals; looked directly at them when they spoke, gave them their full attention and actually listened to what they said. She recognized that for now, it is a man's world. They made the rules, at least for the time being. She didn't like it but there it was. All that was required of her was to make her boys conscious of their roles, somewhat tempered by awareness and prepare them to go out there, into their world, with a little bit more dignity and sensitivity than most, to join the brotherhood of men. Boys didn't present a challenge in her mind; their lives were clearly defined and more or less guaranteed as long as they played by the rules – their rules. She had a plan.

Instead, she got me.

That is not to say I was a major disappointment by any means – just an unexpected surprise. I was, by all accounts a beautiful, normal, healthy baby girl with the requisite number of fingers and toes, big blue eyes and those strawberry blond curls. I was just not part of her original design. I was a pleasant, unplanned for and unanticipated surprise. She would have to drop back, rather quickly, change her position on child rearing and proceed in an entirely different direction- taking me with her. But like everything else she did, she threw herself wholeheartedly into it. As far as she was concerned, if she was going to be as successful raising a girl as she had hoped to be with our boys, it was going to be all or nothing. Everything she had planned for the boys would serve me just as well. And why not? Never one to shy away from a challenge, regardless of the enormity, she rose to the occasion and made a conscious decision, then and there.

I was not going to be a shrinking violet; some delicate, will-of-the wisp little thing, sitting ramrod straight on a piano bench dressed in white lace and satin ribbons, quietly whiling away the afternoon entertaining a small table of stuffed animals with make believe tea parties. I would never be afraid or show fear. Neither would I cower in dark corners, reluctant to voice my opinion or terrified by my own shadow. Hell no! It may be a man's world but she would personally see to it that I was strong and independent; and more than able to hold my own amongst them, compete with them on their level and quite possibly change a few of their rules along the way. By the time she finished with me, I would be able to stand tall with my head held high, confident in my own ability to contend with whatever they threw at me no matter how uneven the playing field going in. She had revised her plan, redefined her goal and had only eighteen years, in her mind to accomplish that goal.

With renewed enthusiasm and dedicated to the task at hand, she launched into her newly revised plan. As a child, of course, I was unaware of her long term intentions and completely underestimated the full extent of her determination. As far as she was concerned, I was not going to get through this life on either my looks or on my back. I would think for myself, be dependent upon only myself and above all, I would never allow myself to be defined by a man - any man.

Today, my mother is the first to admit she may have been overly enthusiastic with her initial plan and, in doing so; went too far. According to her, I am too strong, too independent, too opinionated and far too outspoken. All of which have a tendency to send any young man who shows the slightest interest in me running in the opposite direction. According to her, I need to temper myself and show just a little more self-restraint as well as a desire to compromise. She may be right but I see no reason to change who I am just to attract a man. I want the opportunity to judge for myself who I am and where I've been so far in this life and what I've managed to accomplish entirely on my own. In all good conscience, I answer only to myself and for the time being that suits me just fine. Take me as I am or not at all. But I have yet to meet a man who will accept me as I am. They all insist on making changes. Do they ever stop to consider even for a moment, that they may need to change or at the very least, meet me half-way? Is there no such thing as compromise? Why must I be the one to change?

Chapter Six

I come from a very long line of determined, opinionated, and strong women who were never satisfied with the status quo but rather committed to it's change.

Both of my great grandmothers held college degrees, graduating in 1909 and 1911 respectively. An unheard - of accomplishment at the time when educating women was seen as suspect and completely unnecessary. Under what I would consider deplorable and extremely trying conditions, my paternal great grandmother somehow managed to raise nine children on the plains of North Dakota, three miles from the Canadian border while taking advantage of the Homestead Act of 1861. The Federal Government had granted my great grandparents 640 acres of flat, scrubby, tundra, on the condition that they agree to physically occupy the land for a minimum of seven years, dig a well and install a windmill.

My Great- Grand mother had her first baby when she was twenty years old and watched, hopelessly as that child died tragically after a polio epidemic swept across the Mid-West, crippling or killing thousands of children. She and he husband alone had brought her into this world and now, alone they would bury her. They slowly chipped away at the frozen earth a pick axe and a shovel, borrowed from a neighbor, to carve out a semblance of a grave. There is no marble headstone or marker to give notice of her passing. She had simply ceased to exist. Years later, the town of Ambrose, North Dakota burned to the ground, forever obliterating all record of marriages, deaths or births. It too had ceased to exist. Not long after the fire, my great grandmother left her husband behind, bundled herself and eight remaining children into the back of a horse drawn wagon and drove away from what was left of Ambrose to Fargo, North Dakota.

There they boarded the newly connected Great Northern Railroad to return to St. Paul and her family. She would never forgive herself for leaving her first born child behind, alone and buried in the frozen tundra that is North Dakota. Her last child, her ninth, died of pneumonia when he was just five years old after falling through the frozen ice of a nearby lake.

She and her husband, delivered all nine of their children without the benefit of a nearby hospital, a doctor or even a local midwife. They were pioneer stock; strong , determined and capable. She alone, held onto those windswept acres with only her children, a goat, and a single horse for five days each a week while her husband rode 60 miles into the nearest town to practice law on the frontier, returning every weekend. More than a hundred years later, as I listen to these family stories and I can't help but wonder at the strength she showed or her perseverance in the face of such adversity. Her life had been so full of hardship and deprivation. The remaining seven of their children all attended college and every one of them became more than successful in their chosen fields. Education in my family was never debatable. It was understood and never questioned, from a very young age, that my brother and I would go onto college – not attending, for whatever reason was not an option. My parents agreed to pay for everything as long as we stayed in school and ultimately finished. It was more than a necessity, it was crucial, especially for the women in my family.

Both of my Great grandmothers were not women who lived in beautiful homes on tree lined boulevards in the city; overseeing large household staffs and entertaining lavishly on a regular basis, quietly holding card parties or afternoon soirees. Both women were out-spoken, well respected social activists and later, defiant Suffragettes who actively campaigned for Women's Rights. They both enjoyed material comfort and social standing but above all, they shared a conscience that would compel them tirelessly toward reform, the fight for injustice and discrimination, primarily against women. They followed in the footsteps of the outspoken British political activist Emmeline Pankhurst; the forerunner of the American movement advocating rights for women that included Elizabeth Cady Stanton and Mary Baker Eddy.. All of whom believed women were more than capable of benefiting from a higher education, married life and a career. After successfully securing the passage of the 19th Amendment in 1920, they directed their attention and energy to a women's right to choose, believing that a woman's body was her own. My great aunt worked side by side with Margaret Sanger in Chicago to fight for access to birth control. They organized rallies, campaigned loudly and non-stop for recognition and went so far as to pound on neighboring doors when necessary to have their voices heard. They were known to go into the slums of St. Paul to convince poverty stricken women to raise their awareness and support for the cause of women's rights. They never took "no" for an answer and more often than not, they each had at least a few of their children tagging along behind them.

My Great Grand-mothers were comfortable, educated, married women with several children to raise and the confidence and support of their husbands. Yet they refused to accept their current conditions as defined for them. Both were firmly opposed and determined to eradicate child labor as well as the deplorable factory conditions for women throughout this country in the early part of the nineteenth century. They argued long and hard to abolish, or at least, legislate prostitution, if for no other reason than to control the rampant spread of venereal disease that affected so many women at the time and subsequently their children. That, in turn, drew them into the struggle for proper health care for women and children as well as equality. My Grandmother carried their fight into the 1950's with my mother by her side. It is difficult to imagine these women and picture their lives as they lived them when compared to my own life.

My mother, like so many others, burned her bra in the late 60's while she was in college, fought for a women's right to choose, supported abortion and was an out-spoken advocate of Roe v. Wade. While openly protesting the war in

Vietnam on the streets of New York, she was "detained" twice for her political views in the late 60's and early 70's. To this day she continues to be an active advocate for equal pay for women in the work place and the elimination of the so-called glass ceiling. Lately she has become equally outraged by the abusive treatment directed toward young women in every branch of our military and the all too blatant disregard with which it is dismissed by the government. She is equally outspoken on the existence of human trafficking and particularly domestic violence against women and defenseless children.

Needless to say, I grew up surrounded by and exposed to my mother's friends, all of whom are well educated and accomplished women in their own right. They are doctors, lawyers, an assistant district attorney, as well as, authors, architects, designers and politicians – women who are managing their own businesses, raising their children and actively contributing to society while committed to change. I am convinced my mother and her cadre of friends could rule the world, given the opportunity. Every one of them believe, as I do, that women are 50% of any population and as such cannot and should not be ignored as an vital resource in any country. Women's contributions to the over all integrity and fabric of any society cannot be understated or ignored. Considering our collective history and past, I can completely understand my mother's initial reluctance to raise a young woman in today's world. Would she be as successful as they had been or would I marry the first boy who asked and start popping out babies, one a year, with a total disregard for my full potential? Would I turn my back on an education and become just another statistic; disappointing the previous generations by my indifference to what had gone before? Could I live up to what had gone before?

My destiny pre-determined, the course set, it only remained for her to implement her plan – one day at a time.

I never wore pink. It was not my first choice and I never owned a Barbie doll because my mother refused to allow one in the house. To her, Barbie was a slick, commercial ideal of perfection that no young woman could ever hope to emulate. She represented a strong, negative body image, cleverly forced upon all young women by toy company executives. She was nothing but big boobs and long legs, probably a size 0 – all grossly out of proportion. Her sole purpose in her make - believe life was to undermine a young girl's confidence and destroy her self esteem before she even had the opportunity to develop either. My mother wasn't going to have it! As vehement as she was on the subject of Barbie, I was actually indifferent – you don't miss what you done have. Until a friend brought Barbie to the house for an afternoon play date. I discovered she was indeed a leggy, skinny, top heavy piece of plastic.

Between the two of us, we decided Barbie needed to learn how to ride. We tried in vain to wrap her thin legs with her stiletto feet around the barrel of my Breyer plastic horse models but no matter how hard we tried or what creative devises we applied, including hair elastics, wire or duct tape, Barbie continued to pop of the horse, fly across the room and ricochet off the walls. Her bendable legs wouldn't bend! She refused to cooperate much less adapt to her new circumstances. We decided at some point to separate her head from her body, believing that would improve her balance. I was horrified to discover her head was hollow! Of course it was hollow, what was I expecting? I was stunned and disappointed by the reality. I immediately went back to the security of my plastic horses and Barbie went home at the end of the day, never to return.

I had a beautiful, 3 story, Victorian, antique doll house that had been handed down through the family; and bequeathed by a great-aunt. I immediately filled it with bits of straw carefully cut to fit the tiny rooms and turned it into a very elegant barn, complete with a separate tack room and a pretend wash stall, which I filled with several, small porcelain horses. Unfortunately, Barbie had already proven she wouldn't fit into the small rooms, even when folded in half. She was awkward and strangely out of place in the whole backdrop that I had so painstakingly created, so she was never again allowed to enter.

My bedroom was not papered in subtle floral prints or decorated in an array of rosy pastels like the rooms of my friends and it didn't reek of lavender toilet water or hand milled Old English soap. Instead there were piles of my smelly sports equipment in every corner; saddles, bridles, the occasional girth, lead lines and a basket of heavy stirrups. Whips and sticks, helmets and boots; all giving off the smell of well oiled leather and permeating the air in my room. Saddle soap, linseed oil and cleaning rags were my perfume of choice.

I would adamantly refuse, under any circumstances, to wear a dress or a cute little outfit carefully coordinated for any occasion. I did, once have a long drawn out battle with my mother that lasted for days. I finally agreed to wear a black velvet dress to my Grandmother's funeral with a pair of cut-off jean shorts discreetly hidden under the skirt. My mother was so distraught at the loss of her own mother; I could tell her heart wasn't in the fight so I acquiesced; just this once but, on condition that I be allowed to wear my paddock boots instead of the highly polished, black patent leather Mary Jane's that had magically appeared in my closet. And absolutely no hair ribbons or bows in my hair – that was going too far! To my parents, this was classified as "let her make her own decisions". Left to my own devices and trusting my own instincts, I much preferred to wear my standard outfit of well worn jeans, a reasonably clean t-shirt and my paddock boots. Not surprisingly, I have always felt uncomfortable and more than conspicuous in a dress. I still do to this day.

Most of my girlfriends were preoccupied with hair, make-up and clothes. Hanging out at the Mall for hours, going from store to store, coveting this or that latest fad while I spent hours pouring over the latest tack catalogues that arrived almost daily.

I desperately wanted a horse of my own. Not a pony, but a full grown horse. I knew what breed I wanted; what size and color and, I had a name picked out; all I lacked was the actual horse. A pony is just a scaled down version; a miniature horse with a bad temperament that may appear to be cute and cuddly but they have a hidden agenda that more often than not does not include a rider. Offer a pony a carrot and you are more than likely to lose a finger or two. Ponies bite and kick for no reason. My mother believed ponies were unpredictable nasty little creatures that were obligated by nature to throw you or scrape you off their backs at the first opportunity just to get you off their backs. They are unreasonable and not particularly known for their intelligence – if it exists at all. They don't have the sense they were born with, and their sole purpose in life is to get you off as quickly as possible and if you got hurt in the process, they have been successful.

If I wanted to ride – then I would ride a full- size horse. They are much safer in the long run and less likely to decide they had had enough of you and toss you off just to see you go splat in the dirt. At least you could reason with a horse, they weren't completely mindless like a pony. A pony was out of the question. My father believed soccer to be much safer sport in the long run. The only equipment required is a ball and a level bit of grass and soccer would be a lot less time consuming and considerably less expensive. And you don't have to feed or care for a ball!

Everything they had hoped to teach the four boys was now redirected and channeled in my direction. My father would spend every spare moment he could manage; doing something in the garage, having recognized it was his refuge from the high levels of estrogen he encountered in the house. He always had several projects in various states of disrepair covering every surface and counter top. If he couldn't fix whatever was broken, he usually decided we probably didn't need it anyway and, hoping no one would notice, he'd just throw it out. If my mother asked how a particular repair was going, he'd run out and buy her a new whatever it was that was unfixable and hope she didn't notice. She always did.

When the front doorbell ceased to function, rather than hire an electrician, my father decided to fix it himself. By the time he was finished, whenever anyone rang the front bell, the garbage disposal in the kitchen would start to whirl. For months, the disposal whirling incessantly was the only indication we had that there may be someone at the front door. Finally he gave up on electrical wiring and installed a beautiful, heavy antique brass knocker that fairly shook the house whenever it was put to use.

My father dreamed for years of one day owning a classic car. And when the opportunity finally presented itself, he purchased a 1955, candy apple red, black ragtop, Porsche Speedster that he and I worked on together for years until it was completely restored to its original, pristine condition and Concours ready. He would scoop me up and plop me into the car or I'd scoot under the bonnet or sit in the boot with a sippy cup while we spent endless hours together. I was just happy to be near him, rummaging around in the garage, listening to him and without realizing it; learning almost everything there is know about cars and tools of every kind. To this day, I am still confused as to why many of the tools have men's names. There is a Jack in the trunk of the car, a Chuck attached to the power drill, a Phillips and a Jacobs screwdriver and a box of Brads in his tool box.

My father is a die-hard 49er fan that refuses to surrender his season tickets. During the season, the two of us would watch every televised game, huddled together on the couch. Occasionally he would take me with him to Candlestick Park – just the two of us. Over the years, my mother had taught him the ins and outs of professional hockey and he firmly believed he had the ability to become a professional hockey player until my mother quietly pointed out that would require he learn to skate and it was a little too late for him. That ship had sailed long ago!

For many years, we had a beautiful, antique pool table, originally built in San Francisco in 1870. By strategically arranging a series of empty, wooden wine crates around the table, I was able to jump from one to the other to take a shot until I was tall enough to lean over the table myself. My father taught me well but I was a very competitive little girl who hated to lose at anything or to anyone. It wasn't too long before I was winning consistently and looking around for someone else to "hustle" into a game. More importantly, I learned how to win gratefully and lose graciously, particularly in games that men consider their own. He taught me to fly fish; catch and release, shoot a shotgun and field clean quail. He also taught me the value of trust, honesty and fair play regardless of gender. Apparently, most men have difficulty losing to a woman under any circumstances; in pool, poker or even something as simple dominoes. As competitive as they think they are, they are unwilling to admit to themselves or to each other that they can be beaten by a woman. A woman has to be acutely aware, and on guard at all times, of that extremely fragile male ego lurking just under the surface, waiting to spring out at the slightest provocation. I have yet to meet a man, who will concede defeat with any degree of courtesy or integrity, except my father.

We were off to a good start. By the time my mother finished with her project, namely me, I would stand tall on my own two feet, confident and capable of competing in any arena. To be successful and thrive, I would have to be stronger than most men, at least mentally; more self-assured and independent and able to out-run them, out think them and anticipate their every move if I intended to survive in their world and succeed. I wasn't going to depend or count on anyone but myself for anything – ever. I believed there was absolutely nothing standing in my way; no deterrent or obstacle that I couldn't overcome. I was well on my way and when the day came, I would be armed and ready – my mother would see to it. She never hesitated to remind me that there was "nothing a man could do that I couldn't do just as well, except pee-pee standing up!"

The lofty dream of a farmhouse in the country slowly receded to be considered another day. For the time being, we lived in one of the few existing Victorian homes in Pacific Heights that had survived the 1906 San Francisco earthquake and fire relatively intact. My parents had spent years of painstaking research to carefully renovate the house from the foundation to the roof and everything in-between. Now, fully restored to its original glory, it was generally accepted as one of the finest examples of the architecture of the period and often photographed for one publication or another; a stunning example of San Francisco's Golden years.

It was also very small and very tall; three stories stacked up and topped by a deeply sloping peaked roof and common walls. Our neighbors on either side were just inches away; enough room for a city raccoon to wiggle through. The contractor could never quite alleviate the creaking in the three flights of stairs or remedy the tight, narrow closets; barely the width of a standard clothes hanger. It was cold and drafty; the windows often shook in the wind and most of the doors were so badly warped, they were difficult to open and close. As is the custom with all Victorians in the City, it was painted the requisite three colors; a deep burgundy with nautical, navy blue trim with the gingerbread cut-outs, window frames and decorative moldings meticulously highlighted in simulated gold.

It was situated on a beautiful tree, lined street in a residential neighborhood that wasn't particularly steep for San Francisco but on a hill high enough to offer spectacular views of the Golden Gate Bridge, Sausalito, Belvedere Island and Alcatraz. We were fortunate to have a small, fenced back yard that the sun never seemed to penetrate and the fog more often than not claimed for its own. It was more of a stepping stone for the fat, raucous raccoons that would pass through our yard on their nightly journey to the next house; jumping from fence to fence in the middle of the night to rummage through and tip over trash cans. Needless to say, it didn't lend itself to the garden my mother imagined or the rolling green acres of her dreams.

The chaos and confusion my mother had hoped for had become a reality with the three of us; one large Irish Setter and a cat all in one small house. She had the disorder she longed for but not the space. All too soon, it became apparent that the house was too small for all of us.

The City, while one of the most stunningly beautiful and diverse cities in the world, was becoming increasingly overcrowded and difficult to live in on a day to day basis especially with small children who had to be shuttled here and there, from one activity to another, regularly. Parking was an increasing battle if not a nightmare, and the constant noise of sirens and glaring street lights were becoming more and more unbearable. When the neighbors, on one side of us, decided to keep several chickens in their backyard we were all naturally concerned. When they introduced a few roosters, their incessant crowing was particularly unnerving and the smell was so bad, we didn't dare open the windows on their side of the house. When they introduced what appeared to be fighting cocks we starting calling the SPCA on a regular basis.

Early every fall, our neighbors on the opposite side of the fence, would adopt a lamb and keep it in their yard. Prior to the Greek Orthodox Easter, it would strangely disappear. We never dared to ask what became of it because we didn't want to know. We were supportive of ethnic diversity and religious tolerance but raising fighting cocks and slaughtering lambs in the heart of San Francisco was pushing our level of tolerance to the maximum. We all agreed it was time to move.

Stella Benson

Chapter Seven

I have a tendency to become involved in long-term, long distance relationships that have a way of ending in utter disaster. Considering the amount of time I've devoted to each one, there seems to be a definite pattern developing. Off hand, and I can't recall my high school physics, but I'm sure there must be some obscure law that relates time to distance; the greater the distance, the more time devoted to the relationship. If such a theory does exist, then I am the perfect, living testament to its accuracy. If there is a correlation between the two, whether logical or natural, then I'm it. However, time is never what it seems – neither is distance. To further complicate the issue, I have definite affinity and an uncanny ability to attract only young men who are currently serving in any branch our military; which explains the distance and to some degree, the time. I apparently have a soft spot in my heart for the basic enlisted man. Officers for the most part have eluded me. I do admit, however to a very brief, yet perfectly innocent affair, with a charming young man who was a Midshipman at the Naval Academy in Annapolis. And a short lived, rather tumultuous fling with a handsome West Point Cadet who periodically required an uncomplicated date for the seasonal Academy Balls. Both of whom would graduate, of course, as officers – a completely different world from that of my somewhat limited experience. My mother, who I can count on to reduce everything to the bottom line, sums up my preoccupation with the military, by saying "I have a thing for a man in uniform."

She often convinced me to watch several classic movies that portrayed the inherent dangers of such relationships; hoping to dissuade me or at least, steer me away from any further such associations; especially now with this country involved in more wars and conflicts than we can count. Never one to play it safe, I'm afraid it had the opposite effect. I don't claim to understand my infatuation or the origins of my attraction but I am slowly beginning to realize that I am indeed attracted to that particular type of man. It maybe something of a stretch but my grandfather was in the Army his entire life, finally retiring as a Lieutenant Colonel. Unfortunately, I never had the opportunity to know him; he passed away less than twelve hours after I was born. My mother is convinced that his passing and my birth shortly thereafter is too much of a coincidence. His strength and spirit may have left him but it somehow found its way into me. How bad could that be? Something more for me to come to terms with about myself.

My last three years of high school were spent in a private, all girls, extremely competitive, college prep, boarding school, forty miles north of Baltimore. An incredibly beautiful location with miles and miles of painted, white fences enclosing rolling green acres, and horses of every breed, grazing peacefully. It was a school situated in the heart of the Maryland hunt country and one of the few high schools in the country that offered a nationally recognized equestrian program as an integral part of their curriculum. As beautiful and remote as it was, it was a not situation that lent itself to meeting boys much less dating. The exception being several "mixers" with neighboring boys schools that we were encouraged to attend on a regular basis.

If you rode, and boarded your horse at school, you were required to sign-in at the barn every morning at exactly 6 am; feed your horse, clean his stall, scoop manure and make sure your tack trunk, the tack room and the entire barn were in perfect working order before the breakfast bell. If you didn't board your own horse at school, you tended the resident schooling horses. The process was repeated every evening before 6 pm. There were no grooms casually loitering around waiting to do your work for you or give you "a leg-up" – you were your own groom. You took responsibility for your own horse every day, including Sunday and if you didn't, you didn't ride. It was that simple. I rode before breakfast and after dinner, during P.E, with a team preparing for local competitions and as an extra curricular activity, I chose to play polo. It amounted to four or five hours a day in the saddle. With such a rigorous riding schedule and the expected academics, there never seemed to be enough time much less the opportunity to even consider dating.

My first real, serious, adult, boyfriend and I went to the same high school for a year together in California before I transferred to boarding school in Maryland. I was several years behind him and far too young for him to have noticed me at the time. In fact, he barely remembered me being in the same school. As I recall, I was in eighth grade when he was a senior and understandably he wouldn't have had anything to do with someone so much younger than himself. It wasn't until a few years after his graduation that we were introduced by a mutual friend and even then we were surprised to learn we had, at one time, attended the same school, and grown up in the same community with many of the same friends.

Following his graduation he attended San Jose State for a year and shortly after the tragic events of 9/11, he felt compelled to follow his conscience and dropped out of college to enlist in the U.S. Army. He was briefly stationed at Fort Meyers outside of Washington DC. while I finished my last year of high school in Baltimore. Considering the strict rules, regulations and the near impossibility of obtaining a highly sanctioned weekend pass because of his duty schedule, we were seldom, if ever, able to coordinate a weekend together. It didn't help that neither one of us had access to a car. No sooner did I return to California for the summer holiday, than he was immediately deployed to Iraq for nine months. When I started college at Colorado State in Fort Collins as an Equine Major the following fall, he was deployed yet again to Afghanistan for fifteen months. By the time he returned, too much time had passed and we realized we hardly knew each other. I had grown up; and was finally free of the rigidity of boarding school and my parents' surveillance. Colorado State was the largest school I had ever attended, with an enrollment of over 25,000 students, and so much to offer. I fully planned to take advantage of every minute that I was there.

Fort Collins was a small, lovely college town with a distinctive Midwestern air, completely devoted to the college and its resident students. Not surprisingly, his experiences during both deployments the last two years couldn't be further from mine and it had changed his priorities dramatically. He needed time to process all that he had witnessed and experienced. He wanted to decide his future without the entanglement of what was beginning to look like a failing relationship. I had to agree; we had grown apart, our lives had gone in two different directions with no apparent way of reconnecting. It became increasingly more difficult for me to communicate my collegiate triumphs or disappointments to someone half way around the world; whose goal each day was to simply survive. My secure, sheltered existence at school appeared to be so shallow compared to everything he had seen and done. I couldn't begin to relate, on any level, to his present life any more than he could relate to mine. While I was safely enjoying my first year of college; taking advantage of the very freedom he was fighting for, he was living day to day in an extremely dangerous combat zone, having been trained as a sniper. We both agreed that our lives had changed direction and it was time to call it a day. What had once existed between us had long since dissipated as he tried to readjust to civilian life and return to college himself. For both of us, our priorities had changed dramatically.

Unfortunately no pain of conscience or overwhelming sense of patriotism was to influence my next boyfriend's decision to enlist but rather a dramatic and, as it turned out, a life-changing experience. He had simply run out of options – with no where else to turn other than the military. Nat had graduated from a very small, county, public high school in rural Southern Virginia, and won an athletic scholarship to an even smaller local community college to play baseball. By the end of his first year, he had so severely injured one knee that he could no longer play, forcing him to forfeit his scholarship. He was, of course, devastated at first, believing he had the natural ability, the potential and the determination to become a professional baseball player.

His parents, neither of which attended college, refused to recognize the value of a higher education, took a stand and steadfastly refused to pay his tuition, if he chose to continue. They believed an education beyond high school, was not only a waste of time but money. They clung to a deeply ingrained distrust of education and books; the exception, of course, being the Bible. Lacking their support, he had no choice but to leave school behind and find some sort of gainful employment. They would support him only when he did what they wanted him to do. If he deviated from their plan, they would not hesitate to express their overall disappointment and quickly withdraw their support. It was straightforward and completely understood by all concerned. Doing what he wanted to do with his life was never a factor or even a consideration for his parents. He always, always did what they expected him to do with the possible exception of enlisting, which came as a complete surprise to them and not an altogether acceptable alternative to what they had intended for him.

Prior to his completely unsanctioned enlistment, they encouraged him to apply for a job on the loading dock at their local Home Depot; driving a fork lift day in and day out. In a few years, they reasoned, if he was diligent, he could very well secure a position as a floor manager. Or he could stock shelves at Costco with the same result. If all else failed, he could always follow his older brother down into the coal mines of Southern Virginia. To their absolute surprise and shock, he refused to consider their suggestions and at nineteen, enlisted in the Air Force for a term of six years. It was the first time he had gone against their wishes and it would be the last.

Following his basic training in Texas, he was immediately sent to Warren Air Force Base outside of Cheyenne, Wyoming; just 40 miles from Fort Collins and Colorado State University. Warren Air Force Base is one of three Strategic Missile Bases in the U.S. other than Montana or Minot, North Dakota, that is responsible for the operation of more than 150 Minuteman lll Intercontinental Ballistic Missiles actively maintained for the defense of this country. As young as he was, he was trained in computer navigational systems and logistical support as well as supervising the calibration of those nuclear weapons. I first met him in a bar, in Fort Collins, after his much anticipated return from a four month tour of duty in Afghanistan where he briefly worked construction, well out of harms way.

The distance between Fort Collins and Cheyenne doesn't seem insurmountable but once again, between my classes and his erratic schedule we had difficulty getting together with any regularity. With a top security clearance, he had a consistently rotating work schedule and was usually in the dark as to when and where he would be called upon to report to duty. We managed to drive back and forth between both cities for several months whenever we could before I decided to transfer to a smaller college, nationally recognized for its riding program in, of all places, Southern Virginia.

Bristol, Virginia, is a small community; half of the city is in Virginia, the other half in Tennessee and less than twenty minutes from his Nat's parents' home. Needless to say, the irony was not lost on my parents. When I moved from Fort Collins to Bristol to enroll in their equine program, Nat remained in Cheyenne until his term of enlistment expired, creating another distance between us. Fortunately throughout his enlistment, he had used his time wisely and had successfully completed enough college courses on-line to consider finishing his B.S. when he was discharged. No sooner did I graduate from college in Bristol with a B.A. in Equine Studies and return to California to accept a position as a trainer, than he was accepted to the University of Tennessee, in Knoxville. He had accumulated enough credits; leaving just a year and a half to obtain a degree in Political Science. I returned to California and he remained in Tennessee. Once again we were separated by a distance too great to overcome.

My parents and I were all acutely aware and somewhat confused about his parents' reluctance to support Nat's desire to pursue an education and as a result, my mother, agreed to help him wherever and whenever she could. To her, Nat was a bird with a broken wing that had somehow mysteriously landed on her doorstep. She couldn't be of any help to him with the foreign language requirement for his degree since he had chosen Spanish but she was there to help him with his English and writing classes. She was convinced basic English had taken a backseat to dance lessons in the High School curriculum of the South just as having a baby in High School seemed to be a prerequisite to graduation. She felt sorry for him and was determined to walk him through the most elementary principles of writing. She spent countless hours on the phone and in front of her computer discussing each and every assignment he was given. He would dutifully jot down a jumble of thoughts, in random order, and then email it to her for her recommendations and suggestions. She, in turn, would completely reorganize it, rewrite it and attempt to make some sense of it, correct the grammar and punctuation, which was typically non-existent and email the finished product back to him just in time to hand in to his professor. I would often overhear her trying in vain, to teach him the proper usage of "good" versus "well", when to use "their and there" and the difference between "to and too." Her perseverance and determination to see him succeed was all-consuming. He slowly began to understand that it would be a struggle to move forward without an education and just as difficult to successfully obtain a degree. I had often noticed when he wasn't aware that I was watching him, that he had a tendency to move his lips when he read. And often, unfamiliar with new vocabulary, he would slowly enunciate and sound out those words that were new to him. Rather than admit reading was a hardship for him, he chose to gloss over most of what he read. To this day, he has never admitted nor has he recognized that without our participation and support, he would never have completed his degree. As difficult as it was, he finally graduated with Honors and near the top of his class.

His family, however, refused to acknowledge his accomplishment and, taking it a step further, steadfastly refused to attend his graduation ceremony- just to drive home their overall dissatisfaction. As hard as he tried to convince them otherwise, he was devastated by their indifference and somewhat embarrassed by their attitude. They felt it was a waste of their time to drive the short distance from their home in Castlehill, Virginia to Knoxville, Tennessee simply to watch their son graduate.

He was the first in his family to have ever achieved that goal. An achievement that should have been a cause for celebration. For some unknown reason I was not invited though I longed to be there. Instead, I sent him a large, beautiful, crystal Revere bowl, monogrammed with his name, the University of Tennessee and the date of his graduation. It was a sorry substitute for my presence but I wanted him to know I was thinking about him on such an important day. Looking back, I was trying to compensate for his parent's glaring indifference to his success. As the first member of his family ever to attend college much less graduate with a degree and I was so proud of his achievement. He was ambitious and had more than accomplished all that he had set out to do by making a conscious decision to alter the course of his life for the better. The coal mines were no longer threatening to engulf him in a life of drudgery. He had finally realized his own potential and was moving in a different, more meaningful direction, with or without his parent's approval. A decision that changed everything and led to something else, altogether unexpected.

Much later in our relationship, he confessed to me he had come to agree with his family on the subject of education. He firmly believed his newly obtained degree had not been the stepping stone to the corporate level job he had recently accepted. It was indeed a waste of time and money. He had convinced himself that the first time he attempted college, he had sustained an injury that had cost him his athletic scholarship and the second attempt at the University of Tennessee, had cost him me. Or so he chose to believe. As the day of his graduation ceremony grew closer, a sense of enthusiasm, pride and hopefully shame suddenly overwhelmed his family and they finally agreed to attend the ceremony and acknowledge his success. I was about to find out the real reason for their sudden change of heart and the reason why I hadn't received an invitation.

Glancing at my Facebook page one afternoon a few months before, I was shocked to find a picture of Nat with that roguish smile on his face, in a bar, with a rather chubby, somewhat non-descript, brunette, sitting precariously on his lap while he embraced her with a distinct air of possession. It didn't appear to be a random barroom antic; they looked like they knew each other and knew each other well. She looked starry-eyed and at the same time, somewhat pitiful and desperate. Perhaps a childhood friend or someone else's date for the evening joining in the brawl. When I asked him about the photo later that evening, he feigned indifference and casually brushed it off by telling me, he had no idea who she was. He HAD been in a bar, watching a football game, drinking beer with his buddies when this woman plopped herself down in his lap just in time for someone else to take the picture. It was obviously a joke, and not worth discussing. However if you know someone well enough, you can see what they are hiding by how hard they try to hide it. And he was trying much too hard. He had no idea how the photo had appeared on Facebook. But he hadn't hidden it very well – his secret was out and this particular indiscretion was out there for all to see, including me or perhaps it was meant for me. He went to great deal of time and trouble to reassure me that this particular episode was just a joke. And, as usual, I was the one overacting.

The more I listened to him, the more I wanted to believe him. I thought if I listened long enough to his hollow protestations, I'd find a way to convince myself that this, most recent incident, was exactly what he said it was. I wanted to believe him with all of my heart, so I did, somewhat reluctantly and then dropped the subject altogether. I did wonder, very briefly, if this wasn't another lie, another disguised attempt to get inside my head. For what reason or why, I'll never know. I had, by now, developed a sixth sense and always knew when he was about to lie. I had grown accustomed to waiting for it and then prepared to hear it. It has to be the worst feeling in the world. His need for constant affirmation was beginning to wear thin. How insecure can one person be? A few days later, out of nowhere, in the middle of another conversation, and completely unrelated, he confessed he had run into this woman in the FaceBook photo at a local gas station near his parent's home, while filling his truck. So he did know her after all! This was a pattern I had seen before on several occasions and one I never quite understood.

His initial, vehement denial followed by a few days of guilt then a few more days of remorse and finally a truth or rather, his version of the truth was becoming all too familiar. We had had this argument so many times before; it was beginning to be very tiresome. I had argued repeatedly that there are no versions of the truth, it was or it wasn't and putting your own spin on it didn't necessarily make it right, even if you believed it yourself. It would be far easier in the long run and save both of us a lot of anguish if he just told the truth in the beginning. I've never understood the reasoning behind lying. Why suffer days of anguish, guilt and remorse when stating the truth in the first pace is so much more honest and infinitely easier in the long run. It may not be quite what the other person wants to hear but if it's the truth without embellishment or a spin on it, it is just that; the truth. No complicated web that can leave you exposed to a series of often troubling discrepancies. I honestly believe he thought lies were easier in the long run, though how he managed to keep them all straight in his own mind, I'll never know.

Deciding I required further clarification, he went on to explain that as they pumped gas, he realized she was the younger sister of a friend he had known in high school. She was a member in good standing in the local chapter of 4H, a participant in her church choir, leader of the Pep Club, and active in the Home Economics Club. If their High School had been large enough to have a marching band, I'm sure she would have felt compelled to join that as well. She had also been one of several prom princesses; the title of Queen having eluded her. In my mind, she had conspicuously avoided any activity that required a brain or academic excellence leaving her as empty as Barbie. She was now an emergency room attendant or Para-medic of some sort in a local clinic, who had recently gone through a traumatic break up with her boyfriend of nine years. It had been an ongoing, physically and mentally abusive relationship and she was still recovering; not yet convinced she had done the right thing by leaving him. It may have been a chance encounter at the local E-Z Gas out on the Interstate but she obviously made a lasting impression on Nat. After his unsolicited and detailed description of their meeting, I had a picture in my mind of a barefoot, Daisy Mae in a gingham frock covered with ruffles and either barefoot or wearing scruffy, brown cowboy boots; her dark ponytail swinging from side to side. Knowing Nat as well as I did, she had to be a brunette. Her eyelashes batting in veiled naiveté while her biological clock resounded loudly in her ears. Her sole objective, I was sure, to ensnare any unsuspecting man into a loveless marriage. I could almost hear the desperation in her voice as she poured out her tale of woe to him. She was clearly one of those women born to yield and bred to be obsequious. After her long, somewhat turbulent, previous involvement in what was apparently an already abusive relationship; it wouldn't surprise me to know that the occasional slap would appear to be normal. Being slapped around just to remind her of her "place" would undoubtedly be perfectly acceptable to her, at least. A reminder, I shudder to remember, Nat would never hesitate to administer. It was imperative that he be seen as the one in control of the relationship – always vying for control. Between his need to dominate and an uncontrollable, volatile temper, it wouldn't surprise me in the least if he resorted to physical violence. I have often wondered and to this day continue to wonder what his father would think, or say or do if he ever knew that Nat had actually reared back, hauled off and hit me in the face – once. Just once and for no other reason than to make sure I clearly understood that he was the one in charge . I should have confronted Nat, at that moment – through my tears or at the very least, run. But I didn't. After that particular incident, I made sure we were never alone together and for over a year, I refused to let him touch me. For the first time in my dating history, I was glad of the distance between us.

No amount of begging, pleading, groveling or more false promises on his part could convince me that it wouldn't happen again. I considered, briefly, confiding in his father but reconsidered when I realized that type of physically abusive behavior was most likely learned at his father's knee – no matter how god-fearing he claimed to be. Scripture may fly out of his father's mouth with surprising ease and on any and every occasion but I had no doubt he could come up with a quote that would justify Nat's behavior. He would find a way to justify it. The entire incident should have raised a red flag in my mind or sounded a siren of impeding alarm but it didn't.

I wouldn't go so far as to say Nat was edgy; he was simply wound too tight and enormously insecure. He had assured me that this woman he was seeing was merely a distraction; an annoyance whom he seldom ran into unless he happened to be visiting his parents and even then, she just seemed to show up unannounced, like a bad penny. According to him, she was a sweet, pathetic messed up woman who needed a shoulder to cry on. He didn't hesitate to point out that I had my regular poker playing buddies and my pool playing companions, all of whom I refused to give up for him, so – why couldn't he have a friend who happened to be a woman in need of a shoulder to cry on? He saw every man I had ever known or would ever encounter as a potential threat to himself. He never told me her name nor did I care to know. To me she was irrelevant. If I put a name to her face in the photo, she would become a reality and I would be forced to acknowledge her presence between us and recognize her existence. That was the one thing I was not prepared to do. I didn't want her in our lives, coming between us. Not now – not ever. I wished I was closer to him or he was nearer to me so he could explain himself – in person, rather than over the phone. But he was always better over the phone. It was much less confrontational, something he had learned to avoid, and an escape easily accomplished by simply ringing off.

Out of no where, at some point during one conversation, he loudly declared that he was not sleeping with her. I had not asked and yet this particular piece of information was volunteered, raising my suspicions even further. I may be young and inexperienced in matters of the heart but, I'm not stupid. It doesn't take much to figure out that the only way one woman can successfully lure a man away from another woman is through sex. I knew Nat well enough to know that when it came to sex, casual or otherwise, it wouldn't take much to turn his head. He was an extremely sexual person; one of those men who only needs a place, not necessarily a time and he radiated sexuality, fully aware of the impact it had on other women. He had an undeniable charisma that was practiced and carefully perfected over the years. He could be shy, appear removed, wary and somewhat tense or completely disappear into himself and still heads would snap up or spin around whenever he walked into a room or passed by. Pairs of eyes admiring his long legs, tiny waist and perfect ass. It was something more than basic charisma; he literally wreaked raw, shameless, palpable sexuality and he knew it. Sexual energy emanated from him like a horse radiates heat and he used it to his advantage at every opportunity. He had the innate ability to charm the pants off any woman he chose, regardless of her age. I had found him irresistible so I could hardly blame other women, even those on the street, in a bar or a restaurant, who wouldn't hesitate to trample me and leave me in the dust just for the opportunity to get his attention or catch his eye. If they were alive and had a pulse, they noticed him immediately, and most were far from subtle in their approach while making their intentions perfectly clear even in front of me. He was definitely hard to ignore. He could easily, without even trying, devastate any woman in the room. Whoever this woman was, she must have a very unique skill set or be very good at what she does to have so completely turned his head. I knew from long experience, turning his head wasn't the biggest challenge, holding his interest for any length of time was another matter altogether. I have always believed there is a special place in hell for women who steal from other woman. I had held his interest for over six years; that had to be some sort of a record!

Monogamy and chivalry were concepts Nat neither recognized nor embraced because he truly believed both concepts did not, as yet, apply to him. The idea of one woman with one man was either beyond his limit of understanding or too far beneath him to warrant consideration. If one is accustomed to the simple courtesy of having a door opened for you or your groceries carried; he is not your man. Perhaps one day he would reconsider both but that day had yet to come. Someday he might find them necessary and quite possibly embrace both but that day seems too far off for him to imagine. For the time being, he was too busy drinking, carousing and scheming. He had however; made it very clear early in our relationship that monogamy and all of its implications did, of course, apply to me. "Steppin' out" on me was routine and duplicity appeared to come naturally to him. Every one of his indiscretions, infidelities, chance encounters or flirtations eventually found their way back to me via social media. I doubt he suspected that I knew about each one but by this point I had grown tired of confrontation. It wasn't the first time and I knew, in my heart, that it wouldn't be the last. If he knew or even cared that I had been made aware of his blatant indiscretions; it never caused the slightest hesitation on his part. It was just another occasion for more lies. The denial, followed by my forgiveness had long ago been established as a pattern in our relationship. Each time, his response was the same. Deny, deny and deny it again and continue to deny it until I was thoroughly convinced and believed every word he said. Was he trying to convince me or persuade himself that nothing meaningful had ever really occurred? He loudly, repeatedly, proclaimed he was never unfaithful to me - in his heart. Apparently his mind and body were completely unrelated; separated by convenience and opportunity.

When we were both invited to attend the wedding of a mutual friend in Illinois, I was unable to get away but the bridesmaid he spent the entire weekend with was kind enough to text me often with a detailed description of his indiscretion, complete with photos. Why are we the last to recognize what we should have seen all along? How many lies and how many indiscretions does it take before we see the light? If I wanted to be kind, I would have to acknowledge his highly selective sense of morality. If I was completely honest, especially with myself, I would have to admit that he had the morals of a feral tom cat. Ethics or even the principle of rules regarding right and wrong were foreign to him. Somewhere along the way, he had lost his moral compass. I have often wondered if he simply lacked a conscience. Yet I looked the other way every time and continued to do so. I have no plausible explanation for either my behavior or his. The larger question in my mind has to be, if I knew all this about him and recognized it for what it was, why then, did I continue in this relationship? Was it his looks – possibly? Was it the sex – definitely? Was it his sense of humor – maybe? Or had this relationship somehow just become convenient and routine as the years of our involvement slipped by, unnoticed? Was this an on-going infatuation or a novelty that I refused to relinquish? Was I really so shallow or so desperate myself that I held on? Eventually I became numb, immune to his protestations but I never, never came to accept the full extent of his deceit. It was a balancing act that I never fully understood. Where were trust, honor and commitment in our relationship?

Is it possible we cannot chose who we fall in love with? He was, to me, a young, wild stallion, impossible to geld, running unfettered across the plains of Wyoming. He was not a Thoroughbred – he never would be. Perhaps that's why I fell in love with him in the first place. We were complete opposites in every way that mattered.

This woman, his latest conquest in a very long line of conquests, was from the same small town as he; a home town girl. On more than one occasion, I had tried to explain to my mother that curious and often confusing long standing Southern tradition of giving a child two Christian names, followed, of course, by the surname. But more often than not, the middle name falls into common usage. If your husband's first name was William and his father's name was Robert, it stands to reason that your first born son would be named William Robert, which would quickly deteriorate into Billy Bob. Following this explanation, I recall my mother quietly saying, "Let me be as clear as I can and please make sure you hear me on this; NO grandson of mine will ever be referred to as Billy Bob or any other quaint, regional combination you care to come up with. And Bubba is, without a doubt, out of the question."

The two of them had attended the same high school, and knew many of the same people. I'm surprised they weren't somehow related! Returning home from Cheyenne after six years in the Air Force, and having seen a little bit of the world outside of his home town, single and never married at 26, made him something of a catch to the local talent. There apparently was no shortage of competition. The well known fact, courtesy of his parents, that he was involved in a long distance relationship with someone from as far away as California only heightened their overall curiosity and made him that much more interesting. He presented a challenge; obviously one worth pursuing. I envisioned this latest in a long line of women, as a predator turned poacher who had set her trap well with just the right amount of attractant; namely pity and apathy. It would seem the local girls have the uncanny ability to quickly sniff out an unsuspecting male and close the deal as soon as possible by producing a baby in record time, usually before marriage. More or less sealing their collective fate. Most men don't even see it coming. The fact that she hadn't had at least one baby, with or without the benefit of a spouse, while still in high school, made her something of a novelty. No doubt heightening her overall appeal to him and causing considerable embarrassment to her family.

Her parents knew his parents; everybody knew everybody else. Of course they did. She knew the small town rules, she knew the game inside out and more importantly, she knew her place - she fit in. She was a local, a townie. Not a "Yankee" or a "foreigner" from somewhere as distant as California. I have been called many things but I found "Yankee" to be more a source of pride than denigration. If we're going to live in the past; at least I was born on the winning side! To me, it was simply a matter of geography. I was to learn that his mother believed there existed a cultural divide between us and no matter how we felt about each other or how much we loved each other, that gap could not be bridged. I was a threat to the mediocrity that was her life; a life she was determined to perpetuate through her son. I had succeeded in convincing him to finish college and that, in her opinion, was to be the full extent of my influence. She would not tolerate another decision made on his own and directly opposed to her wishes. What unreasonable idea would I come up with next that would further derail her plans for her son and break the bonds that held him?

His mother was not about to hand off the reins to me quietly. If nothing else, he and this latest flirtation, shared the same zip code and the same Southern comfort zone. His mother, not surprisingly, adored her at first sight and felt a bond immediately. She could talk to her, when she had always felt the two of us had very little in common. She had been born and raised in the same community as he, whereas I was new in town. I was a temporary transplant in Bristol; living there just long enough to finish my degree in Equine Science. This was her territory, her turf and I was a "damned Yankee". Damned if I did and damned if I didn't. She knew everyone in the county, having been born and raised in Bristol while I had only a few friends from school, as a result, I couldn't contribute much in the way of local gossip. His mother showed little or no interest in my family, my life in California or my equestrian pursuits. We never engaged in a lively dialogue or debate on any topic, current or otherwise nor did we ever exchange ideas or opinions. My presence in her home, on rare occasions, was merely tolerated and often ignored as though she questioned my motives for being there in the first place. The only topic we seemed to have in common was her son. His mother felt no need to ask me if I preferred tofu to red meat or sushi to catfish.

This woman was one of them, she belonged there and I couldn't have been more alien. There was nothing "foreign" about this girl, in fact, quite the opposite. She could make ketchup from scratch, "put up" jam; turn cucumbers into pickles, "can" beans and fry a catfish to crispy oblivion just as well as his mother, if not better. I am somewhat proud of my own culinary skills but unfortunately, I don't count canning among them and I seldom, if ever, fry anything. She posed no threat to anyone, quite the opposite and the twang in her voice was as identifiable as his; her Southern-ness as deeply rooted as his own. One of those Southern belles, I had come to know so well while in school in Virginia, who steadfastly stand by their man, and accept every word he says as gospel. They seem to lack the spine or the nerve to question, and wake up every morning with the express purpose of making every day of his life as carefree and delightful as a Disney Cruise. To me she was unmistakably docile, cowering and subservient without an original thought of her own. This was all more than I cared to know. Under the circumstances, I doubt he bothered to protest his parent's decision not to attend his graduation. One rebellion; the choice to return to school, in the last year and a half was his limit. In fact I'm relatively certain he was purposely kept in the dark by his parents. To his surprise as well as my own, it was she they invited to accompany them at his graduation. In my absence, she had successfully managed to wiggle her way into the family and slowly ingratiate herself.

Until the morning of his graduation ceremony, he was on his phone pleading with me to fly out for the ceremony. Poor planning on my part to be sure, but I couldn't possibly get away. My training schedule had locked me in. Something he could not understand much less tolerate. Once again I had disappointed him. His family planned to drive from UT, following the ceremony, back to Castlehill for one of their typical, large scale, family B.B.Q.'s.

These were usually rebel-rousing affairs that brought very aunt, uncle, and cousin, no matter how far removed and no matter how distant; out of the woodwork with nothing more to contribute than a six-pack of beer and a voracious appetite for free food. Occasions, that more often than not, flared into hostile controversy among the family as the day went on and the beer continued to flow. I had spent so many weekends as a witness to, but never really a participant in, all the highs and lows of his family drama that had been going on since probably before the Civil War and definitely long before I had arrived. A perpetual, loud, long-standing family dynamic that as a guest, I was aware of and never quite able to piece together.

To a man, they would arrive in worn out pick-up trucks, usually in desperate need of repair with several dogs of questionable breeding; the exception being the occasional Blue Tick Hound, loosely tethered in the flatbed. Legions of squabbling, barely-clad, barefoot children, again of questionable breeding, would ratchet up the volume as they clamored, across the dirt of a long neglected lawn. Several dilapidated and unsteady picnic tables, lined up end to end covered in red and white checked, plastic table cloths and heavily laden with carbohydrates and all things fried, provided the only shade for several drowsy hounds patiently waiting for crumbs to fall into their gaping jowls. If the dogs lingered long enough, someone would invariably toss them a discarded B.B.Q'ed rib bone, a fried chicken bone or the skeletal structure of a catfish fried in lard and recently flayed. Pitchers of cherry Kool-Aid stood quietly sweating in the sun; the cups and cups of sugar visibly crystallizing in the bottom of each pitcher and crusting the rim while the fluid itself slowly separated. Deep plastic bowls held dozens of peeled, pickled hard boiled eggs and a bowl of soggy boiled peanuts sat next to large open jar of okra pickles. Biscuits and corn bread lay exposed and slowly dried out in the sun. In the place of honor in this cholesterol laden, culinary feast sat a the piece de resistence; a well worn, warped cookie sheet, piled at least five inches high with flash frozen hash brown potatoes, generously sprayed with Velveeta from an aerosol can and then baked beyond recognition or until the cheese bubbled, burped and burned. Up until then, I never knew it was possible for cheese to squeeze out of a spray can and I was fascinated. Deciding it was for regional distribution only, I was determined to obtain a can as a novelty to add to my mother's Christmas stocking. If she didn't throw it at my head, she too may be fascinated. This potatoe surprise was Nat's favorite childhood dish and one his mother continually whipped up just for him as a special treat. An elbow macaroni salad, made with what appeared to be a great deal of mayonnaise and chopped, chunks of yet more hard boiled eggs had been tossed with pickle relish, turning the entire salad an unappetizing, glaring shade of green. A can of Spam was carefully sliced and fanned out on a large paper plate and then perfectly cut, round slices of pineapple, fresh from the can, were piled on top; the round holes of the pineapple packed with brown sugar. At its side sat a large Pyrex dish of brown lumpy gravy, the clumps of flour slowly floating to the surface. Boiled collared greens, boiled corn on the cob, and the inevitable grits, that to me, tasted more and more like buttered kitty litter were always present.. A family-sized, plastic bag of fried pork rinds rounded out the menu. Large balls of fried cheese, no doubt government issued, served as hors'd oeuvres and the blue and white coolers of beer, safely stowed out of the sun under the raised porch, kept the beer iced. An enormous, three tiered, chocolate, layered cake, on the verge of collapsing in the sun, listed dangerously to starboard, threatening to slide into the anxious mouths of the flop-eared, drooling mongrel's patiently congregated below. Next to it stood a large can of Redi-Whip, always at the ready. For what, I could never be sure. The orange jello mold had long ago melted into a puddle, causing the miniature marshmallows to bob along in the orange liquid remaining. Everything farm to table except for a slight, detour through a deep fat fryer. Is it any wonder they were, for the most part, grossly overweight and suffering from any number of cardiac maladies? I may have been only 26 but I could hear my arteries screaming for relief or at the very least, for a simple, tossed, green salad! The first time I was invited to attend one of Nat's family's gatherings, I was unsure of the etiquette required for the occasion. Nat pulled me aside to explain that the women would serve the men, at least those lounging around the picnic tables in undershirts, first. They would then retreat to the kitchen to dine and gossip amongst themselves but they were required to stay within shouting range, in the event the food ran out or someone require "seconds." It was expected that I would join the other women in the kitchen. I was speechless, stunned and confused; consumed by anger and humiliation and nearly in tears! I had never before been so summarily dismissed nor had I ever felt the sting of inequality to that degree. This was a far cry from being invited by my parents to join them on the veranda for a glass of Port! That memory seemed so distant and obscure.

They all shared the same genetic material and obviously the same rather shallow pool which by now was probably more of a murky, muddy mosquito ridden puddle. I can't help but wonder what they would have done had I showed up completely unannounced and uninvited. How welcome would I have been or how awkward my presence?

Shortly after his graduation from the University of Tennessee, he was hired by the railroad. As it happened, it was the same company that had employed his father for over thirty years. He was immediately sent to Savannah, Georgia to begin a year long, intensive, management training program that would prove to be both time consuming and extremely demanding; leaving him little or no time for a life outside the company. Except for the brief, somewhat disastrous few months that we lived together in Cheyenne, I could probably count, on one hand, the number of times we have actually been in each others presence. Now that I'm back in California with my client list steadily growing and busier than I want to be as a trainer, he is living in a small apartment and working non-stop in Savannah. We couldn't be further apart if we had planned it. East Coast versus West Coast. For the time being, there seemed to be no way around our current situation but we had to find a workable solution and soon. With our educations behind us and our respective jobs somewhat secure – the only remaining obstacle was to somehow be together – somewhere, and soon.

Neither one of us could afford to fly back and forth across the country on a regular basis to maintain this long-distance relationship. And all the emailing, texting, Skyping and phone calls couldn't make up for the distance between us and the lack of physical nearness. I felt something was terribly wrong with us and this on-going situation but I didn't know how to fix it. I only knew I couldn't ignore it any longer. It was not going to go away and it seemed to be more than the distance between us – it was something else, but what? Something had to change. Perhaps it was her. The woman on his lap in the photo posted on FaceBook? I envisioned her as a chubby, grey, little mouse silently nibbling away at the tapestry of our relationship in my absence. Whether to chew a hole large enough to wiggle through or simply to cause the fabric to unravel - I couldn't be sure, I had no way of knowing – only my suspicions which grew larger every day we were apart. I wanted to believe her presence wasn't just another one of his lies; he'd been caught in too many over the last few years. For the last six months after his graduation, he had been insisting that we get together in the same place, at the same time, and make a serious plan for the rest of our lives. He had things to say that I needed to hear from him, in person – face to face – not over the phone and not on Skype.

He decided the time had come to determine what we were doing and where we were going before the distance between us grew out of proportion and we lost all perspective. We owed it to ourselves if we intended to move forward. The situation and this on-going, long distance relationship could not go on indefinitely. Something had to change. Under the circumstances, it was mutually unsatisfactory and far from manageable for both of us. We agreed one of us had to change. But which one? I had the distinct impression from the tone of his voice whenever this particular controversy came up in conversation that it wasn't going to be him. There was never any question in his mind which one of us would concede. But several hundred questions lingered in my mind.

Stella Benson

Chapter Eight

The opportunity for Nat and I to finally be together in the same place at the same time came up rather unexpectedly when my oldest and dearest friend, Sybil, announced her intention to be married in Denver in early June. She had asked me to be one of her bridesmaids and Nat, who she knew well from our days at Colorado State, was to be invited as well. For over sixteen months she had let her engagement drag on while she meticulously planned the ideal, picture perfect wedding and both excitement and expectations were running high. No detail was overlooked and no expense spared including the small photograph of her and the soon-to-be groom printed on the postage stamps on the invitations, the monogrammed linen napkins and the carefully chosen wine complete with commemorative labels. It was expected to be a whirl-wind three day event; four days for those of us coming from out of town. Every moment was accounted for in one way or another with a wide selection of activities to keep all the guests properly entertained. As a bridesmaid, my duties to the bride and her family were very clearly defined and my time already spoken for. It was imperative that I fulfill my responsibilities as an attentive bridesmaid and yet equally important that I spend as much time alone with Nat as possible, regardless of all the scheduled activities that invariably accompany a huge, extravagant, society wedding.

Nat and I had been together for over six years and we both agreed this was the right time in our lives to move forward. This wedding would give us the perfect opportunity and just the excuse we needed to finally spend some long over due time together. We had been separated for one reason or another for far too long. It was decision time. I was helplessly and hopelessly in love with him committed, with every fiber of being to our relationship and unquestionably devoted to him. I knew it; I could see it, feel it and I couldn't stop it if I wanted to. I had no desire to change what we had or the experiences we had shared over the years. I had no reason to believe he felt any differently about me or our relationship. And I believed him when he assured me that this home-town girl meant absolutely nothing to him; she had never been a threat to our relationship and never would be. We only had three days together and I had no intention of wasting what precious little time we had, discussing her. I already knew more than I cared to know. I had had more than enough of the subject. This weekend would be about us and us alone I was not about to let her come between us and ruin our weekend together. When one woman strikes at the heart of another woman, she had better be damn sure her aim is true because if she misses, it is unlikely she will ever have another opportunity. For at least this weekend, he was mine and mine alone and as far as I was concerned, she had missed her mark.

When my mother and I finally arrived at the hotel in Denver early Thursday afternoon, we were immediately swept into the welcome champagne lunch, held exclusively for the sixty out of town guests. It lasted just long enough to coincide with the cocktail hour and hors' d'ouvers, followed by a full five course dinner. The wine and champagne never ceased to flow. By ten o'clock that evening, my mother was exhausted, completely talked out, and a little the worse for the wine. Claiming a roaring headache; she politely excused herself and headed to our room for a hot bath and a good night's sleep. I was excited, equally exhausted and more than a little nervous about seeing Nat the next day after so many months of separation. I couldn't wait for us to be together – actually together. I had missed him every minute that we were apart and all the texting and phone calls couldn't make up for the feeling of being in his arms again. I wondered if he would look the same, if he would feel the way I remembered and if he would smell that smell so uniquely is own. I don't know what he wore, but he always managed to smell distinctly woodsy; as if he'd just come in on a cold day from chopping wood, or damp woolen mittens drying on a radiator. To me, it seemed to be a blend of cedar or pine sap with a dash of Sweet Baby Rays B.B.Q. sauce and a slight whiff of chocolate; a very distinctive aroma that even now, years later, I associate with him. Would it be awkward at first or would we just pick up where we had left off so long ago? Would the specter of this other woman continue to loom between us or was she really just a minor indiscretion not worthy of discussion? Easily forgotten. I had already decided to take the high road and not be the first to bring her up in any conversation. She meant nothing to us – not now. It occurred to me for one very brief moment that this entire incident with her, trying to come between us, at this particular time, was just another one of his games. He was a master game player who truly enjoyed getting into my head. Was she just another excuse or a futile effort to infuriate me and conceal his own insecurities? Insecurities veiled in arrogance. Whatever his game, I didn't want to play. He plays by his own rules which have a tendency to fluctuate in his favor. I refuse to dwell in petty jealousy or open competition with anyone, especially another woman unless it's on the back of a horse in an enclosed arena, and on a level playing field, which this was not. Once again, given the distance, I was at a definite disadvantage. Jealousy, to me, is a wasted emotion and he knew that but it never stopped him from trying to elicit a reaction from me. In his mind, if I couldn't be coerced into jealousy then clearly I didn't care enough about him. It was a constant challenge he couldn't resist. I have always felt, if you have something to say and have the courage of your convictions, then stand up and say it. To my face! I may be many things, but I'd like to think stupid isn't one of them. I'm not an idiot. I would like to think I have a fairly high functioning, well disciplined mind and I'm more than secure in my own skin so don't try to spare my feelings. Spare me the sugar coating! I'm not a shrinking violet who might wilt under your gaze or melt into a puddle at your disapproval. I suppose it's possible he was trying to keep me on my toes and in my "place" whatever that was. Only he seemed to know and he seldom chose to share it with me. That was the essence of the game. The question was, why now? Why the sudden need to plan our future?

Nat was scheduled to arrive at the hotel at 10 o'clock the following morning, after flying the red-eye all night from Savannah. I was expected in the hotel lobby, an hour before his arrival, at 9 o'clock, to take the limousine with the rest of the bridal party to the full dress rehearsal. I was hoping the rehearsal would go smoothly, with just one walk through and I'd be able to get away as soon as I could politely excuse myself. I had no choice but to ask my mother to keep Nat entertained when he arrived until I could feasibly excuse myself from the rehearsal and return to the hotel.

Over the last year or so, Nat and my mother had become somewhat close though guardedly, at least from my mother's perspective. She wasn't entirely convinced "he was the one for me." The first time he came to visit my parents a few years ago, somewhere between the airport and my parent's home; he had decided to stop off and buy a six pack of courage in a can. By the time he arrived at my parent's home, he was drunk and wreaked of beer. Needless to say, my parents weren't particularly impressed with my current beau; the so-called love of my life that they had heard so much about for the past two or three years. My father graciously shook Nat's hand and then disappeared back into the safety of his library. My mother shot me a disapproving look as if to say, "Seriously! This is the love if your life and he's to be a guest in my home for how long? He's drunk and it's barely noon! This is going to be a problem." I just stood by his side, too embarrassed to come to his rescue or offer an explanation. Nat was capable of cranking up the charm when it suited him but so far it was lost on my mother and she was far from won over and even less impressed. He was the type of man, in her mind, who would, sooner or later, disappoint me and inevitably let me down. It was just a matter of time before he showed his true colors and she could afford to wait. I was hoping this weekend and this wedding would give her the opportunity to get to know him as I did. During one of their previous phone conversations, my mother had admitted to Nat that she knew absolutely nothing about Country and Western music. She preferred classical music or the music of the 60's that she had known growing up. He took this admission as an opportunity to get back into her good graces by "burning" a total of 26 CD's, fully loaded with every country song he thought she should know, including a few songs by his brother who played guitar and was an aspiring country/western singer. He scored a few points with her but it didn't quite put him over the top. I suspect she looked upon this occasion and this long wedding weekend as an opportunity for up close and personal scrutiny.

Whether he knew it or nor not, by agreeing to attend this wedding, he was clearly out of his social element, over his head, fully exposed and vulnerable. Too many beers, any off-color jokes or the slightest social faux pas and my mother was ready to pounce, like a duck on a June bug, as Nat would say. As far as she was concerned, I had yet to meet a man worthy of me much less one who could afford me; my two horses and one rather hyperactive puppy. In other words, according to my parents, I came with a lot of baggage. Unless I intended to marry well or become somebody's trophy wife, which I had no intention of doing, I had to, in all fairness; give this guy a serious heads-up. She believed he had every right to know, in great detail, just what he was "getting into" so that there were no surprises anywhere down the road. And, if I didn't enlighten him, she was there; ready to jump in at a moments notice to make sure he got the full picture. Life with me wasn't going to be easy and he should know everything there was to know, now, rather than later. If all this information scared him off – better to find out now. Either he loved me or he didn't. You take it all; you can't pick through and chose what suits you and disregard or change whatever you disagree with. Everyone has a good side as well as a bad side and you have to accept and embrace both equally if you love them. That's how it should be. Throughout this weekend, she had absolutely no desire to bond or connect with him, instead her goal was to quietly discover exactly "what he was made of" and whether or not he had what it would take "to go the distance." All of which she intended to relay to my father in great detail the minute we got home. She was prepared to observe his every move, listen to every word, try to understand what he was saying, regardless of his accent and carefully analyze everything from his obvious lack of table manners to his black dress cowboy boots with the well worn heels. Nothing was going to get past her; she was armed and ready, locked and loaded. She knew practically everyone at the wedding with the exception of groom's immediate family and she had no intention of being embarrassed or humiliated by Nat. Neither did she intend to make excuses or apologize for whatever shortcomings he might take this opportunity to display. This was his one chance to redeem himself after their first, beer soaked meeting and she hoped he'd take advantage of it. One slip and he was history. Since their first disastrous meeting a few years ago, she had her doubts about him and so far he hadn't done much to alleviate her skepticism. As far as she was concerned, this was his last chance, his best chance and his only opportunity to prove his sincerity.

My mother had spent too much time and energy on my upbringing and my education; not to mention subsidizing my passion to ride. She was determined not to let some guy, who came from goodness knows where and that I had met in some cowboy bar in Fort Collins, lead me down a path to obscurity. That hadn't been part of her original plan. I was entitled to something more and deserved more out of life. For the most part, I had to agree with her. I had no intention of "settling". I had enough on my plate as it was and there was so much more I wanted to accomplish before settling down. Babies and diapers could wait and wait a long time as far as I was concerned. Besides, I knew babies, unlike horses could vomit. A very scary thought that I didn't want to consider, just yet. I had already seen a few of my girlfriends marry young, have a baby within a few months and file for divorce shortly thereafter. In the end, they had no choice but to move back in with their parents and hand their child over to be raised by its grandparents. The whole, tragic scenario scared the wits out of me, so much so that I was determined not to let it happen . My mother never hesitated to remind me that she was far too young to be anyone's grandmother.

Divorce was absolutely out of the question, not an option worthy of discussion in my mind. No one in my family had ever been divorced and my mother had no intention of me becoming the first to be burdened with that rather dubious honor. As a rule, she didn't give a tinkers damn what people thought about her but she cared deeply about the rest of the family. I had to look at this relationship calmly and rationally, weigh the pros and cons and make an informed decision regarding my future with Nat, if there was to be one. If I insisted on marrying

Nat she would support that decision as long as it wasn't based purely on emotion, sex or simply an infatuation. I had to know there would be bumps in the road, we wouldn't always agree on everything but if you were committed to your relationship, you "worked it out". You just didn't cut and run, you stayed the course. Her greatest fear was that I would become just another statistic. Married and divorced by 30 with a 4 year old, living at home with my parents, working long hours at some low level job, and leaving my child all day, very day, with it's grandparents. That was absolutely out of the question, to her and to me. The only way to avoid that particular situation was to be as sure as I possibly could be before I agreed to whatever he was proposing – if indeed that was what he had in mind.

Of course, the rehearsal ran on and on, ad nauseum. It was very late in the afternoon by the time I was able to get back to the hotel and I realized I had left Nat, unprotected and completely vulnerable, with my mother for well over five hours! If I was nervous before, I was beyond nervous now; I was coming up quickly on pure hysteria. My curiosity about him and us and my mother alone with Nat for so long only added to my apprehension. The minute I came through the door of our hotel room, I was in his arms. It felt so right, so natural; his was where I was meant to be, where I wanted to be. The sparkle in his eyes was all I needed to see to believe he felt the same way. All our fights, arguments, disagreements, and the months spent apart, melted away in a single moment, all but forgotten. We were together, that's all that mattered. There couldn't be more than this – anything more than this moment, or this feeling. He was just as handsome as I remembered, even more so, if that's possible. There was a noticeable bit of grey at his temples that wasn't there before but it only made him that much more appealing and somehow more sophisticated. And that smell – his smell - the smell I remembered so well, was all over him and now all over me.

We were together and if only for this weekend, that had to be more than enough for both of us. Nothing else mattered as long as we had each other. No obstacle could be too great if we faced it together. This was the way it was supposed to be

– the way I had dreamed it would be one day. Now I had everything I had ever wanted and nothing and no one could possibly come between us. He looked a bit worn around the edges, whether from having flown the red-eye or from spending the last several hours in my mother's company, I couldn't be sure. He was hungry and tired and all he wanted was something to eat; a hot shower and me by his side. Once in his room, we ordered room service and then just lay on his bed all afternoon staring at each other – rediscovering each other all over again. We didn't talk much; we were content to just look at each other for hours. We had so much to talk about, so many decisions to make and so many plans to consider, but we didn't address any of them. It could all wait. It was satisfying to know again what it feels like to be with someone who wants to be with me - just me - not out of a sense of obligation but sheer desire. He was my lover, my friend, my balance and my desire. I wanted to hear again, all about his life since his graduation; his new job, his cramped, dumpy apartment in Savannah and his bizarre roommate who paid his share of the rent on time but seldom if ever actually lived there. His new job and the training program were exhausting and as a new hire, he was often required to keep demanding and unusual hours. I couldn't help but notice that this new job and the last six months had somehow matured him. Gone were the insecurities and the indecisiveness that had plagued him since the day of his discharge from the Air Force. He had finally grown up. He seemed somehow older, more in control and I admired his new found confidence and his desire to be successful. Back too, was the Top Gun/Tom Cruise swagger that I had fallen in love with when we first met.

He wanted to know all about my horses and my clients; the long hours I spent at the barn often feeling more like a babysitter to some or an amateur, fortune cookie psychiatrist to others. Their over - zealous and increasingly impatient parents with their unrealistic expectations and hopes for their children's rapid rise to success and recognition. My constant frustration in trying to keep the children motivated and moving along, at the same time trying to appease their parents- convincing them that their little darlings were indeed making progress – however slowly.

The remainder of the afternoon literally flew by and all too soon we realized that we were both expected to attend the rehearsal dinner that evening. There was no way out of it, no acceptable excuse we could offer though we would have given anything to just stay where we were, as we were. We were so content in each others arms, reluctant to disrupt what we had at that moment – neither one of us wanted to be the first to break the mood. If we made some excuse not to attend the rehearsal dinner our absence would not go noticed by Sybil, John or more importantly Sybil's mother who would make sure my mother knew about it in minutes. I really didn't want to go down that road. It was, after all, the reason we were here. This was Sybil and John's weekend, their celebration, their wedding. We couldn't, in good conscience, disappoint everyone and I was expected to give a toast. I'd never hear the end of it, and my mother, I was sure, would probably blame him for our collective rudeness. There was no satisfactory explanation or acceptable reason not to attend.

We sat side by side at the dinner, holding hands under the table as though we were two high school sweethearts who had just decided to go steady. I'm afraid we may have appeared somewhat impolite to the other guests but all eyes were firmly focused on Sybil and John. No one seemed to notice or pay much attention to the two of us. We enjoyed the obligatory five course fabulous dinner and drank enough wine and champagne to make us question our ability to find our way back to the hotel safely. We endured what seemed to be the endless toasts to the happy couple and their future until I thought I'd scream if we didn't find a way out of there soon. We'd clap politely after every toast, and then kiss each other with probably more ardor than necessary and obviously more for our mutual benefit than to Sybil and John's happiness. Finally, thankfully, we were able to slip away unnoticed and head back to his room in the hotel.

That night when we came up for air and as I lay in his arms, our legs entwined and our noses two inches apart, he quietly said, "Marry me". Here we were, finally together, happier than we ever had been in a long time. I looked at him and as calmly as I could, though my heart was beating furiously, I said, "Yes."

His reaction was not at all what I expected. You would think by agreeing to marry him, I had finally punched the right code into the system and pushed a button that, like his missiles, caused him to explode. This is what had been so important to him; why he had insisted we be together. This is what he had wanted to say that was so important it couldn't wait. He had thought about all this and now he had a plan.

He wanted to elope that night – immediately! Never mind that it was 2 o'clock in the morning. We were here, my mother was here – what more did we need? The decision had been made; I had accepted his proposal, so why wait? Apparently he'd given this a lot of thought and proceeded to outline his overall plan for my benefit. He seemed to always have a plan. We simply had to drag my mother out of her bed, grab a few friends who were still partying upstairs in Sybil and John's suite, find a Justice of the Peace and we'd get this done before the sun rose on another day. He had learned from the front desk at the hotel, that this weekend, the hotel was hosting a convention of over three hundred Lutheran ministers - one of them must be available even at this hour. Didn't hotels usually keep a minister or a priest on staff? Maybe if we checked the bar we'd find one that was willing to perform an impromptu ceremony. Or we could jump into my mother's rental car and drive to Cheyenne and the Fort Warren Air Force Base to roust the base Chaplain. The fact that it was a four hour drive there and back was possible as long as we were back in time for the wedding that afternoon.

While I found his enthusiasm infectious, I decided one of us had to be sensible about this. It was after all, very late and though I didn't want to dampen his mood, one of us had to be the voice of reason. As patiently and carefully as I could, and as happy as I was, I started to carefully explain all the reasons why what he was proposing wasn't feasible – not here and definitely not now.

First of all, and possibly the most important issue, was the fact that anyone who knew my mother and valued their life would never consider "dragging her out of her bed" at this hour – no matter how important. That wasn't going to happen! And, if we went ahead and eloped here and now, without her, she'd be on her cell phone at first light to her attorney and have it annulled before Sybil got half down the aisle! This was Sybil and John's weekend – their wedding and we were here to celebrate with them and their families. I didn't feel comfortable stealing their thunder, ruining their big day or Sybil's months of planning by announcing our engagement or possible elopement. She'd never forgive me. My mother would invariably have a great deal to say about our lousy timing and the idea of incurring Sybil's mothers' wrath, who I had known all my life, was too scary to even consider. Neither one of us were Lutherans, even if we could convince one of the ministers wondering around in the hotel lobby to agree. Furthermore, the idea of getting married in an Air Force Base chapel without any of our family present and in front of a handful of strangers dragged in to bear witness wasn't exactly what I had in mind. And, not to put to fine a point on it, but Nat had not yet asked my father for my hand. Maybe the ring could wait but my father's opinion on the subject certainly would not. Nat may think that particular tradition was outdated but I knew my father was looking forward to that conversation and was not going to be denied the opportunity to express his opinions on life, love and marriage to any serious suitor I might bring home. He was not about to blindly hand me over to some guy he hardly knew without a thorough investigation. He had questions and serious concerns about Nat. Having met him only once, and he had not come away from that first encounter overly impressed or at all convinced that Nat, in any way, deserved me. He wanted each and every one of his concerns properly addressed before he would agree to anything.

His own experience with my grandfather, when he finally asked for my mother's hand, was too vivid in his own mind, even if it was 40 years ago. It was a right of passage and a matter of respect, one Nat couldn't possibly avoid. According to my father, when he finally approached my Grandfather, my mother's father, he'd been too nervous and unsure of what to expect. And my grandfather, knowing full well what my father intended to ask, couldn't resist the temptation to drag out the conversation and make my father squirm by asking innumerable questions; starting with how he intended to support my mother, his gross annual income, his religion, if any, his politics, if any, and his thoughts on the war in Vietnam. My father was, thankfully, a Republican. There was no way in hell my Grandfather was going to let his only daughter, my mother, marry a Democrat or a Catholic! My grandfather summed it up with "if a bird marries a fish, where are they going to live?" It didn't help that they were having this conversation while sitting on the back porch of my Grandparent's home in Minnesota in late December with a bottle of Aquavit between them and a six pack of beer.

Between the beer and the shots of Aquavit, by the time my grandfather finished firing questions at him; my father was so confused he had all but forgotten what his original question had been and why he was there in the first place. His resolve had, by this time, all but dissipated. My grandfather had to steer the conversation back to the subject at hand. By the time my father received my grandfather's blessing, and being unfamiliar with the full impact of Swedish Vodka, he was suffering from a blinding headache and a deep desire to lie down somewhere, even a nearby snow bank would do. He was, in the end, successful in receiving my grandfathers blessing, he just can't quite remember how he'd managed to do it. My father was not going to be denied a similar experience; he felt it was his due; waiting for this day and planning this conversation since the day I was born with all his questions firmly in his mind. Nat would just have to endure the ritual. I knew my father had a lot of concerns about Nat but as long as he didn't bring up the bird and the fish, as my grandfather had so many years ago, I thought Nat would survive. At least, I had given him some idea what to expect from my father. I made it very clear to Nat that if he avoided politics and religion he would survive. I knew too, that my father was looking forward to walking me down the aisle – any aisle. Nat's current plan didn't seem to include an aisle of any sort. And, it might be a pesky little detail, but we couldn't avoid the fact that we didn't have a valid marriage license and no possibility of obtaining one on a Saturday afternoon much less a Sunday morning.

When I first started to date, my father took enormous pleasure in telling any boy who dared come through the front door, that if he ever made me cry, he'd blow his knee caps off with a .22 and if, god help him, he ever laid his hands on me, in anger or otherwise, he'd shoot him where he stood. Quietly explaining to them that he didn't give a damn if his actions did violate his parole! They never knew he was joking but most weren't exactly in a position to argue the point and few hung around long enough to test his theory. Once he had successfully outlined the ground rules he would calmly announce to me that my date had arrived, pump air and stroll back to his library to wait and see who stood their ground and who ran like hell. He believed this would eliminate the riff-raff and hose boys whose intentions were less than honorable. All he managed to do was to eliminate most of my dates and I'd spend yet another Saturday night on the couch wedged between my parents holding a bowl of popcorn, watching a classic war movie or a foreign film. I couldn't begin to count the number of times I've been dateless on a Friday or Saturday night, watching "The Hunt for Red October" or "Run Silent – Run Deep." I could probably recite the entire dialogue of "Das Boot", verbatim, in German, if called upon to do so. If the film was a classic and involved a submarine, ear-splitting alarms and sweaty, clammy men in cramped quarters yelling "Dive, dive", we watched it over and over again. My mother favored Scandinavian Noir. Any film reflecting a collaboration of Ingmar Bergman and Sven Nykist became an instant must –see in our house. They, at least, included subtitles. My Swedish, at this point, was limited to simple expletives, learned from my mother and to be used with great discretion.

A handsome young man in high school that I had been flirting with for weeks actually had the nerve to pull into the driveway, stand along side his mother's champagne colored, Mercedes SUV, and honk the horn repeatedly. From my bedroom window, I could see he was dressed in very tight black jeans, biker boots with a thick chain wrapped around his waist, a white t-shirt that said FU across the front and to complete the look, a pack of Marlboro Reds rolled up in his sleeve. My father, annoyed at this particular specter, opened the front door and yelled "Dude! You better be dropping something off because you're not picking anything up.". I watched, fully dressed as another date peeled out of the driveway, never to return while my father calmly closed the front door, turned off the front lights and retreated to his library very satisfied with himself. He had successfully chased off and discouraged yet another beau. Listening to Nat,

I was convinced this plan of his to elope, while wildly spontaneous and very romantic was just his way of avoiding my father. No such luck. There was no way out of this one.

Every Christmas Eve, without fail, my mother would appear with the bottle of Aquavit, determined to give her traditional Christmas toast to our collective health and happiness. My brother refused to touch it, the smell alone made me instantly nauseous and my father could feel that old familiar headache lurking under the surface, just waiting to reappear. He was convinced it wasn't vodka at all, just disguised high octane diesel fuel cleverly packaged in a pretty bottle. My mother had to be the only person west of the Mississippi who would actually pay good money for it. It was the one tradition he hoped to avoid every year. Yet, I knew, if he suspected a young man was going to ask for my hand, he would immediately start rummaging around in the bar until he found that bottle safely stowed somewhere near the back. He intended to lure Nat out on our back porch with a six pack, which he knew by now Nat was partial to, and introduce him to Swedish Vodka, just as my grandfather had done to him, while he peppered him relentlessly with the his laundry list of questions. He was determined to make a tradition out of this particular ritual and I knew he couldn't wait and had no intention of being denied the opportunity for any reason. He secretly hoped Nat would collapse under the pressure, succumb to the subtle effect of the vodka and if he forgot why he was there, my father, unlike my grandfather, had no intention of reminding him.

After what seemed like hours of arguing, I finally convinced Nat we had no choice but to wait until after Sybil's wedding and reception to announce our news. We'd have to keep all this to ourselves until we could work through some of the details confronting us. He agreed he would call his parents the minute he arrived in Savannah on Sunday night and I agreed I wouldn't say a word until my mother and I arrived back in San Francisco. My father had arranged to pick us up at San Francisco Airport and then intended to drive directly into the City for dinner.

Bix restaurant was one of my parent's favorite restaurants in San Francisco. Once an upscale, civilized speakeasy in the 1930's and then a very sophisticated supper club in the 40's, it was hidden in an alley in Jackson Square that tourists could seldom find and most local cab drivers refused to admit even existed. It was dark, mysterious and sultry; like stepping back in time; far from the hustle and bustle of North Beach. It traditionally showcased local, live jazz or a solo pianist every night of the week. It had a quiet, elegant ambiance, cozy booths and a typical San Francisco menu of primarily locally caught, fresh seafood. One of the finest restaurants in San Francisco and, at the same time, one of the City's best kept secrets. You had to know the City very well in order to find it and the doorman even better to get in. It occurred to me this would be the perfect opportunity to tell them both exactly what had happened and everything that had been said over the weekend. It would be a quiet, public setting; eliminating the possibility of a loud discussion and any drama. It would be the perfect opportunity for me to tell them both everything. I just had to wait and hold my tongue until we arrived.

The bride and all the bridesmaids were picked up at the hotel in a limousine early Saturday morning for a full day of preparation prior to the actual wedding that evening. We were all treated to lavish, full body massage and then a manicure and pedicure, followed by a stylist brought in to do our hair. As it happened, we were all brunettes with long hair and Sybil had very specific ideas of exactly how she wanted our hair styled; flowers carefully woven into our plaits. Throughout the day we munched on light, cucumber and watercress finger sandwiches, mimosas and a continually replenished tray of hors d'oeuvres. The groom and his attendants arrived a few hours later to dress for the photographs which were all taken that afternoon prior to the wedding. The entire bridal party had been asked by the photographer to casually cavort through an aspen forest like a flock of overdressed wood nymphs.

The ceremony itself was performed on an adjoining stone courtyard with a fountain quietly cascading into a water lily pond, and beneath an ivy and flower laden pergola, covered in bright, white twinkle lights. Facing due west, with the Rocky Mountains as a natural backdrop and timed to the setting sun, it was breathtakingly beautiful in its simplicity. The wedding was, of course, perfection even though it was over 96 degrees. Sybil's months of planning were reflected in every detail; the heavy, floor to ceiling doors of the dining room and dance floor were open to the warm evening breeze as thousands of twinkle lights sparkled from every tree. She had chosen purple, black and silver and her color scheme was reflected throughout the room. Our simple, long dresses were black and strapless with a wide, satin silver sash. All of the tables were covered in creamy white antique linens with huge arrangements of Japanese anemones, pale lavender peonies, dahlias, white stephanotis and lily of the valley, surrounded by luxuriant greens and encircling a single, glowing silver pillar candle. Given the heat, even at that evening hour, combined with the sheer number of floral arrangements, the overwhelming scent was intoxicating. The five-tiered, wedding cake stood elegantly by itself on a single table in a broad, windowed alcove; glistening in silver frosting and covered with large chocolate covered purple and black polka-dots. Even the aisle was carefully lined with large vases of trailing green ivy and fragrant, pastel campanulas. The food was incomparable, compliments of one of Denver's premier chefs hired just for the occasion.

Apparently, just a few days before the wedding, the battle lines were drawn when John's family insisted on serving only beer and bourbon while Sybil's family felt strongly that fine California wines and French champagne, not domestic, should be included. They all finally compromised by serving both and the bar never stopped pouring. Their quiet, non-denominational ceremony lasted exactly eleven minutes, which Nat conveniently timed and, with a sigh of relief, grateful to be in out of the heat, we all strolled back inside for more chilled champagne before dinner.

Early on in her child-rearing career, my mother had discovered that children, safely buckled into a booster seat or strapped into a car seat, gave her what amounted to a captive audience. She and she alone, controlled the door and window locks as well as the radio channels and the CD selection, which could include anything from the Bob Dylan's Greatest Hits to her favorite series of piano concertos or her Rosetta Stone Level 4 Advanced French CD's. More importantly, she controlled the volume. Unfortunately her choice of music gave us absolutely no indication of her mood or what was to follow. We could roll our eyes all we wanted, she wouldn't notice as her eyes were focused on the road. Like it or not, she had our full attention – we were in a vacuum of her own making, trapped and with no way out until we reached our final destination. As I look back, I realize many of the most important conversations between my mother and myself, occurred while we were driving in the car. It didn't happen all the time and certainly not every time but my brother and I never knew what to expect when we climbed into her car with her, which I'm sure was probably her intention. It did occur often enough, however, to be memorable for both of us.

I knew I would be preoccupied attending to the bride prior to the wedding, so Nat willingly agreed to arrive at the appointed hour, driving my mother's rental car. He had no idea what was to come and in all the confusion of the wedding, I had not had the opportunity to warn him. An oversight he would never let me forget. The minute the car door slammed, he was trapped for a full twenty minutes for the drive from the hotel. Recognizing she was once again in control and finally had what she hoped was his full attention, my mother decided to seize the opportunity to give him a few pointers regarding the proper etiquette required for a social gathering of this caliber.

Stella Benson

Chapter Nine

Casually, she said, "Ecoute! Sparky; you're not in Dogpatch any longer so it might behoove you to pay attention to what I have to say. I don't have the time to fill in the obvious, glaring gaps in your education, but there a few things I'd like to go over before we arrive. So listen closely."

"Shit naw, momma, I shouda node y'all was gonna cook my grits the very minute this here car door done slammed shut. I jus' knew me an' you was gonna have a problem what with Jory goin' on ahead of us to the weddin' in that limo. Y'all jus' want me all to yourself fur a spell doncha? He replied.

"I am not cookin' your grits! Whatever that means? Do not flatter yourself by over estimating your seductive prowess! I am more than immune. To put it simply, and in terms even you can understand, you are pissing on the wrong tree! I'm going to pause and give you a minute to remember who you are talking to. There are a few things you should be aware of; a few things I'd like to point out before you make a complete fool out of yourself or embarrass all of us. As far as I can determine, your social skills are basically non-existent. This wedding is neither a barracks nor a church social. And this good ole boy, aw shucks, dig our toe in the dirt demeanor of yours isn't going to impress anyone. Now would be a good time to dig down deep for that shiny veneer of Southern civility which, against all odds, you have somehow managed to perfect."

"Where to start? First of all, and most importantly, you have no insight opinions or a position on anything - especially religion, politics or current events. Please try to limit your conversation exclusively to the weather or sports and that's all! If you can't do that, then keep your mouth shut." She continued.

"Do not volunteer any personal information to anyone regarding your past, your future, your hopes or dreams, your home town, your upbringing, or the lack of it.

Could you possibly get the grits out of your mouth long enough to speak something vaguely resembling English? Have you ever considered taking a basic grammar course? I'm curious, are you intellectually indolent by nature or is it a condition you have to work at to maintain? Either way, it must be exhausting. Is it possible you are functioning in a parallel universe? Were you dropped on your head as an infant or possibly struck by lightning? Whatever the cause, I don't feel as though I have your full attention. You seem to have a head full of disconnected wiring! Are you listening?' " She asked.

"Shucks, I can't hep but listen. I ain't got nowheres else to go an' y'all are the only one in this here car doin' all the talkin. Y'all got me trapped like a possum in a stump!" He said.

"Do not, under any circumstances, stick your fingers in your ears or your nose.

Neither is this the time nor the place to explore the contents or your belly button or any other cavity. There will be no expressions, audible or otherwise that are a direct result of your digestive process and that includes armpit noises spitting, burping or belching. And, don't scratch anything!"

"Because you are my daughters date for the evening, you will be seated at the head table with the rest of the bridal party. When you sit down there will be a napkin folded on your left. Pick it up and gently place it in your lap. Do not tuck it into your collar, stuff it into the waistband of your pants or tie it around your neck like a bib because you will undoubtedly forget it is there until you stand up. When you have finished your dinner, fold it and place it back on the table. Do not roll it into a ball and throw it into the remnants of your dinner. And please make a concerted effort to keep your elbows off the table, chew with your mouth shut and don't you dare steal the silverware!" She advised.

"There will be three glasses in front of you. The largest one is for water. The second is for red wine and the last, smaller glass is for white wine. Drink red or white but not both! Rest assured, the wine will not come out of a box. Do not, under any circumstances, bring your usual Whiskey Pickle to the table with you when we're asked to sit down to dinner. Hard liquor is neither allowed nor tolerated at the table. And, do not stand around chomping on your ice cubes! Do not grab your wine glass with your fist as if it was a can of beer. Champagne is to be sipped, not chugged! There will be no drinking contests, tequila shots or liars dice included in this evening's activities!"

"I took the liberty of pre-ordering the filet mignon– rare, for you." She said.

"Fish! We're gonna be eatin' raw fish at a weddin' supper? All this time 'an money ta get this shindig offa the ground 'an that's the best they gots ta offer! Y'all are shittin' me right? He gasped.

"Filet mignon is not fish! Seriously! How do you get from one day to the next with such obviously limited intelligence? You are either living in a bubble of your own making or you are surrounded by a deep fog of indifference. I can't decide which and I doubt even you know. As I was saying, do not attack your steak as though you are gutting an elk. Cut it into small bite-sized pieces and please try not to talk with your mouth full! It will not be a .22 ounce steak smothered with a can of baked beans, or slathered with that lumpy, brown gelatinous gravy that you are so fond of. I specifically did not order the salmon for you because I knew a fish fork would only confuse you and probably send you into sensory overload. If you are at all unsure about the silverware: what fork to use with what course, watch my daughter. And do not ask for seconds – there are no seconds!

Eat what is put in front of you without comment or criticism. There will also be no salt, pepper or red and yellow plastic squirt bottles of mustard and Ketchum, A1 Sauce, Duke's mayonnaise, vinegar or any other familiar, regional condiments on the table so don't even ask. And, I can guarantee you, grits, chitlins, and pork rinds will not be on the menu! There will undoubtedly be an appetizer before the entrée, probably fried calamari or possibly pate de fois gras in aspic. I'm going to assume that you have never had calamari so it might be a good idea to try it, without making a face or questioning its origins or preparation. I may be going out on a limb here but I'm told you prefer most everything you consume to be deep fat fried. Am I right?'

"What the hell's calamari? Y'all are enjoyin' this ain'tcha, makin' a fool outta me 'an pointin' out my shortcomin's?"

"I must admit I do enjoy it to some extent because you make it so easy. It's hard to resist. Your obvious shortcomings are too numerous to mention and I don't have that kind of time. As for making a fool out of you; you don't need any help from me. You do a wonderful job all by yourself. There isn't enough time to address those and I honestly wouldn't know where to begin." She responded.

"To answer your question, calamari is a cephalopod, commonly called squid. The body of the squid is sliced into rings and the tentacles are eaten whole. It's lightly breaded, seasoned and fried – so you should enjoy it. It's usually served with tartar sauce or a light remoulade sauce which has an anchovy base. It is considered a delicacy.

"Shit naw! Ugh! I ain't gonna eat no friggin squid! An' I ain't eatin nobodys or othins' tubes 'an tentacles neither! I don't care what y'all do 'em or where all they come from! Y'all can put whatever sauce ya want on them things cuz I ain't eatin' none of that shit! How in the hell do y'all make sauce outta anchovies? I ain't touchin' no sauce made outta them slimy little fishes! Them ain't nothin' but bait fur my catfish line! Don' y'all ever eat anything like normal people? How 'bout chicken fried steak wit biscuits an' gravy, collards an' maybe some corn fritters on the side or sweet tater fires? That there y'all are talkin' 'bout jus' ain't natural. It ain't even Amurican! Y'all get yurselves all dressed up 'an stand 'round eatin' that there crap cuz somebody tole y'all is was fancy 'an expensive 'an all yur really doin' is givin' yurselves fancy airs! Slimy shit like that would gag a maggot! Did y'all know, when me an' your daughter was movin' our stuff from Cheyenne down ta her school there in Virginia, when we was driving 'cross't country, we pulled up outsida Lincoln, Nebraska somewheres 'long the highway, at a Howard Johnson's fur somethin' ta eat an' she ordered them fired clams they all got on the menu there. Well, I tried one of them thin's an' I ain't lying when I tell y'all it struck me as tastin' like chewy, fried snot! I don' care how delicate y'all think that shit is. An' if them clams tasted like snot then I got it in my head that fried squid ain't gonna be that far different an' is gonna be more 'n likely akin to fired boogers! No ma'am I gotta pass on that. No way in hell, I'm eatin' that shit! Y'all are shinin' me agin' ain'tcha? Y'all think I'm stupid enuff ta fall fur that!"

"Where to begin! You really don't want to know what I think! Those were clams, this is calamari! There is a significant difference. Unfortunately, I am completely unfamiliar with the inherent differences between snot and boogers. Until I met you, I hadn't given the subject much consideration. If pressed, I would have to say boogers are clumpy or crusty, requiring a bit of scraping, while snot is far more viscous and has a tendency to run. If left unchecked, it settles on one's upper lip in a disgusting yellow rivulet until it is wiped off with the back of one's hand or shirt sleeve. Wouldn't you agree? Obviously you have given this a great deal more thought than I have. I'm not even going to ask where you stand on the subject of goobers. But all this is makes for riveting conversation – please continue.

"An what the hells pate de foy grass? And aspic? Are them more of y'alls foreign words or what? I jus' can't get my mouth around them kinda words! I'm thinkin' cuz of yur age an' all, y'all seem to have lapses of some sort every now 'an again' causin' ya ta forget who the hell y'all are talkin' to." He said.

"I sincerely wish I could forget to whom I am speaking but unfortunately you are here and as such, impossible to ignore. And what does my age have to do with anything? Foie gras is basically the diseased liver of an artificially fattened duck, or more often, a goose, and then very delicately prepared.

Let's just keep our fingers crossed, for your sake, and pray it's the calamari appetizer – not the foie gras. That will spare me yet another lengthy explanation. Remind me to introduce you someday to lutefisk!" She said.

"F---in' A! There gots to be sumptin' wrong wit y'all! If y'all already knows what the hell that foy gras shit is, an' ya knows it's diseased, why the hell would ya go ahead and eat it! Y'alls bound ta get some damn, nasty crud left over from that diseased ducks liver! That there don' make no sense a'tall goin in. Shit naw! I ain't gonna eat that shit! Y'alls jus' funning wit me, messin' it my head, ain'tcha? You folks don' really eat that crap!! Y'all think I don' know shit from shinola. Well, I'm here ta tell y'all I been aroun' the block more'n y'all knows an' I know a lot more 'n ya'll think I do. I cen do this! I gots me the shanks fur this."

"If only that were true. Regardless of your shanks, I have my doubts. Why don't you reserve judgment until you have at least tasted the calamari? You may be pleasantly surprised. If you don't care for it, quietly pass your plate to my daughter with out calling attention to yourself. She was practically raised on calamari and she loves it. It is probably the only fried food she would ever consider eating. The salade, of course, will be served following the entrée – not before, so don't ask for it. There will probably be a basket of dinner rolls on the table, or small slices of a baguette or bruschetta but no biscuits and gravy. Do not rip the baguette into little pieces and impale them with your fork and proceed to mop up whatever remains of your dinner. If you should happen to drop anything on the floor, other than crumbs, do not dive under the table to retrieve it! Just leave it there and quietly ask the server to replace it. Are you getting all of this? Need I remind you, there are only two things you are allowed to eat with your fingers - chilled asparagus and fried chicken -neither of which will be on the menu. So please pay attention to your flatware.

"Yes ma'am. I'm hearin' y'all. Notin' wrong wit my ears, one of 'em least ways - but t'other one is holdin' up purty damn good." He said.

"If any one of the women at your table rises and excuses herself to go to the powder room, stand up until she has left. When she returns, stand again and hold her chair for her." She said.

"What the hell fur? What is she, crippled? Are y'all tellin' me I gots to stand up every time some gal heads for the can? I'm gonna be jumpin' up and down all night long while I'm 'ttemptin' ta eat my supper! Kinda like one of them bobbers gots on my catfish line back home. How am I supposed ta eat wit all that goin on? Bless yur heart, Momma, y'all are sure as shit shinin' me, ain't cha? Y'all don' think I know what yur doin' here? He replied. "I really don' gotta do that. Y'all are jus' waitin' for me ta make a fool outta myself an' mess this up."

"You don't have to stand for every woman in the room, just those at your table." She said.

"At some point in the evening, if you have the opportunity, go out of your way to ask the bride to dance and then her mother, in that order. Speaking of dancing, there will be no jerking or anything remotely sensual, sexual or provocative. If I see your hands wander anywhere north or south of my daughter's waist, it will be the last thing you ever remember. It's going to be very hot, especially when you two are dancing, so if you perspire, that tie, such as it is, is not hanging around your neck on a rubber band to wipe the sweat off your face!

"Furthermore, if you are detained outside in the parking lot or anywhere else for that matter, with an uncontrolled or illegal substance in your possession, you're on your own! I have no intention of bailing you out! Are we clear so far? She said.

"Y'all sure gotta shitload of rules." He said

"Every waking hour of your life in the Air Force for the last six years has been governed by rules! Why is it you don't know these things? Didn't your parents teach you anything? There is absolutely no excuse for bad manners. That being said, I'm curious; how have you managed to get this far? How did you ever graduate from college, any college, let alone the University of Tennessee? Were you initially accepted into a remedial program of some sort or a special program for intellectually challenged adults? I only ask because you appear to be a little bit thick. Oh! Come on! Why are you looking at me like that? You have to admit you are clearly not the brightest bulb in the box! Keep your eyes on the road or we'll both end up in a ditch! And how were you ever accepted into the Air Force? I am aware of you're knee injury but my daughter tells me you have limited hearing in one ear, less than 20/20 vision, some degree of scoliosis of the spine and a history of heart disease in your family. For someone about to turn thirty, you're not holding up very well. Just how long do you expect to last?"

She also tells me you don't swim, ski, skate, surf or ride. So what do you do for fun besides the obvious?' She asked.

"Shit! That there jus' ain't so! I cen ride! I done me some bull ridin' years back 'an my uncles gots him some horses that I been ridin' since I was jus' a mite. I don' ride like yur daughter rides though – all that fancy, prancey shit. She always looks ta me like she gots a corn cob shoved up her ass. Don' appear too comfortable from where I sit. Watchin' her do that there ain't much different from watchin' paint dry! Damn! I knows which end of a horse shits!"

"An' shucks naw. Hey! I put in ma' time at UT an' I got me a fur real diploma in Poolitical Science, signed by the Head of the school 'an everything. Even got me this here orange watch an' a matchin' orange class ring, that my ole man give ta me. An' as far as the Air Force went, they was more'n glad fur me ta sign up. Truth be told, they was pleased as punch ta have me. Even give me a big ole signin' bonus! He responded.

I ain't lying when I tell y'all I ain't never been to such a fancy, high-falootin' white-table cloth shindig as this. It jus' never come up afore. Last time I recall being this here all gussied up was at a weddin' fur my second cousin on my momma's side but we don't mention him much in polite company cuz he's illegitimate which ain't no fault a his. We all had to truck on out ta the local VFW Hall in Johnston City or maybe it was the American Legion Post in Bristol. I don' rightly recollect. We' all don' usually step out like this here. We's happy as a fat tick on a wet dog ta jus' make do witout all this trouble. Seems like a whole lotta fuss fur jus' one day! Makes me fell like summthin' plucked outta the Mississippi mud, hosed off, 'an dumped in a bucket on the back stoop. Could be I'm a tad outta my element, maybe even over my head here but shit ain't gonna stick ta me. I cen make this work. Don' y'all pay me no never mind." He answered.

"For the love of God, will you focus? Am I taxing your attention, such as it is, beyond its normal limits? Pay attention to what I'm saying! Having a calm, diversified conversation with you is like talking to a pinball machine or a wind up toy! Are you on any medication that we should be aware of? And another thing, and this is important, please try limiting the folksy, albeit charming references to wildlife and farm animals that have a tendency to colour your conversation." She said.

"So far, y'all are tellin' me I ain't got no manners, I dress funny cuz my clothes don' fit none too good, I talk funny, an' y'all think I'm kinda slow. Y'all are shinin' me from here to thar' ain'tcha? Heck, I do believe I embarrass y'all. Bet yur ashamed of me too, ain'tcha. Bless your heart, momma, y'all are jus' the sweetest thing." He replied.

"Watch yourself Sparky, I may not know much about the South but I know what that means and you are skating on very thin ice as it is." She answered.

"Don' know how ta skate. Never learnt. Ain't much of a swimmer neither, 'specially in oceans. All we gots for swimmin' down home is rivers 'an water towers come summer. Thar's all sorts of weird critters down thar in that ocean like that squid shit ya'll was talkin' 'bout or them slimy clams y'all are so fond of. That an' I know theres sharks in them waters offa California. My luck, bein' what it is, the very minute I steps in that ocean one of them big ole suckers is gonna cruise by an' take me off at my knees! Y'all never gonna know what's gonna come atcha or when. Gots to be on your toes every damn minute. That ain't 'xactly my idea of fun, if ya get my meanin'!"

"Focus! The depth of your ignorance and your complete lack of sophistication clearly has no match. But ... to answer your question, the fact of you; your very existence and your continued presence in my life is indeed a constant source of embarrassment. You are vaguely reminiscent of an insidious canker or a gangrenous pustule on my derrière. Pausing she said, I'm sorry, did that shaft go a little too wide for you"?

"Say what. Momma?"

"My point exactly."

"I betcha y'all are ashamed of me too." He said.

"Bien sur! I don't know you well enough to be ashamed of you - but the night is young. I think we can both agree that you obviously lack something! N'est-ce-pas?? Which puts you at a serious disadvantage. Now that you are aware of the hurdles that lay before you, let's see if we can move forward this evening without incident.

"Don' y'all worry yorself no more, Momma. I ain't gonna do a thang wrong. I ain't here ta embarrass y'all! I got my shanks all ready! He replied.

"Your shanks not withstanding, stop calling me momma! Thankfully, I am not your mother. The responsibility for your upbringing or the lack of it, lies elsewhere. That particular burden is not mine!" She said.

"Do not do or say anything to call attention to yourself. You're enough of a novelty just walking in. That camo flask in your breast pocket, filled, no doubt, with moonshine – leave it behind in the car. And, for the love of God, take that Colts baseball hat off – it doesn't do anything for the suit and remove that toothpick from your mouth or is that a cracker? It must be obvious, even to you, that I haven't spent much time in the South with the exception of an occasional long weekend in New Orleans. And I have never had the opportunity, before you, to really get to know anyone from the Deep South. That being said, I am the first to admit I probably have a somewhat idealized, romantic idea of life south of the Mason-Dixon Line and I can't begin to tell you just how disappointed I am. It is taking a remarkable amount of restraint on my part not to burst out laughing! If nothing else, you are amusing. Let me say this as simply as I can so there is no misunderstanding. It's just an initial observation on my part, not a judgment, by any means - you are no Rhett Butler! I was under the impression Southerner men were steeped in good manners from the day they were born. Imagine my surprise on meeting you?"

"Well, shit, naw. Rhett Butler weren't a fur real person. Jus' some ole guy in an ole movie an' I hear tell there was a book too. Hell, me an' my buddies woulda hauled his bony, white ass right outta town an' dumped it jus' across't the county line faster 'an the wind outta a ducks ass iff'n he'd a showed his face 'round our parts". He replied.

"Hey, Momma. Didja ya'll know me 'an yur daughter been corn-holin'?"

"Yep! I been teachin' her 'an she's already gettin' the hang of it. She's a fast learner that one, gots to give her that. Even my ole man thinks she's gotta whole lotta potential".

"I beg your pardon! Need I remind you that while my daughter may be an adult, I am still her mother! What she does or does not do in the privacy of her own bedroom is none of my concern nor do I care to hear any details, sordid or otherwise, from you – especially you!"

"Shit naw. What are y'all talkin'? No! Momma y'all gots it all wrong. It's a game. Ya throw little square bags fulla beans inta round holes cut outta a piece of plywood is all. My momma makes them bags 'an my ole man cuts the holes."

"Why? To what end?"

"Jus' ta see if ya cen. I reckon. Or ya can play fur points if yur so inclined."

"It's real popular back home."

"So, it's considered a leisure pursuit? A simulating past time best left too the locals, no doubt! She answered.

Nat had driven my mother's rental car to the wedding and no sooner had they pulled up under the porte cochere than the parking attendant came running over to their car.

"Good evening sir. How are you this evening?"

"Hey man, I'm doin' jus' great. Happy as a short-peckered loon. Hows 'bout yurself?"

"I'm fine, thank you sir. Thank you for asking"

Nat had lowered his window and stared at the parking attendant who stared back; a contest that went on for several seconds while my mother waited patiently.

"Excuse me for interrupting. Do the two of you want some time alone together or are you and I going to attend this wedding?" She said.

Finally Nat, turning to look at my mother said. "Momma, do y'all know this guy?"

"Stop calling me Momma! And no, of course I don't know him! He's the valet parking attendant! He's probably from one of the local colleges, putting himself through school by working as a valet on the weekends. Give him the car keys." My other insisted.

"What the hell fur? I ain't givin' him shit." Nat replied.

"He's going to park the car for us".

"The hell ya say! I can park this here car by my own self."

"You could but you won't".

"The hell ya say! Why in the hell not?"

"Because that's the attendants job and I have no intention of walking across this hot, steaming, asphalt parking lot in this heat or in these heels! Just hand him the car keys!"

"So what? This is, like, this guy's career or something! Parkin' other peoples cars fur 'em when they sure as shit' is probably more'n able ta park it themselves. Why don' ya'll jus' hop outta this here car an' skeedaddle over there 'an stand under that big ole shade tree. I'll go park the car an' swing on back by for y'all. That gonna work?"

"Sadly, I never hop! Nor have I ever been known to skedaddle! If this job with the railroad doesn't work out for you, you should definitely consider a career as a parking valet. Can we discuss your future another time? Right now, we have a wedding to attend. Do you have five dollars with you?"

"What do y'all need, momma? I got me five bucks. Why? Aint'cha got no cash on ya?"

"In this little bag? No. I don't have any cash with me! I have a credit card. Give the parking attendant five dollars when you give him the keys."

"What the hell fur? Shit naw. I ain't givin that dude no five bucks! I'll park the damn car myself 'fore I pay some dumb ass college boy to do it! Shit, five bucks is five bucks, y'all hear what I'm sayin?"

"I do and you're starting to scare me! Just give him the keys and the five dollars so we can get out of this heat or are we going to sit here all night debating this. Allez!"

"How we 'sposed ta get the car back from this dude when we's ready to leave? How's he gonna know who's car is who's - it being a rental n' all?"

"When you give him the keys, he'll give you a little piece of paper; a claim check, with a number on it. Don't lose it! When we're ready to leave, you hand him the little piece of paper and he will get the car that has the corresponding number and bring it around to the front. Is that clear? Oh! And when we leave, give him another five dollars."

"Now y'all is jus' shinin" me! Yur tellin' me this dudes gonna make ten bucks offa me, jus' for parkin' yur car. This car ain't even mine for shits sake. He gonna get that kinda money otta everybody that shows up to this thin'? I gots to look into this! Never heard of such a thin'. Y'all surely do have some purty strange ways of doin' shit. An' y'all think I'm a dumb peckerwood."

"What can I say? That's the way it works. Nat?"

"Yes, ma'am."

"You're baseball cap."

"Yeah, whata 'bout it?"

"Take if off! D'accord!"

With the car safely consigned to the valet, the five dollar gratuity reluctantly surrendered and the stub securely in Nat's breast pocket, the two of them started up the sweeping marble staircase, cascading with bright flowers and lengths of flowing ivy, into the reception. Half way up the stairs, my mother had another thought. Turning to Nat, she said, "Are you familiar with Guerlain?"

"Shit, now what? I was beginnin' ta think ya'll was done wit me. Who?" Y'all gots to give it a rest, momma! I don' know who in the hell that is. Ain'tcha y'all jus' 'bout finished messin' wit my head."

"Guerlain is not a who but rather a what. It's Eau de parfum. It's my daughter's favorite. It's the only perfume she will wear."

"What's that all gotta do wit me? So what! Do I look like I give a rat's ass?" He said.

"If you care as much about my daughter as you say you do, you would be aware of all the small details that make her who she is!"

"I don' git where ya'll are goin' wit this, Momma. Y'all wanna run that by me one more time."

"No, I don't think so. You have just told me everything I need to know."

Following the ceremony, as the bride and groom turned to start down the aisle, the guests stood to follow; relieved to me out of the heat and anxiously anticipating another glass of champagne and the dinner and dancing that would follow.

As my mother and Nat approached the wide open doors of the entry to the reception, Nat stopped abruptly, forcing a backup of guests who were either forced to step around the two of them or wait for them to continue on into the room.

"Lookey here, Momma. There's little slices of cucumbers floatin' in this here upside down water jug! How's they suppose'da get on outta there? That there little faucet ain't big enough fur 'em ta pass. Better questions is, how'd they get 'em in there in the first place? Don' believe I've ever seen the like. Is this stuff free or do I got's to pay fur a glass of water too?

Apologizing to those backed up behind her, my mother just stared at him, a look of disbelief on her face. My duties as a bridesmaid, were, for the time being, suspended and I was free to enjoy the reception with the rest of the guests. I quickly helped myself to three glasses of champagne from a passing waiter and set out to find them in the crowd.

By the time I found them in the courtyard, my mother was standing, watching Nat as he was bent over, fascinated by the ice- water dispenser, completely focused, as the cool water slowly trickled into the small crystal cup he held. As I handed her a glass of champagne, she looked at me incredulously, rolled her eyes upward and said, very calmly. "That's it! I'm done! He's all yours! But if I were you, I'd throw him back and cast your net a little wider next time."

With that, she quietly walked into the room, leaving the two of us alone for the first time since they had arrived. Nat, ignoring the other guests, grabbed me around the waist and twirled me around the courtyard, layers of black taffeta swirling around our legs. Then he kissed me on the cheek and said, Ain'tcha y'all jus' a sight fur sore eyes! God damn, I surely did miss ya'll! That drive over here with your momma plumb wore me out. Ain't ya jus' the one! Y'all look so damn purty! Y'all are wearin' Guerlain, ain'tcha. Y'all smell better 'an a new bottle of furniture polish!"

"Yes. Shalimar. I always wear it. I'm surprised you noticed. You have never noticed before. But I don't believe it's ever been compared to furniture polish!"

"Ya'lled be blown away by what all I take notice of. If'in it's important to y'all then I'm sure as hell gonna know 'bout it. Come on. Y'all have done your part in this circus. What say me 'an you head on outta here 'an mosey on back to my room at the hotel 'an have a party of our own, if y'all get meanin'."

"Nat! You know we can't do that! What's gotten into you? Everyone would notice if we were both missing. We haven't had dinner yet! Sybil would be disappointed if we left now."

"Shit! There gots to be at least seven other bridesmaids flittin' 'round here but y'all are the prettiest one! Lets us sneak off somewheres so's we cen be alone. Ain't nobody gonna notice if we was ta disappear fur a spell. Lets us head on out to yur momma's car. We jus' gotta get that parkin' dude ta tell us where in the hell he put yur momma's rental. I gots me the claim check fur it right here in my pocket. I cen hep' ya'll get outta that there dress. Ain't nobody in this crowd gonna notice we's gone or pay the two of us no mind. Work wit me here, darling. Come on."

"It has to be over a hundred and twenty degrees by now in that car! And, getting out of this dress isn't the problem. Getting back into it is! What's gotten into you? Behave yourself! We're not sneaking off anywhere! Let's just go to the bar and get another glass of champagne. Have I told you how handsome you look this evening? I don't think I have ever seen you so dressed up! You look very dashing and somehow, dangerous."

"I ain't drinkin' no more'a that champagne! Them little bubbles go straight on my nose 'an send me inta a sneezin' fit. Ya'll cen fetch me a Bud Lite, if they got, 'an don' worry 'bout no glass unless standin' around wit a beer is against the rules. Looky 'round this room! Ain't no other guy better lookin' 'an me. 'An sure as shit, I may be dangerous, but I'm all yours, darlin'. Face it, I'm yur destiny. You 'an me was sure as shit meant to be."

As I waited at the bar for another glass of champagne and a beer, I put my hand on Nat's arm and said. "By the way, I haven't had a chance to ask you. How was the drive over with my mother – just the two of you in the car together? How are the two of you getting on?"

"We was chattin' it up jus' fine til I tole her me 'an you been cornholin'. I reckon she kinda lost it at that."

"Nat, you said that to my mother! Seriously! Please tell me you didn't say that! She doesn't know it's a silly bean-bag game! She's going to assume you are some sort of a sexual pervert or something! You're on awfully thin ice with my mother as it is!"

"Yep! She done tole me that too! What is it wit you people an' ice anyways? Don' go gettin' those pretty little drawers of yurs all in a bunch! She sure as shit knows what cornholin' is now cuz I went ahead 'an straightened her on out. But Christ Almighty! Let's don' talk 'bout yur momma jus' now. That woman cen make more noise than a she-hound in heat! I ain't one ta speak poorly of folks, 'an she's a mighty fine lookin' woman fur her age 'an all, kinda skinny though, not much meat on them bones an' I ain't inta blonds. <u>I gotta believe yur momma is at least ten years older 'an my momma but she sure as shit looks a whole lot younger. My momma got herself an early start. Hell, she had my brother when she was barely outta high school 'an he's nine years older 'an me. She's even havin' trouble now wit her ticker. Ya'll sure do take mighty good care of yurselves, I'll say that fur ya. When yur momma finished bustin' my balls, goin on 'an on 'bout the rules fur this here rodeo ya'll got goin' on, she as much as dragged</u> my sorry ass through a keg a' rusty nails. That's all I'm sayin'! But don' ya'll worry none, darlin'. Me a' yur momma gonna git along jus' fine. Sometimes I gets me a real sour feelin' in my gut tellin' me I ain't 'xactly what yur momma had in mind fur y'all. But I ain't met a women yet I can't bring aroun' ta my way a thinkin' one way or 'ther. Jus' gots ta give her some time ta get used ta the whole idea a me. She'll come around – y'all don' need ta worry 'bout that. It's yur ole man that kinda gives me pause.

"Nat! Be careful – please. You may have just met your match in my mother." I replied.

Chapter Ten

Nat arrived sans baseball cap, looking a little worse for the wear after his conversation with my mother in the car. He was a little shaken but still breathtakingly handsome in a three piece suit, purchased just for the occasion, and, as always, his black dress cowboy boots. It was the first real suit he had ever owned and he didn't look particularly comfortable as he tugged constantly at the collar. The jacket was obviously too small; the sleeves far too long, allowing the cuffs of his new, crisp white oxford shirt to shoot out and nearly cover his hands. By the way he kept tugging at his shirt collar; it was obvious he was unaccustomed to the feel of starch. His trousers were too big and so long they dragged on the ground regardless of the one inch heels on his boots. The vest seemed to be the only garment to fit properly. His outfit, combined with a few days worth of scruffy black stubble, gave him an air of casual, yet calculated dishevelment that was very appealing to every woman in the room. My mother spent a greater part of the evening reminding him to stop fidgeting and fussing, until she finally gave up and resigned him to his fate. At one point, she confided to me that she was sorry she hadn't thought to buy him a razor at the little shop of sundries in the hotel.

It didn't take too long for the jacket to come off, the vest to disappear, the tie to go missing and the sleeves to roll up. The DJ played non-stop country and western music; including, 'Living Our Love Song - our song - that Sybil had included in her play list as a favor to me. That night I was his "fairytale princess" and he was my "backwoods boy". Together we believed we would 'shatter all doubts and prove 'em all wrong.' Not long after dinner, many of the guests left for their respective hotels, and the D.J. immediately increased the volume as the evening wore on, for the rest of the guests. We danced and bumped with sheer abandon, following Sybil and John's example. Nat and I were oblivious to everyone else in the room as we danced together for hours. Still hoping to score a few extra points with my mother, he had, at one point in the evening, graciously asked her to dance. However, when he decided this was the perfect opportunity to teach her the Texas Two Step, he went too far. Her glare alone was enough to peel the paint off the walls from across the room. He was coming perilously close to that faux pas she had been anticipating. Any points he may have scored earlier were considerably diminished.

Sybil looked radiant and deliriously happy in her size 24 Vera Wang gown with layer upon layer of white satin poufs trailing to the floor, Swarovski crystals encircling her waist and laboriously woven into her hair. She floated around the dance floor like a cloud of meringue; a gliding confection, while John, unsure of what exactly was expected of him, looked somewhat overwhelmed and a bit shocky; but he never left her side. There were a few moments of drama here and there but that always seems to occur at any gathering, no matter how well planned.

One of the groomsmen said something offensive to one of the bridesmaids that no one else overheard. Outraged and to everyone's surprise she retaliated by throwing a full glass of bourbon in his face, ice cubes and all, causing the wait-staff to scramble, as inconspicuously as possible, to mop it up. Another couple unexpectedly had a loud argument on the dance floor and decided this was as good a time as any to break up. She was later found huddled on the floor of the ladies lounge, crying her eyes out, while he took up a permanent position at the bar and started openly flirting with one of the bar tenders. There was a rumor going around at one point that Sybil's younger brother was out in the parking lot with a bunch of his buddies, smoking weed but no one was particularly inclined to follow up on the rumor. It was a beautiful evening and

Sybil and John were so blissfully happy, we couldn't help but be happy for them. Nat and I danced all night, looking, I'm sure, like two Cheshire cats sharing a secret. We couldn't stop smiling. We did have a secret and for the time being, it was ours and ours alone, although I occasionally caught my mother watching us a little too closely. I'm sure she suspected something but neither one of us had any intention of exposing our secret engagement and for the most part Nat, behaved himself.

Bright and early on Sunday morning, I reluctantly drove Nat to the Denver airport to catch his flight back to Savannah. We had slept less than three hours and the entire weekend had gone by so fast with hardly any time to catch our breaths. It wasn't enough time but what we had was more than enough and better than nothing. After his proposal, we agreed that I would move, as soon as possible, to Savannah to be with him. We'd start over, just the two of us; a new life together in a place that was new to both of us. An adventure of our own making. I walked with him as far the security line and when we kissed, one last time, I couldn't let go of him. I was terrified I'd never see him again; afraid I'd lose him; possibly forever.

Over the years we had said goodbye far more often than we had said hello and here we were saying goodbye again when it seemed we had just said hello. This time it would only be for two weeks at the most and we'd be together for the rest of our lives. As I watched him slowly saunter down the concourse toward his gate, turning every so often to smile that mischievous smile of his, my heart ached, and I tried to freeze that picture in my mind to keep it from fading. I wanted to hold that image in my mind forever, believing if I could hold onto it, it would never fade.

Standing there, watching him walk away, I briefly felt a shadow pass over me. Looking down at the goose bumps on my arms, I hastily shook it off, blaming the airport air conditioning. I was so close to my dream and excited about our future together but the shadow continued and refused to move on, leaving me with a distinctive chill. If I was this close to my dream, why did the shadow linger with such a chilling presence?

I couldn't help but think of that age-old, well established and universally accepted Scandinavian truth, an ingrained principle that clearly states: if you are in good spirits, full of joy and everything in your life is going well, you have obviously overlooked something. Brace yourself because it is all going to heck! That is not to say that Swedes, as a whole are overly dark, icy or pessimistic or that they appear to be "the glass is half empty" kind of people. Rather, they are more circumspect than most, believing that if you are extremely happy then everything in your life is about to go sideways. Before you know it, your life will be circling the drain. Too much joy or too much happiness is definitely not a good thing. No one deserves to be that happy. Happiness is fleeting, unsure and should be kept safely tucked away – somewhere. Do as little as possible to call attention to yourself or the results will be, devastating. Keep your emotions hidden, safely bottled up inside and your life will be easier and you, much more content with the outcome. It may not be particularly wholesome or a sound philosophy but such an attitude does, somehow, keep life's little disappointments to a minimum. It's not a negative mindset but rather, a cautionary one. Do not become overly secure in your happiness, believing it is guaranteed; to do so only makes you that much more vulnerable. It is Nordic pragmatism. What had I overlooked?

It had all happened so fast, my head was spinning and my heart was racing. The full extent of everything I agreed to with Nat had yet to filter completely into my consciousness. There were so many decisions to make, so many details to address. I wasn't sure where to start or even how to go about making so many drastic changes to my life. It didn't take long for me to realize that, without knowing it, I had stepped off the Ferris wheel and climbed aboard a merry-go- round. I wanted it to stop or, at the very least, slow down so that I could jump off. But it continued to go round and round with no end in sight while I sat on an oversized, brightly painted wooden horse, pumping up and down rhythmically. This garish carnival atmosphere that was my life accompanied by the loud, repetitive music roaring in my head was too much for me to process. If there was a brass ring somewhere in my future, I was having trouble keeping it my sights. What was so close and within my grasp, was now whirling by, barely distinguishable and slipping in and out of my grasp. I had no way of knowing if I was on the right path or any path for that matter. While the most important decision appeared to have been made, and mutually agreed upon, the ensuing circumstances appeared overly complex and insurmountable. Would Nat and I ever be able to make all the decisions that were confronting us? Would we be able to do it together? Could we agree on anything?

How long would this euphoria last?

Stella Benson

Chapter Eleven

Before we checked out of the hotel on the Sunday morning after the wedding, my mother and I were expected to attend a farewell brunch in the hotel dining room to say goodbye to the rest of the out-of-town guests and the bride and groom. Neither of us felt particularly inclined to attend; too much food, too much wine and too little sleep had my stomach in turmoil; that and everything else I was holding in, had my head spinning. The thought of the impending three hour flight back to San Francisco didn't do much to alleviate my queasiness.

As we headed out of the hotel parking lot and toward the airport, I'm sure I was nervous, and visibly anxious. I thought I would fly apart at the seams if I didn't tell my mother everything. Another conversation in the car but this time, my mother was my captive audience with no way out and no choice but to listen to me. With as much calm in my voice as I could muster, I announced that Nat had asked me to marry him. The rental car suddenly accelerated, bumped up over the curb and came to a dead stop in the middle of the sidewalk just inches from a parking meter, as my mother looked at me unbelievingly. By the time we reached the car rental return kiosk at the airport, she knew all there was to know and then some. There were a few details I had left out but she didn't need to know absolutely everything even though she couldn't help but notice that I hadn't spent one night the entire weekend in our room.

Stella Benson

Predictably, her first response was "are you out of your mind? Have you ever head that old adage, "Love who you will but marry your own kind?" It is more than apropos in this situation. The two of you are polar opposites! It will never work, I will never allow it and your father will be dead-set against it! Why do you have this insatiable need to rescue every stray that lands on your doorstep? You pick up every little bird with a broken wing or tiny, cold, abandoned mouse in an attempt to save it. In the past, it's been guys that are just a little bit screwed up and seem to need you to unscrew them. You have dated some real weirdoes and more than a few losers but this one really takes the cake! He has rabbit in his blood, amongst God knows what else, and sooner or later that boy is going to run like hell! He's a bolter! And when he does he'll break your heart! Those Southern boys may be slow with their words and even slower to think but they are incredibly fast on their feet. When Daddy and I encouraged you to learn a foreign language, we were thinking something practical like French or Italian, not Southern Appalachian English! He can't be rehabilitated! He's broken, toxic, tarnished and twisted! He can't compete with you on your level so he has no choice but to bring you down to his. You know too little about him and you believe far too much of what you do know! If you insist upon marrying him, your life as you know it will never be the same! You're too far apart and you come from two different worlds! Do you really see yourself living in a double-wide trailer at the end of a narrow dirt road, two minutes away from his parents' home and surrounded by a litter of dirty, snot-nosed little brats, suffering from rickets and probably riddled with pin worms? Or maybe a mobile home in a holler down by the crick – assuming, of course, that the crick doesn't rise!

What are you supposed to do all day when you're not taking care of all the children I'm sure he wants? Learn to fry pickles? Here's a thought – with your culinary skills, perhaps you could perfect that endearing Southern delicacy commonly referred to as the knife and fork sandwich! If a sandwich requires a knife and fork, it is no longer a sandwich – is it? Sooner or later, he'll suggest you get a part-time job; probably weekends, as a check-out girl at the local Winn-Dixie just to make ends meet. Or maybe you could waitress nights at the IHOP in Johnston City, carefully counting your tips until you hand them over to him.

There's a career path I know you haven't considered. One that has been unjustly maligned and that you are seriously overqualified for. He's the type of guy who will eventually insist that you turn over all your paychecks to him each and every month and then subtly suggest putting you on an allowance, of his own making!

He is unmistakably a notch-on-the-bedpost kind of guy and I'm sorry to be the one to tell you, but you are just one of many notches and there will be more! Can you live with that because it's not going to change anytime soon? This is a guy who does not hesitate to tell anyone who will listen that he has "screwed" – and that's his word, not mine - a former Miss Maryland! As a rule, a gentleman, and I use the term loosely when referring to him, does not kiss and tell! Is that the future you had in mind for yourself? Do you honestly believe your father and I are going to quietly stand by and let you throw your life away on someone like him! If you do, you obviously don't know me at all and you have grossly underestimated your father. Daddy had him pegged the first time he met him when he came to the house. Do you remember? Who shows up to meet the parents stinking drunk and reeking of beer? Since then Nat has done nothing to change your father's opinion. Daddy is convinced he will break your heart or at least try to destroy you because he has absolutely no honor. He's not good enough for you and marrying him won't change that! Date him, sleep with him, live with him, if you must – do whatever you have to do to get him out of your system but do not, under any circumstances, agree to marry him!

That southern charm of his won't last! Believe me, you will outgrow him! You can bet your grandmother's silver on that! He may have a brain, it has to in there somewhere, but he as yet to learn to use if effectively. He is nothing more than a predator hiding behind all that charm! You, on the other hand, possess a very highly developed, active thought process. You care deeply about everything from the oceans to the ozone layer and everything in-between. He cares about nothing but himself and it is painfully obvious to everyone. He is just a novelty, an infatuation, but that too will wear off. You've never known anyone quite like him and you're curious. I get that! You're intrigued by the very idea of him – not the reality of exactly who and what he is.

Actually, I suspect he's gay and all this posturing and bravado are just an attempt to cover it up. He may very well be confused about his own sexuality, which would go a long way toward explaining his underlying anger. If you stop and think about it, what exactly do you two have in common? I also suspect he is an inconsiderate and selfish lover, given his temperament. Someone as self-absorbed as he is cannot begin to comprehend the needs or desires of another. And, he's almost 30 so we can't exactly blame it on immaturity! There is no room in his head or heart for anyone other than himself! If you carefully consider these last six years rationally, you have to admit to having experienced both. Forgive me for saying so, but you will always be an afterthought, running a close second and nothing you say or do will change that! If you persist in this, you will regret your decision the rest of your life!

It doesn't really matter where you come from. What matters is where you are going. But you will never be happy if you follow him where he wants to go. If he stays in Savannah, you might have a squeak of a chance but if he returns to his home and to his parents, your life will be miserable! Where is that nice boy who recently graduated from the Naval Academy? Why don't you give him a call? He had a lot of snap and he absolutely adored you." She asked.

"For the love of God mother, take a breath! You're going to have a heart attack! That "nice boy" who just graduated from the Naval Academy was the reason you and I ended up in the Headmasters Office in sixth grade. Remember?" I replied.

"You see, exactly my point, you two have a history!"

"Nat and I have a history. We've been together over six years." I said.

"If you think about it, in reality, you've been together a total of about six months! All this texting, emailing, Skyping and hours on the phone, is hardly my idea of a stable relationship. Communicating with a screen does not constitute a stable relationship! How can you have any kind of a relationship with someone if you never actually talk to each other – face to face? I have a feeling there is something definitely wrong with that boy. A short or a crimp in his wiring! He's too uncertain about himself, too insecure and it shows. There are probably monsters prowling around under his bed or in his head that even he doesn't recognize!" She said.

"We lived together in Cheyenne for three months! There is nothing wrong with him and there are no monsters that I am aware of, prowling around anywhere. You just don't like him" I said.

"You may have lived with him for three months but consider how well that turned out! You know as well as I do that you couldn't get out of there fast enough and you were only nineteen! Do you really want to go through that again? You were nothing but the live-in help – with benefits, if you know what I mean. You did everything for him and his two roommates; the shopping, cooking, cleaning and laundry, even rolling his socks into little balls for him while holding down two jobs. And, that's not true, I am trying very hard to like him but he isn't giving me much to work with, especially when I can barely understand a word he says." She replied.

"I am going to move to Savannah next week and marry him - and there is nothing you can do to stop me." I said.

"I don't think I like your tone, young lady. Keep in mind; I am still your mother! Let me ask you this, is he a Democrat? Or does his family have a long-standing, close association with the Klan? Maybe he should consider going into politics. He can turn that good, ole boy country charm of his, off and on; he is a consummate liar and he clearly has no conscience. He'd make a fine Southern Democrat! The only element he lacks right now is the ability to give away everything he has or ever will have to anyone with their hands out. But that too, will come. Who knows, it wouldn't surprise me to learn that he has a relative in the local County Court House who could quietly expunge his latest DUI, thereby clearing his way to run for some regional office or another. " She said.

"Mother, what do his politics have to do with anything?" I nearly shouted

"There is a lot of anger and hostility in that boy. He has a very dark side. He's absolutely smoldering; doing a slow burn over something, and when he blows, I don't want you in the same room. That's why I suspect he may very well be gay. Didn't he have to undergo a comprehensive battery of psychological testing of some sort by the FBI or be properly vetted by the NSA before some misguided bureaucrat in Washington handed him the codes to our nuclear missile silos? That's terrifying! That boy is a walking time bomb himself with our missile codes in his pocket!" She replied.

"Mother, as usual you're over-reacting! He's not angry, he doesn't have a dark side and I can personally guarantee you, he is not gay! We just want to move on with our lives." I said.

"Is English his second language or is he speaking an obscure, regional Appalachian dialect that I'm unfamiliar with because I can only understand about every third word that comes out of his mouth. I ask because he seems incapable of maintaining any consistency with his verb tenses and his pronouns are all over the map. Is it possible he has a mild, somewhat chronic speech impediment? Could it be genetic? He also seems incapable of focusing for very long. She said.

"Mother, you're exaggerating; blowing all this out of reasonable proportion." I said.

"That brings up another question. Why, on earth are you in such a hurry to get married? Or is this all his idea? You have your whole life ahead of you! Mark my words; he's going to want a baby as soon as possible, which will more or less seal the deal. Are you ready for that? You are both just caught up in wedding fever and Sybil and John's fantasy, society wedding. Marriage is a leap of faith as it is but the very least you can do is be as sure of each other as you can possibly be. There are too many unknowns here." She said.

"If it's right and we love each other, why should we wait?" I answered.

"We really don't know anything about him or his family. I've only met his parents once, very briefly and under very difficult and certainly not ideal circumstances. Remember you were competing at the Nationals in Lexington last year when they drove up from – wherever – to see you ride? You were in your competition "zone" and unapproachable and I was once again in my role as your groom. I regret we didn't have more time to get acquainted because they seem like decent people, a bit quiet and detached and not particularly sophisticated, but I didn't come away feeling as though I knew them at all. And your father has never met either one of them. For all we know, Nat may have been raised in a rabbit hutch somewhere! Sometimes I feel like I don't know you at all! When did you become so completely infatuated with him and beyond all reason? What kind of a hold does he have on you? This isn't at all like you."

"He strikes me as selfish and extremely insecure and that's not going to change anytime soon. If anything, it will only get worse! It isn't something you can rectify no matter how hard you try. He has a feigned confidence bordering on arrogance yet he never seems at ease. I suspect he was the kind of child who spent his spare time pulling the wings off of butterflies, stomping on ladybugs and tormenting the neighbor's puppy. He has a definite penchant for cruelty and quite frankly, it scares me to death! He can't be fixed and if you try, he'll take you down with him and, I, for one, refuse to let that happen!" She said.

"I admit he's extraordinarily good looking and a very smooth talker. Butter does indeed melt in his mouth. But that's an acquired skill! How many times have I told you to never, ever, date a man who is better looking than you are? That's just asking for trouble! He would be considerably more appealing if he kept his mouth shut and just stood around looking pretty, quietly oozing all that Southern charm. But something is still not right. He's a little too smooth; and I get the distinct impression he's hiding something. I don't know what it is and I just spent three days with him! That boy can change moods mid-sentence and I find it exhausting trying to anticipate where he is going much less keep up with him. It isn't difficult for anyone to sense the chemistry that exists between the two of you but it is obviously of a sexual nature. I hope that lasts, for your sake, but what if it doesn't? Fireworks aren't enough to sustain a lasting relationship. If that goes, what are you left with?" She asked.

"Why can't you be happy for me? I don't need your permission to marry him. I'm over twenty-one!" I practically screamed

"I am trying very hard to be happy for you. But you make it so difficult! Of course, your father and I want you to be happy. That's all we care about. If, and it's a big if, he makes you happy, which I can't believe he does, we will, of course support you no matter what. I just want you to be sure of what you're doing. He is a nothing short of a roué, a back country rogue, and I do not intend to idly stand by and watch you throw your life away. He is not who and what you think he is! Not to belabor the point, but I strongly suspect he is something of a control freak. He is asking you to give up everything you love; your family, your home, your whole way of life! What about your horses? And exactly what is he giving up? What's he bringing to the table, other than his charming, adorable self? That is not meeting you half way? Why can't you fall in love with someone who isn't so blatantly needy and insecure? Someone who doesn't need you for his own purposes but simply wants you by his side for the rest of your life. There is a huge difference. Marriage is a two-way street, and so far, I see nothing equitable about this relationship. How many times have I told you to never kiss a fool and never be fooled by his kisses? This time, you have managed to do both! He's a runner, and mark my words, sooner or later, he's going to bolt! The sooner the better as far as I'm concerned."

"And, if you'll slow down and think this through, I don't see how you can feasibly move anywhere before the end of the summer. You are completely booked until mid-October. You have been training all year for the Regional Championships coming up in two weeks in Reno. You are expected to represent the barn at the Canadian Nationals in Manitoba, followed almost immediately by the Sport Horse Nationals, in August. Then you have the Pacific Slope Championships scheduled in early September. You have also agreed to compete in several local dressage shows on top of that. Your younger clients are depending upon you to be there for them. I have already paid the fees to have Odie hauled the length and breadth of California and up to Canada and back, none of which is refundable. Your plate is full at least until the end of September. All of your classes have been registered and the entry fees have been paid, in advance, I might add. Odie has been in training for months and you've both worked so hard to qualify. What about your clients? You have to supervise them and help them through their classes, not to mention the contracts you've already signed to show the horses for other clients. You can't just walk away from those contracts – they are legally binding! We have already booked your airline, hotel and rental car reservations and put down deposits on all of them; it's too late to withdraw or forfeit all that. You can't scratch all those competitions! You have a responsibility to yourself and other people. Are you so much in love that you are prepared to disappoint all the people who are depending upon you and go running off to Savannah, chasing after Nat? Think about what he's asking you to give up and why now?

And – I'm sorry but I don't see a ring on your left hand. He hasn't had a conversation with your father that I know of, to ask his permission. If Nat knew he was going to ask you to marry him in Denver, why didn't he come prepared? It breaks my heart to tell you this, but he's playing you. Don't be a fool! I don't know how and I don't know when, but believe me, sooner or later, he's going to let you down. There's too much ego and far too much vanity involved here. He's drawing on your strength to support his own insecurities and he'll suck you dry if you let him. And you are so besotted that you won't see it coming. There is "Danger" written all over that boy." She said.

"He can't afford to take time off from his job training to fly out here for a weekend just to talk to Daddy. What is the point of some stupid, rigid rule from a stuffy and obsolete era? It makes no sense! And he can't afford a ring – yet" I said.

" That, in itself, should tell you all you need to know! Let me understand this, he can afford to fly to Denver for the weekend for Sybil's wedding but he can't make similar arrangements to fly out to talk your father? Who behaves like this? He has the manners of a field hand and a complete lack of respect, not just for us as a family but more importantly for you. Can't you see that? It seems to me, this is a very volatile and contentious relationship. All you two do is argue and fight over the most mundane things. I've over heard the two of you on the phone, one loud argument after another. Starting with that most recent blow-up when you thought he was going through your phone; checking on previous calls. What's up with that? You don't trust him anymore than he trusts you and that is not a foundation for a marriage; that's a very slippery slope leading to a downward spiral. You can't possibly be that insecure and if you are, you've got a bigger problem than you know.

You will never change him. He is what he is! Whatever that is, and we don't really know, do we? The only thing you can change about a man is the way he dresses and you've already got your hands full there! Did you notice, at the wedding, his tie was permanently tied in a knot and then threaded onto a large elastic band that he just pulled over his head and tucked under his shirt collar? And that suit – where do you suppose he got that? Sears? He looked like a walking scarecrow! He doesn't even know how to properly tie a tie! Where on earth did you ever find this one? No wait – he found you didn't he? In some bar in Fort Collins? What was the bet?

"Mother, you're not being particularly helpful! Please help me work through this. It's important to me and to both of us. And, I think he's intimidated by Daddy and a little bit afraid of him." I said.

"Of course he's afraid to talk to Daddy and he should be! He knows he's way out of his league and he knows Daddy knows he knows. That's the whole point of the exercise. Daddy just wants to make sure he is afraid." She replied

"But why?" What difference does it make?" I said

"This isn't some patriarchal conspiracy where two men casually sit down over a six pack of beer to determine your fate. It is, however, a guy thing; a right of passage as well as a matter of respect and above all, a common courtesy. It's an indication of integrity, or the lack of it. Apparently you've already decided and made a commitment to him by agreeing to marry him. He needs to know that Daddy has your back. If anything happens to you, if Nat screws this up, he has to understand that he will answer, under no uncertain terms, to your father. Open your eyes! Can't you see what Nat is doing? He's on a campaign to systematically alienate you from everything you know and love; first your family and then your friends and finally your horses! And for what? Him! He may be good in bed but he can't be that good! He's clearly not worth all this! Sooner or later he will move on – if he hasn't already. When do you intend to tell your father about all of this?" She asked.

"Tonight at dinner." I said.

"What do you honestly think your father will say?" She asked.

"Knowing daddy, he'll probably make some lame reference to a bird and a fish." I answered.

Stella Benson

Chapter Twelve

From the moment we left the hotel until the wheels of the plane touched down at San Francisco International, I didn't let my mother out of my sight. I was convinced, if I left her alone or turned my back, she'd be on the phone to my father and, with her usual resolve, reduce everything I had said to simply, "She's getting married and moving to Savannah – next week! She has an uncanny ability to cut right to the meat of the matter – an instinct for the bottom line. If she got a hold of him before I had a chance to explain, he would have all afternoon to consider everything before he heard my side! I couldn't afford it let that happen.

Once again I had completely misjudged my mothers' reaction to my news. I thought she'd be happy about Nat and I and immediately throw herself into planning an extravagant wedding; an occasion that would rival Sybil's ceremony and reception in either San Francisco or Savannah. At the very least, I expected her to start calling everyone she knew to announce our engagement. Instead, she had launched into a tirade of everything she thought was wrong with Nat – which I really didn't want to hear. I hadn't anticipated her arguments or even considered the possibility that she may be reluctant to endorse our plan. I should have waited until we were all together, as I had promised Nat, and safely in the restaurant before I blurted out our intentions. I had hoped to sit down with both my parents and quietly, rationally explain everything from the beginning to the end – without interpretation. Hoping to have her on my side before confronting my father.

I used the two and a half hour flight to make a comprehensive list, in my own head, of what I wanted to say to my father. Getting my thoughts in some kind of order so I could make a calm, intelligent presentation without the slightest hint of drama. When I thought I had that conversation well played out in my mind, I started to make a list of what had to be done and when.

If I was going to move as soon as possible, there was so much to do. Would I throw just the things I would need initially into my twelve year old 1999 Mustang with the puppy riding shot gun and drive across the country myself or fly with just a simple carry on and send for everything else once we were settled? My mind was spinning with all the possibilities and options. What would I do with my horses and my job? How would I explain the situation and all the sudden changes to my clients? What was I going to do about the entire summer show season, and on and on it went with very little resolution. The more I thought about it, the more muddled I became. It was all too overwhelming to consider and I had no idea here to begin. As usual, I had more questions than answers.

Why does everything I try to do become so confusing? I knew Nat had, by now, arrived back in Savannah and couldn't help but wonder how his conversation with his parents had gone and what, if anything, their reaction had been.

First things first and one step at a time. I had to get through this dinner with my parents with as little emotion and as few hysterics as possible. Keep it simple and straightforward. Steer the conversation in my direction with my arguments and impress upon them our sincerity to move forward as soon as possible.

My father picked us up at the airport and on the drive into the City, we filled my father in on all the wedding gossip. Who was there, who wasn't, who should have been and who had crashed? My dress and hair, Sybils dress and her hair, the heat, the flowers, the bourbon throwing incident. the wine and the food. By the time we finally reached Bix restaurant we were all, thankfully, in a fairly festive mood. My mother and I hadn't spoken much on the plane – each of us more or less consumed by our own thoughts. Now it was my turn - where to start?

Fortunately, my father had reserved a quiet booth upstairs, far from the bustling bar and just far enough away from the jazz trio to barely hear the music playing softly in the background. I couldn't help but remember how many times, as a child, I had fallen asleep, nestled in one of these deeply upholstered booths. Things seemed so much simpler then. No confusion, no responsibilities, no drama and no major, life changing decisions to make. I talked and talked all the way through dinner as my father listened quietly, obviously relishing his trout tartare and truffle frittes as much as the conversation and my enthusiasm. I talked and talked and my grilled salmon went untouched. Occasionally he glanced at my mother and then back to me but I knew that I had managed to capture his full attention. I thought I was calm, rational and more than convincing in my explanation and "the plan." If he was surprised, he didn't show it, maybe my mother had gotten to him after all? He didn't ask any questions - just waited patiently for me to finish. My mother sat there quietly relishing her stripped bass with tomatoe tapenade, glancing from my father to me and back again. You'd think she was Center Court at Wimbledon! Fortunately she had nothing to add and didn't interject at any point. I was on my own. Half way through his chocolate brioche bread pudding, my father calmly put his spoon down, folded his napkin and asked, "So, when is Nat coming? There are some things I'd like to discuss with him before this goes any further"

"I don't think he is, Daddy. He's very busy. I answered. Maybe he'll call."

For a moment his eyebrows shot up as he looked first in my mother's direction, then directly at me.

"If he doesn't come – you don't go." He quietly said.

I started to protest. "But Da…"

Ever so slowly, he raised his hand and looking directly at me, said, "Waiter, the check please. We're done here."

With that, I knew this conversation had abruptly come to an end. We were indeed done here. I had seen the sadness in his eyes and heard the disappointment in his voice mixed with just a hint of anger, directed at whom, I wasn't sure but I wasn't going to push him any further. I knew my father well enough to know when to back off. As we were leaving the restaurant, my mother quietly came up to me and said, "That's enough for tonight. It's a lot to digest in one sitting. He needs time to process everything you've said and everything the two of you are proposing – we all do. Needless to say, this isn't exactly the scenario he envisioned. Leave it alone for now. Don't push him into a corner. He'll come around sooner or later if this is really what you want to do but don't expect him to like it."

Throughout dinner and the drive home, I kept glancing at my cell, hoping for either a call or text from Nat. He had to be back in Savannah by now and must have called his parents with the news - as promised. For whatever reason, this wasn't going the way we had planned. It had never been our intention to hurt or disappoint anyone and yet my parents were not exactly jumping for joy over the possibility of my moving across the country and marrying a relative stranger. I knew by now that I wasn't his parents first choice either but if we could convince everyone concerned and present a united front, we should, hopefully, be able to persuade them all of our sincerity and determination. Once again I found myself waiting for a phone call. I was praying he had been more successful with his parents than I had been with mine.

He called very early the next morning to tell me he had spoken to his parents the minute he landed in Savannah. He had informed them he intended to marry me and that I was moving to Savannah. From the tone of his voice I knew he didn't get the reaction he was hoping for any more than I had. Apparently they were not surprised and neither were they particularly overjoyed. His mother, as usual, had very little to say and his father, somewhat resigned, apparently kept it simple by saying. "If marryin' that gal is what y'all wanna do, we aint gonna try ta put a stop to ya. But hear me on this, y'all are makin' a big mistake takin' up wit the likes of her. She ain't one of us – pure and simple. Ya ain't never gonna be able ta control her. She gots her own, stubborn way of doin' things 'an it ain't our way! Y'all are bitin' off more'n y'all can chew wit that gal, is all I'm sayin."

We talked for hours, going back and forth on how we were going to do this without creating any more friction than was necessary. We had to somehow systematically eliminate as many complications as possible. We were both determined to find a reasonable solution that would be acceptable to everyone. As we spoke, I knew we were both aware of how much easier it would have been had we eloped in Denver. We were thinking the same thing but neither one of us wanted to be the first to admit it. We were reluctant to bring it up and admit to each other that we may have lost that opportunity. This shouldn't be this difficult! It occurred to us, briefly, that is was entirely possible we were so concerned with keeping everybody else happy that we were losing sight of our own happiness.

Stella Benson

Chapter Thirteen

We were young, full of vitality and madly in love. We had made a commitment to each other, so no problem should be too much for us to face; no obstacle too great that we couldn't overcome it together. Not time and definitely not distance, not now. Both the time and the distance between us would finally come together as we planned for our future. But would it be soon enough? This was going to be our first major stumbling block; a test of our collective strength and love. We could survive this. I was completely confident in my own decision and secure in his love.

I dreaded telling him that is wasn't going to be possible for me to move or for us to get married before the middle of September, given my summer schedule. I had an idea what his reaction would be and I wasn't looking forward to that conversation in the least. The next three months of summer were the height of the scheduled show season and I was already too heavily committed to even entertain the thought of just taking off and leaving my clients without a trainer - high and dry. They had all worked too hard for too many months; they didn't deserve to be abandoned by me. I couldn't bear to see the veiled disappointment on their faces, their eyes slowly tearing up, especially the younger ones, most of who were showing for the first time. They depended upon me to get them and their horses through their classes. I too, had too many competitions scheduled for myself and too many previously signed contracts to show for other people. I couldn't, in good conscience, let all of them down. Nat would just have to try to understand and together we'd work it all out - somehow. We had to. It occurred to me it may be a blessing in disguise though I knew in my heart he would never agree with me. This respite would give us both a little more time and the opportunity to carefully plan our future. It would also give both my parents and his the time they obviously needed to get used to the idea.

The next two weeks passed in a mad flurry of activity as Nat and I tried to make sense of what we were doing. Going back and forth several times a day back to our all too familiar routine of calling, texting and spending endless hours Skyping late into the night. I more or less lived at the barn; sleeping on the cot in my trainer's office and running out between clients for junk food. All of my younger clients had to be thoroughly prepared, as did their horses and their respective parents. I spent hours quizzing them on the dressage patterns, schooling them over fences and reminding them of the importance of the proper form the judges expected to see. They had to be appropriately dressed, confident in their own ability and trust their horses to do what they had been trained to do. Above all, they had to breathe and smile. No matter how terrified or unsure they may be, they had to at least give the appearance that they were in control and having fun. And, most importantly, never, never forget they were sitting, rather precariously, on the back of a large animal that is probably just as nervous as you are and depending upon them for guidance and direction. You are two bodies of one mind competing to win a ribbon to tie on your horse's bridle not in your hair! At the end of the day, it's not about the ribbons you win or lose its you learn by trying. A smile goes a long way in convincing any judge that you know what you are doing. If nothing else, you have to appear to be enjoying yourself.

For myself, I had at least six horses a day to exercise and prepare, not including Odie. In between rides, I spent every possible minute on my computer, researching and reading everything I could get my hands on about Savannah. I wanted to know as much as possible about the city before my arrival and subsequent transplant. I read "Midnight in the Garden of Good and Evil" and watched the movie at least five times, hoping to get a glimpse of the city.

I knew I was just scratching the surface of everything I wanted to know but I was surprised to learn that it is not unlike San Francisco in a many ways. At one point, I was called away, forgetting my laptop on a bale of hay in Odie's stall. When I finally returned, it was covered in sticky slobber; slimy apple juice and the occasional bit of carrot wedged in the keyboard. Fortunately, he hadn't knocked it off the hay bale, trampled it to death or taken a bite out of it. I think he was initially fascinated and finally annoyed by its presence because it wasn't edible. Whatever it was, he didn't want it in his stall with him!

Nat and I argued incessantly and loudly over whether I would drive across the country myself with my four month old, Australian Shepard puppy in the car or fly. I wasn't enthusiastic about driving across the country alone but if that's what it took, that's what I was prepared to do. I pleaded with Nat to consider flying out to California, spend a little time with my parents, have that long over - due conversation with my father and then drive across the country to Savannah with me. He finally, rather half-heartedly, agreed to work around his schedule and if possible get permission for another long weekend off. When I arrived and more or less got the lay of the land, I could send for everything I needed that wouldn't fit in my car. When I found a suitable stable, I could easily arrange for my horses to be hauled across the country. I just needed a destination. This was Plan A.

Encouraged by the possibility that Nat was at least trying to meet me half way, and confident he may yet have the opportunity to have a conversation with him, my father dug out the bottle of Aquavit to let it "breathe" in anticipation of Nat's arrival. He was concerned for my safety if I decided to drive alone. Fearing my car would finally give up in the middle of the night on some deserted, dirt road somewhere in the middle of Kansas, he immediately decided to take my old, 1999 silver Mustang to his mechanic for a complete over haul. He had two new windshield wipers, a new battery and four new tires installed. They also changed the oil and completely rebuilt the air conditioner and defroster, all at my father's expense. It was now road ready.

If we decided not to drive I spent several hours researching airline schedules and fares as well as the regulations for shipping a dog. My uncle, who has lived in Alaska for many years, routinely ships his Labrador from Anchorage to Northfield, Minnesota for three months each summer for comprehensive gun dog training. With his help and based on his experience, I was able to purchase the appropriate size kennel, complete with two interchangeable water dishes, security identification labels and the regulation zip lock ties. I made an appointment for the puppy at the vet for a complete physical, to document his shots and obtain an airline approved, signed veterinarian health certificate that would be valid for a maximum ninety days; allowing him to travel on the same flight as mine, in the temperature controlled cargo hold. Then I started a search for commercial, long distance trucking companies that would be able to haul both Odie and Sundae across the country and deliver them safely to a barn in or near Savannah. When I was reasonably sure that was possible, considering the expense; I contacted their usual vet to administer the shots they would require to travel and issue all the necessary travel documents. That was Plan B. It wasn't ideal but it could work.

Once I felt secure in the knowledge that I had made progress as to when and how to ship the horses, I began to explore possible barns and stable facilities around Savannah. I spent hours on-line between riding and training, researching local facilities that may have two stalls available immediately. When I found a site that appeared to be promising, I would send the link to Nat who promised to stop by whenever he could to look at each one and report back to me. While there, he would casually ask if any of the barns were hiring, especially a qualified dressage trainer with years of experience. Fortunately, Nat had spent a few years bull riding on the rodeo circuit and knew something about horses. He also knew my particular preferences as far as my horses were concerned. He knew the right questions to ask potential stables regarding boarding, feed, the farrier and whether or not they kept a veterinarian on staff.

While I attempted to solidify my travel plans, Nat had one job and only one. He was to find a larger, two bedroom apartment for us that accepted pets. If and when he ever encountered his somewhat elusive roommate, he intended to inform him of his new plans and his change of circumstances. Hopefully, Nat would be able to break his current lease and move into something larger and more suitable by the time I arrived. We were no longer in a hurry. We could take our time without any pressure or time constraints to find something that would do for the time being and suitable for ourselves and my horses.

As well as researching stables, I began an intensive on-line search for a job for myself. People in Savannah must ride and I was sure they kept horses. Someone somewhere had to need a trainer or a stable manager! My resume was literally flying out the door into cyberspace.

I was completely overwhelmed and nearly reduced to tears one evening when my father casually handed me an opened-ended, round-trip ticket from San Francisco to Savannah, again at his expense. I tried, for hours that night to convince him that I didn't need a round trip ticket. When I left, I was leaving for good. He was adamant, however, saying, "If this doesn't work out, for whatever reason, you can always come home. Hold onto the ticket but if you do come home, leave that nut-case, hyper-active, puppy with Nat." He said. "They deserve each other!"

After the initial shock of what he kept referring to as "another one of my crack-pot ideas or a fool's errand," my father, slowly began to support my impending move to Savannah and subsequent marriage to Nat. I had worn him down with my determination. He and Nat weren't close by any stretch of the imagination; there hadn't been many opportunities to develop any kind of a relationship. Instead, Nat was hesitant around my father; choosing his words carefully, and clearly intimidated. My father, on the other hand, at first appeared indifferent, believing Nat was just another in a long line of young men who either couldn't afford me and "my baggage" or didn't posses the strength of character to appreciate me for who I was. He wasn't happy about any of our plans, just resigned. And, reminiscent of the day I insisted on changing my hair color, he had finally decided to drop the reins and let me have my head. I knew his primary concern was for my safety and happiness; even though he wasn't at all convinced Nat could or would be able to provide either to his satisfaction. Unlike my mother, who remained out-spoken on the subject of Nat, my father, quietly acquiesced. He intended to watch and wait to see just how this was going to play out.

Never a believer in either fate of destiny, he was determined to let things unfold without his opinion or interference. I don't believe he had yet had the opportunity to inform Nat of his usual dictum; threatening either his knee caps or his very life if he screwed this up.

I had a fairly good idea that the conversation regarding any delay in my departure wasn't going to sit well with Nat. He may thrive on conflict but it was usually of his own making, not mine. My responsibilities and commitments were never quite as important as his. In his mind, my position as a trainer never amounted to a "real" job; just a lot of senseless horseplay that people with too much time on their hands and too much money enjoyed and didn't hesitate to pay for. I thought he, of all people, would understand my passion for my horses and my desire to compete. He had, at one time pursued a similar dream on the baseball field.

Lately his support wavered and I often sensed a bit of jealousy as though he was threatened by my competitiveness. He had made it very clear that when we were married, he was to be my first and only priority and he would the primary bread winner. Wives belonged at home; their job clearly defined and their sole responsibility to be a wife, mother and homemaker, in that order. His job was infinitely more important than mine in the long run. On the other hand, I didn't feel the same sense of urgency that Nat was displaying. Now that we had made a commitment to each other and had two workable, alternative plans in place, it was simply a matter of navigating our way through the details. We were, after all, making headway and things were beginning to fall into place. We'd managed to come this far and the entire process no longer seemed quite so difficult to overcome or as daunting as it had first appeared to be.

I wasn't wrong. The ensuing battle over the phone was epic in proportion and lasted for several hours. He couldn't seem to understand that I had previous, long-standing obligations that I couldn't and wouldn't break. I couldn't imagine the faces of my little clients if I had to tell them I was leaving them high and dry, completely on their own, without honoring my promises to see many of them compete for the first time. They were depending upon me to be there for them and I knew from previous experience just how important that can be. He, of course, was absolutely outraged at the delay; believing instead that I was making excuses to avoid moving. At one point, he even went so far as to accuse me of not loving him enough to "git on wit it" and went even further by intimating that my mother was "holding me back and interfering in our relationship" Nothing could have been further than the truth. My parents had been nothing if not supportive. My father had already gone to great expense between buying plane tickets and having my car more or less rebuilt. How could Nat be so callous as to not see that? He argued, that if I had a ticket in my hand, why wasn't I on a plane – that night. He had given up the Air Force for me, why couldn't I bring myself to give up California for him? I couldn't make him understand that was exactly what I was in the process of doing!

After his discharge from the Air Force, Nat began, in my mind to change almost imperceptivity. He slowly isolated himself from most of his friends and withdrew into himself, becoming more and more sullen and moody. He would have moments when he would visibly become distracted and almost lost. It was as if the previous six years in the Air Force and the careful indoctrination had deserted him and left him confused, unable to make even the simplest decisions concerning his own life. Since his enlistment at nineteen, he had been told when to get up in the morning, what to do and when to do it; when to eat, what to wear and when to sleep. The Air Force had done most of his thinking for him. Somehow, he had misplaced his ability to think rationally for himself. Now, on his own, he felt that while he had honorably served his country, he was more or less set adrift; unsure how to approach the most basic, daily tasks that the rest of us usually take for granted. He had somehow lost his anchor and, it scared him to death, so much so that he would experience moments of sheer panic.

The decision to leave the military when his term of enlistment ended and return to college had been an agonizing one that he argued back and forth with himself for weeks on end while we were in Cheyenne. He had looked at the pros and cons and debated for months before deciding that not re-enlisting was the right thing to do. With that decision; the world suddenly became a very terrifying place. The idea of walking away from all the security the Air Force had to offer frightened him beyond reason. The fact that there was a rumor flying around the base that he would probably be sent to a similar base in North Dakota if he chose to re-enlist became the over-riding factor and forced him to finally make the decision not to re-enlist. That was all he needed. Once he did leave the Air Force, and pursue his education at the University of Tennessee in Knoxville, he questioned the validity of that decision every day.

At the University he suddenly he found himself on a large, bustling campus at least ten years older than the average sophomore and in a new, strange city. Living alone in a small, sparsely furnished, studio apartment with absolutely no support from his parents either emotionally or financially and surrounded by all those perky little co-eds. His only companions during that time was a dog named Duke and a large, green lizard of some sort, confined to a glass enclosure.

I know he doubted whether or not he was doing the right thing and I know, based on our conversations during that time, that he was lonely and felt abandoned by his friends, family and especially me. I could feel him pulling away from everything that had once been so familiar no matter how much I impressed upon him the need to continue and finish his degree. I was the one, after all, who had encouraged him to be better than he was, to stretch himself as far as he was able, promising that in the long run, he would benefit enormously. Without a degree, he would severely limit his employment options. With a degree, in something- it didn't really matter what - six years experience in the Air Force, an honorable discharge and the highest security clearance possible, he could literally write his own ticket. But with the subtle disconnect between us came anger and the more frequent manifestation of an already volatile temper.

It didn't take much to set him off, a sideways glance, a misspoken word or a thoughtless shrug of my shoulders could escalate into a full blown tantrum, not unlike a disgruntled six year old sentenced to a time-out. All reason was immediately pushed aside as raw emotion and irrationality slowly took over.

After a time, he slowly embraced the routine of college life but in doing so, lost contact with most of his military friends and those he didn't purposely ignore, he shunned. No one, least of all me, understood, why? As a result, he became somewhat distant and detached. Many thought he had simply chosen to immerse himself in his studies and campus life but to me it appeared to be it a longstanding insecurity, a feeling he had to prove himself to his friends, his family and me. He desperately wanted to make something more of himself. But he was unsure how to go about it. He didn't want to end up like his father in a thankless, menial job, but his anger, fear of failure and his own insecurities held him back. It suddenly became much easier to blame anyone other than himself for his decision and immediate hardship. He couldn't see the light at the end of the tunnel and the inherent benefits of his education. Nothing I said could convince him that he was doing this for himself; not for his family, not for my parents and definitely not for me. He was the one, in the long-run who would ultimately benefit.

While we were in Denver for Sybil's wedding, I thought we were once again connected. I saw very little of his anger, no uncontrolled outbursts and no temper tantrums. Either he was learning how to control his anger, holding it at bay, covering it up or perhaps he had finally outgrown the need for such blatant and unreasonable displays. I thought he may have finally reached a point in his life where he felt confident and secure. During that brief weekend, he was the same person I had fallen in love with; that cocky, somewhat arrogant guy who could charm my socks off.

I dreaded telling him I wouldn't be able to leave until the middle of September at the very earliest. I couldn't predict which way he'd go. Once again, from a distance and over the phone, it was becoming harder and harder to anticipate his moods or his reactions. There seemed to be too many factors, that from a distance, I was unaware of. Somehow I knew the delay in our plans would be my fault. He would become immediately accusatory, blaming me as if my life and responsibilities meant nothing. We weren't in this together; this was his life and his plan and I was not moving along fast enough to satisfy him. I felt as though I was tiptoeing on eggshells or constantly peeking around a corner, never knowing what was about to come my way. Carefully trying to gauge his mood before I said or did anything; living in a state of fear and never quite knowing what to expect.

When I finally called, I wasn't too far off the mark in my estimation. His anger was palpable and, of course this delay was entirely my fault. I alone was to blame; I was completely responsible. Finally after what seemed like hours spent with the phone in my ear, I was able to placate his anger and he gradually began to listen to reason. Reason was followed by agreement, eventual acceptance and finally, thankfully, he saw the benefits of a delay. For myself, I was once again, exhausted and emotionally drained. How many times had we had this conversation and how many times more would we repeat this exercise in the future? Was this destined to be the pattern of my life? I felt so helpless, unsure how to put an end to it.

Two days later he called, briefly, to tell me he had considered conversation very carefully and now felt he needed time for himself to "think about whar' exactly we was 'aheadin." He admitted it was entirely possible that we were "movin' too fast." At his request, I agreed that we would not communicate with each other, in any form, for one entire week. He promised to call the following Sunday evening. We had both been in our respective cities just two weeks to the day. Two weeks since Sybil's wedding and our weekend together in Denver! It seemed so much longer – a lifetime of confusion and decision making packed into two weeks and now we were at a mutually agreed standstill.

With Plan A and Plan B firmly in place and a week of forced, albeit agreed upon silence, looming in front of me, I decided to make use of the opportunity to continue to explore several wedding venues in Savannah. In point of fact, throughout all of our conversations, heated or otherwise, we had yet to actually discuss a wedding date. We both assumed it would be just three months away; sometime in September. I saw no harm in researching what Savannah had to offer. At one point, Nat had suggested we get "hitched" at the local county courthouse in his small hometown. He wanted a quiet, simple ceremony with just our families present. No lavish, extravagant, society affair similar to the event we had just experienced in Denver. Followed by one of his families typical on – going, never ending B.B.Q's in the backyard. At first, I thought he was joking; once again testing me. I could no more consent to that idea than to a ceremony at the base Chapel even if his older brother would agree to wear a clean t-shirt under his coveralls for the occasion! He also made it very clear that a honeymoon was, at this point in time, out of the question. Between my relocating, getting my horses safely ensconced somewhere, his work schedule, and the overall expenses involved, the honeymoon would just have to wait a few years.

I think a girl has only one white wedding in her lifetime. Only one opportunity to wear a beautiful, long, flowing white dress and declare her love surrounded by family, friends, flowers and music. Just one time in her life to share her happiness surrounded by those she loves most. Now it would seem he was asking me to give that up as well. If I took the time to carefully consider a tally sheet, at this point, it would be grossly out of balance on my side and far from equitable. Not only was I giving up my home, my family, my life as I had known it, my friends and everything I loved, I was now expected to concede a wedding, a honeymoon and an engagement ring! I was beginning to realize that little by little, piece by piece and day by day, in these last few weeks of turmoil, I was giving up everything for him. I was quickly running out of things to surrender - except, of course, myself. Each day, I was losing a little piece of myself. At this rate there wouldn't be much left. Perhaps that was his original plan, his ultimate goal. I am not an empty vessel waiting to be filled by someone else. How much more was I expected to give up? I was slowly running out of concessions and without leaving the safety of Odie's stall, beginning to feel abandoned and alone; alienated from everything I knew and loved as I felt myself slowly slipping away into oblivion – barely recognizable even to myself. How had I let this happen? How had I come to this place?

Chapter Fourteen

I knew my parents had their hearts set on a wedding at either the St. Francis Yacht Club in San Francisco or The Lodge at Pebble Beach; both of which my mother was convinced she could organize on a moments notice. The idea of the Russell County Courthouse in Castlehill, Virginia, Nat's hometown, was not within her realm of possibilities. Savannah, of course, would be more difficult but she had every confidence that it could be done – the distance not withstanding. Anything was possible; it was simply a matter of organization.

There is no one place in San Francisco more beautiful than The St. Francis Yacht Club. As a private, members only club it is definitely not included in any tour nor are the tour buses allowed anywhere near it. Unless you are member yourself or know someone who is, you're chances of getting though the huge glass front doors are non-existent. Built in 1927 on a jetty just off of Chrissy Field in the Marina District of the City, it holds a commanding presence on the Bay with views of Angel Island, Alcatraz, the Golden Gate Bridge and the City skyline – all visible from what appears to be literally sea level. If the tide is running high, the deck and walkways are just inches above the water. Waves crash, sending spray up over the rocks in a fine mist that give the City a distinctive view that few can imagine or have the opportunity to enjoy. The marina itself is home to every type of boat afloat, including small, one-man kayaks and sleek, ocean going yachts displaying world-wide registries. Growing up, I spent many summers subjected to the cold and wind while learning to sail first in the yacht basin and later on the Bay.

Elegant and formal in a historic setting it is considered one of the most prestigious yacht clubs in the world and was recently completely renovated in classic navy blue and white to celebrate the America's Cup Races. The interior is filled with antique boat models of every type, classical nautical antiques, photographs of historic San Francisco and anything remotely associated with sailing. It is perhaps one of the most beautiful and intimate settings in the City for a wedding.

At the same time, there is nowhere more glamorous and classically elegant than the equally historic Lodge at Pebble Beach. It's distinctive, natural beauty, sitting high above the cliffs of the Pacific Ocean takes your breath away in its simplicity. The dramatic coastline, the incomparable scenery, the legendary mystical forest shrouded in fog and the stately, iconic architecture all carry you back to a gentler time of grandeur and romance. Once through the marble foyer, you immediately find yourself in a grand ballroom of glass that faces due west onto a sweeping lawn high above the cliffs and the ocean. The sunsets alone from this room are unparalleled. It is, without a doubt, one the most spectacular corners of the world. On one of Nat's rare visits, my parents had taken us to dinner at the Lodge and though I was to discover Nat was not a big fan of oceans in general, even he had to admit he was impressed and completely overcome by its beauty. He had no idea such places existed.

My on-going research on-line into various wedding venues had led me to believe that Savannah too offered several equally beautiful options. I was more familiar with and naturally biased toward the places I knew, having grown up spending time at both the Yacht Club and The Lodge. But the rolling green acres, the obvious gracious lifestyle and the gentle ways of the South, steeped in tradition, were equally intriguing. Antebellum mansions, like the Mackey House, surrounded by lush gardens, pavilions with fountains, 200 hundred year old oak trees, dripping with moss and flowered arbors all suggested an old world elegance that I longed to explore. The idea of arriving at the ceremony in a horse drawn carriage covered in magnolias; the horses decked out in top hats and a driver in full livery was very appealing. If we kept it small, there was even the possibility of being married on a riverboat, floating gently down the Savannah River - reliving a by gone era, mint julep in hand and surrounded by Southern hospitality and cuisine.

While I was thrilled and excited by all the possibilities and discussed each one at length with Nat for hours, he kept extolling the virtues of his local county courthouse. Unfortunately, I can't see myself barefoot, in a filmy cotton shift, clutching a handful of daisies, stolen, no doubt, from a neighbor's garden or purchased from the local grocery. Judging from Nat's insistence on the County Court House and his resistance to my ideas, I was beginning to think that maybe both he and his family were intimidated by my parent's wedding options. He was obviously uncomfortable with the sheer scope of our plans even though I had tried repeatedly to reassure him that organizing a wedding, especially on such short notice required making several decisions quickly if it was going to come together in time. While I felt comfortable with marrying in California, I had to recognize the fact that he too probably felt more at ease with what he knew and loved. We were poles apart once again and there didn't appear to be a compromise anywhere on this issue – unless we eloped. But we had already had that conversation and that ship had sailed two weeks ago in Denver.

It was hot; hotter than usual for the end of June and I was tired and dirty. I had been at the barn before dawn preparing the schooling horses for the day to come. I had several clients who were scheduled to ride regardless of the heat and two summer camps full of activities for children to supervise before I could ride myself or even attempt to work with Odie or Sundae. I had hoped to ride early in the morning before the heat of the day but one thing led to another and I finally decided to wait until the cool of the evening.

I'd spoken to Nat no less than three times during the day. Each call more frantic than the last. The first call, earlier that morning was simple, straight forward and to the point. He casually, almost offhandedly outlined this new development; another crisis, today's crossroad; with his usual ease. The second call was definitely more pleading and included many more details, explanations and apologies. By the third call, the desperation in his voice and his despondent tone were clearly palpable and couldn't be ignored. It fell to me to inform my parents of this new development; the content of our three conversations and pray they would have a workable solution or agree to be somewhat accommodating. Driving home, up over the hill, just as the sun slipped behind the hills, I decided the only way to broach the subject was to just blurt it out and hope for the best. I knew somehow my mother would be able to find a way around this. Years of experience had taught me the direct approach was the most effective.

As usual, the front door was wide open in the hope of catching the evening breeze, as was every other door in the house. My mother sat on the colonnaded terrace off the kitchen, overlooking the sparkling blue pool and the rolling green lawn. Her rose garden ablaze with color on one side and the champagne grapes, full and ripe, gentling sloping down the other, – all carefully fenced against the potential threat of marauding deer. The view of San Francisco Bay glistening in the early evening as the sun began to fade over the Bay, had turned the water the water a pale pink. In her crisp white, linen tennis shorts and a pale blue silk shirt – she looked as cool and relaxed as the glass of pinot grigio next to her. Her long legs, perfectly tanned from hours in the sun tending her roses and nurturing her grapes, stretched out beneath the oval, glass table, crossed at the ankles. As I walked in, she held up one finger, signaling me to wait until she had finished her call. Covering the phone with one hand she said, "Pour yourself a glass of wine and come join me. It's much cooler out here and there's finally a breeze coming up off the ocean."

I poured myself a cool glass of chardonnay and plopped down – as dirty and dusty as I was– on one of her newly reupholstered deep teak chairs, waiting for her to finish her call.

When she finished, I asked, "Who were you talking to?"

"I was calling the San Francisco Conservatory of Music to look into the possibility of hiring a string quartet to play Mendelssohn's Wedding March for the wedding as well as background music during dinner. Or would you prefer Pachelbel's Canon? It's up to you. What do you think? Goodness, you look like hell! You're getting far too much sun! Can't you at least wear a hat or something? You're going to be all wrinkled and pruney before you're thirty! You have to learn to take better care of your skin."

"Please don't start, mother. I'm exhausted and dirty and absolutely starving. Why do kids have to be so loud and sweaty? Are they always like that? I swear I'm never going to have any children – they're horrid, obnoxious little monsters! Today, two of them found a tray of ice cubes in the freezer in my office and decided it would be fun to feed them to the horses. When they ran out of ice cubes, they started giving them banana and root beer popsicles. It was chaos! I couldn't get any time in the covered arena so I was out in the full sun all day. Odie refused to go forward and Sundae refused to go backwards. I finally gave up and came home. It's just too hot to ride! I spoke to Nat three times during the day. There is something we need to discuss. Something's come up." I replied.

Snapping her lap-top closed and taking off her glasses she said, "Okay, you have my full attention. What's up?"

Tired, frazzled and determined to get through this conversation with as little drama as possible, I continued. "According to Nat, this has got to be a dry wedding."

"A what? She replied, clearly surprised at this new development.

"A dry wedding. No wine, champagne or alcohol of any sort can be served. I said.

"Ah! Desole! Shall I alert the staff and have Alejandro kennel the dogs? Jory, we live in California. We live in wine country. We have friends in the wine industry, we grow our own table grapes and we have invested in a few local wineries. People come to California from all over the world just for the wine and we are very fortunate to live here. I had hoped his parents would welcome the opportunity to experience everything we have to offer. Of course we're going to serve wine and champagne! It is a wedding, after all! You only get one opportunity like this. Make the most of it! If you and Nat don't want a full bar – that's entirely up to you. Your father will be thrilled to avoid that expense. But just out of curiosity, where is this coming from?"

"Mother, you don't understand. Nat's parents don't drink." I said in response.

"Don't tell me, the local IRS agent finally found their still and confiscated their stash of moonshine! Now they are high and dry. Quelle horreur!" She said.

"Not funny mother! This is serious!" I said.

"Is that what's causing those nasty little furrows to form on your sweaty little brow? I fully intend to have both sparkling and still water on each table. I'll even arrange to have a few pitchers of Sweet Iced Tea available or would they prefer Kool-Aid? Though I'll need to know what flavor. And, in the spirit of compromise, I'll even throw in a few cases of Cherry Coke, or RC Cola and maybe a few moon pies for them if they have an aversion to cake. Where do they stand on butter cream frosting? Et viola! Problem solved. You worry too much! This is, after all, a wedding – a day of celebration! What part of that don't they understand?"

"Mother, I practically screamed, it's you who doesn't understand! Nat's parents are as much as saying, if we insist on serving alcohol, they may very well refuse to attend the wedding!"

"Oh, now I see. Didn't we go through this last December when they refused to attend his graduation? Who are these people? Would they seriously use the occasion of their youngest sons wedding to take a stand on alcohol? Are they aware of the fact that Nat, as we well know, has never been one to pass up a cold beer – especially if somebody else is buying? And, from what you've told me, his brother doesn't seem to hesitate to put Jesus back on the shelf long enough to consume a six pack of Bud Lite. It occurs to me, there is something more going on here other than the issue of alcohol consumption.

Are they so insecure that they won't leave that bible-thumping backwater town for just one weekend to celebrate their youngest son's wedding without fabricating such a shallow excuse not to attend? We know from past experience that supporting him has never been their highest priority but to impose their beliefs on the rest of us is going too far. Take a look at that invitation list I've been working on for the last few days. These are all people you know. Friends and family you've known all your life. Tell me, who on that list of two hundred do you think will agree to attend if we don't serve wine and champagne? Do you honestly believe Gloria and Scott will agree to fly in from St. Paul if there isn't a glass of wine at the end of the road? Or that Kathy and Peter will come from Dallas to attend a dry wedding! Jory, think about what you're asking! Do you seriously think your uncle will fly down from Anchorage without the promise, at the very least, of a glass of chilled Sauvignon Blanc for his trouble? Good God! I suspect even your Aunt Debbie will have a glass or two of champagne and she's a Mormon!" she said.

"Nat is very upset and doesn't know what to do and neither do I." I said.

"Of course he's upset. I don't blame him in the least. I find this kind of behavior very unsettling and totally uncalled for, especially at this point in the planning. They are obviously feeling somewhat left out of the decision making process. It doesn't help that we've never actually had the opportunity to get to know them and all this is happening so fast. I suppose it's possible they are uncomfortable and unsure of what they are walking into and rather than put all they're reservations aside for one weekend for the two of you they seem to be looking for a way out; an excuse not to attend and this is it. They're taking the focus off of you and Nat - basically stealing your thunder. They ought to be ashamed of themselves! At least now we know where Nat gets his need to control!" She replied.

"But what are we going to do?" I cried.

"We're not going to do anything except continue to plan the wedding the two of you want. If they chose to turn this into a cause celebre and decide not to attend there's nothing anyone can do. It's their decision and ultimately their loss. Whatever they decide – it's up to them. Of course, we'd love to have them attend but if not, we'll manage. Let's try to focus on the positive and not let this become such an issue. They may very well change their minds as we get closer. We'll have to wait and see."

"There's something else Mom."

"There's more? I've about reached my limit for today. I don't know how you handle all this drama on a daily basis. But before you tell me; please pour me another glass of wine." She said.

"Speaking of feeling left out, Nat is beginning to scare me. I think he's freaking out a little bit with all of this going on. He wants to be more involved, and wants to know every detail and make even the smallest decision. Then, when I explain everything, and ask his opinion, he gets all wishy - washy and seems incapable of making any decision at all. It's driving me crazy!" I said."

"Well, that's to be expected. Men, in my experience, don't easily embrace change, or progress especially when it comes to planning a wedding. It's inherent in their nature and, I suspect, it's a control issue. All Nat really needs to know is when and where to show up. Don't ask him to choose between black wicker or silver mesh bread baskets. He doesn't really care. And I suspect he doesn't even know what a bread basket is in the first place. When you ask his opinion on the color of the tablecloths and the overlays, all you're really doing him is confusing him. God knows, his little brain is easily muddled. He feels like he should know these things but he really doesn't know and rather than admit he doesn't know, he waffles on the decision. Then you're upset and it ultimately leads to yet another argument which could have easily been avoided if you hadn't asked his opinion in the first place. Don't fill his head with minutiae. He can't process it and it confuses him – which, truth be told, isn't at all hard to do." She replied.

"Mom, that's not particularly helpful." I cried".

"Sorry, I couldn't resist. He makes it too easy. Come on, you know it's true. The point is, men have a tendency to go with what they know; what is most familiar. When you ask Nat's preference on things like tablecloths and coordinating napkin colors or bread baskets, he's going to respond with what is most comfortable to him. In his case, that would be red and white checked plastic, purchased by the yard, no doubt, and easily trimmed for your convenience to fit the picnic table or the folding card tables. And, it goes without saying that paper napkins or paper towels obviously work just as well as linen and are considerably less expensive. He is aware, isn't he, that we are paying for this – not him? Give him a project of his own so he that feels more involved. How about the honeymoon. How's that coming? Has he made any progress or decisions regarding that?" She said.

"Mother, I've already told you, there isn't going to be any honeymoon! He didn't seem to have any trouble making that particular decision. Until I move to Savannah, get us settled in a new, larger apartment, find a job as well as a barn for my horses and save some money, it's out of the question. There just isn't enough time to do everything." I said.

"I'm very sorry to hear that. Every girl deserves a honeymoon and an engagement ring! I remember telling him on at least one occasion that the women in our family will not accept anything less than two carats. It was the same conversation that I brought up the subject of the pre-nuptial agreement. Was all that completely lost on him? It's a family tradition! What part of that didn't he get? Because as far as I can see, you have nothing!

Put him in charge of the music. Have him look into hiring a DJ and make it his job to select all the music for the reception. That will give him something to do and take his mind off these other issues. Just make sure he understands that this is a wedding reception, not a ho-down or a revival meeting and his brother and his band, the Appalachian Apple Cores or whatever they call themselves, are definitely not the headliner for the evening. If his brother wants to strum his banjo and sing a song or two at some point during the evening – that would be lovely. But that is the full extent of his contribution to the entertainment. Do you think Nat can handle that or is it too much to ask?" She said.

"Mom, this is not the way I thought it would be! Not at all what I imagined! Is being in love supposed to be this difficult or this much work? They say you can't repeat the past and yet every time we're together, we fall in love all over again. Then, when we're away from each other for what ever reason, everything falls apart. If we could just get back to where we started maybe everything would fall back into place. That's why this wedding and this move to Savannah are so crucial. All we seem do is argue. All day, every day – it never stops. I wake up every morning dreading what today's crisis will be. All this non-stop drama! Where is the passion, the romance and the spontaneity? Why does every conversation turn into an argument? Is this going to continue for the rest of my life? I want the passion back in my life and all this quarreling and drama has to stop! Is that so unreasonable? I'm not entirely sure I can go through with this. There has to be something more! The last few weeks, I've felt as though the merry –go-round that is my life, was actually slowing down and I could finally step off and walk into a relatively normal life. Instead, it seems to have picked up speed, whirling faster and more out of control. I just don't know if any of this is worth it. My god! Do I sound as whinny and pitiful to you as I do to myself?" I replied.

She slowly reached out for my hand and looking over her glasses calmly said, "You're hot and tired and you smell like a horse which makes you a little bit pitiful. You've got a lot going on right now and a lot of decisions to make rather quickly, so if you feel like whining – I think you're entitled. Just don't make a habit of it. It doesn't become you. And, I suspect you're a little on edge because you haven't spoken to him in over a week. Why don't you call him? I have been thinking about all of this and it seems to me there is far too much conflict in this relationship. It's not a coincidence that you haven't heard from him. There is more going on here than meets the eye and think it's possible someone, probably his parents, have gotten to him. I suspect they are trying to convince him to marry his own kind – a local girl, no doubt. They probably already have someone suitable picked out for the job. All he has to do is go along and keep his mouth shut. Some sweet, doe-eyed cousin who is as malleable and easy to control as he is to manipulate. But first they have to be rid of you. What better way than to start throwing roadblocks into your wedding plans? I'm sorry to say -these people have an agenda that does not include you.

They are so desperate for grandchildren I can practically smell it from this distance. And they want them sooner rather than later because they know that will keep him home- their home. They have no intention of seeing their grandchildren shuttled between Virginia and California. What the two of you want isn't really a consideration for them. Don't ever make the mistake of under estimating his mother or the amount of influence she has over him. She may come across as a bumpkin but she's no fool. She knows her son far better than you do and she has no intention of letting go quite that easily. You have to understand that when you marry someone, you marry their family as well and the dynamics of your relationship inevitably change. Every family has at least one black sheep and from everything he has told me about his family, they appear to be a flock of black sheep with a Shepard who seems to have lost sight of his purpose, wondered into the woods, and left his charges to their own devices.

Harmless flirtation is one thing that his mother cannot control but forever is quite another and you are not exactly what she has in mind for her son. In other words, you're not forever material. Whether he gives in to their pressure or not remains to be seen but it wouldn't surprise me in the least. He asked for a week to think and to consider. He hasn't had a complete thought of his own since he enlisted in the Air Force but now his brain kicks in! Why now? It seems obvious that someone else is doing his thinking for him. You are the only one who can decide if he's worth all this. I can't make that decision for you. I wish I could, but I can't. You know where I stand on the subject and if you want to think about it and reconsider, take all the time you need. I can put a stop all these plans inside of ten minutes with just a few phone calls so please don't feel obligated. That boy really has you chasing your tail! These differences aren't going to go away just because you move from here to there. They have a tendency to follow you - wherever you go."

"Mom how can you be so cool and calm about all this? Everyday it's something new! How do you manage to stay so in control"? I asked desperately.

"Forgive me for saying so but since you asked - the answer is quite simple. I simply don't believe any of this is ever going to happen. I'm sorry but Nat is going to bolt. He's going to run as fast as he can to wherever it is he came from and he won't be checking the rearview on his way out. He'll never go through with it. He's too feral!."

I had the opportunity to step back and rethink the last six years but I hadn't taken advantage of it until now. I had been listening to my heart for too long and it had brought me to this place. Now, it was time to listen to my head. So here I sit on my bale of hay in Odie's stall, waiting for that phone call that is now three days late. I have finally forced myself to stand back and consider every last aspect of our relationship and it has finally all fallen into place. For the first time in a very long while, I'm calm. My thoughts are clear and there is no longer any confusion or indecision in my mind. I have managed to answer most of my own questions. I don't know what I'm going to say when he calls and I am determined not to let the sound of his voice dissuade me but I know now what I have to do. Sometimes, no matter how difficult it may be, we have to look long and hard at the reality in front of us and either accept it or reject it. We all have a tendency to make what we believe are good decisions for the wrong reasons or bad decisions for what we think are the right reasons. The trick, I suppose, is to recognize the difference.

Sitting here, safely in the stall surrounded by all that I love, I've gone over and over every detail of our long, torturous relationship. I can remember every detail of every day we spent together and I can clearly see the mistakes I've made over the years. I hardly recognize the girl I was when Nat and I first met any more than the woman I have become. I don't have as many questions unanswered. Most seem to have been answered. Everything has quietly fallen into place nd I can see clearly now. The merry-go-round has, without warning, abruptly come to a stop. The wooden carousel horses are frozen in an assortment of ungainly positions, no longer graceful in their physical movement and the deafening music has abruptly ceased to play. The carnival atmosphere has gone. I can continue on or step off and walk away. I alone will have to live with the consequences. The most salient factor now is can I live with the consequences of either continuing on or –what? What exactly is the alternative? He is apparently thinking exactly the same thing at the same time. Why else would he suddenly and without any warning ask for more time? I thought all the questions lately spinning around in my head had been answered. One question remained and the answer would very well define the rest of my life. To me, this was about getting my life back and gaining some control but was I prepared to let go - if need be? Either I would take back the reins and define my own life or I'd stand by quietly and let him define me.

I must have dozed off for a time, when I opened my eyes Odie had quietly turned and was standing directly in front of me, his big eyes unblinking, intent upon staring. I could see my own reflection in his large, liquid brown eyes and at last, for the first time, in a very long time, I liked what I saw. He nodded his head once and looked up at me as if to say, "You've been gone a long time, welcome back."

STELLA BENSON

Chapter Fifteen

The endless search for a home in the country was not progressing as smoothly or as quickly as we had all hoped. As the months dragged on, we became increasingly more frustrated while our little Victorian house in the City continued to shrink and become more and more choked; every square foot filled up with recent furniture acquisitions; stacks of books piled in every corner that seemed to multiply on their own, and occupying every possible surface; art work, prints, maps and canvases filling every inch of wall space or leaning precariously against the walls. Rolled up Persian rugs lay the length of the foyer, stacked on top of each other, creating a risk to everyone's toes.

Each and every morning, like clock-work, my parents would diligently peruse the Multiple Listings, hoping to find something new; a house they hadn't yet seen or that appeared remotely interesting. They had at least four realtors scouring every neighborhood within a forty mile radius of San Francisco; as far north as Mill Valley and down the Peninsula, as far south as Palo Alto. From the listings and based on their realtors weekly recommendations, they would compile a comprehensive list of possible properties and spend most of every weekend trotting through other people's homes; most in various stages of disrepair, creatively and expensively staged or completely under construction. This weekly ritual was followed by any number of often tedious, Sunday Open Houses to show our Victorian house to prospective buyers. At some point in this process, my parents reluctantly gave up and decided, rather than take on another costly renovation; they would instead design and build, from the ground up, the house of their dreams. But where? Buildable land in the Bay Area was virtually non-existent and if it could be found, at what cost?

Shortly after I was born, my mother started riding again and while the stables in Golden Gate Park were convenient and the scenic trails through the park lovely, the horses themselves didn't offer much of a challenge to her. Determined to find a stable within reasonable driving distance of the City, she set aside one day a week, for almost a year, to search for a suitable barn that offered a training program and horses more compatible with her capabilities. I, of course, was routinely nestled into my car seat: bottle in hand, diapers in the glove box and baby wipes readily available as we set off for the day.

What she discovered - what she inadvertently stumbled into, turned out to be a small, yet up-scale residential community, just thirty miles south of San Francisco and twenty minutes north of San Jose. An entire sleepy community tucked into the hills above Stanford University. Beautiful homes discretely hidden behind old, crumbling, stone walls with massive iron gates rusted off their hinges and seldom locked. The tree-lined, narrow roads wound over worn, wooden bridges, through barely discernable vineyards and what had once been cattle ranches and fruit orchards. It didn't take long for my parents to realize this was where they wanted to be. Within a relatively short period of time, they had found and purchased several acres of land ; heavily wooded with Sequoia redwood trees, half way up the side of what was commonly referred to by the locals, as a mountain – though it was far too modest to be considered a mountain.

As the oldest English speaking settlement on the Peninsula, the community had originally been established as a lumbering area with several active saw mills, as well as a few ranches, orchards, farms and lush vineyards. As early as the late 1850's the giant, Sequoia redwood trees had been cut down and dragged by cart and oxen, across the Peninsula to be floated up the Bay in order to provide building lumber for the burgeoning new City of San Francisco. Miners shacks, small businesses and several homes built from that first cut can, to this day, be found in San Francisco. Our Victorian in San Francisco had been one of them.

Following the Earthquake and subsequent fire that destroyed the San Franciso in 1906, the trees were felled a second time and again floated up the Bay; this time to rebuild the City. Fortunately, those who harvested the trees had the foresight, even then, to plant two trees for every one they cut. By the time my parents purchased their property, the third generations of redwoods were again gigantic and strictly protected by law as were the scrub oaks and pungent eucalyptus.

By the 1880's the most prosperous families of San Francisco had discovered the area; buffered against the Pacific fog so prevalent in the City. It soon became fashionable to build elegant country estates or small, quaint, thatched summer cottages that benefited from the warmer, milder climate. Until regular stagecoach service in 1852, many set out from the City early, in a horse drawn carriage, stopped briefly in Half Moon Bay for a picnic lunch on the beach and then continued on, easily arriving before dusk. As a result, horses were and continue to be, a large part of the community and deeply ingrained in the local culture.

Mile upon mile of well used and worn trails wove throughout the small community. Some were easily recognizable as the old, long established logging trails beneath the towering redwoods. Others still bore the faint footprints of cattle, winding from the flats over the crest of the hill to the open pastures near San Gregorio beach: a narrow climb on a precarious path through the Coastal Range. Many of the trails were increased by more recent property owners who wished to extend the existing network and connect to those trails already twisting through the adjoining State Park. All were heavily trodden by the locals, most of whom kept horses, if not on their own property, then stabled nearby at local boarding facilities. There were no maps or sign posts available to delineate the trails because every horse owner in town knew just where they started, where they ended and where to pick them up at any point. There was a series of no less than 52 gates, installed just high enough to be reached while on horseback. Several residents had been successful in teaching their horses to grasp the leather thong and slip it over the post to open the gates for them. No one could ever remember the gates being bolted closed or locked to deny access to the riders.

The maze of trails zigzagged beneath the cover of the redwood trees, over wooden bridges and, eventually led down into the small commercial district of town. Every small business provided a hitching post, a trough of fresh water and a bale or two of hay. It was commonplace to ride to the local restaurant, tie up your horse and enjoy a glass of wine before heading home. Teenage boys were often sent to the grocery store, their mother's list in hand, to fill their saddlebags with groceries. The Police were more often than not, mounted, and the traffic was strictly regulated giving those on horseback the right of way. Manure for gardens and vineyards was plentiful, readily available and usually free for the taking.

Most local women didn't participate in anything as sedentary as book clubs, instead they organized riding clubs. Children, often as young as six, spent their summers participating in riding camps and many businessmen were known to ride to their offices each morning. Small, gleaming horse drawn carriages and buggies clogged the church parking lots every Sunday while the horses waited patiently in the shade of olive or apple orchards for the service to end. Every discipline was represented to some extent, depending upon the interest of the rider; cutting horses, hunt seat, trotters, hunters and jumpers, polo ponies and dressage, from training level to Prix St. George. Side saddle was very fashionable for many ladies and the Annual Fox Hunt, complete with packs of howling dogs and blaring horns was the high point of the fall season; drawing large crowds of basket toting spectators ready to spread out their lunches on the lawn at the nearby Horse Park.

Within our little community of just over five thousand residents, an involvement with horses comprised the livelihood of many and the chosen sport of most; both attacked with what can only be described as equal intensity and enthusiasm. There were three tack shops selling the latest equestrian fashions as well as saddles, bridles, boots and the most basic necessities of horse care. At least four Feed and Seed stores supplied every horse owner with bales of hay, bags of oats and stall shavings as well as rabbits, ducklings and chickens. It wasn't unusual to find a box of puppies or kittens available for adoption just inside the front door. There were more large animal veterinarians specializing in equine medicine than any other area in the state and just as many physicians whose major field of study specifically included sports injuries directly resulting from horse related accidents.

The only exception to this excess of available services was the provincial farrier who had managed to corner the market for his professional care well over fifty years ago. No horse owner would dare hire anyone else, even if there was anyone else, to properly see to their horses hooves. In order to insure his farm calls you were required to pay cash, in full, at the time or he would simply refuse to show up. He knew who paid and who didn't. He was a little man, hunched-over from years and years of bending up a hoof. He would tolerate neither your questions nor your opinions any more than your advice. He was a man of few words. He knew more about horses and their hooves than you could ever hope to learn in your lifetime. Hooves were hooves regardless of their age or breeding; mules to thoroughbreds – they were all the same to him. He knew every horse and pony in town by name and every possible malady that could attack a hoof. Even the local large animal veterinarians would quietly defer to his opinion. It came as no surprise that he was first on everyone's Christmas list and with good reason. He preferred Knob Creek Bourbon but feigned surprise every year when he received cases and cases of it.

The three restaurants in town, including the most recent addition that boasted 5 Star Michelin recognition, proudly installed hitching posts for the residents as well as designated "parking" for your horse and a groom readily available to tend your horse while you dined. If you rode into town and left a little the worse for the wine, our one local bar, built to resemble a Wild West Saloon, complete with a false front and saw dust and peanut shells on the floor, was gracious enough to lend you an orange, neon, reflective vest on the condition that you return it on your next visit. If not, they added it to your bar tab. Everyone assumed your horse would eventually find its own way home. If not, our local, mounted police would lead you and your horse back to your home and unceremoniously drop you in your barn. You would invariably awaken to a hefty fine for riding under the influence of alcohol with impaired faculties and an even larger penalty for potential animal endangerment.

In the fall, those residents with productive apple orchards would generously donate a portion of their crop to the community at large by filling several old wine barrels, strategically placed, around town. And the grocery store maintained an overflowing trough of carrots for the horses tied outside, patiently waiting for shoppers. A large, rather battered sign hanging above specified just two carrots per horse. No one dared take more than two and abuse the generosity of the owner of the grocery store.

Every breed of horse from Clydesdales to thoroughbreds, quarter horses to small Welsh Cobbs could be seen lolling in private pastures or clopping through town. Every possible discipline was actively pursued to some degree. The local polo club rotated between members' fields and pastures until an old-time resident bequeathed several hundred acres for the development of a proper horse park. One large enough for a proper polo field.

There were too may training facilities and boarding stables to count and too many trainers offering lessons in every discipline; from calf-roping and barrel racing to side-saddle, fox hunting and hunter jumpers. Several well-know and nationally recognized jockeys quietly lived among us and almost every barn proudly boasted at least one former member of the U.S. Olympic Equestrian Team on its staff. Not surprisingly, there was also a nationally recognized center equine facilitated therapy that offered extensive physical therapy for children and adults with neurophysiological, cognitive and psychosocial challenges. Exhaustive medical research has proven the inherent benefits of the repetitive, rhythmic movement of a horse that simulates normal human movement of the pelvis and spine. The repetition of that movement while sitting on a horse stimulates the muscles and reminds them of their function no matter how badly damaged. The center had recently expanded its therapeutic services to include recently returning veterans suffering from both physical and traumatic injuries and PTSD's.

Every holiday presented yet another occasion for a parade though town. The opportunity to show off your horse and your ability was just too much to resist for the locals. Very early, often before dawn, trucks hauling horse trailers would congregate in the parking lot of our little City Hall. Those who had managed to enter the parade before the designated cut-off date and even those who were last minute entries would either ride into town ready to begin or could be seen off-loading their horses in a morass of confusion. Chaos seemed to be the order of the day no matter how hard the organizers tried to maintain some degree of order. The local fire department, stationed in one corner of the parking lot, offered a hot pancake breakfast, at a nominal fee to everyone. Many people would show up just for the breakfast and the opportunity to observe the pandemonium prior to the actual event, which more often than not, proved to be more entertaining. To the locals, the preparation and the preliminaries where more entertaining than the parade itself. There was only one rule that everyone adhered to: no motorized vehicles allowed. Other than that, it was more or less, a free for all. Seeking to circumvent that rule, many children insisted on participating on bicycles, tricycles and little red wagons. Flexi-Flyers, roller skates, skate boards and often strollers, were all suitably decorated to reflect the occasion.

The first of May, May Day, would kick off the season with a somewhat subdued parade from City Hall. It being the first scheduled event of the year, people hadn't yet quite hit their stride. They were just warming up. Participation was somewhat lower but enthusiasm never flagged. The designated parade route would continue down the main street, past the commercial district, around the Episcopal Church, over the wooden bridge and end in the parking lot of the elementary school. A distance of approximately six blocks through the heart of town and would last anywhere from twenty minutes to two hours. Every horse was covered in pastel ribbons, painstakingly braided into tails, manes and forelocks. Saddles, bridles and bits reflected hours of careful polishing and were tied with long, flowing ribbons. Pastel seemed to be the order of the day and flowers were creatively attached everywhere and anywhere possible. Blankets of flowers replaced saddle pads and many horses sported straw hats covered in flowers with holes cut to accommodate their ears, loosely tied under their chins with even larger ribbons, causing a constant irritation. Saddle bags would be overflowing with greenery as the first blooms of spring cascaded to the street. The sweet smell of daisies, freesias and tulips competing with the overwhelming aroma of manure. The riders themselves were dressed in their finest, reflecting their respective interests or their own personal interruption of the rights of Spring. It could vary and it usually did. There didn't seem to be any rules governing the riders or their horses. It was entirely open to interpretation.

Those who chose not to actively ride in the parade would show up early to secure a suitable viewing spot along the parade route. Collapsible beach chairs sprung up to line the curb, many put out the night before to guarantee the best viewing position for the coming festivities. Everyone knew that the parade seldom, if ever, started on time but no one seemed to care. The fun lie in the anticipation and the chaos that was inevitable.

It was left to the mounted patrol to set the pace and maintain some degree of order but that never happened. Just getting everyone lined up in some sort of order and out to the parade route proved to a challenge. Usually the horses themselves would have their own ideas and set their own pace. The fresh flowers were too great a temptation as were the bales of hay, the bins of carrots or the water troughs. Some horses simply stop to munch the flowers off one another horse, have a drink of water or casually grab a carrot along the way, causing a delay or worse, a back-up in the parades progress. Empty water bottles, trampled under hooves and crumbled potato chip bags were a constant concern. Tempers would flare as many horses didn't anticipate the close proximity of other horses. Some horses didn't like ponies, some ponies didn't like horses. The unfurled American flag proudly carried by the Sheriff and flapping in the breeze was often enough to send at least three horses looking for a suitable escape, taking others with them and changing the route altogether. If you happened to live along the designated parade route, more than one horse would often decide he'd had enough for the day and just turn off to head home to the security of his stall, with half the parade following him. Many would rear, some would just lie down in the road, a few would decide on their own to pick up the pace and be done with this, causing others to scatter or bump into each other. Bicycles would collide with horses or sink into a newly deposited pile of horse manure, ponies would nip a child on a tricycle, and red wagons would topple over, spilling children into the path of an on-coming horse while parents scrambled to their rescue. You never knew what was going to happen but you didn't dare miss a minute of it. After each event, the organizers, once again outraged by the lack of discipline, would attempt to institute new rules to determine how many horses could actually participate and in what order. But each successive parade was a reflection of the last. Too many local people enjoyed and looked forward to the spectacle. Our parades soon became a tradition, an occasion not to be missed. They had grown and grown out of all proportion, taking on a life of their own, much to the dismay of the organizers but to the endless delight of the spectators.

By far, the biggest parade of the season was that of the 4th of July. The May Day parade was just the preliminary; a warm-up of sorts for this debacle. Residents scheduled their summer activities around it, local anticipation ran high and observation spots were at a premium. The parade route itself was extended to end at the stables and the official grounds of the County Mounted Patrol.

Every year, the elementary school students were responsible for constructing a life-sized version of the Statue of Liberty out of papier-mache. In the dark of night and veiled in secrecy, Lady Liberty would be transferred from the school to the back of the red, hay wagon belonging to the Feed & Seed Store that had been newly painted for the occasion. Driven by the owner of the Feed & Seed, fully dressed as Uncle Sam and pulled by two matching, grey Clydesdales with feet the size of dinner plates, Lady Liberty had the honor of leading the parade each year. The first in line, ostensibly to set the pace which was more leisurely given the increased length of the route. Unfortunately, after the horrific events of July 4th 1958, her flame had been doused and she had to stand flameless - but no one noticed. A hot summer day, horses and an open flame, never mix well.

Children painted their faces, teenage girls dyed their hair – temporarily – red, white or blue and teenage boys painted American flags on their hairless, sunburned chests. The third graders could be counted on to man a lemonade stand somewhere along the route, the fifth graders sold homemade popcorn balls and the local chapter of the Boy Scouts sold chocolate bars, slowly melting in the sun while the curate of the Episcopal Church canvassed for converts.

The horses were draped and beribboned in red, white and blue. Uncle Sam stove pipe hats were somehow secured around ears and bunting hung from every saddle while flowing white beards hung under horses chins. Open carriages, phaetons, broughams, surreys and buggies of every description were dragged from barns, stalls and garages; then cleaned and spit polished until they shined. American flags were visible everywhere from the shop windows to replacing saddle pads. Balloons, fireworks and sparklers had long ago been banned. The popping noise causing too many horses to rear and the deflated residue; a choking hazard for the horses.

At the end of the road lay the mini fair grounds, generously donated each year by the Mounted Patrol who immediately took over the rest of the day's festivities and the rodeo. Speeches were given by local dignitaries but seldom heard and all the horses were properly blessed, courtesy of the Episcopal pastor. The high point of the afternoon was by far the mutton bustin' competition; open to any child, boy or girl, between five and seven years old and weighing less than 55 lbs. Carefully seated on sheep, and holding on for dear life they would tear into the arena to the shouts of encouragement of parents and bystanders alike. The object was to hold on for at least six seconds, similar to bull, bronc or rough stock riding but on a much less dangerous scale. There are no set rules and no National organization responsible for policing the sport. The ASPCA and PETA however, have both been quite outspoken on the event on the grounds that it does not promote kindness or respect for the animals and they openly discouraged its practice and participation. They needn't have worried. The sheep belonged to a local farmer who, every year lent them to the rodeo for the children to ride. Almost pets, most would step into the area and just lie down or wonder aimlessly around completely unfazed by their passengers. Very few ever bucked or posed any threat to the children.

If the May Day parade celebrated the Rite of Spring and the 4th of July parade was for the benefit of families, and the community at large, the Annual Halloween Parade was exclusively for the children. The competition was fierce as children attempted to out do each other in costumes for themselves and their horses to win the highly coveted First Place prize of a $100.00 gift certificate donated by the local Chamber of Commerce.

Carved pumpkins lined the street and fresh hay bales replaced the need for collapsible beach chairs. Bubbling black cauldrons of hot apple cider; the sticky, sweet aroma filling the air, was available to everyone. Black and orange were the colors of the day as filmy spider webs dangled from every tree and life-sized, glow in the dark skeletons lurked around every corner. The creativity, time and energy that went into designing each costume escalated each year with some amazing results. Black horses were painted with water soluble white paint, outlining their skeletal structure and ponies were doused in neon colors, particularly orange. Little girls appeared to be enamored with Disney favorites; one going so far as to dress as a mermaid, riding side-saddle with her huge, blue, satin fin carefully draped to one side. Her horse trotting along with a multitude of colorful, cardboard fish and crabs and a mass of green, plastic kelp hanging from the saddle to the bridle. Another, child cleverly put four white, ruffled pantaloons, one on each leg of her horse; a bonnet on its head with holes cut for its ears and herself as Little Bo Peep, complete with a Shepard's hook. Ponies draped in white sheets with holes cut out for their eyes, pulled wagons of smaller children, dressed for some reason as vegetables; peas-in-a-pod, an ear of corn and even a potatoe. The potatoe won 4th prize one year in the 4 year olds and under division. Boys favored either Star Wars, particularly Darth Vader or Pirates of the Caribbean. Their horses were covered in yards of black fabric with helmets artfully created out of black foam or painted brown paper grocery bags. It can be rather intimidating to see several large horses trotting down the road dressed entirely in black and ridden by furry, little Chewbaccas only to be followed be three or four little white ponies painted with black spots. A nod, we had to assume, to 101 Dalmatians. The parade ended every year with the rather ominous appearance of Ichabod Crane as the headless horseman, carrying a pumpkin under one arm and thundering down the street, just at dusk, to the delight of everyone and the horror of the smaller children. True to Washington Irving's story, no one really knew who he was; no one ever determined his true identity but every year he was eagerly anticipated and he never failed to scare the entire populace. Some chose to believe he was the butcher in the deli. Others were convinced he was a member of the fire brigade but to this day, no one is sure and his legacy lives on.

By Christmas, everyone had more or less had their fill of parades.

But Santa Claus had yet to come. Once again, the owner of the Feed and Seed Store, who was a large, heavyset man to begin with, would drag out his red delivery wagon and hitch up his two monstrous Clydesdales. Twelve days before Christmas, he would dress up, his grandchildren in the back of the wagon as elves, and head down the street to the fire station, tossing hard candies to the crowds who waited. The horse's legs were artfully wrapped with red and white leg wraps to resemble candy canes and floppy, red velvet hats with white pom-poms balanced on their heads. His reins and bridle as well as the horse's hooves were covered with jingle bells to announce his arrival. From Thanksgiving forward everyone's horse wore bells and the sound was festive even though we lacked the snow to complete the occasion.

When I was very young, not yet eight years old, I was allowed to ride my bicycle from elementary school to the barn. I'd stay there, riding, hanging out and underfoot until it was dark and my mother somehow knew it was time to pick me up. There was an older woman, who rode everyday at dusk, rain or shine, without fail. Tall, thin, very elegant and soft spoken, she kept to herself most if the time. She rode, what seemed to me to be an enormous black stallion, nearly 18 hands tall, suitably named Diablo. She may have appeared to be quietly concentrating on her own ride but she didn't miss anything that went on in the barn or in the other arenas. She carefully watched us all grow and progress in our lessons. Often she would shake her head, seeming to know instinctively who had what it would take to be successful and who was just hanging out for the sake of hanging out. Very few met her approval. For some unknown reason, I was one of the few who passed her scrutiny. I was to learn many years later from my trainer, that of all the children she had observed over the years, I alone had caught her eye. She believed I had the dedication and the talent to one day becomes a world class equestrian. Given time, the proper training, and something other than a schooling horse, I had the potential to be successful where others were just playing at the sport.

No one dared question her prophesy but suddenly everyone looked at me just a little bit differently. The pressure increased as did the frequency of my lessons and the quality of the schooling horses I was allowed to ride. While many others rode the same horse for years and years, I learned to ride every horse in the barn. I wasn't allowed to become too familiar with just one animal. The idea being, I would learn to handle any horse regardless of its size or nature.

When she rode, we would all run to watch her through the slates of the fence of the main arena which was always cleared just for her. Her equitation was beyond reproach, her hands quiet and more often than not, she held a glass of white wine in one hand and a cigarette in the other. She never wore a helmet as the rest of us were required to do, but no one dared point that out to her. Her ability to communicate her wishes to Diablo through her legs was too subtle to observe and impossible to emulate. She was the epitome of grace and other professional trainers on the grounds would often stop what they were doing to watch her. We all knew it would take years of patient practice to achieve the same degree of control and elegance that she displayed so effortlessly. She was the old guard; born and raised in the community and from one of its oldest families. She could trace her roots back to the original Spanish land grants.

She rode for the love of riding and her love for her horses, not because it was fashionable to do so.

She let it be known that she fully intended to die in the saddle, on the back of her beloved Diablo so no one was surprised when she did just that. Unexpectedly, she quietly suffered a massive stroke while on Diablo and slowly slid out of the saddle to the ground. Diablo was observed to stop, dead in his tracks, and bend to softly nudge her several times before standing over her until help arrived. A memorial was held in her honor in the center arena on a beautiful day in April. The shops in town had closed for the day as the entire town attended to honor her memory; including my parents and me. All three of her horses, including Diablo were tied to the fence railing, black satin ribbon woven into the braids of their manes and tails. The stirrups crossed over her highly polished, empty saddle. According to her wishes, white wine was served. At the time of her death, we learned she was 87 years old, something most of us could never have guessed. She had such a deep respect for horses and knew more about their behavior than anyone, including the farrier who, some whispered, had once been her sweetheart.

She made a lasting impression on me that continues to this day. She was the first to encourage me and applaud my success no matter how small or trivial and she was always there for advice. For years I had followed her around like a puppy, making a nuisance of myself in order to learn all that she knew. She quietly radiated grace and dignity; her influence understated but constant. She set the standard for excellence, and raised my expectations to what they are to this day. Not just in riding but I'd like to think in life as well. I was devastated when I learned she had passed away. Not believing that, on any given day, she would not be in the ring, riding Diablo at dusk, a glass of white wine in her hand.

I never knew what became of Diablo. One day, he was just gone from the barn, his usual stall empty. In truth, I didn't want to know, it was too painful to bear. I wanted to hold onto my own memories of the two of them and I couldn't imagine anyone else on his back. They are both with me to this day and I'd like to think she would be proud of me and all I've accomplished thus far.

For all of our outward displays of excitement and support for the community that we now called our own, we all struggled to jealously guard and protect our anonymity, both individually and collectively. When asked where we lived, we'd lie through our teeth and swear up and down we came from the next town over, the next exit down the highway. We wanted to believe we lived in a private, exclusive, gated community - without the gate. We were anxious to protect the simple life we shared in a quiet, rural community so close to San Francisco and San Jose. But that was to change dramatically in just a few short years. We could feel it coming; there was something in the wind that couldn't be ignored much longer. A vague, uneasy feeling that life as we knew it was about to change dramatically. We weren't sure what direction it would come from or what form it would take when it did arrive. But change of some sort was definitely in the wind.

Stella Benson

Chapter Sixteen

Once the decision to build the house of their dreams had been made, and the land purchased and cleared, the actual construction proceed rather quickly with very few delays or changes from the original specifications. The fact that the seven acres of heavily wooded property was just a quarter of a mile from the San Andreas Fault proved to be problematic but not one that was insurmountable. My parents had carefully covered every aspect of construction; the steel support beams; copper drains and downspouts to the door knobs and the crews that held them in place. Nothing was going to be left to chance and there would be no surprises along the way that would result in delays. No substitutions and absolutely no deviations from their original design. The fact that my parents had done their homework and researched every possible aspect of the construction; hired a very reputable architect with a background in late 18th century and early 19th century American architecture and a contractor, who was painfully honest, contributed, to the overall ease of the project. And, the contract my father negotiated with both the architect and the contractor included a bonus/penalty clause to keep things moving along and within the specified construction time.

The house was completely finished in just over ten months and we moved from the City down the Peninsula to our new home in the country. Our little Victorian had sold very quickly, in less than three days without ever being listed or advertised. An overly zealous realtor within the listing office readily agreed to pay considerably more than the asking price for the privilege of owning an original. Pre-Earthquake, San Francisco Victorian. No For Sale sign ever went up in the little gated front yard; there were no more Sunday Open Houses to endure and no looky-loos trotting though the house at awkward hours.

While we were sad to leave the City, we were more than excited at the prospect of a bigger house, with room to spread out and in the country. No more glaring street lights that required black-out drapes or the blaring sirens of police cars and ambulances roaring throughout the night. No more fighting over parking spaces or wondering up and down the street in an attempt to determine who had managed to block our driveway. Our bizarre neighbors who insisted upon keeping chickens and fighting cocks or raising sheep for their holiday table were left behind. The chickens would have to fend for themselves. The little lambs, their fate a foregone conclusion, and destined for the rotisserie were no longer our concern. And the raccoons would have to survive with one less garbage can to rummage through and topple over on their regular nocturnal visits. We had no idea what we were about to encounter and we were blissfully unaware of what lie ahead but our enthusiasm far outweighed our naiveté.

Unbeknownst to us, our new life in the country would include deer; more than comfortable with the human population, and not at all deterred by the presence of people. They hovered, patiently on the edge of the newly laid lawn, waiting for my mother to plant something, anything edible. The minute her back was turned whatever she had put in the ground, would be gone. The dining room windows, in particular, were covered with wet deer nose smudges on most of the lower panes as they followed a path under the portico and gazed into the house at all hours of the day, usually dinner. The rabbits, prolific as ever, would nibble away at struggling and unprotected vegetables and the moles, voles and gophers would decimate the roots of anything that hadn't been initially planted in a wire mesh basket, including the roses. Feral pigs were known to occasionally wander out of the hills and through the redwood forest to quietly peal back the newly laid sod, in the middle of the night. Looking for grubs, bugs and worms, they would curl the lawn back very neatly at every corner and leave it looking like toast. Hordes of marauding woodpeckers would routinely attack the champagne grapes the minute they had set if they hadn't first been draped in fine black mesh. By far, our greatest challenge was a mountain lion that seemed to be exercising some degree of territorial imperative and was not at all happy with our presence. She would wonder, very leisurely, through the yard, calmly drink from the pool and occasionally lie down to take a bit of sun on the warm stone deck. More or less defying us to confront her. My mother was convinced a call to the Department of Fish and Game would only resort in her death and refused to make that call. As a result, the dogs and the cat would be called into the house no later than dusk. No one dared walk after dark; no tricycles or bike riding was allowed and small children could not be left unaccompanied. Only a city slicker – which we were – would install a pet door - an open invitation to the smaller, marauding, nocturnal wildlife. That, in itself would give anything wild and small enough to pass through, immediate access to the entire house.

My mother, determined, as always, to come to some sort of compromise, would often sit on the front lawn with her cup of tea, very close to the deer while they grazed. She hoped to discuss with them the feasibility of our co-existing peacefully in the same environment. They would listen, unafraid, to her proposal while intently munching on her roses, thorns and all, completely unfazed by her argument. Research lead her to believe the deer were creatures of habit, and territorial, so she convinced my father to install a large water trough on the front lawn. They seemed grateful for the gesture but remained undeterred. Finally, she laid out large blocks of rock salt, delivered by the local Feed & Seed on a regular basis; believing they would come to our house for the water and salt and then, once satiated, mosey on over to our nearest neighbors' house to eat their roses and geraniums, thereby protecting what she had planted but leaving the neighbors vulnerable. When that failed to have any effect, she reluctantly gave up, and conceded defeat. The battle that had raged was lost. She has never been able to understand how she and my father: two obviously well educated, fairly intelligent and reasoning adults with at least six degrees between them, couldn't seem to outwit the deer!

Compared to the Victorian house we had left behind, our new home was enormous and somewhat overwhelming. We had all been involved in the construction process so its overall size shouldn't have come as a surprise to us when it was completed. The original intent had been to build a new, old house. That goal was realized when many people casually driving by would assume it was one of the original estates, built over a hundred years ago by a prominent San Franciscan that had recently undergone a complete renovation. Except for the lack of landscaping and the debris of recent construction, it looked as though it had been there, in the forest for many, many generations.

It was not a typical California ranch house by any stretch of the imagination, but more an example of a classic East Coast, center hall Colonial adapted to California. A white clapboard exterior with black shutters, four large pillars in the front supporting a balcony above the front door and four more pillars of equal proportion reaching to the peak of the roof. It dominated the landscape and yet had been designed to blend into the existing forest.

An oversized, large front door with a brass knocker that could raise the dead when utilized as it reverberated throughout the entire house, replaced the need for a bothersome doorbell. Over eight thousand square feet of empty space waiting to be filled. We were no longer bumping into each other or tripping over rolled rugs and piles of books or a bicycle in the hallway. The entire house smelled of fresh paint, recently hewn lumber and the dry, chalky scent of stone. Sleek, stainless steel appliances in the kitchen, and a huge custom designed pot rack suspended from the ceiling held my mother's collection of French, Mauviel copper pots and pans. Everything my parents had ever dreamed of in a house was now a reality. The twelve foot ceilings, large-scale rooms with highly polished plank floors and the rustic French kitchen had all been carefully designed and meticulously executed to take advantage of the country setting and, at the same time, resemble a centuries-old homestead.

The black and white checked painted floor in the double foyer led to a sweeping, staircase which, after considerable argument with the contractor, was installed in such a way that it actually creaked. A facet of construction that I became increasing more aware of as a teenager trying to sneak in after curfew. The wide plank, hardwood floors, stained a deep coffee brown, covered the floors in every room except those laid in stone. There were six bedrooms, all en suite and each with a huge walk in closet and a balcony leading outside. The twelve foot ceilings soared with classic 6 over 6, full mullioned, floor to ceiling windows, every one with a window seat and a bookcase. Several pairs of French doors, opened to reveal the thick forest beyond and occasional breeze off the ocean.

The three full masonry fireplaces all in pale, blond stone, quarried locally, stood in the family room, the downstairs pool room and the master bedroom and all three actually burned wood as opposed to gas. The full butler's pantry off the kitchen housed a climate controlled wine seller capable of storing over 500 bottles of wine.

With the furniture arranged, the rugs laid, the pictures, paintings and lithographs hung, the house still echoed. Everything was new and functioned as it should. I could safely flush my toilet without fear of scalding my father if he happened to be in the shower. And the dishwasher was not mysteriously connected to the doorbell because we had alleviated that particular electrical issue by not installing a doorbell in the first place. There were no drafts, leaks or unexplained breezes to be stuffed with towels and every bedroom opened up to view terraces. An extensive porch, immediately off the kitchen and family room had been designed to take full advantage of the sweeping views of San Francisco Bay and was accessible through no less than four sets of French doors. The entire house with its stark white walls, and sparking clean surfaces was designed to take full advantage of as much natural light as possible.

The Victorian, in contrast, had been long and narrow with common walls; a tunnel with light at both ends and only a front and back door. This house had no less than 19 doors! A security companies worst wiring nightmare. Situated as it was, in the middle of seven, heavily wooded acres, and encircled by redwood trees, we had absolute privacy. Our neighbors were far distant; no prying eyes and no need for shutters or drapes to obscure the view or limit the light. We were as remote as we could possibly be and still have access to everything the City and the Peninsula had to offer.

There was no need to give up everything we had come to love except the practical, day to day trials of actually living in a large, cosmopolitan City. My mother was still able to meet her girlfriends on a regular basis for lunch at the Elite Café or LaColonial – they're usual haunts; and attend the occasional gallery opening, maintain her position on more than one Board and continue her participation in various charities. My father's monthly poker game at the Pacific Union Club wasn't disrupted and Candlestick Park was actually now much closer and easier to access for the 49er games than it had been. The annual summer functions, at least those that would allow women and families at the Bohemian Grove, required only a bit more planning and a little more driving time but they were still within our reach. Their season tickets to the theatre, the ballet, the opera and the symphony would not be forfeited because of our move. And my parents' annual appearance at the annual Black and White Ball or the much anticipated Hookers Ball was never in jeopardy. Everything would remain the same except the location. The ocean was nine miles, over the hill and tough we couldn't see it or hear it we could smell it in the salt air. The fog that slowly creeps through the Golden Gate to envelope San Francisco most of the time, seldom, if ever, reached us. The only thing we did miss was the lonely wail of a distant fog horn that had been so much a part of life in the City. All things considered, we felt we had gained more and sacrificed less to be where we wanted to be and happily settled into a contented routine.

Chapter Seventeen

Every morning, five days a week, my father would drop me off at the Episcopal Church nursery school, down the hill, on his way to his office. My mother would ride three days a week and come by immediately following her lesson and pick me up at noon. She always brought a picnic basket; usually a cold, crisp, Granny Smith apple, cut in half with a schmear of room temperature, soft camembert or a flaked, white albacore sandwich on nine grain whole wheat bread without mayonnaise and an organic juice box.

It is common knowledge in the Midwest that hordes of hungry rats routinely invade the silos where the grain is stored. When processed and turned into white bread, there lurks the possibility that anyone could, unknowingly, ingest all that nasty bacteria and the virulent microbes present in the rat's feces. That's wasn't going to happen. My brother and I were never allowed to have potatoe chips, Fritos, Cheetos, candy or chocolate. My mother had read somewhere, that chocolate, by itself, could impede the development of brain cells in a child and ultimately have a lasting impact on the synapse of the brain. And she had been boycotting tuna for so long, even she had forgotten why. As far as she could remember, it had something to do with the excessive number of dolphins that were caught and needlessly slaughtered in the skein nets of careless fishermen while harvesting tuna. With our lunch in tow, we would drive back to the barn to enjoy our lunch, al fresco, on the sprawling lawn surrounding the outdoor ring to watch the other horses and riders.

On one very ordinary morning, in the early Spring, her lesson was moved back forcing us to have lunch before she rode. Armed with my albacore sandwich and juice box, I was unceremoniously strapped into my stroller and parked under the eave of the barn in the shade. While I hated that stroller with a passion and resisted the straps that confined me to it, it did give me the opportunity to observe the goings on at the barn as well as my mothers' lesson, completely unnoticed. I was, by now, well known to most of the grooms and trainers working at the barn as well as all the scraggly barn cats that usually skittered away but on that day showed a renewed interest in me and my albacore sandwich. From my position, just outside the ring, I had a full view of my mother jumping and the conversation that passed between her and her trainer. A constant stream of instructions, barked out loud enough for me to hear, went on non-stop as my mother adjusted and readjusted until she performed to her trainers' satisfaction. I sat, fascinated by the exchange, envious and determined to ride one day. The sheer size of the horse and its controlled movement was mesmerizing. How was it possible to command such a large animal and appear confident and in control while doing it? On that day, forever seared into my memory, circumstances were in my favor and the pattern of my life was determined.

My father had barely come through the front door that evening when I ran into his arms with my news.

"Daddy, daddy, today I rode Nevada, all by myself, just like momma!" I screamed.

"Okay, slow down. You sat in the saddle with your mother and the two of you went for a ride together. Am I right? That must have been exciting!" He said as he let me slide back down to the floor.

"No, No! I rode! Momma was outside the ring with her trainer talking while I rode Nevada all by myself!"

"Well, that is big news. I can't wait to hear all about it. Where is your mother now?" He asked.

"She's out in the vineyard talking to Alejandro about her grapes. They aren't happy."

"Who isn't happy? Alejandro, your mother or her grapes?" He laughed.

Just as we came around the corner into the kitchen, my mother came up the back stairs, brushing dirt from her knees. A clump of shriveled grapes clutched in one hand, hanging from a single, puny, black stem.

"My God! I'm glad she gave me a heads up! You don't look happy at all and those grapes, if that's what you call them, look even worse. What's wrong with them? Aren't they supposed to be green? He said. If that's what you have to work with, you and Alejandro might want to consider diversifying into champagne raisins. You'd corner the market and make a fortune"!

My mother rolled her eyes and said, "Birds and blight."

"And how, I'm afraid to ask, is Alejandro holding up considering today's horticultural crisis?" He asked, trying to control his laughter. "Not to change the subject but I'm told the two of you had quite a day. It's amazing the amount of information I pick up by just coming through the front door at the end of the day. It's like going through a portal into another world!" He said as he winked at me.

My mother, with overly exaggerated calm said, "Can I get you a glass a wine?"

"Of course, he replied, as long it wasn't pressed from those grapes! And don't think for a minute, you can ply me with wine before you tell me you put her on a horse by herself, especially Nevada! That animal is enormous – he even scares me!"

"What you know about horses wouldn't fill a thimble. And - you think every horse is enormous and every horse you come near scares the wits out of you simply because you know absolutely nothing about horses and you're not particularly inclined to learn. You should talk to someone about that fear you're harboring. It's not healthy! That being said, to answer you're question; yes! She did ride today, by herself, and she was absolutely amazing!"

"My fear, as you call it, is well founded, thank you very much, in limited exposure and even less experience. That and I value my life just a little bit more than my manhood. You must be out of your mind! She's much too little to ride! What were you thinking? How did this even come about?" He said.

"Calm down. My trainer rang this morning after you dropped her off at school and asked to move my lesson back until later this afternoon. I picked her up at school and we went to the barn and had lunch on the lawn as usual. After that, I parked her stroller near the barn in the shade while I rode. She sat there quietly, talking to the barn cats until I came out of the ring. We had left the gate open so I could see her every minute and I was the only one in the ring so there was no traffic. No other horses coming or going. The minute I rode out of the ring, she started rocking that stroller back and forth with such a vengeance that I thought she'd end up face first in the dirt, tangled in the straps if I didn't release her. So I scooped her up and put her in the saddle. My trainer and I were just standing there with Nevada, talking." She said.

"And then? Go on."

"At some point, while we were talking, she picked up the reins and clicked her tongue, which I didn't even know she could do. Nevada responded by walking right back into the ring. She held the reins, sat straight up, scooted her bum deep into the saddle, even though its too large, held her head high and never lowered her eyes as they just walked around the ring at least three times. But she was so happy! You should have seen the smile on her face! She was absolutely beaming and so sure of herself! She was focused - not just playing around. The two of us were amazed and just stood there watching. Neither of us was quite sure what to do so we just let them walk. I had one heck of a time trying to get her off that horse though." She said

I had been listening to this conversation, back and forth, somewhat surprised at my father's reaction. I thought he would be pleased and surprised. Throughout this entire exchange, my mother had been in the process of preparing dinner. She had carefully sliced a small baguette into thin slices, placed them on a cookie sheet and slid it toward me as I sat in a stool at the center island. My job was to brush it lightly with a mixture of Olio Basilico, balsamic vinegar and sea salt before she put it under the broiler to brown. It hadn't occurred to me that my father wouldn't be as excited as I was about today's events so without hesitating, I jumped into the conversation and said, "Daddy, my trainer says I'm a natural."

He looked at my mother, somewhat stunned and said, "She has a trainer? She didn't have one when I left this morning!"

"She does now! My trainer has agreed to take her on as long as she listens and does exactly as she's told. She can start at three days a week – beginning tomorrow." My mother replied.

"This is crazy! She'll kill herself! What if she falls? It's a long way down for someone as small as she is! He replied.

"She won't kill herself and she will fall sooner or later – everyone does. The first thing she's going to learn is how to properly fall. These days the rings are engineered to be cushioned. She's not going to be riding on asphalt or concrete or a bridle path through the forest. Give me a little credit! Plus as young as she is, her bones haven't completely formed so she'll probably bounce like a ball. And she's definitely not too young to start. She's the perfect age simply because she has no fear, or preconceptions, unlike some people." She responded.

"There's a proper way to fall off a horse? How long does that take to learn and how, exactly does one learn? Do you actually practice falling off? I think you're crazy to even go near a horse let alone pay good money for the privilege!" He said looking surprised.

My mother, not to be distracted, replied. "Her size is unquestionably an issue but we can work through it. The barn doesn't have a saddle small enough to fit her so she will start bareback – which, when you think about it, is a good thing, She'll learn to balance herself without depending upon her legs because right now they are too short to wrap around the barrel of the horse. They just sort of stick straight out. I doubt I'll be able to find any riding boots small enough to fit her and she needs something with a heel. But she can't reach the stirrups anyway so, for now, she can wear her little rain boots. The green ones with the bugged-eyed frog faces on the toes. And, I can put some tissue paper or bubble wrap in the top of one of my old helmets so it fits her head more snuggly."

"This is madness! You've actually thought about all this. Why can't you put her on smaller horse? How about starting her out on a pony? They are only two feet off the ground. Less distance to fall - cushioned or not. I can get behind that but not a horse the size of Nevada!" He said.

"Daddy, I don't want to ride some fat, stupid little pony! They're mean and nasty. I want to learn to ride a regular horse!" I said.

"She got that from you. I hope you're satisfied. She's been brainwashed!" He said, glancing in my mother's direction.

"Well. She's right. It's nearly impossible to coax a cantering, chubby pony over even the lowest of fences. They are far too unpredictable and she understands that. At least she has a healthy respect for those nasty little beasts. And, in my experience, they are stupid and ornery! I really don't understand how parents, can, in good conscience, blindly allow their children to ride ponies! All it takes is for one of them to kick out and you've got a chain reaction; sooner or later, their kids are definitely going to get hurt. Those children would be so much safer on a merry-go-round, pumping up and down on a wooden carousel horse that is bolted to the floor. There are a few other considerations to discuss if she's going to start taking lessons." She said.

"I can't wait. What are they, since the two of you seem determined to pursue this?" He answered.

"Right now, she to young to know her right hand from her left so it occurred to me to put a big R on her right hand and an L on her left hand with a black marking pen. That way when her trainer tells her to use her right rein, she'll know which is which. I'll do the same to an old pair of her jeans so she learns her right leg from her left. Make sense?" She explained.

"That's the first thing you have said since I walked through the door that does make sense - in a very strange way. I'm sure there's more. Go on." He answered

"She's much too small for the mounting box. So, I or we, wanted to ask you if, on your way home tomorrow, you could stop at the hardware store and buy a step ladder?"

"What on earth for? You can't lean an aluminum ladder up against a horse! He's not just going to stand there and tolerate that."

"Of course he is. We do it all the time. It depends upon the horse. Nevada wouldn't hurt a fly. He's a schooling horse and more than accustomed to trotting around with children on his back. He's just a big, ole teddy bear. He won't hurt her – believe me. All the kids spoil him terribly with apples and carrots. And I'm not going to lean the ladder up against him; I'm going to put it to one side, next to him, so she can climb up on his back. I'm not asking you to buy an aluminum, 54 foot extension ladder, just a small, wooden step ladder. A groom could give her a leg up but it would be better, in the long run, if she learned to mount by herself. Besides, I can never seem to find a groom when I need one" She said.

Now, completely taken aback by this request, my father asked, "If Nevada is such an old softy why do you ride him? I thought you liked a challenge – though why, on the back of a horse, I'll never understand! That's not a challenge, it's a death wish!"

"There are a few things I need to work through and Nevada doesn't mind the repetition which is why, obviously, he's a schooling horse. If you ask a horse to do something over and over again, especially in the space of a one hour lesson, after four or five times, if you cant get it right, he's going to assume you're an idiot! He's doing what you ask, but if you're wrong, he's going to think you're the one with the problem, not him, and in my case, he's right. Nevada will repeat the same move all day long and not give it a thought because he's been doing it for so long. That's why he's so good with novices and children. He's very mild mannered and patient and there's not a mean bone in his body." She answered.

By this time, we had moved into the breakfast room off the kitchen and nearly finished dinner. I was exhausted; if not from all the days' excitement but from following the back and forth banter of their conversation. I could sense my father was about to yield but I couldn't be sure. Between my mother and me we had managed to counter every one of his objections. Either that or we had simply worn him down. I wasn't sure which but I couldn't keep my eyes open any longer. I knew as soon as I was safely bundled up to bed and out of ear-shot, their conversation would continue when they moved to the library with their coffee. I would have to wait until the morning for their final decision; their conversation was too distant and too muffled to be heard from my bedroom.

My father scooped me up under my arms and lifted me off the floor as the two of us started up the stairs to my room. I threw my arms around his neck and said, "Daddy, Nevada is my best friend, and he wouldn't ever hurt me. Please, please let me learn to ride. I'll be really, really careful. I promise."

"I'm glad he's your best friend but he's awfully big for a best friend and he has four very large feet. I don't know what I would do if something happened to you. I would feel better about this if we waited a few years until you have grown a little." He whispered.

"No, it has to be tomorrow, Daddy! If we wait for me to grow up, it will be too late. You wait and see; someday I'm going to be on the Olympic riding team!" I said, as I fell asleep snuggled in his arms.

Chapter Eighteen

I have to believe it was a trade-off from the beginning or at the very least an agreement between my parents during the design phase of the house. My mother had an enormous, round Jacuzzi bath tub capable of seating six people comfortably, installed in the master bath, though who exactly she intended to share it with, I have no idea There were eighteen jets, directed in every possible direction to guarantee complete therapeutic relief from whatever may ail you. In exchange for the tub, my father designed his library to his own specifications.

By far my most favorite room in the house; the library was a room of peace and tranquility that was indelibly printed into my memory from a very young age. To me it was a sanctuary of safety and quiet. The high ceilinged room was always a little bit shrouded from direct sunlight by heavy plantation shutters to protect my father's rare books and first editions. The dry, musty, smell of old leather and paper was so familiar to me and so reassuring. True to Scandinavian tradition, the entire interior of the house had been painted in a bright, almost industrial white; not ecru, eggshell or champagne, to take full advantage of all the natural light flowing through the large paned windows.

The Library was the exception or possibly the concession. Paneled in a deep, rich cherry wood that continued to a mitered, coffered ceiling, it held floor to ceiling bookcases for my father's ever expanding collection of California history.

A tall ladder on wheels suspended on a track from the ceiling ran around the entire perimeter of the room and his massive, Chippendale partners' desk, purchased at auction from Christies, sat at one end of the room opposite a large bay window. Directly behind his desk, over a bookcase, hung a large water colour of his beloved Porsche, commissioned by the artist and given to him by my mother. Behind the painting he hid the rarest of his rare books – his collection of valuable first editions. The deep cushions on the window seat were upholstered in a soft, pale, tapestry fabric my mother had purchased years ago in the South of France. In front of the window seat, lined with over-stuffed pillows stood two large, matching wing back chairs with a beautiful, antique Queen Ann tea table standing between them.

I have such warm memories of that room. Every important moment of my life was discussed and decided in the safety of that room. It was a haven of warmth and security for the entire family and my own personal sanctuary. I spent countless hours on the antique, Persian Bakhatiari rug playing chess with my father and later learned to play poker, eventually well enough to sit on his games if one of his friends unexpectedly cancelled. I can still hear the gentle thud of the red, white and blue clay poker chips as they accumulated in little piles on that rug.

His books, thousands of them, were rare, first editions which no one was allowed to handle. They lined the shelves like so many colorful soldiers; sentinel and stoic. Family photos stood gleaming in polished silver frames, a stuffed valley quail, a preserved blowfish and even the fossilized partial remnant of an elephants jaw, discovered on the Masi Mara and carefully shipped home from Kenya, filled the blank spaces in the shelves.

The entire room, with its soft, diffused light, gave off a distinct aura of cultured masculinity. A bar, carefully built in one corner of the bookcase displayed an array of glittering decanters and several sparkling, crystal bar glasses competed for space with a humidor. A small refrigerator had been cleverly hidden in the opposite corner bookcase, topped by a small, shining brass sink that usually held ice. The room had the subtle but pervading odor of cigar smoke and Bay Rum; a pleasant mixture that lingered.

It was here that my parents usually retreated in the evening to discuss the big and small issues of family life while classical music or soft jazz quietly filled the room. Given today's events, I assumed my riding adventure was to be the main topic of this evening's conversation. I desperately longed to eavesdrop on this particular conversation, convinced it concerned me. I had been known to slip out of bed and creep down the stairs, silently. Along the long corridor and around the corner in my pajamas, only to be stopped, dead in my tracks by the loud creak built into the forth stair down from the second landing. No amount of stealth on my part could navigate around that subtle trap. I would have to be content to wait for my parent's decision regarding my riding lessons in the morning.

My mother could be extremely persuasive but my father was a master at stone-walling – and a man of few words. They were too evenly matched. Before I had been carried upstairs and tucked in, I had no indication which way their conversant would go or if the scales would tip in my favor or not. Perhaps another compromise could be reached. I could only hope and dream of tomorrow.

In the following years I would spend a great deal of time in the libraries of other men but none as dear to me as my father's. I found the forbidding library of my first Headmaster with it's imposing array of crucifixes, assorted icons, and a very large portrait of a white, blond, blue-eyed Christ to be terrifying as it gazed down at whoever happened to be squirming in one of the over-sized leather armchairs . The Headmaster's library offered none of the warmth or security that I had come to expect. The more I looked at that portrait of Christ, which, as it happened turned out to be quite often, the more it bore a strange and unsettling resemblance to Brad Pitt. The pervading darkness of the room, the looming shadows and the nauseating odor of incense that was so foreign to me aroused nothing but fear. It was a monastic cell: its Draconian severity purposely designed not to be conducive to an exchange of truth but rather dread of what was to come.

Later, the subtle library of my high school Headmaster filled with faux New England antiques, flowery chintz fabric, and a salvaged crab pot disguised a coffee table encouraged conversation, and an exchange of ideas and trust as opposed to sheer terror.

Neither ever came close to the security and familiarity of my father's library. Over the years, I quickly leaned to judge my current situation quickly whenever my mother, in a very soft, monotone voice would calmly say. "Your father would like to see you in the library." Years later, she would use the same tone to say," Would you care to join us on the gallery for a glass of port?"

Presenting myself in my father's library could be a positive experience, an occasion for praise or it could not bode well. Had I been caught in the middle of something or betrayed – somehow? I never knew what to expect whenever I went through the door. My father, usually quietly sitting behind his desk, studying an auction catalogue or reading a current medical journal, would casually gesture toward one of the chairs and taking off his reading glasses, close whatever he was looking at and say, "Tell me about your day." That was my opening; and it never varied regardless of the situation. I was either completely unaware of what was to come or I would brace myself to vehemently deny it – whatever it was. As I saw it, I had three options; start to cry, which never had any effect on my father, blink in mock confusion which was even less effective than tears, or flat out lie, which I learned, at a very young age, proved to be the least effective option. Either way, I felt the warmth and security that I had grown accustomed to.

I could just imagine my mothers opening salvo on this conversion. She would start out slowly, then warm to her argument and finally end with a fiery but convincing conclusion. My father didn't stand a chance and he knew it.

"I knew this was coming, I'm just as surprised as you are that it has happened so soon. I've been thinking about it all day and I don't see any serious drawbacks.

In fact there are far more long term advantages to her riding now as opposed to making her wait a few years to start." She said with as much conviction as she could muster.

"She's much too young and she's too small. That, in itself, is a huge drawback as far as I'm concerned!" My father argued.

"At least give me a chance to explain. We're both fully aware of the downside of starting so young but you should be aware of the upside. You know how headstrong she is and how stubborn she can be. When she sets her mind to something, there's no dissuading her and she is determined to do this. It's not just a passing fancy. If we say no now, she'll be devastated because she wants it so badly and she won't understand our reluctance much less our reasons for saying no. I think it's important that we, at the very least, let her try. If she is too young and too small, let's let her come to that conclusion on her own. She can always stop the lessons and start again in a few years but it would be her decision, and hers alone, not ours. I'm not pushing her into this, it was entirely her idea. But I have to admit that I'm thrilled she wants to ride."

"How old were you when you started riding?" He asked.

"Seven or eight. But it was exactly the same situation. My mother rode all her life and she'd drag me along every weekend until one day I got bored hanging around the barn and crawled up on a horse by myself. I had watched and waited until I was ready and then I climbed on the nearest horse I could find. After that riding was something she and I shared for years, just as she and I can share this. I know you're afraid she'll fall and hurt herself and I'm telling you she will definitely fall off at some point and she will most certainly get hurt but the question is, will she get up, brush herself off and get back on or will she give up and walk away from it? Does she have the strength and determination to stick with it? I think it's important that we find out. And this gives us the perfect opportunity – either way".

"What if she's bucked off or scraped against an exposed fence post?" He asked.

"Schooling horses usually don't buck for absolutely no reason unless they are stung by a bee or something and there are no exposed fence posts inside the ring. Outside, yes, but inside, no. They are designed to be as safe as they can be. If anything, she'll slip off and go plop in the dirt which is not particularly dangerous"

"What if the horse steps on her?"

"He knows where his feet are and he knows she is on his back. He also senses that she is a young, small person and if anything, his first instinct is to protect her not hurt her."

"How can you be so sure?" He asked.

"Because I've been riding most of my life and I'd like to think I have some idea of what I'm doing. Do you honestly believe I would let her do this if there was the slightest chance that she could be hurt? I'm hoping her desire to do this will far outweigh the occasional fall because she is a very strong little kid! Not only that, but you have to admit the barn is a much healthier environment for a child than hanging out at some Mall or playing video games."

"How so?"

"She'll be outdoors, rain or shine, working with animals; doing chores and caring for the horses instead of cruising some Mall comparing nail colours with her girlfriends or lusting after a pair of $200.00 designer jeans. She'll learn what hard work is and more importantly, she'll learn responsibility. It will be up to her to get the horse out of its stall before each lesson, tack it up properly, cool it down, pick its feet, brush it and return it to its stall when she has finished. No one is going to do that for her. She'll also be responsible for cleaning out the stall, putting away her tack and making sure her horse has food and water."

"How can you expect her to do all that? Have you been in her room lately? I can barely push the door open because of all the stuff on the floor and yet you expect her to keep a stall clean! It's not going to happen. You're expecting far too much of her".

"That's the point. If she wants to ride, she'll have to do all that and more. If she doesn't carry her own weight with her horses' care and chores she won't be allowed to ride – barn rules. And that applies to everyone regardless of their age."

"You don't do all that! I can't remember the last time you actually schlepped out a stall! You just arrive and your horse is tacked up, waiting for you. You lope around the ring, jump a few jumps and then hand the reins to some guy who seems to be just standing around waiting for you to finish."

"Fortunately, I have the luxury of being able to afford a groom to do those things for me. That doesn't mean I didn't do it for years or that I couldn't do it again if I had too."

"Dare I ask how long this groom of yours – Miguel is it, - has been on the payroll? That horse of yours survives on a mulch of $100.00 bills as it is and now you're telling me that I'm supporting Miguel as well! Is he related, by any chance, to your gardener, Alejandro?"

"That's irrelevant. I couldn't ride without him. The point is, riding is something she will be able to do anywhere, anytime, and by herself for the rest of her life. It doesn't require a partner like tennis, three other people for a foursome or several other people to make up a team. It's just you and your horse. You're not dependent upon anyone else. I rode in Central Park in New York when I was at school and I rode regularly in the Bois de Boulogne when I was living in Paris and occasionally in Hyde Park whenever I happened to be in London. It gives you an entirely different perspective when you travel and the opportunity to meet people you normally wouldn't encounter as just a tourist, which has its advantages."

"There are so many advantages and any number of opportunities that will be available to her, assuming she continues and riding holds her interest. Every barn, including mine, offer summer camps, Christmas camps, Easter Break camps as well as classes, courses and clinics all year round; for every age and ability. In the years to come there will be all sorts of interesting opportunities that will expand her overall knowledge and skill. This entire community is devoted and completely immersed in every aspect of horsemanship and anything remotely related to horses. Surely you know that?"

"What sort of classes – exactly?" He asked.

"There will be courses in Basic Horsemanship, of course, as well as equine physiology, anatomy, animal behavior and nutrition. All of which are very important to any horse owner." She said.

"Aren't you getting just a little bit ahead of yourself? She can't even read yet and you're got her enrolled in an equine physiology class." He said incredulously.

"I'm just giving you an idea of what will be available in the years to come. They also offer classes in things like braiding, which is different for every discipline, hoof cleaning, basic ownership, how to properly clean and oil your tack, sweat scraping and shaft cleaning . The possibilities in this community alone to learn are endless."

"Wait a minute. What was the last thing you motioned?

"The shaft cleaning? What about it? She said.

"What exactly are we talking about here? Whose shaft are you referring to?

"The horses shaft, of course. For goodness sake, it has to be cleaned. It's a very important part of overall health care. Have you ever seen a horse clean its own hooves or shaft"?

"I never really thought about it. I just assumed it was something they did in private like any other self respecting animal. Discretion and all that. While we're on the subject, tell me why that cat of yours waits until he has my undivided attention to raise his hind paw up over his head and proceed to attend to his shaft, as you call it? And why does he have to do it on our bed?

"There – that's a perfect example. A cat has the ability to clean himself while a horse, obviously, does not. Besides, the cat likes you; I think he's reaching out to you. Trying to bond. Maybe it's a guy thing."

"I don't want the cat reaching out to me and I certainly don't care to bond over his shaft nor do I want him cleaning his shaft on our bed! Do you do that – to your horse?"

"Of course not, at least not any more – Miguel does it for me. There is a special tool available for just that purpose. It's a long metal thing with an adjustable, rather sharp ring in the middle. You slide it up and over and then gently, with a downward motion start to …

"Alright, I've heard enough on the subject. And what does he charge for that particular service?

"The shaft is a very sensitive area and a breeding ground for bacteria which makes it ripe for infection. It has to be cleaned on a regular basis because you don't want an accumulation of smegma or beans. It can be very painful to a horse and have a serious effect on his performance."

"I agree. To the uninitiated, it sounds extremely painful but I cannot speak to his performance level. So, I'm not even going to ask what smegma and beans are because I don't want to know. It all sounds nasty".

"Why are you sitting like that – all hunched over? Is this making you uncomfortable?"

This entire conversation has, in my opinion, taken a turn for the worse. And yes, I'm incredibly uncomfortable. You're not doing much to convince me that she is capable of all this. And I can tell you, unequivocally, that my daughter is not going to clean anyone or anything's shaft until she's over twenty-one and even then I don't want to know about it. If Miguel does that for you, he's a better man than I am - remind me to give him a bonus at Christmas.

"You already do – give him a bonus." "

"I do – what?"

"He has a passion for sweets and three little kids at home, so you usually give him a two pound box of assorted Godiva chocolates"

"Is there anyone else on my Christmas list that I should know about?"

"Well, you traditionally give the farrier a bottle of Knob Creek every year. If you didn't we'd be in a very bad way. He's the only game in town and we can't afford to neglect or slight him. He could easily refuse to show up when we need him the most. We can't have that!"

"No, of course not. Anyone else I should know about?"

"You give Alejandro a case of Bernardus chardonnay. Though I suspect he keeps half of it for himself and gives the other gardeners a bottle or two. Which is fine. It's his to do with what he pleases. He is, after all, the head gardener and he's here at least once a week overseeing the grapes. He's worth every penny of it."

"An entire case!! Since when? How long have I been doing this? No wonder these guys are so friendly when I run into them in town. Complete strangers shake my hand, bump fists or clap me on the back. Now, I know why! They all think I'm the biggest chump in this community. Is there anyone in this town who isn't on my payroll?"

"The vet, for one. He sends his bill to me because he is somewhat fond of me. We've served on a few Boards together and you'll be happy to learn, because of our past, he doesn't charge you a fee for a farm call."

"Caught a break there, didn't I. What do you mean, he's fond of you? I thought you told me he was gay."

"He is gay but I think he likes me because you sponsor one of the mutton bustin' class at the Fourth of July Rodeo every year. We also support the end of season Hunt. And – just to prove my point, did you know there is an older woman at the barn who rides every day, regardless of the weather? Every day –

without fail! And she's been doing it all her life! She's very elusive, no one knows very much about her. She just shows up and rides an enormous black stallion named Diablo. If you think Nevada is huge, you should see Diablo! He's got to be at least eighteen hands! I suspect she is rather old but you wouldn't know it to watch her. All the kids are fascinated by her because she rides so beautifully with a glass of white wine in one hand and often a cigarette in the other. Rumor has it, she was once very much in love with the farrier and they had a very horrid, somewhat scandalous affair that her family refused to acknowledge."

"No doubt he seduced her with my Bourbon. How long has this been going on?"

"Their affair – I have no idea. It's really none of my business. I'm just repeating barn gossip."

"Not their affair! I was referring to all this Christmas gift giving."

"Years. Of course. Ever since we moved down from the City. I have told you all this several times before but as soon as I start taking to you about horses, your eyes glaze over, you tune me out and then stick you nose in an auction catalogue. But we're getting way off topic here."

"How long do you seriously think these riding lessons will last? What are you going to do when she turns sixteen and discovers boys? She'll give it up in a minute and all of those lessons will have been for nothing."

"I don't think so. In fact, I'm more afraid she won't want anything to do with any boy unless he can also sit a horse. She'll want to find a guy who can ride as well as she and by then, that may be very difficult unless he rides western or the rodeo circuit; roping calves or riding bulls or something. If he can't ride, she'll leave him in the dust – he won't hold her interest for long".

"Like any other sport, riding can be recreational and fun or it can be extremely competitive but you have to start somewhere. The earlier the better as far as I'm concerned. If this is what she wants to do, there is no end to where it could lead. It also has a definite career possibilities – who knows how far she'll go. We'll just have to wait and see. She may decide it's not right for her after just a few lessons or it may become a lifetime pursuit. There are a few, not too many, but at least three universities in the country that offer a B.S. in Equine Science or a B.A. in Equine Studies. There is one in southern Virginia and Colorado State in Fort Collins. They are very competitive programs and very difficult to get into and they don't accept just anyone. You have to be extremely accomplished or don't even bother to apply. They require a comprehensive history of your competitions and those results as well as a recent video of your performance in the ring. In fact, you have to be nationally ranked and recognized in at least the Top 10 of the country before you can submit an application."

"A B.S. in Equine Science! – There's a lucrative major. What about a business degree?"

"She can get a dual major in business which includes stable and barn management."

"Again – lucrative."

"Or she could go to law school, perhaps Stanford, and with a law degree pursue breeding and stud contracts. From what I understand, that is very lucrative. And there is also the possibility of vet school. She could go to UC Davis or perhaps the University of Minnesota and become a large animal veterinarian specializing in horses or she could pursue a career as a Blood Stock agent. By that time, I'm sure she'll know everything there is to know about horses."

"Why didn't you go to vet school?

"I wanted to and I tried to apply. After I graduated, I called the University of Minnesota to request an application. I'll never forget it! The woman I spoke to actually laughed and told me, and I'm quoting here, 'we do not accept applications from women into the veterinary program at this time'. Can you imagine how I felt? I was outraged!"

"I understand your outrage; I'm just sorry for the poor woman on the other end of that phone line when you finished with her. What exactly is a Bloodstock agent?"

"It's someone who is incredibly knowledgeable about horses and is paid, quite a healthy commission, I understand, or a percentage, to buy and sell horses for other people. They evaluate the horses, based on their pedigree and conformation for the owner who wants to sell as well as potential buyers. There aren't too many women in that field yet but that won't stop her. Perhaps, in a few years, there will be more women involved. One can only hope".

"Wait a minute. Before you go crashing through any more glass ceilings or blazing new trails to empower women, stop and consider the fact that you have her whole life planned out and she may not want a thing to do with any of this" He replied.

"I'm just trying to make you aware of the possibilities. It's not a matter of sitting on the horses back, all dressed up and looking pretty while the horse does all the work. There is great deal more involved. I think now, you'll agree. We have to decide if we're going to let her start taking lessons or not. I think we should at least let her try and see how it goes"

"Alright – I can't fight both of you. If I say no, she'll end up blaming me for the rest of her life. It will be my fault, I alone will be responsible for holding her back and I don't want that. We'll start slow and try a few lessons but the minute she falls or gets hurt – that's where it ends and instead of buying a ladder, I'll buy her a soccer ball. She would be much safer on a soccer field as opposed to bobbing around, five feet off the ground, on the back of a 1500 pound animal! Agreed?"

"We won't be sorry. I think she'll surprise us both. She can feel it. She has an instinct and a passion. She's too young to be afraid of any thing or anyone and that can work to her advantage here. She doesn't know how to be afraid and that, in itself, will be her strength."

"And what is this new-found passion of hers going to cost me?"

"For the time being, just the price of one small, wooden step-ladder."

I was two and a half years old!

Within six months, I entered my first horse show and took a first in an equitation class for six year olds and under. No one asked my age and neither my mother nor I offered any explanation regarding my size. We silently prayed everyone would assume I was just small. The blue and gold ribbon I was awarded was longer than I was tall and dragged through the dust when I clipped it on the waistband of my jeans as I had seen the older girls do so often. It was all I could do to avoid tripping over it as I walked Nevada back to his stall. It was my first blue ribbon but it would not be my last. The small silver cup, awarded with the ribbon, remains one of my most prized possessions – filled with paper clips and sitting on my desk, while the ribbon hangs in a place of honor in my father's library.

I rode everyday after school, sometimes more often, for the next twelve and a half years until I went off to boarding school. Once there, I rode twice and day, morning and evening as well as playing polo until I graduated. My father's fears concerning boys proved to be completely unfounded as the boys came and went with alarming regularity. Once they discovered they were neither my first priority nor my passion, to a man, they would leave a mumbled, weak excuse or a garbled apology on my voice mail. Not one had the decency to offer an explanation to my face. They just quietly drifted away.

I never cared to learn the social nuances of flirting, or the delicate dance surrounding dating that is played out on a daily basis on every high school campus in the country. I had absolutely no interest and even less desire to participate in the petty jealousies and on-going dramas that were the life-blood and the grit of my girlfriends lives.

My nails were dry, split and more often than not, caked with dirt, making a visit to a nail salon more of a reclamation project than a manicure. Had I ever appeared at the barn in couture jeans, splashed with a designer label, I would never have been able to live it down. Nail polish and designer jeans were both gaudy flourishes that simply weren't practical and held no interest for me. I had no need of either. Instead of hanging out at the nearest, upscale Mall, I preferred to spend my free time at the local Feed and Seed debating the nutritional value of oats versus hay.

I did fall occasionally, as predicted, but not with any regularity. My arm, broken in two places, was the result of a bee sting to the rump of a horse who tossed me into the air, throwing me to the ground. Yet I somehow managed to compete three days later with a full cast encasing my left arm. Not long after I healed, I was exercising horses for my neighbors while they were in Europe, when an unexpected kick to my face didn't quite break my jaw but fractured three teeth and cracked six ribs when I fell. Less than a week later, I competed in the Canadian Nationals in Manitoba with a black eye, slowly turning purple, a swollen jaw, twelve itchy stitches under my chin and my chest wrapped so tightly in tape that I could barely breathe. By the time I was nineteen, having ridden for nearly seventeen years, my father would have to add an orthopedic surgeon to his payroll as well as his Christmas list because of the chronic deterioration to both of my knees.

My instincts grew stronger and developed with each year, commensurate with my skill and much to my father's dismay; my passion never wavered, if anything, it became all consuming. Eventually I outgrew the necessity for the small, wooden step ladder he had so reluctantly agreed to purchase and passed it down to those who came after me. And I have never owned a soccer ball.

Stella Benson

Chapter Nineteen

Jumping into the car one afternoon after school, I was surprised when my mother immediately turned to me and asked, "What's a PDA?"

"I don't know. What is it?" I replied.

"I don't know either, that's why I'm asking you"

"I have no idea. Is it important?"

"How can I know if it's important if I don't know what it is? The Headmasters secretary called a few minutes ago on my cell to invite us both to join the Headmaster in his library, first thing tomorrow morning for a 'chat'. It would seem you have been given a PDA. I'm beginning to feel as though I've slipped into in the middle of game of Clue! Meet the Headmaster in the Library – all I'm missing is a candlestick! That's why I need to know what PDA stands for. Is it possible they are giving you an award for something? Could it mean Perfect Daily Attendance? Maybe they're giving you a gold star for consistently being punctual."

"Mom – this is middle school not grammar school! They don't give out gold stars any more. And, this is my first semester at this school. I haven't been here long enough to win any sort of an award! Could it be someone's initials?

"I suppose that's possible. Is there anyone in your class whose last name starts with an A?"

"The only one I can think of is Billy Andrews - but the first two initials don't fit. I've only been here a few weeks so I haven't met everyone in the upper grades yet – just my class."

"I'm happy to meet with the Headmaster but I'd like to know what I'm walking into and so far, I have no idea. I need more information. Where is that Student Handbook they gave us at orientation? Maybe there's an explanation or a definition in it."

"It's somewhere in my room, I think."

"The minute we get home, see if you can find it. Hopefully it will offer some insight. I have no intention of walking in there cold and completely uniformed the first thing tomorrow morning!"

I sprinted into the house, taking the stairs two at a time, threw open my bedroom door and frantically rummaged around until I found the unread and unopened Student Handbook at the bottom of a basket full of tack catalogues safely stored under my bed, and out of my brother's reach. Sitting on the floor and flipping through it, I found the definition of a PDA in Chapter Seven, page 39, paragraph 16 under the heading Acceptable/ Unacceptable Behavior. My head snapped back as I read and reread the definition over and over again. What! This cant be! This has to be a mistake! A PDA was a Public Display of Affection! I wasn't in the habit of displaying affection publicly or anywhere else for that matter. Being half Swedish, I was raised not to display emotion at any time or under any circumstances, much less publicly, with the possible exception of a funeral. And even then with great reserve. So far I had only been to my Grandmothers funeral. We had been taught to hold everything in; to be addressed another day, in private. Clutching the Handbook, I tore back down the stairs to find my mother on the back porch watering her little pots of kitchen herbs.

"Mom! I screamed, I found it! According to the Handbook a PDA is a Public Display of Affection!"

"Well – that's good to know but I don't understand what that has to do with you? Did anything happen today; something unusual or anything you can think of that was out of the ordinary?"

"No! It was just a normal, average day! I went to class, had lunch, and then went to PE. and met you in the parking lot. That's all I can think of except…

"Except what?"

"I didn't think it was important, but after the last bell, I crossed the quad to my locker to get my backpack and Billy Andrews was standing at his locker, which is right next to mine and he started talking to me. He's the coolest guy in my class and I didn't think he had even noticed me. Then we walked together across the Commons toward the stairs. When we got to the top, he said 'see ya tomorrow' and started talking to three guys from our class who were just standing there - hanging out. I continued down the stairs, heading for the parking lot because I knew you were waiting."

"And then?"

"As soon as I reached the landing half way down the stairs, out of nowhere, Billy ran past and kissed me".

"Why would he do that?"

"I don't know, I replied, boys are just weird!"

"Did anyone see him kiss you? Where were the three boys you passed at the top of the stairs? Could they have seen all this?

"I think I heard them laughing. But it was no big deal"

"Apparently the Headmaster would disagree. That is obviously what this is all about. Though it seems to be more of a public display of affection on Billy's part – not yours! All we can do is wait and see what the Headmaster has to say tomorrow morning. We'll get to the bottom of this one way or another. Where, exactly did Billy kiss you?"

"I told you, on the stair landing!"

"Not where on campus! Where, on your person?"

"On my cheek. It was sort of dry and pishty!"

"Did he grab you anywhere – by your shoulders or around your waist?"

"No – nothing like that! Just the one kiss, then he raced down the rest of stairs headed toward the parking lot. I think his mother was waiting there too to pick him up."

Seven-thirty the following morning found us sitting outside the Headmasters library as requested, waiting to be shown into his inner sanctum. Early morning is not my mother's finest hour. She is not a morning person; she never has been and sees absolutely no intention of changing her ways. She has been known to fly around the house cleaning at eleven o'clock at night, water the garden at midnight and then read until 3 am. Any decision that required her full attention was better considered after 10 am. Whatever it was, crucial or mundane, it could wait until a reasonable hour. Clattering skillets or the sound of sizzling bacon at an early hour was best left to our full-time housekeeper. Children sleepily crunching on toast or cold cereal would often send her fleeing from the room. As a result, we were introduced to warm, soft and noiseless croissants, slathered in butter, Devonshire clotted crème and marmalade. Or, on a cold, foggy morning we would be treated to a steaming, hot bowl of havremjöl covered in melting brown sugar. Were it not for a succession of no less than five Austrian au pair girls, it is a miracle my brother and I ever got to school on time.

Being summoned to the Headmasters office this early in the morning was problematic for her from the initial request. Whatever we were there to discuss had damn well be important enough to interrupt her routine or heads would inevitably roll. Being asked to wait was not an option she would entertain lightly or patiently. The situation was further exacerbated by her not having had at least three cups of her fully caffeinated, detoxifying, all natural, 100% organic, specially blended green tea. So far this morning wasn't going well.

My stomach was in turmoil, boiling over with nervous tension at the thought of what was to come. I battled to keep my organic granola, peach yogurt and orange juice from coming up and out while my mouth felt as though I'd been chewing pennies for days. I desperately contemplated an escape route to give myself and my stomach a chance to stop churning. Finally, after what seemed a lengthy wait, we were ushered into the Headmasters library by his scowling secretary.

We were both immediately struck by the oppressive darkness and overpowering smell of stale incense. My nostrils rebelled, my eyes watered and my nausea rose. Our eyes struggled to adjust to the lack of light – especially at this early hour. This was not a library – though the extent of my experience was only that of my father's. This was a cave; a dark, oppressive dungeon. I couldn't be sure, it was so dim, but I was reasonably certain there were wooden gargoyles with large blank eyes sprouting from every corner of the room. There were no bookshelves, lined with colorful books, no silver-framed photographs or personal mementos of any sort- simply bare wooden walls. The only book visible stood across the room on what appeared to be a bookstand. It was obviously a very old, very large Bible. The Headmaster sat directly across the room at his long desk; stoically, a high shiny forehead, balding on top, a less than prominent nose, a tight, narrow slit of a mouth with a pasty white pallor, little or no chin and sad, heavily lidded eyes behind wire glasses. His glasses were perched half way down his nose, forcing him to look down and puffy, little grey tufts of hair near his ears gave him the look of an old, intemperate owl. His eyes were not bright but rather a dull grey with absolutely no spark of life in them and not large but furtive and beady, flitting around the room until they settled on me. His shoulders slumped as though the burden of maintaining order and discipline in a private school was too much for him to bear. His grey, mottled skin reminiscent of the grey flecked feathers of an old owl.

Two lamps at either end of his desk gave off the only light in the room with the exception of a small framing light illuminating a life-sized portrait of Christ hanging to his left. There he hung, his bright, blue eyes glistening, his porcelain white skin glowing and his long blond hair cascading past his shoulders. His countenance at once benevolent and yet vaguely condemning. My mother glanced briefly at the portrait and then to me, rising one eyebrow. Opposite Christ hung an equally large and glorious portrait of the current Pope, trying with every fiber of his being to look as saintly as Christ. At the other end of the barren room stood a stone, garden statue of St. Francis of Assisi; a concrete bird on one shoulder, head bowed, his hands cupped in front of him but holding the Headmasters business cards rather than birdseed. We are not Catholic and such obvious displays of religious relics have a tendency to unnerve me, my present state of upheaval not withstanding.

The Headmaster did not rise as we entered. Instead, he glanced in our direction, acknowledged our presence with a slight nod of his head and said, "Good morning ladies. Please be seated."

Our seating options were limited to the only two large chairs in the room, both directly in front of his desk. My mother settled in one, her back straight, her feet firmly on the floor and her hands resting quietly in her lap. I dropped my backpack and attempted to slip into the other. By the time I had managed to scoot back, deeply into the chair, my legs were straight out in front of me giving me the opportunity to study, at great length, the little round rivets that held my shoelaces in place. Something I had failed to notice until now. Finally settled, and glancing up, I was immediately drawn to an overly large crucifix hanging to the right of the Headmaster. A disproportionately small, shiny, metal Christ, in the obvious throes of agony, appeared to be nailed to a burned and charred 2 X 4. More importantly, I noticed that the one large, clerestory window in the room, located directly behind the Headmaster, was perfectly level with the landing and the stairs, giving him an unobstructed view. So, he had been the one to witness my alleged indiscretion!

"Shall we begin?" He said, very seriously.

"Aren't we going to wait for the others?" My mother asked.

"What others?" He replied.

"Billy Andrews, his parents, the three other boys involved and their parents. I assumed they would be joining this morning for this little chat."

"They will not be joining us. Their presence was not requested. Yours was!" He replied."

"Why is that? My mother responded. Do you intend to speak to them about his at another time?"

"We don't consider their presence germane to this proceeding. I have no intention of speaking to them at all." He answered.

"I happen to think their presence is more than germane and their involvement and possible participation implicit to this proceeding." She responded

For the first time since sitting down I dared to glance over at my mother. I desperately wanted to know what 'germane" meant. Regardless of what it meant, it was now seared into my memory as I continued to be preoccupied with my shoelaces, feigning fascination with their purpose. It was safer to look at them than the Headmaster.

"We are acutely aware of the fact that you and your family are new to this institution. As such, we attempt to extend to every new student a period of adjustment as well as an opportunity to adapt to our methods. Discipline here is paramount, in accordance with our Founders mission statement and our code of conduct. In consideration of the needs of others we …"

"Who exactly is 'we'? My mother interrupted.

"Myself, the entire faculty as well as the monastic brotherhood presently in situ of course. As I was saying, while we recognize each new student's requirement for a period of adjustment, it is not, nor will it ever be, within our purview to condone this type of behavior."

I realized this conversation concerned me and what was quickly shaping up to be my somewhat tenuous status at this school so I struggled to stay focused but between germane and purview, I was lost. I still wasn't exactly sure what I had done to warrant this exchange between my mother and the Headmaster. Or why we were even here. As I contemplated my current situation rather than my shoelaces, I couldn't help but notice that Christ was glaring fiercely at the Pope, the Pope ignored the crucifix and the crucified Christ appeared far too mortified with his own wretched suffering to acknowledge either. My chair had been perfectly placed in such a way that I was in their immediate cross-fire which did nothing to alleviate my growing anxiety. As far as I could determine, there was no escape.

"And what type of behavior is that exactly?" My mother countered.

"We expect the young women enrolled here and under our tutelage to behave like young ladies - at all times. Your daughter's behavior of yesterday afternoon sets a precedent we will not tolerate much less condone."

"And what, do you expect of the young men enrolled here."

"We assume they will, in turn, comport themselves as gentlemen at all times. That being said, we also recognize that young men are, by their very nature, given to a letting off of steam, if you will – hijinks and pranks are quite often the result. By the end of the day, tempers often flare and clashes are bound to occur - which is to be expected. Boys will be boys, after all. We have a zero-tolerance policy in place here for just that reason. We want to nip this in the bud – here and now before it escalates completely out of our control. We cannot allow this sort of behavior to metastasize within our community! Wouldn't you agree?"

"No, I'm afraid I do not agree, not in the least. Let me understand this, Billy Andrews, full of youthful, male exuberance at the end of the day, accepts a dare from three other boys to run down the stairs and kiss my daughter, in full view of your window. And yet here I sit at this ungodly hour! It is my belief, under the circumstances, that it is Billy's bud that wants nipping, not my daughters! Wouldn't you agree?"

"I would most adamantly not agree. No more than you with me. Young William is beyond reproach – as is his family. We have agreed to do nothing that may besmirch or cause blight to his name or his family's reputation. They have been overly generous in their on-going contributions and continued support of this institution and as such we have no intention of creating a rift on that score."

Germane, purview, metastasize and now besmirch – I was quickly losing track of my growing vocabulary list and realizing I had more or less exhausted the examination of my shoelaces, decided my fingernails warranted scrutiny. I couldn't help but wonder if a blight on William was at all similar to the blight on my mothers champagne grapes? Did the Headmaster have the power to cause blight or head one off? Sitting in the cross hairs of the Pope, Christ and the crucifix, I was beginning to believe he did indeed have it within himself to do just that if he chose to do so. The tension in this room was, by now, noticeably tangible. Either my mother was suffering from serious caffeine withdrawal or she was preparing for battle. It was hard to tell at this point as she sat so stoically in an oversized chair. The Headmaster too was beginning to question whether he had miscalculated this morning's particular opponent.

"So, you vehemently deny any culpability on Williams's part and chose instead to take advantage of this incident to make an example of my daughter. Is that right? Has it occurred to you or is it at all within the realm of possibility that she may be a victim?"

"It is our collective opinion that your daughter must have done something or said something that led William to believe she would be amenable to his overture. Perhaps she fell back upon her feminine wiles in some manner that initiated his action toward her. We can find no fault with William. She was observed by other students talking to William immediately after class and walking across the commons with him shortly before the incident occurred.

"Are you listening to yourself? She is twelve yeas old, for god's sake! She hasn't developed any "feminine wiles' to fall back on. You seriously can't believe that she asked for this to happen? Or that she somehow initiated this ridiculous exercise. He kissed her! You just admitted young Williams's so-called overture! She didn't kiss him! She was minding her own business until he ran by her on the stairs. You seem overly anxious to accuse her! But I happen to think it goes both ways. Given the ridiculous nature of this accusation, and if I was at all inclined, I could very easily turn this back on you and accuse Billy of assault? Perhaps sexual assault? How about bullying or harassment? Your choice. Do you really want to go down that road?"

"It was he who displayed affection publicly toward her – not the other way around. Surely you can see that? Perhaps if you had had the wherewithal to invite Billy and his parents to this morning's little chat, he could offer a credible explanation for his behavior. Either way, I fully expect to have a conversation with his parents whether you intend to or not. Maybe he simply likes her! Has that occurred to you or do you have a policy against that as well? These are children, we're talking about. You make it sound as though the two of them were caught rolling around, buck naked in the bushes behind the Science Building! In my opinion, you are blowing this out of all reasonable proportion. It was just one kiss, for the love of god! Children this age do that – whether you condone it or not, it's going to happen. You can not legislate human nature or adolescent behavior! Perhaps your time would be better spent investigating what goes on during lunch in the redwood grove near the tennis courts amongst the juniors and seniors. There are enough public displays of affectation going on up there to curl your toes. What is it exactly that you are so afraid of and by that, I am, of course, the "collective you?"

Ignoring her question, he said, "Never the less, we have principles and tenets in place; guidelines necessary to govern and restrict this sort of outward display. This type of behavior cannot be allowed to continue on this campus and at this institution! Who knows what might come of it – where it may lead?"

"Of course. It's becoming all too clear. Now I see where you are going, I just can't believe it! Let me take a minute to make sure my daughter understands. This does, after all, concern her."

With that, both my mother and the Headmaster turned their full attention to me. My immediate response was to wiggle deeper into the cushion of the chair, hoping it might swallow me up. Forgotten were my nails and my shoelaces as both my mother and the Headmaster leveled their gaze at me.

"Do you understand what the Headmaster is saying? She asked looking directly at me while the Headmaster looked at his watch and readjusted his glasses.

I managed to lift my chin off my chest long enough to squeak out, "Not really."

"Well. I'm not surprised. I don't quite believe it myself. It's a lot to take in this early in the morning but let me see if I can explain. Okay? We'll talk more about this tonight but listen to me for now."

"As far as I can determine, there are apparently three things going on here that you should be aware of. The Headmaster, in his infinite wisdom, has chosen to make more of this than a simple kiss on the cheek. I wish it was that simple but it's not – not now. First of all, there is the issue of the Church, and then something I know you know nothing about but it is called the double standard and lastly, money.

Jarred out of my complacency, I starred at my mother. The Church! Billy had kissed me and somehow I had offended the Church! I had purposely avoided any participation in this conversation between my mother and the Headmaster but now I found myself seething at the implication. This was getting out of control or so I believed. But my mother wasn't finished. As she continued, I could do nothing to defend myself but sit there like a lump and hope this was all a horrible mistake.

"You are aware, that this is a Catholic school – not my first choice –because we are not Catholic- but recognized as the best private, college preparatory school in this community. I, personally, don't believe religion belongs in the schools for the simple reason that those being taught will question the teachings of those who are doing the teaching. Eventually, if you don't bow to their way of thinking, if you dare to question, the teachers will lose all credibility and finally the trust of their students. Ones faith, in whatever they chose to believe, is a highly personal decision. Not a specific one to be crammed down throats at an early age sprinkled with fear and aced with guilt. As with any highly organized religion, especially one as wealthy and powerful as this one, they're primary objective is to control the way you think as well as the way you behave through fear and intimidation. And failing that, they can always fall back on guilt – which as it happens, is my personal favorite. Any system of authority based on control is, in itself, infused with fear. Our being here this morning is nothing short of an exercise in fear and intimidation. The guilt will probably come later. The Headmaster is doing his best to intimidate me and, at the same time, terrify you. What he doesn't seem to understand is that I am not easily intimidated by either him or his religion and you cannot be frightened or bullied because you know in your heart that you have done nothing wrong. When I was in school, I spent enough time in my own Headmasters office, for one reason or another, to be very familiar with this particular game and I cannot be brought to my knees by whatever he has to throw at me. I am also far too secure in my own faith to be threatened in any way by his. As a result, I'm not about to sit here and allow him to accuse you of something we all know you did not do.

Add to that, the fact that this school is run by priests, brothers and monks, all of whom have chosen to devote their lives to God – which is, all in all, admirable. Or not? They have all taken a vow to love God above all else which means they have no love left over to give or share with a wife or a family. They have also taken a vow of chastity. Do you know what that means?"

"No." I said quietly. But I had a feeling I was about to find out. She was far from finished and visibly warming to her subject. I had witnessed this mood often enough to know what was coming. The Headmaster, however, had no idea of what lay before him.

"It means they have chosen, of their own free will, to be virtuous and decent, pure and most importantly, unmarried. Now, if they are not married, they cannot have children and because they have no children of their own, they clearly have no idea how to raise children. They are completely at a loss as to know how to talk to children or reason with them let alone how to handle all that child-rearing involves on a day to day basis. They are afraid to admit that they are baffled by children, so every summer they take classes in childhood development and adolescent behavior, hoping to gain some insight that will guide them. They claim to be educators but that's the full extent of their knowledge concerning children. And frankly that's all they care to know. To them, children are nothing more than pliant little souls, and something of a nuisance, to be merely tolerated until they are old enough to commit to and embrace the Church – unquestionably. They live a very sheltered, cloistered life here, safely ensconced on this campus, immune to real life as they strive to be faithful to the Church. Are you following me?

I was very uncertain, having absolutely no idea what any of this had to do with me or where she was going so I boldly answered, "What does any of that have to do with me or Billy?"

"I'm getting to that – bear with me." She answered.

"If they are unable to communicate with you or reason with you or even begin to understand you, how then are they going to control you? She asked." This obviously directed toward me.

It occurred to me that fear was the right answer but I was too afraid to say as much out loud. So far, the Headmaster, this chat we were having and this room had done a thorough job of scaring me half to death. Instead I shrugged my shoulders in response; falling back on that; pre-teen attitude of indifference; the hopelessness of adolescence that never failed to infuriate my mother and illicit a reaction. I was beginning to understand that my mother was seething, growing more angry by the minute and, given the choice, I would rather she redirect her anger away from me and in the direction of the Headmaster. With a quick glance toward the Headmaster, I turned back to my mother and managed to whisper one word – "fear."

"Bingo! Their ultimate goal is to control you and your thoughts with fear; hell fire, eternal damnation, excommunication and guilt. All of which are designed to scare the wits out of you. They have a laundry list of terror they will not hesitate to use and they have centuries of practice to back them up. They believe God gave you a brain and their mission in life is to train you how to use it, the way they want you to use it. There is absolutely no room here for free will! This is nothing more than a control issue! You must never, never be afraid to think for yourself! Now, how do they convince you to think and behave the way they want you to? She asked.

"Rules, I suppose. Lots of them." I said getting braver by the minute.

"Right again. Rules! They all sit around like a flock of crows, their black cassocks artfully disguising their false piety and proceed to anticipate any and all likely situations. Then, they come up with a set of rules regarding both the positive and the negative aspects of those scenarios. It doesn't matter how ridiculous the situation as long as they have given it their consideration and decided upon a course of action in the event it comes up. And once they have a set of rules they will adhere to them beyond question and without deviation. There are absolutely no exceptions and the surrounding circumstances have no bearing on the situation.

This PDA is a perfect example of a situation that screams absurdity. But, there is nothing wrong with rules per say. We need rules because without them there is confusion. Confusion can lead to chaos, chaos leads to anarchy; anarchy, in turn, leads to the downfall of democracy and the downfall of democracy leads to the decline of Western Civilization as we know it. And the Church will never, ever allow that to happen because where would that leave them? The Headmaster is on a campaign to consign your soul, such as it is, to the Church. His Church. And he won't give up or concede defeat until he has successfully converted you to his God and his Church. What he doesn't' know is your soul has been already been safely consigned to the Anglican Church. COE."

I couldn't help but smile to myself. This wasn't the first time I had heard this and I realized, finally, where she was going. This was her favorite quote. My mother has always been overly concerned with the state of Western Civilization – especially these days with so much turmoil in the world. Glancing at the Headmaster however, brought me up short, my smile instantly fading. He had removed his glasses and sat polishing them with a white linen handkerchief, a look of disbelief clearly on his face. I suddenly hoped she wouldn't go a step further and finish her line of thought but she continued on undeterred, and looking squarely at the Headmaster said, "Life is nasty, brutish and short so keep your bowels open and your powder dry." She may have been mixing her metaphors and combining quotes; tacking Oliver Cromwell arbitrarily onto Thomas Hobbs, but she didn't care as long the message was clear. It never ceased to bring a smile to my face or my brothers, no matter how many times we heard it. For years we had no idea what she meant. As far as the two of us could determine, our lives had indeed been relatively short but not particularly nasty and certainly not brutish. Our bowels were something we chose to ignore for the time being, not quite sure exactly where they were or what their function was. Gripping the arms of the leather armchair, I silently pleaded with her not ask the Headmaster how his bowels were faring this morning.

"The second thing confronting us this morning is something called the double standard. I know you don't know what that means and I was hoping you wouldn't encounter it for some time but here we are so let me explain. I'll try to be brief."

"It means there is an unwritten code of behavior or a set of rules that are applied in very different ways to boys and to girls. It is very subtle; so subtle that you are usually unaware of it until it confronts you or you confront it. Then, understandably, you are surprised and you're surprise is followed by outrage and anger. You are surprised because you didn't see it coming and outraged that it has settled on you. These rules basically favor boys over girls, because, for now, boys make the rules to suit themselves. In other words, boys have the freedom to do things that you do not. Boys are often praised for their behavior while girls would be considered promiscuous for exactly that same behavior. Because of these rules, boys have more sexual freedom than girls."

I couldn't believe my mother was talking about sex in front of the Headmaster! What sex? I had just turned twelve! I had, by this time spent enough time at the barn to have a basic grasp of the birds and the bees but failed to see what Billy's kissing me had to do with sex??

"As the Headmaster said earlier, he sees nothing wrong with Billy kissing you but you are definitely not allowed to kiss Billy. Do you see the difference? I know it can be confusing but there it is. Billy is their Golden Boy. In their eyes, he can do no wrong and if he does, they are right there to either sweep it under the rug, gloss over it or find someone else to blame. That would be you. Which is why we are here this morning. Billy is not to blame for this – you are! The only explanation the Headmaster can come up with to explain why Billy kissed you in the first place is that you made him do it. Left to his own devices, Billy would never do such a thing unless you did or said something to encourage him. In other words, the Headmaster believes you initiated this ridiculous exercise. You and you alone are to blame for Billy's behavior. Somehow you made him do what he did. Never mind the fact that the Headmaster has to be the last person in this community to know that Billy's father, for all his wealth and influence, keeps an impressive collection of pornography – in alphabetical order – in a closet in his home! But that, apparently, is a conversation best left for another day. Do you understand so far? No, of course you don't and I can't really blame you. Neither do I and I've been dealing with this all my life. It is purposely vague, for what reason, I have no idea. But it is real and it does exist. Believe me, when I tell you, you'll recognize it when you're confronted with it. Which, I'm sure, only makes it that much more confusing and I'm sorry for that. So you are left with only two choices; either play by their rules or change them. Change inevitably comes slowly because they are not inclined to give up whatever power they think they have. So for the time being, the best thing you can do and in fact, the only thing you can do in a situation such as this is to learn both sets of rules. Watch the boys, study them like bugs under glass, listen to them and learn from them.

Then put all that knowledge into a tiny drawer in the back of your mind and store it there for another day. Believe me, the day will come when you'll need all that information and when you do, it will be there waiting for you.

"That's not fair! That sucks! I didn't make Billy do anything! He kissed me! I didn't ask him to do that! I have hardly ever spoken to him!" I replied, now angry and embarrassed.

"No – it isn't fair at all. And, I agree with you. It does suck! But the Headmaster seems determined to punish one of you for this and believe me when I say, it will not be Billy. It's you! If he has his way, you're going to take the fall for this. As a man, he will always have Billy's back - not yours. The brotherhood of men and all that crap. You heard him. He has no intention of even discussing this with Billy much less his parents - why do you suppose that is? Because in his mind, Billy has the freedom to do something that you do not. Make sense?"

"No – it doesn't make any sense at all. I didn't do anything wrong! Billy kissed me!" My eyes were, by now, burning with the threat of tears but I refused to cry – not here and not now. I wouldn't give the Headmaster the satisfaction of making me cry. This was too much to take in all in one morning. But my mother was far from finished. Quite the opposite, she was on a roll and she knew it. The Headmaster hadn't moved to interrupt her though she occasionally glanced from me to him – probably more for emphasis than anything else.

"Unfortunately your father and I have been led to believe this school was more progressive in their thinking and practice than most. Imagine our surprise to learn the double standard is alive and well and thriving on this campus. Another important factor which only serves to complicate the issue before us is the fact that the Headmasters world, due in large part to his vow of celibacy, is one of God and men. He understands boys and feels far more comfortable in his dealings with boys than he does with girls. Women terrify him and little girls inevitably grow into women! All in all, a very scary thought as far as he's concerned. That fact alone scares le merde out of him because he doesn't understand how women think – if indeed they do. He can't be too sure.

He has very little knowledge and even less experience with women and, not only is it perfectly obvious but it puts him at a serious disadvantage – one he is reluctant to admit." She said.

"Now, pay attention because this is where it gets interesting. We're not finished quite yet. The third issue confronting us this morning is money. Money is always involved and today is no exception. Did I mention the fact that they also take a vow of poverty? Which I find ironic considering the Headmaster is often seen driving around town in a new Jaguar XKE. No doubt a generous gift from a grateful parent. But let's just chalk that up to one more example of the hypocrisy in the Church of Rome and leave it alone for now.

You have told me yourself that Billy is considered the 'coolest boy' in your class. Apparently the Headmaster agrees with you. I understand, from his mother, that Billy has better than a 4.2 grade point average and he's only in sixth grade! He is also your classes rising star - athletically. He's on the football team, the soccer team, the baseball team, the track team and the swim team and, if that isn't enough, he's one badge away from becoming an Eagle Scout. The Headmaster, as well as the faculty, has a vested interest in making sure he is successful academically, athletically and socially because if Billy is successful then they have been successful. They can put his picture on the glossy brochure they hand out to prospective parents and take full credit for what he has become. He is what they have made him! If they can do all that for Billy, they can do it for other boys as well and their parents will be tripping all over themselves to get their sons admitted to this school. All of them will gladly pay the tuition and then some.

Someday, Billy will graduate and go on to college, probably an Ivy League School back East or perhaps the Naval Academy in Annapolis. With all the support they offer anything is possible - for him. How can he fail? You – not so much. They have no such high hopes for you. Then, long after Billy has graduated he'll inevitably look back with longing on all the years he spent here and remember how happy he was and, to show his appreciation, he'll start to respond to those endless pleas for money and donations. They will educate you because we are paying them to do just that but they don't give a tinkers damn if you are successful or not. As far as the Headmaster is concerned, the best you can hope for, once you graduate, is to marry well and then somehow, convince your husband to write those checks for you. In other words, your success will be measured by that of your husband's.

Your father and I pay the five-figure tuition here as do Billy's parents. Basically we're paying them to educate you because we have been led to believe, as a college prep school; you will receive a much better education here than you would at our local public school. Billy's parents have chosen to take that a step further. Think of it as very subtle, unspoken extortion or protection money; willingly paid to guarantee nothing unseemly happens to Billy that may show up on his permanent record, his college applications or come to the attention of a college admissions board someday.

For example, just last week we attended a dedication ceremony here in the courtyard. Billy's parents generously donated a lovely, redwood bench, carved by a local chain-saw artist, renowned for his craftsmanship, which was installed in the meditation garden by the chapel. We want you to be successful based on your own merit and hard work. We have no intention of greasing the skids for you. What you accomplish will be yours and yours alone. We refuse to buy your success by subtlety donating to every cause or project they come up with and the Headmaster knows that and it infuriates him. That's not to say, we won't help where we can. I'll be more than happy to help collect canned goods for the needy at Thanksgiving and gently worn clothing for the homeless at Christmas and your father and I will even go so far as to volunteer to chaperone your school dances. We'll do anything we can do but we will not throw more money into their coffers. It is our job as parents to give you every opportunity to be successful at whatever you chose to do but you have to take advantage of it. We won't buy your success for you – unlike Billy's parents. It will be what you make of it. Do you understand?"

There will undoubtedly be many of obstacles in your life. But this is not one of them! This is nothing more than an exercise in tyranny. Think of each obstacle you encounter as a series of jumps on a proscribed course. There will be low brush boxes, oxers and cross rails. Large or small, it doesn't make any difference. What is important is that you clear each one cleanly with courage and above all, honesty. You must sail over each one as it comes up without hesitation and without dropping a rail. If you hesitate, for whatever reason, you circle around, take a deep breath and approach it again, this time with more determination and you keep trying until it is safely behind you. It is what it is until it's behind you! Never look back!"

I was just about to say. "Mom, your not giving a closing argument to a jury" when she stopped speaking – abruptly. So abruptly that both the Headmaster and I were both suddenly jarred out of our reverie. The sudden silence lingered for several minutes. The only sound in the room, a clock somewhere in the room- ticking ominously. Each one of us feared being the first to break the silence, especially me. So I waited. The Headmaster stared at my mother and my mother stared at the Headmaster. Fortunately neither one stared at me. I was all but forgotten. Christ continued to radiate his heavenly glow, the Pope, in his little, white beanie, waved to the devout beneath him in St. Peter's Square and the crucifix, nailed on the wall, remain forever cast in his own misery. Even St. Francis seemed unmoved by these proceedings, staring blankly across the room. Finally, my mother, focusing her attention on the Headmaster said "I think that about sums it up. Wouldn't you agree?"

I turned to the Headmaster who sat with his hands pressed down in front of him, flat on his desk top. His shoulders slumped under the heavy burden he believed he carried. His wire rimmed glasses had slipped down his long patrician nose, barely balancing on the tip and his mouth hung open while little bubbles of white saliva formed in one corner. He looked almost rabid. His face was as pale as the white clerical collar that seemed to have a self-imposed grip around his neck causing it to bulge. It was not difficult to read his reaction.

His jaw was firmly clenched causing his mouth to be nothing more than a thin slit in his face while he stared at my mother, who stared back at him with equal, if not greater intensity. He clearly had no idea how to proceed and questioned how this morning's conversation had gotten so completely out of his control. This was to have been a brief meeting; the first on his calendar for the day to determine suitable punishment for my supposed participation in my supposed crime. He clearly had no idea how this conversation had slipped out of his hands. I was forgotten – no longer in the room and as far as he was concerned, I had ceased to exist. After what seemed like several minutes, he broke the silence and when he did, he made a fatal mistake. Still staring, he said to my mother, "Perhaps if I had this conversation with her father, he and I could come to some agreement regarding appropriate punishment, commensurate with the situation before us."

Punishment for what? Billy had kissed me. It was his display of affection, toward me – not mine toward him. Punish him – not me! I screamed in my head. I stole a sideways glance at my mother to gage her reaction. Her back had arched at the obvious insult; her eyes, appeared to be wider and a large vein in her neck that I had never noticed before was visibly pulsating, while her nails threatened to puncture the leather upholstery of the armchair.

The Headmaster, finally realizing he had seriously misjudged this mornings opponent, should not have been surprised by my mother's reaction when, very slowly and deliberately, without another word, she pushed back her chair and stood up. Reaching for my hand, she pulled me up and out of my chair and together we started across the room toward the door. But the Head-master wasn't finished. Just as we reached the door he said, "Excuse me, you ladies have not been dismissed and I'm not finished."

"Well, I am! You, sir, are no man of the cloth! You are a wolf in sheep's clothing and an embarrassment to your calling!" Opening the door with one hand and still holding onto mine with the other, she turned around and said, rather caustically, "How dare you? You should be ashamed of yourself! This is bullshit and you know it as well as I. Find another scapegoat; someone other than my daughter for this little morality play you've got going on!"

The Headmasters head snapped up and his eyes narrowed to thin slits as he drew a bead on my mother. A profound silence followed; a tangible hush of quiet as they stared at each other. "Are you threatening me, madam?" He asked quietly.

"No more than you are threatening me." Rather than continue this mornings charade, why don't you address the rampant drug situation on this campus. And, I'm told you have a "flasher" in the girl's locker room that appears with some regularity. Perhaps your time would be better spent investigating that public display of misguided affection!

With that, the Headmaster was up and out of his chair like a shot. He flew across the room, his black robe billowing behind him. He looked like a giant, red-faced crow and stopped just inches from my mother and I.

"What drugs? What are you talking about? There are no drugs here! What flasher? We have no flasher," he sputtered, spit flying from his mouth.

My mother looked at him quietly, with the slightest hint of a smile and said, "You really have no idea do you?"

We walked out the door, across the office and into the parking lot, I ran to keep up with her as she stormed toward the car. As soon as we were safely clear of prying eyes, I grabbed the sleeve of her jacket and said, "Mom, you just swore at the Headmaster and in English! Why couldn't you swear at him in Swedish? What were you thinking?"

"That man is an angry, bitter man! He shouldn't be allowed anywhere near children. He deserved every word."

"Mom, once this gets around; I'll never be able to show my face at this school again! My life is over! I'm going to have to move to Minnesota and live with Grandmother or maybe we can find a boarding school somewhere in Siberia."

"Calm down and get a hold of yourself. You are not moving to Minnesota and you're definitely not going to boarding school in Siberia because there are no boarding schools in Siberia. – just gulags."

"What's a gulag?" I asked.

"You really don't want to know."

"I'll be a piranha! No one will have anything to do with me. I'll be a social outcast! I won't have any friends!" I cried.

"A piranha is an omnivorous fish with very sharp teeth. I think you mean a pariah."

"I may as well walk around campus with a dead abalone hanging around my neck!" I continued, almost hysterically.

"If you're going to make a literary reference, at least get it right. An abalone is a sea snail that lives in the ocean You are referring to an albatross – which is a bird. In this case a dead bird!"

"Whatever! The point is - my life is ruined!"

"You're really upset about this aren't you? If you're going to beat yourself up – why not a Scarlet A, embroidered on your chest? I believe that has always been the acceptable symbol for martyrs. Keep in mind there were only three of us in that room. I have no intention of discussing this with anyone except your father and I'm sure you won't be talking to anyone so, if this does get out, we'll certainly know were it came from! Nothing is going to come of this, at least not for the time being. But, I'm afraid this is only the beginning." She said.

"The beginning of what?" I whimpered. This was beginning to get scary and I could feel the tears that I had held back welling up in my eyes, threatening to spill over.

"I'm afraid your days at this school here are numbered because of this incident and our conversation this morning. The Headmaster is not going to forget this.

He's going to back off for now, then watch and bide his time – however long it takes. He is going to wait for you to give him an excuse, any excuse, and then he will take the necessary steps to see that you are expelled. He doesn't have the nerve to come after me, directly, so he will go after you in order to get to me. If you do anything, say anything or give him just cause, he will use that against you simply because you are a threat to everything he believes in and the only way to eliminate a threat is to get rid of it."

"How am I a threat to him? I'm just a kid!"

"Which makes you the worst kind of threat! You may be just a kid, but you are not a Catholic kid, nor are you ever likely to become one. Add to that the fact that you are a young woman who can think for herself, which absolutely terrifies him. And daddy and I refuse to play his game by buying your success for you. All in all, a disastrous combination as far as he's concerned. One that he cannot, nor will he, tolerate. You may as well walk around campus with a bull's eye on your back. All this talk of encouraging each student to explore their individual potential, develop their unique personalities and capitalize on their personal talents while encouraging diversity is just that; talk. Shallow rhetoric, full of false promises on a glossy brochure designed to draw wealthy parents into the fold. We have just informed him, in no uncertain terms, that you cannot be pushed into his mold so he has no choice but to back you into a corner and eventually, out the door."

"All this because Billy kissed me on the cheek in broad daylight?"

"That's right! All this because Billy kissed you." She answered.

My mother was right. Less than three years later I was expelled. They had found a way to be rid of me and I had found a way to be rid of them. It was mutual.

Chapter Twenty

I passed the rest of the morning in slow motion – in a daze; trying to make some sense of the entire conversation that had taken place earlier. I was surprised at my mother's reaction and unsure what the Headmaster had said that had triggered her reaction? Or how it was all going to affect me in the long run. The whole episode was confusing and beyond my comprehension.

Once or twice, in class, Billy had tried to attract my attention with a broad grin, flashing a mouthful of brackets and wires in my direction, as though we shared a secret. I didn't want to have anything to do with him or the secret he thought we now shared. I wanted to be left alone and out of his sight long enough to process all that had been said. To me, he was the reason for my embarrassment and humiliation. Without realizing it, and probably without thinking, he had made a fool out of me and I didn't like the feeling. How dare he smile so mischievously and so knowingly!

By noon, instead of heading to the dining room for lunch, I sought out the mediation garden behind the chapel, hoping it would be deserted at that hour. I wanted a quiet place to think without interruption; without the mid-day boisterous break that seemed to come with lunch. I wanted to be alone for a time, not obligated to participate in the constant, somehow mandatory ritual that accompanies lunch. Above all, I wanted to avoid the Headmaster – at any cost. He would undoubtedly give the blessing followed by a litany of daily, boring announcements regarding the events of the day and then shoot a knowing glare in my direction, if I happened to be in his sights.

I found the newly dedicated, redwood bench, standing alone under the canopy of two gigantic redwood trees and covered in nettles. While the last of the fall flowers slowly wilted under the first threat of winter. Another wind-worn St. Francis stood quietly behind it. Its base showing a few cracks and moss creeping over his face. At least this one held birdseed in his cupped hands which was not lost on a lone squirrel balancing on a low tree limb. It was hard to believe this bench, as beautiful as it was, had once been a tree; but now stood as a testament to Billy's parents and their continued generosity to the school. As serene as it was, it did nothing but infuriate me further. There it stood as tangible proof of their money well spent. That seemed to answer any question I may have had regarding the monetary aspect of the equation. The involvement of the Church and the realty of the double standard, however, continued to elude me.

I was not overly concerned about having offended the Church, if indeed I had. In my naiveté I believed I was well beyond the reach of the long arm of the Catholic Church and could not be influenced by the hollow threat of hell fire and damnation. We were Protestants and my fragile soul had been spoken for long ago and consigned to the Anglican Church by baptism, shortly after I was born.

If God had nothing better to do than cast his eye on the comings and goings of two middle school students on the steps of a school then I couldn't help but wonder at his purpose, divine or otherwise. Maybe that was the point, I wasn't supposed to question – but I did. Too many wars had been fought in his name. There was too much poverty, famine and disease in the world. What kind of a benevolent god is that? Why must I be held to his standard when he himself chooses to ignore the very laws he created? If they are his laws shouldn't he be the first to uphold them? If we are so imperfect, by his own design, why doesn't he set an example rather than condemn our frailties? Who is he to stand in judgment? He is what we have chosen to make him – which doesn't say much about us. If indeed we are created in his own image, it is no wonder we are so deeply flawed. It stands to reason he is as equally defective and as marred as we are or is that a figment of our collective imagination, something we chose to believe for our own sakes? I am not at all sure when exactly I stopped believing but I am reasonably sure that the incident of Billy's kiss, the conversation with the Headmaster and the dogmatic rhetoric pounded into me at that school was the turning point. Rather than suck me into their vortex, I chose instead to find my own way.

There was a roar swelling in my ears that I couldn't ignore. Lying on this bench, in this quiet place, I was consumed by an anger I had never experienced before. I wasn't inclined to let this go or rise above it. I wanted to get down and dirty, if that's what it would take to show Billy he couldn't get away with causing my humiliation. He wasn't going to make a fool out of me, and make me feel so small. I was angrier than I had ever been and, at the same time, very sad.

Being only twelve years old, I was relatively unfamiliar with the whole concept of revenge unless stealing the occasional French fry from my brother or hiding his pet turtle under the covers his bed, counted. That was child's play - this was serious. Until now, I had never felt the need to seek revenge against anyone in earnest but the more I thought about it, the more appealing the entire concept became. If the idea was to hurt someone as badly as I had been hurt – I could do that. What could happen? After all, how much havoc can one twelve year old reek? It seemed to me, all I needed was a plan. It had to appear to be spontaneous, but well thought out and quickly executed. I couldn't waiver. If I started down that path, I had to follow through without hesitation, if I was going to be successful. I had to hurt Billy as badly as he had hurt me, regardless of the Church or his parent's money. I would have just one opportunity to put a dent in the double standard. I had to force myself to remain distant, emotionally detached and cold, regardless of my anger.

I thought about nothing else for the rest of the day. Gradually a plan, so simple and so complete came to me. It would drive home the point in no uncertain terms and Billy would know once and for all that he could not target me in the future with either his smiles or his blatant displays of affection – public or otherwise.

That evening as I sat at the long, worn , plank trestle table, in the sunroom, across from my younger brother, doing my homework; I decided now was as good a time as any to share my plan with my mother. I was sure she, of all people, would understand my anger and endorse my plan. It did, after all, require her participation in a small way.

Looking across the table at my brother, who was completely engrossed in something, I said, "What are you doing?"

My younger brother rarely spoke. It took my parents years to understand that he just didn't have anything to say. They had dragged him to every specialist and speech therapist from L.A to San Francisco when he was younger but the diagnosis was always the same. "He will speak when he has something to say." We all knew he had the capacity for speech but seldom said very much, preferring instead to keep to himself. If asked a direct question, he would invariably respond with a one word answer. a groan or a grunt. Full sentences from him were rare and an occasion for celebration, causing our heads to snap up as we waited for whatever would follow. His intellect was such that he didn't have the patience for useless conversation and he was, more often than not, a good three sentences ahead of you – finishing your thought before you even knew you had one. He was possessed of a highly developed, hyperactive brain that, for many years did not co-ordinate with his speech. Add to that, the fact that he was convinced he was surrounded by idiots and refused to engage in tiresome, pointless conversation, believing it was beneath him. As a result, having a meaningful conversation with him was difficult at best and something best not pursued lightly.

I repeated my question, "What are you doing? Looking for more typos?"

My little brother, losing patience with my mother years ago, had taught himself to read when he was barely three yeas old. As a result, he read everything he could lay his hands on; from the New York Times and the Wall Street Journal to Economics Today and everything in between, often perusing my father's medical journals as well.

In second grade, when the other children were let loose in the school library and encouraged to pick out a book for their first book report, my brother chose Moby Dick while the other children scrambled to find "See Spot Run" or something comparable and grade level. My brother chose not the Young Readers edition or the condensed, simplified comic book version but rather the complete, unabridged novel. The comprehensive twelve page report he subsequently handed in was, no doubt the reason he skipped a grade. Now, he spent every waking moment carefully scrutinizing the pages of whatever he was reading, looking for typographical or punctuation errors. When he found them, and he did with amazing regularity, he would insist my mother write or at the very least call the editor to complain and demand a correction.

"Translating." He quietly answered, without looking up.

"Translating what?" I asked, not really caring what he was up to. I had a head full of my own thoughts.

"The Cat in the Hat – from English into Latin".

"Why?"

"For the Talent Show."

"And that's your talent? What are you going to do, read aloud to all those little kids?"

"Exactly! I'll show them the pictures, read each page in English and then read it again in Latin. I'm trying to make it rhyme." He quietly explained.

"That doesn't count! That's not talent! That is so B O R I N G! You'll never be able to make it rhyme in Latin anyway! All those little kids don't care! You're such a dweeb!" I practically screamed.

"At least I have a talent." He responded.

"I've got lots of talent." I said, growing more frustrated by the minute. Why did I ever bother to engage him in conversation in the first place?

"Anybody can sit on a horse!"

My little brother's IQ had finally leveled off at the genius level. He knew it and he never let the rest of us forget it. By the time he graduated from high school, he would speak at least six languages, fluently, and despite my parents refusal to donate a gazillion dollars to the school to insure his first choice of college or the Headmasters reluctance to support him, he would go on to American University in Washington DC. Then attend Waseda University in Tokyo for a year and graduate in three years with honors; majoring in Japanese and Global Economics.

"Mom! I screamed. Make him shut up!"

Coming around the corner from the kitchen she said. "What's going on in here?

"Mom, I need to talk to you about something really, really important. Make him go away or at least go somewhere else!"

"He's not going anywhere. What's so important that it can't wait until you have finished with your homework?"

"Tomorrow is a uniform free day and I have a riding lesson right after school - right?"

"Yes. As far as I know – why?" She said.

"Then I can wear my breeches and paddock boots to school. The ones with the re-enforced steel toes."

"I suppose so. It would be easier than changing at the barn."

"Well. I've got a plan." I said growing more and more anxious by the minute. I had no intention of discussing my plan in front of my brother but by this time, he had gone back to his Latin translation and seemed impervious to our conversation.

"A plan for what?" She answered

"For Billy Andrews." I exclaimed little too loudly.

"I see, and what do your paddock boots have to do with this plan?" She asked.

"This is going to be good!" My brother said under his breath just loud enough for me to hear.

"I know I'll probably regret this but, let's hear it." My mother responded.

"You know about the path at school that leads from the parking lot up to the tennis courts? Right? The narrow trail through the redwood grove where all the seniors go to make-out during lunch?"

"And yet, you've been given a PDA!." She said.

"Maybe it's o.k., if you're a senior." I said.

"No! It is not o.k. even if you are a senior! The rules should apply to anyone and everyone, equally, regardless of their age or sex. Rules are rules, as we're finding out."

"What's a PDA?" My brother quietly asked without looking up.

My mother looked at him patiently and said. "Yesterday, after school, Billy Andrews kissed your sister and, as the Headmaster was quick to point out to us this morning, that is considered a Public Display of Affection, a PDA, which is not allowed and seriously frowned upon." She informed him.

"Why would anyone want to kiss you? You always smell like horse shit! Someone must have paid him to do that." My brother said, starting to laugh. "Somebody must have dared him or maybe it's some sort of lame initiation ritual into the jock-of-the-month club. My moneys on the dare because no guy in his right mind would ever kiss you! There's got to be something more going on here."

"Mom! Seriously! Can't you sell him or something? Maybe you could give him away. Why don't you take him out in the forest and let him go"! I screamed

"Your brother is not for sale! He's a keeper! Besides, I happen to know he walks around with a pocketful of those little packages of oyster crackers for just such an eventuality. You've threatened him once too often. He'd find is way home in no time."

"What if we put a big cardboard sign around his neck that says "Free to a Good Home" or just "Free". It doesn't have to be a good home – just somewhere else! Then tie him to the front gate. Maybe someone will feel sorry for him and drive by and haul him away in the middle of the night. We just have to leave him out there long enough. I'm about to be kicked out of school for something I didn't do and all he can do is gloat! I'm having a major crisis here that could very well ruin my life forever and he's sitting there calmly conjugating Latin verbs for his stupid translation. It's infuriating! Can't you call the Mother ship and ask them to beam him back up to wherever he came from?"

"He's not going anywhere! Both of you calm down. Let's hear the rest of your plan." She responded.

I was resigned to my bother's presence but determined to continue. "Tomorrow, right after the last bell, I'm going to lure Billy up to the"...

Interrupting, she asked, "Lure – how are you going to lure him?"

"I'm going to use my wiles, of course." I said, confidently.

"You're what?" She said, staring at me incredulously.

"My wiles." I responded. "If the Headmaster is going to accuse me of using them when I didn't, then I may as well go ahead and use them now." I said.

"How many times do I have to say this? You don't have any wiles, as you call them, and I hope you never do. Some women spend years honing those skills; they aren't something that comes to you in the middle of the night! They are carefully acquired and you're not going to acquire any between now and tomorrow afternoon! Only desperate and insecure women develop feminine wiles and put them to use. You are far from insecure and I doubt you will ever be quite that desperate! By the way, they are commonly referred to as feminine wiles – not just wiles. "But go on" My mother said. I'm curious to see where you are going with this."

"Since this morning, I've thought about it and now I have a plan but it is probably a good idea for me to know what feminine wiles are exactly so I'll know how to use them. Give me a few examples?" I asked.

"They are a bag or a tool box full of all sorts of tricks that many women employ to either capture or entrap a man. The tools they use to play the games they insist upon playing. They aren't anything you can actually see but rather subtle ways of using deceit. Games people play to get what they want or what they think they want. You have to learn how to use them properly to achieve your desired result and more importantly, when to use them. Too much too soon can scare a guy off; too little too late and a guy will lose interest. At the same time they can be very dangerous and if not used properly or over used, someone can and usually does get hurt." She said.

"And why, exactly, do I need these tools" I asked.

"That is exactly my point, you don't need them!" Just be yourself and be honest – that's all you really need. Anything else is just subterfuge. It's a game of sorts and it can be very risky or disappointing and, in my opinion, there is no place for either in a relationship" she responded.

"I'm still not clear. Give me an example."

"I'm not very good at this sort of thing but I'll try. O.K? Say your standing at your locker between classes or after school and Billy comes up to you and starts a conversation. Turn around very slowly, lower your head and look up at him through your eyelashes. Sort of like Lauren Bacall"

"Who?" My brother and I both asked at the same time.

"O.K.. Lets start over. You would need to be a little bit older to pull that off anyway and no one yet has been able to duplicate that sultry, come hither look the way she did."

"Think of all the photographs you've seen of Princess Diana. That's the look I'm referring to - meek and coy."

"And why should I do that? I answered

"Because it will make you appear to be shy, somewhat distant and modest."

"I don't want to be shy, distant or modest! Why should I pretend to be something I obviously am not?"

"Because boys and men like that sort of thing. If you appear to be helpless, it makes them feel they are strong. Billy will feel you need protecting and believe he is just the one to provide it."

"Okay, that's it! I'm out of here." My brother said out of nowhere. "I'm not going to sit here and listen to all this girly stuff. It isn't important for me to know or remember. I've got other, more pressing things to do."

"Sit down – you're not going anywhere. This stuff, as you call it, may come in handy one day for you as well. It wouldn't hurt you to listen and learn. You will, at some point, confront some of these things and it might be helpful it if you saw it coming."

"What else," I asked, trying to ignore my brother. "Go on."

"When Billy speaks to you or asks you a question, don't look directly at him. Don't make eye contact. Look over his ear, off into the distance before you respond."

"Why?" I asked again.

"It will give him the impression that he interrupted your thoughts - surprised you, catching you off-guard – and that you are preoccupied, thinking about something else totally unrelated to him. You're just a little bit dreamy."

"So far, all this is just plain dumb. I'm not going to pretend to be all dreamy and wimpy just for him!" I said.

"When you finally say something to him, speak very slowly and lower your voice to almost a whisper." She continued.

"I'm afraid to ask again, but why? I asked.

"It will force him to lean in closer to hear what you are saying."

"I don't want him to lean in closer to me. And I don't want him breathing on me! Most of the time he smells like B.O. or old, wet gym socks! And little balls and sprays of spit come out of his mouth because of his braces. I could get some horrible disease just being that close to him!"

Undeterred, my mother continued. "If he says something funny or tells you a joke, laugh, but laugh with him, not at him. There's a huge difference. And not a hearty guffaw or a giddy, high pitched, little girl giggle, just a slow smile followed by a low, throaty chuckle – barely a laugh – and don't let it sound practiced. Try to be spontaneous.

If you can do that, he'll be convinced that you think he's funny. Men, are for the most part, easily amused, usually by themselves, but they like to know that their humor is appreciated by others. If he says something offensive or tells you a dirty joke – look shocked - as though you are disgusted and personally offended. You're not the kind of girl who will listen to or laugh at that sort of thing." She said.

"So far, Billy hasn't said anything remotely funny to me. All he does is talk about himself and I can't seem to make him understand that I don't care!"

"Okay, I've heard just about enough of this. All this stuff you're telling her is so manipulative. No guy is going to fall for any of that! Believe me; we're not as stupid as you seem to think we are. Any guy with any smarts would see through all this in a minute. Where's Dad, he'll back me up on this?" Said my brother, who up until now had had very little to say. Quite the opposite, he seemed to be taking it all in, hanging on every word my mother was saying while pretending to be engrossed in this Latin. "Maybe you should invest in a very large net or a rat trap since your tool box appears to be empty. Your success rate might improve. May I be excused now?" He asked my mother.

Ignoring him, my mother continued, "Men have their own set of tricks too that they don't hesitate to use – just as women do. Women aren't the only ones who play games. It's is a two-way street."

Suddenly my brother appeared more interested in the conversation and asked. "Like what?"

"Well, to start with, most men have a tried and true pick-up line that they are particularly fond of and has been proven to work for them."

"Like what, for instance? He asked, his curiosity now piqued for the first time.

"Say you're in a bar and across the room you see a girl that you'd like to talk to. You approach her – slowly. You lean down, not too close and ask, "Do you happen to have a cell phone? To which she will reply, "Yes, of course." Then you ask, "Does that cell phone have a number?"

"And then? So what?" He asked.

"And then, she'll either ask you join her at the bar or she'll get up and slap your face. It could go either way. It all depends on your timing and your delivery. Understand? You have to keep it short and to the point. Try it tomorrow at lunch on Anabel and let me know her reaction. I'm told it is usually foolproof. Ask your father if you don't believe me! Sitting here, at the kitchen table, it doesn't have the effect it would under the right circumstances."

"That's great! Very smooth! Good talk, Mom. Very enlightening and definitely good for thought. I'm going to remember that, maybe I can use it. May I please be excused now? I'm in informational overload at this point." He answered.

"Oh, dream on! Remember it for what?" I asked. That mousey, little, myopic girl with the stringy hair who follows you around like a new born colt and hangs on your every word." The idea of my little brother trying to pick up a girl in a bar was so unlikely, I too started to laugh. He wasn't that smooth. At least, not yet.

"That's enough, my mother said, raising her voice. There is no need to resort to name calling. Anabel is a very sweet little girl who absolutely adores your brother. She just happens to wear heavy, black glasses right now but that could change."

"That mousey little girl, as you call her, happens to be in my three-dimensional Chess Club and the Latin Club. She's incredibly intelligent and would never resort to these sorts of games or any of this other stuff you two are talking about. She has far too much integrity. Something you obviously lack." He explained.

"Before you two get into it, let me finish. My mother interjected. "When Billy is out on the soccer field and kicks a goal that wins the game for the home team, tell him how wonderful he is. Flatter him. Let him know you were watching his every move on the field and how proud you are of his athletic prowess." She continued.

"I'm not going to tell him that! He'll think I'm some kind of a dork! I practically screamed. Besides, he's, he supposed to kick goals; he's the Captain of the team. That's his job! He doesn't seem to be too concerned about flattering me, in fact, quite the opposite." I responded.

Ignoring my outburst, she continued. "Or, if you should happen you see Billy by the side of the pool just before a swim meet, tell him how handsome he looks in his little, navy blue Speedo with the school's logo on his bum. Convince him he is the epitome of virility in your mind. The kind of guy who can turn heads or stop traffic with his good looks and masculine demeanor."

"Mom – he's a mealy-mouthed, pasty-faced milque-toast! He looks like a dead fish that's been lying on the beach in the hot sun for too long! All slimy and white! You seriously want me to stand there and lie to his face? He won't believe a word of it!"

"That's the point of feminine wiles! If you use them correctly, it won't ever occur to him that you may be lying – which you aren't! He'll only hear what he wants to hear, believe me. And it's not lying, exactly – its flattery. He'll eat it up with a spoon. Do something for me – right now". She had changed gears and I wasn't sure where she was going. Stand up and walk across the room" She asked.

"Why, why should I do that? I asked.

"Please, Just do as I ask. There is a point to all this." She said.

Reluctantly, I got up out of my chair and walked across the room, turned and walked back while my brother continued to laugh. "Okay, so what?"

"Look at how you walk! Maybe I should put a book on your head and have you walk around the house for a few minutes every day. Both my mother and my grandmother put me through that for years. You walk as though you are lopping across a pasture trying to avoid gopher holes or cow pies. And after, what – ten years of being in a saddle, you're very nearly bowlegged. "

"There's nothing wrong with the way I walk and if there was, what good would a book on my head do?" I asked

"A heavy book on your head, will force you to stand up straight and improve your balance and your posture. Suck in your stomach, lift your chin, point your toes and glide – don't stomp and keep your eyes forward. Don't look down at your feet; they know where you want them to go. Put a little more wiggle in your bum – a slight swish if you can manage it; part saunter and part sway." She was laughing now. This conversation had gotten completely out of control and she was enjoying herself far too much at my expense.

"I'm not going to walk around with a book on my head and I'm certainly not going to wiggle, swish, sway or saunter. Why on earth would I do that? No guy is worth all this!"

I said, anger starting to get the better of me.

"I think there is something about a women walking away from a man that really excites them. I'm not entirely sure but I believe it has something to do with evolution – a distant, primordial reflex action, locked somewhere in our collective memory. Did you know that when a female baboon feels feisty or flirty and in the mood, so to speak, she has the ability to turn her bum a very bright orange which tells any male who happens to be passing, that she is ready."

"Ready for what?" My brother and I both asked at the same moment. Was she now comparing me to a female baboon? Where as she going with this?

My brother had decided this was his opportunity to gloat and said, "There you go! That's the answer. Now we're making some progress. Since you're already on the fast track to expulsion, why don't you just paint your ass orange and moon Billy? That ought to get his attention. What guy could resist a bright orange ass, assuming he is familiar with the mating habits of a female baboon? And that is definitely is a blatant, public display of affection. If you're going to go down, you may as well go out in a burst of flames." He couldn't stop laughing and I was beginning to find him very annoying.

"Now, you decide to speak in full sentences instead of your usual cryptic monosyllables! There is something definitely wrong with you! Why don't you go somewhere else and calculate the volume of an empty cardboard toilet paper cylinder or something else equally useless." I screamed.

"I've already done that. As it happens, I'm currently working on the cylinder inside the paper towels.' He replied.

"Whatever! Ask me if I care! - can we please discuss my plan?" I asked somewhat desperately.

My brother sat back down and said, "I've come this far, I may as well hear what you're planning for this poor, unsuspecting schmuck".

"Billy is not a schmuch! My mother said, glaring directly at my brother. And where exactly did you learn that word? We don't talk like that in this house!"

Determined to lead the conversation back in my direction, and ignoring my brother, I continued, "Once I lure Billy up to the redwood grove, I'm going to punch him in the nose as hard as I can, kick him right between the legs and then run like hell." I said, growing more confident. I realized that by saying it all out loud it suddenly became more plausible.

"Ouch! That's cold! I like the painted orange ass plan much better." Said, my brother.

"I see now why your paddock boots are so crucial to the success of your plan. Tell me, where exactly are you going to run to when you run like hell?" My mother asked.

"Well, that's where you come in." I said. "I need you to be in your regular spot in the parking lot and keep the car running. I'm going to run back down the path, jump into the car and we'll take off for the barn. What do you think?" I said, now completely relieved that my plan was exposed. "

"That's it? That's the full extent of your plan? That's your revenge?" This from my brother.

"Nobody is asking for your opinion so why don't you just shut up and stay out of this! None of this concerns you." I screamed!

At this point my father wondered into the sunroom. "What are all of you up to in here?" He asked.

"Hey Dad, Jory's going to kick Billy Andrews in the balls tomorrow" my brother called out.

"Why do I always get the feeling that I am walking into the middle of the second act in this family? Why would you do that? If that's your idea of revenge, you would do well to reconsider. Kicking him won't change anything! You may feel better but that's about all you will accomplish. The end result will either be your expulsion from that school or a law suit. And from everything your mother has told me I don't care to engage the Headmaster in one of his little chats! Let it go, but learn from it and don't ever let this happen again." He said, looking directly at me and then at my mother.

"Alright, everybody calm down. No one is going to kick anyone anywhere especially there. If you kick Billy between the legs with those boots on, you'll most likely cripple the boy for life or at the very least, render him sterile. Can we please try to discuss this rationally?" My mother said.

"I know you're upset about all of this and it is unfair but nothing is ever solved by resorting to physical violence. You have to learn from this whole experience and rise above it. If you stop and think about it, did Billy really hurt you in any way?" She continued.

"He embarrassed and humiliated me- isn't that enough? I cried. I have to do something to let him know he can't get away with that! All day today, he just smiled at me, flashing his braces and I'm not going to just rise above it and do nothing. That's sucks!

"Is it possible, he hurt your pride more than anything?" She asked.

"Well, that too. All the more reason to really hit him where it hurts." I said.

"If you go ahead with this plan of yours. you and I will be right back in the Headmasters library – first thing Monday morning and since I now know what you intend to do, you have made me an accomplice. This time I won't be able to defend you and he'll have you dead to rights. He will undoubtedly accuse you of assault with intent to do bodily harm and there won't be anything I could say or do to help you. Billy's parents will most likely become involved and who knows where it will end. Are you prepared to go that far? Don't you see, this is exactly what the Headmaster is expecting you to do? Don't give him the satisfaction of being right. If you do this, you're playing right into his hands. And, I'd rather not spend another minute in that library of his. All those ghastly religious icons give me the creeps. Since when was Christ that white, with long, shiny, blond hair? He looks like a shampoo commercial! And I think it's genetically impossible for him to have had such incredibly blue eyes. He must have been PhotoShopped! The next thing you know, the Church will have us believe that while handing out fishes and loaves to the teeming masses and the great unwashed, he did so speaking the Queen's English rather than Aramaic! It certainly seems to be a religion of convenience which is probably why it has endured. As for myself, I'd rather "laugh with the sinners than cry with the saints." It makes life much more interesting." She said.

"This is obviously one of Mom's teaching moments. So now who's a dweeb!" My bother chimed in with a smirk on his face.

"But I have to do something!" I said, reluctant to give up my well laid plan so easily. I thought it was perfect. Now, exposed to everyone's scrutiny, it seemed terribly flawed and a waste of time.

But my mother wasn't finished. "Someday, when you least expect it, a tall, handsome young man with blond hair, eyes bluer than yours and a pixie smile that reminds you of Puck, will come to the door and daddy won't be able to scare him off. He'll love you just as you are and there won't be any need for games or lies or the use of feminine wiles. All this is completely unnecessary. Just be you and above all – be honest.

The next morning, I was up early dressed in my breeches and paddock boots and more determined than ever to go through with my plan. I was calm and at peace with my decision regardless of the consequences and my family's reluctance to support me. Hang the consequences! I knew what I was going to do.

Shortly after 3 pm. that afternoon, after the last class and the last bell, I casually walked to my mother's waiting car in the parking lot. I don't know how long she had been patiently waiting but the car was running as I had requested and she sat listening, absorbed in her French CD.

"You're not all hot and sweaty, out of breath or all lathered up and you obviously haven't been running like hell. So how did it go?" She asked.

"It didn't" I replied.

"That's probably for the best. I'm glad you reconsidered." She answered.

"No! I didn't reconsider and it's definitely not for the best! I fully intended to go through with it but Billy isn't here! He was dismissed from the last class to go to the orthodontist!" I said, now completely disappointed by this unexpected turn of events that I had never anticipated or figured into my plan.

By Monday morning, my anger was gone. To where, I'm not sure. It had all but evaporated. Since I had missed my opportunity for revenge, the next best thing for me to do would be to watch and learn; to observe boys and their behavior unobserved from a safe distance to determine if indeed they were different. There had to be a reason why they were different and I wanted to know what that reason was. Why were they so difficult to understand? I'd save my revenge for another, more opportune time.

Billy continued to smile his knowing smile and occasionally made vague attempts to engage me in conversation. And I continued to do everything possible to ignore him. He'd taken to lingering just a little bit longer than necessary by our lockers and waited outside of classes for me – hoping to walk with me. It occurred to me, the more I ignored him, the more ardent his pursuit became. As time passed, we reached what became an unspoken truce that slowly developed into a tenuous friendship until I left three years later for boarding school. A chance encounter fifteen years later would bring Billy back into my life.

Stella Benson

Chapter Twenty One

I had all but forgotten the traumatic incident with Billy and the Headmaster that had occurred so many years ago. It was safely stored somewhere in the deep recesses of my memory, collecting dust. The Church continued to flourish without my participation, and the double standard appeared to be alive and well. Money continued to be an on-going influence in every way; but I had successfully filed the entire episode away in that tiny drawer in my head where it lay undisturbed for nearly ten years.

I was three years into a committed, albeit tumultuous relationship with Nat when I decided to spend the Christmas break at home with my family. Standing in a long queue at Starbucks, amongst a throng of holiday shoppers, I felt someone staring directly at me with what appeared to be more than a passing interest. As I looked back at him I thought he looked vaguely familiar but in that crowd it was difficult to be sure. I wasn't about to confront him and he too seemed reluctant to approach me. Picking up my coffee, I found a table outside in the sun, on the sidewalk and no sooner had I sat down when he sat in the chair opposite me, completely uninvited. As I continued to look at him, I couldn't quite put a name to the face but there was something definitely familiar about him. Then it struck me. It was Billy Andrews – though I couldn't quite take in all the changes the years had brought – probably to both of us. He was ram-rod straight, over six feet tall and his eyes, a bright, cerulean blue. They were piercing and direct, not furtive and constantly moving from side to side in anticipation of some unforeseen danger lurking somewhere in the shadows. His relaxed movement, deft and precise, was not lumbering and unsure. His speech was authoritative yet soft. I immediately noticed the F-word was conspicuously absent from his extensive vocabulary. Unlike Nat who believed the F-word to be the most descriptive adjective, verb, or noun in the English language. – applicable in any situation and regardless of the company. Billy's French was perfect and his Italian was flawless. As we sat talking over our coffee, catching up on the previous years, I couldn't help but be struck by the glaring differences between the two of them. I realized a comparison wasn't fair to either Nat or Billy but the discrepancies were so blatant, it was impossible not to notice. Billy was everything Nat was not. He was articulate, gracious, well-read and sophisticated. In other words, he was finished and polished whereas Nat was definitely a work in progress. I wondered if Nat even had it in him to ever reach a similar level – even if he wanted to. He was definitely not a Thoroughbred and he probably never would be. The contrast between the two of them was striking and somewhat unsettling. The discrepancy somehow made me sad and at the same time sorry. Sorry for what – I couldn't be sure - but I was very sad none the less.

Half way through our conversation, I couldn't resist the temptation to ask Billy if he remembered the kiss in sixth grade. Did he or his parents ever know about my confrontation with the Headmaster? Was he aware of how deeply hurt and humiliated I had been all because of a simple kiss on the cheek?

The expression on his face said it all. He had no idea what I was talking about, or what had transpired all those years ago in the Headmaster's library. He was reasonably sure his parents were as much in the dark as he was. When I told him of my well laid plan for revenge and why it never happened, he couldn't stop laughing. He assured me, that for once, he was glad he had been dismissed early for an orthodontist appointment and greatly relieved that he had managed to avoid contact with my paddock boots. When I asked him why it was all so clear to him, as though it had happened yesterday and why he remembered it, he stopped laughing and became serious for a moment and then looking directly at me with those eyes, said.

"We may have been in the sixth grade but I was madly in love with you though I gather now you didn't know it. I know it seems silly now, looking back. but I remember it clearly because you never forget your first love and you never forget your first kiss. All these years have passed and I had no idea what you had gone through. Why didn't you say something to me at the time? I would have come to your defense and spoken to the Headmaster or at least asked my parents to intervene. Is that why you avoided me? As I recall, all of a sudden, you wouldn't speak to me much less acknowledge my existence and I tried everything I could to get your attention. Finally I gave up pursuing you and then you left for boarding school. For a long time, I thought I was the reason you had left. I have thought of you so often over the years, wondering how you were, where you were and if you were happy. It is no wonder you were determined to break my nose and do untold damage to whatever else you could reach with those boots."

I'm relatively sure, sitting there in that bustling crowd of Christmas shoppers and listening to him that I succumbed to that unexplainable human emotion and blushed a deep crimson. I felt my cheeks slowly deepening into a glowing red up to the tips of my ears for all to see. I was speechless at his unabashed confession. All these years had passed and I had no idea he had ever felt that way about me. I suddenly realized that what had been a very traumatic day in my young life; a memory of pain and humiliation was to him a deeply cherished memory.

Reaching across the table, he picked up my hand and said. "Now I have managed to embarrass you, haven't I? I can see that we were at cross purposes when we were younger but consider we were only twelve years old! What did we know about anything? I believed I was truly and deeply in love with you even if it was sixth grade. No question in my mind. I remember very clearly how I felt at the time. Let me make it up to you. I'm graduating from the Naval Academy at the end of May and I have to be in New Orleans by the middle of June to start medical school. Come to my graduation – be my guest and my date for the entire weekend. I'll send you a round trip ticket to Baltimore and have a car pick you up and drive you to Annapolis. It's an important day in my life and I can't think of anyone else I'd rather share it with. It won't make up for what happened years ago but it's a start. I don't know where you are right now – whether you're in a relationship or not and I'm not going to even ask but I'd like you to at least give it some consideration. It's a full weekend of scheduled activities; starting with the actual graduation ceremony on the Commons Saturday morning. The President is giving the Commencement address and that will be followed by a dinner and then the obligatory dress Ball that evening. I've already made arrangements to charter a sailboat boat on Sunday with three friends of mine. We're planning to sail from Annapolis down the Chesapeake Bay to Baltimore's Inner Harbor and stop somewhere along the coast to cook an ice chest full of crabs, lobster and corn on the cob. I won't take no for an answer."

He was looking at me in such a way that I knew he had no idea what he was asking of me; neither did I volunteer any explanation for my current situation. No one was more surprised than I was when I heard myself say, without hesitation, "of course, I'd love to be there."

Billy stood up pulled on his jacket and leaned toward me and gently kissed me on the cheek. The same cheek he had kissed so many years ago. This time there was no humiliation, and no embarrassment. Before he walked away he said, "Whatever you decide, whether you come or not, don't ever change and don't ever let anyone change you. Promise me that much."

When he had left, I sat there for a moment and realized I was ashamed at how quickly I had accepted his invitation. Not for a moment, throughout our entire conversation had I thought of Nat – not once. How was I going to explain this? What could I possibly say to justify a weekend to myself? I'd lie, of course. That is what I'd come to. One lie of my own to offset all Nat's lies. Now we were lying to reach other! I had finally been reduced to playing his game.

I am not an accomplished liar – far from it. It is not a skill I either posses or intend to acquire. It was not included in my bag of tricks. I had, until now, always equated honesty with integrity. I was as good at lying as I was at implementing revenge. To me, lying is an acquired talent, developed over years of practice not unlike my feminine wiles that had so far completely eluded me. It did not come as naturally to me as it did to Nat. He had the innate ability to create such a maze of fabrication with so much sincerity and authenticity that I never knew what was real and what was not. Leaving me in a constant state of confusion.

I shutter to remember the few lies I tried, with disastrous results, at an early age. My mother would look at me, listen carefully to my contrived story that was overly embellished and told with a great deal of physical animation and simply say, " I'm going to give you a few minutes to reconsider and perhaps revise what you have just said until it closely resembles something nearer the truth. When you're ready, I'll be happy to listen to whatever you have to say but I will not tolerate a lie from you. I don't deserve that and it is beneath you. Look at you! Your eyes are dilated, your lip is twitching, your heart is pounding away in your chest and there is moisture of some sort starting to form on your upper lip. All of which tells me you are lying or at least trying to. Give it up – not you're not very good at it. "

Nat, on the other hand, was a consummate liar – an expert in practiced deceit. I had never seen any hesitation on his part, much less his eyes dilate, his heart beat rapidly or any sort on moisture forming on his upper lip. Apparently all visible signs of deceit can be eliminated by practice. It came to him so easily and effortlessly; it often amazed me how he was able to keep them all straight in his mind. I know enough to know that one lie invariably leads to another and another and another until it is impossible to go back and identify the original truth. I have often wondered if he ever felt any remorse or did he ever have any regrets.

How or why Nat came to be so accomplished, I have no idea. Perhaps it was all a rather subtle attempt to make himself appear to be someone he was not or hide what he really was. Perhaps he just didn't know any better, which is not hard to believe. Or perhaps, his father, a self-appointed man of God, with little or no formal education and for all his proselytizing, bible-thumping and scripture spewing, had somehow neglected to instill in his youngest son, a sense or right and wrong as well as a conscience. Right was a matter of what was right for Nat under the existing circumstances. Wrong seldom, if ever, was a factor worthy of consideration. To him, lying was a part of life as necessary as breathing but I had long ago learned to anticipate as well as identify each and every one. Lying came as easily to him as breathing.

If I told one lie now – just one - wasn't I just a little bit entitled? I had been living with Nat's lies for so long. Where's the harm in just one lie from me? I was tired of living in a shabby, rental, track house in the middle of a plot of dirt surround by a rusty cyclone fence in the middle of nowhere Wyoming. Tired of working two jobs to make my portion of the rent and sick of cooking, cleaning and caring for three guys, two of whom I barely knew and didn't really care to know. They were rude, undisciplined, and disrespectful of everything and everyone. And to add insult to injury, neither one of them had any concept of personal hygiene. I was tired of the mundane reality that I had let my life become. I needed a break and this invitation from Billy was my opportunity to take it. I wanted a glimpse of my old life. Was that so wrong?

This was all new to me. Being a novice at lying, nowhere as accomplished as Nat and with absolutely no experience, it occurred to me it had to be a good, believable lie. Very simple, and as close to the truth as possible with just a slight deviation to suit my own purposes. I couldn't make it too elaborate. I had to be aware of my own limitations and keep it simple. More or less an "Oh, by the way, I forgot to tell you"… sort of lie. In other words, I had to keep it casual and light, nothing overly complicated that would find me unduly enmeshed in a complicated web of my own design. However, the fear of being caught, while not particularity rational, overwhelmed the shame if I had to admit to it. Did Nat ever have such fears or was he so immune to shame that it had absolutely no effect on him? Could I live with myself if I went through with this? Or would it eat away at me until I confessed? How did he manage so casually when more often than not, he was caught – dead to rights? Can any relationship survive that much deception or would quilt eventually destroy us both? So far, we had managed to survive. I was determined to take advantage of this opportunity and the devil take the consequences. I was convinced I could say anything at this point and he would believe it. He knew I was incapable of lying. He had the ability to see through me as easily as my mother had years ago.

As the days and the weeks past with no word from Billy, I practiced my lie over and over again in my head and in front of the bathroom mirror; looking for those tell-tale signs, until I finally found a credible, uncomplicated and feasible explanation for a few days respite. But as time went by, I began to worry that Billy had forgotten his invitation. Perhaps I had made it out to be more than it really was. My eager acceptance not withstanding, perhaps I had been overly enthusiastic, reading more into our chance encounter than there really was for my own gratification . Perhaps it was just as well. I was about to give up on the whole idea, when I received an envelope containing a round trip ticket from Denver to Baltimore. I had completely forgotten to give Billy my mailing address in Cheyenne so he sent the ticket to my parent's home and they, in turn, forwarded it on to me. Nat had, by now, developed the curious habit of scrolling through my phone, checking my contacts, messages and email but he had yet to dare to open my mail especially if it bore my parents return address. But that too would come.

With the ticket now in hand, I was committed. And with my practiced lie firmly in place in my mind, one evening I casually said to Nat, "Oh! By the way, my trainer has scheduled me to compete in the California Regionals at Del Mar in San Diego at the end of May. It is the first show of the season and I need to be there if I'm going to qualify for the Nationals. I'll only be gone for four or five days."

I was amazed at how easily the words flowed out of my mouth! And just as amazed at how readily he accepted what I said; without hesitation or question. Apparently I was, far more credible than he was on any given day. This business of lying wasn't as difficult or as nerve wracking as I had anticipated. I had spent so much time and effort; agonizing over every detail. It was no small wonder that Nat lived by it but I promised myself this would be my one and only lie. My conscience couldn't absorb all this intrigue and deception.

When I explained my intentions and the reason for a round-trip ticket to Baltimore from, of all people, Billy Andrews, after all these years, my mother she was predictably, outraged.

"Who are you? That is nothing short of a bold, straight – faced, out and out lie! I don't understand how or why you tolerate that kind of behavior from Nat but now you seem to be doing it too! Tell him the truth! You cannot casually take off and spend a weekend in Annapolis with one man when you are supposedly in a committed relationship and living with another! What are you thinking?" She said calmly.

"Why not? Nat does it to me all the time! Whenever I'm out of town for whatever reason, he invariably finds a way to keep himself entertained and more often than not, with someone I know. The only difference is, he doesn't care if I know or eventually find out. But you and I are the only ones who will ever know. He'll never find out, believe me! This is for me, Mom! You don't understand! It's just a few days with an old friend, that's all! Its one harmless weekend! Please don't turn it into something it is not! I need to do this." I replied.

"You can't have it both ways!" She replied.

"Why not – he does!"

"That doesn't make it right. I don't care what he does or what he has to tell himself to get through the day. Tell him the truth! How you have tolerated all his lies, one after the other, this long is beyond me? And when, exactly did you become so adept at lying? Is that what you've learned from him? How to lie effectively? What will you do if he finds out about this little weekend jaunt to Baltimore?? He has the emotional maturity of a six year old and one of these days he's going to snap! And I don't want you in the same room when he does. I think he's capable of just about anything – if sufficiently provoked!"

"He won't find out! And I sure as hell am not going to be the one to tell him! And neither are you! I need to do this. Billy is an old friend. It's just two friends spending some time together. Besides, retaliatory sex may not be particularly satisfying in the long run but I'm hoping it will be gratifying in the short term as long as I don't think about it too much".

"Who are you? This is what you've become? You are playing a very dangerous game and somebody is bound to get hurt. That being said, I have to admit I'm glad you have finally come to your senses. God knows you can do better."

On the day of my departure, Nat dropped me, rather unceremoniously, at the departure curb of he Denver Airport; casually kissed me on the cheek and said, "ya'll go on out thar an' kick some country club ass 'an ya'll be sure ta come on back with one of them big blue ribbons ya'll are so fond of. "

Instead of turning left for a flight to San Diego, I turned right and boarded a flight to Baltimore where a car was waiting for me, as promised.

Nat never did find out. He showed absolutely no curiosity about where I had been or what I had done. He couldn't help but notice and he didn't bother to mention my scorching sunburn; the result of a days sail on the Chesapeake Bay. He never asked about my success or the lack of it at the supposed horse show. Nor did he comment on the fact that I didn't return with a blue ribbon or a ribbon of any colour. All of which saved me yet another lie.

One lie leads to another and I was fortunately spared the complication. To this day, I'm sure he has no idea. While I had suffered over my lie, vacillating between guilt and shame for days; I was to learn when I returned, that he had spent the entire four days I was gone with a friend of mine. They never came up for air and when I finally ran into her, she couldn't wait to tell me all about it; boasting of her conquest. After four days in his arms, and she was in love with him. She needn't have bothered. I'd been there and I knew how it felt to lie in his arms in the middle of the night; listening to the soft cadence of his speech. A voice made for lies and whispers; one that he used to his advantage at every opportunity. I knew the feeling all too well. I was there still. What she didn't know, what she couldn't have known, was that she was nothing more to him than another temporary diversion - an opportunity ripe for the taking. She was collateral damage that he would cast aside just as easily as he had picked her up. He would throw her to the wind as soon as I returned, which is exactly what he did. I later learned from a mutual friend, that she was devastated by his subsequent rejection. Her sole purpose had been to serve his vanity – nothing more. As it turned out, my lie, that I had agonized over for weeks, debating the right and the wrong of it, did nothing more than give him an opportunity for another indiscretion. When I found out, I did not confront him – not this time. Two wrongs don't make a right but it was close. It was a small victory for me that now and then brought a smile to my face. In the days and weeks to follow, I often caught myself smiling for absolutely no reason.

Lies, like revenge and jealousy aren't worth the effort and the results are more often than not, unsatisfactory. I prefer the truth. It can be painful but at least it's right.

Chapter Twenty Two

The change we had sensed in the air like the salt mist blowing off the ocean from the west, didn't creep up on us and gradually settle slowly over the western hills to blanket the valley below. Instead, it hit us hard and fast right where we lived.

Too everyone's surprise, it came from the South – from Silicon Valley. First one, then another, until they filtered in en mass in a steady stream like ants on a determined march. The first to arrive were the newly made millionaires. The very young, tech nerds and brainiacs; the smart and very creative pioneers who were being advised to move out of their barren condominiums on Santana Row in San Jose and invest in their dreams. They were followed closely by the intellectual entrepreneurs determined to succeed through sheer energy and at any cost. Then came the loyal infrastructure of Stanford University; venture capitalists, bio-tech engineers and billionaire corporate executives. All were driven to succeed through sheer power and over confidence; wealthy, spoiled and demanding, they knew all to well, and they could lose everything in a heartbeat. Their wealth was fleeting and tenuous and it had to be guarded. They were nervous and in a hurry; accustomed to getting their way at any cost. No barrier could or would contain them. They wanted the benefit of our Mediterranean climate but not the distance from their bases of innovation and creativity.

Overnight, our once bucolic community became the target of their desire and greed. This new breed of high strung arrogance shocked us all to our core. Dazed we questioned whether we could absorb the lack of taste and the vulgarities of excessive wealth and the flagrant displays of conspicuous consumption they so naively displayed. Collectively, we all hoped they would, in time, move on to somewhere else, find another target and ultimately leave us in peace. Instead they set about to change everything we knew and had come to love. Everything that defined our community as we knew it and everything we had hoped to protect from just such an onslaught.

Everything was for sale, everything had a price and everything could be bought. Everything except those of us who had made this area our home for so many years prior to their invasion.

Land values soared and existing home prices sky-rocketed as the demand for housing increased. Our nearest neighbors took advantage of the opportunity and put their home on the market with an asking price of sixteen million dollars and saw it sold within three days. During the sale process, they discreetly entertained an offer from Kevin Costner and the scuttlebutt at the Feed and Seed confirmed that Tom Cruise was seen house hunting in the area. Further up the hill, near San Gregorio, an abandoned beautiful old barn, sitting alone on six acres for years was listed by the owners with an asking price of fifty-four million dollars. It too sold within three days!

To meet their insatiable demands, the historic mansions and the quaint cottages, where once the elite of San Francisco had summered came crashing down. We stood by, horrified, as they were tragically dismantled, stone by stone and piece by piece. Most of the small cottages were either plowed under or brutally hauled away intact.

In their place, world famous architects were employed to design and build even larger mansions of steel and glass, imported stone, marble, poured concrete and sustainable woods. Massive homes of eight, ten, fifteen thousand square feet popped up almost overnight, surrounded by acres and acres of exotic trees planted in huge wooden crates, loaded on long flatbed trucks and lowered carefully into the ground by cranes. Hordes of landscape personal were hired to insure their survival and encourage them to flourish in a new, hostile environment. Competition was fierce as each tried to out - do the other in size and cost and design. A few attempted to renovate the existing mansions and one or two purchased small chateaux in the South of France , only to have them numbered, dismantled and reconstructed on land newly cleared and awaiting delivery.

In place of the old, established estates, French Country homes on a sprawling scale sprouted overnight to compete with stately Georgian mansions, faux Tutor manors and more than a few attempts at Early California Mission style haciendas. One extremely successful CEO of a major tech company, not to be bested by his colleagues, spent nine years and in excess of seventy million dollars to build an exact replica of a 16th century Japanese emperor's home, importing and housing skilled stone masons from Japan. Located not far from the center of town and surround by a matching high stone wall, it included ten separate buildings; several matching guest houses, a man-made lake artfully dredged a tea house, a separate bath house, a koi pond loaded with fish and a 24 hour armed guard stationed at the gate, comfortably installed in his own little house. A guard who was paid very well and took his post seriously. The sedate, pea gravel paths were delicately scraped into swirls and sworls with thin bamboo rakes on a twice daily basis by swarms of dedicated Japanese gardeners. They were on duty to snatch any leaf that fell in the wrong place, disrupting the overall harmony of costly perfection. It soon became apparent that neither the reclusive inhabitant nor the guard of this fortress intended to entertain trick or treaters.

The beautiful, antique iron gates; long neglected and rusting off their hinges that had hung neglected and welcoming for years were replaced with electronic, state of the art, impenetrable steel barriers that required a complicated process to gain entry. Large, highly trained Dobermans roamed feely within the confines of many properties as added security; a visible, threatening, paws- on-the ground, back –up deterrent to anyone who dared to enter unannounced. They boldly locked the trail gates, the trails traversed their property, denying horseman the access that they had enjoyed for years. Not surprisingly, tempers soon flared within the equestrian community; long accustomed to a daily lope around town. As a solution, and in the spirit of compromise, our City Hall installed a system of uniform locks and issued a key upon request but most riders instead chose to strap bolt cutters to their saddle.

Once the homes were completed, it follows that they would turn their attention to the grounds. What had always been pasture land was now leveled and covered in acres of flagstone patios and terraces leading gracefully to sparkling, salt water, Olympic-sized pools; with a matching pool house, a guest house or two, and complete out- door, commercial kitchens of gleaming stainless steel. Tennis courts were discreetly constructed just a stones throw from the pool and, looking further a field, the once stately redwood groves were rudely cleared to accommodate a concrete tarmac large enough to safely land a private helicopter.

With the pasture land gobbled up and scheduled for better use; down came the old, weathered barns and stables and with them the livelihood of many long established trainers who had run small, private stables in the community for as long as anyone could remember. Those of us who held fast and resisted, saw our salaries double, then triple and finally quadruple as the need for our expertise and experience increased. Our new, completely ignorant residents suddenly developed an avid interest in horses and encouraged their children to learn to ride and their wives to participate in our local heritage.

Many chose to incorporate barns in their overall estate plan and set about constructing everything from small, traditional, octagonal barns, complete with a cupola and twisting weather vane to staggering structures designed to stable as many as forty horses. Most included a series of wash stalls, an apartment and office for the newly-hired, resident trainer and a small but comprehensive veterinarian clinic for the on-site veterinarian, also recently added to the payroll. Many boasted heavy, mahogany criss-crossed wooden beams, smelling of stain and varnish and carved stall doors with gleaming brass fittings. The floors were carpeted in one inch; thick, soft black rubber and tiered, multi-faceted, crystal chandeliers in shining metal frames hung in a row from the ceiling beams the entire length of the center aisle. Large, arched, multi-paned, beveled windows swung open to let in the summer breeze while a series of thermostats regulated the heat and kept the air-conditioning consistent and at a comfortable level. Extensive surround sound systems, wired throughout, offered a selection of soothing music carefully orchestrated to calm all but the most nervous of occupants.

The horses, imported from England, Germany and Kentucky to occupy these new barns arrived in a constant stream of sleek, 18-wheel rigs that had difficulty navigating our narrow country roads and clogged the freeway exist. The resulting confusion and local traffic soon escalated beyond the control of our local sheriffs department. On more than one occasion, several horses had to be off loaded in the gas station parking lot on the edge of town and either walked or ridden to their perspective new homes by truck drivers who had contracted to drive not ride – a union rule. To all who witnessed this exercise in futility, it proved to be more entertaining than our parades. Their inexperienced owners, baffled as to how to safely relocate and house several hundred thousand dollars worth of quality horse flesh on the hoof immediately called for capable riders to come to their aid and many answered that call, myself among them. Who wouldn't welcome the opportunity to ride animals of that caliber and breeding! A string of eleven polo ponies were unceremoniously dropped in the grocery store parking lot and loosely tied to the nearest tree or the bumpers of patron's cars until several off duty members of the county mounted patrol offered to escort them to their new homes.

What they couldn't buy, they collectively set out to change. These were intelligent, accomplished businessman and women who did not get to where they were through indifference. They had power, influence and the wealth to accomplish whatever they set their minds to and they did not hesitate to use both. They clearly enjoyed their success and were working very had to improve their new-found status – amongst themselves. The rest of us could only shake our heads in amazement- taking it all in stride.

What had originally attracted them to our community in the first place; its charm and relative proximity to their think tanks and their hot-beds of innovation eventually proved to a bit too charming to suit their immediate needs.

Our winding, dirt, country roads not only barred the passage of big wheel rigs, scraping under the canopies of trees but Porches, Maserati's, Lamborghini's and Aston Martin's suffered when gravel flew up from the tires to scratch the paint or crack the windshield. Paving the roads seemed to be the only answer to alleviate that problem. They decided our meandering country lanes needed to be widened and then paved in such a way as to include a designated bicycle lane. After years spent in cubicles, and their fortunes made, our new residents longed to experience the outdoors. Complaints continued to rise when they realized horse poop had a tendency to accumulate and dry in the wheel wells of their Rolls Royce's and Bentleys. We were all advised to restrict our riding to the trails that they had locked and limited or dismount and collect our horses own poop! Piles of manure, dropped here and there in the streets by horses was no longer considered charming or indicative of our country life style. It was declared unsightly, a potential health hazard to their children and difficult to remove from the under carriage of their cars.

Our parades, while encouraging a sense of community, were deemed too many, too noisy and far too chaotic to be tolerated four times a year. They lacked organization, blocked the roads for hours on end and were disruptive. The headless horseman had run his last gauntlet.

To the horror of the aging pastor of the Episcopal Church, who often rode to church himself, and his congregation; a very tall, looming steel structure was unceremoniously installed on the quaint, white steeple of his church.. As the highest point in town, towering over the redwood trees, it was designed to guarantee reliable and consistent WiFi and Internet service. The life blood of our new residents industry.

The hardware store, long a community gathering spot, changed hands and was now a proper store; corporate owned and corporate managed. Gone were the cardboard boxes of puppies and the occasional baskets of kittens as well as the bales of hay, bags of oats, rubber muck boots and gardening supplies. It now strictly adhered to regularly posted hours. The previous owner was no longer available to open at a moments notice to help with little emergencies or last minute home deliveries. And on more than one occasion, my mother, casually looking through the seed display outside the hardware store was mistaken for Michelle Pfieffer.

It didn't take long for our one-stop, corner grocer to become insufficient to meet their everyday needs and wants. The water trough outside the doors, long stocked with carrots and apples, free for the taking, was replaced by another very serious security guard. The hitching posts outside, surrendered to a large, paved parking lot. Feeling the pressure, the grocery store underwent an extensive renovation, and re-opened three months later as a very high-end supermarket offering a finely curated selection of products from local farmers, artisans and purveyors of the best California and the world at large had to offer.

A full time, skilled, butcher, supervising the charcuterie, was on hand to cut whatever cut of meat you desired, including fresh bones for soup or your dog. Your meat was handed over to you wrapped properly in white butcher paper, never shrink wrapped in plastic. The extensive sushi bar spilled over into the fresh caught, sustainable fish section. Fish and shellfish from either local waters or any of the earth's waters for that matter, were displayed on gleaming trays of ice.

We now had a fromagerie as well as a patisserie. With a choice of over four hundred and forty two different cheeses; some locally made, most imported, it took an inordinate amount of time to make the correct choice. Any indecision could of course be immediately alleviated by the expert staff on hand to offer a free sample.

The patisserie offered fresh, baked breads, and pastries, including petite gateaux, tasty verrines, petite fours and tarts. On special request and given a days notice, they would whip up custom made cupcakes for a birthday party or design a six tiered wedding cake, all courtesy of a master pastry chef; himself a recent Cordon Bleu graduate.

The five thousand bottle wine cave offered a staggering selection of wines from around the world, and a full –time sommelier as well as a wine steward. Both were on hand to assist you with your pairings. Those who cared to rent space in the climate controlled storage room to house their own wine collection were subject to a waiting list that included a hefty monthly rental fee. Wine tasting; flights, were offered every Friday night, by invitation only, to those who wished to extend their knowledge of the world's wines or further educate their palate. And for an added fee, small, carefully temperature controlled drawers were available to securely store your cache of imported albeit, illegal Cuban cigars. It was possible to gain access to your private wine collection or visit your cigars without an appointment only.

Children's birthday parties were no longer casual afternoon gatherings in neighbor's backyards or the local park; followed by the ritual of whacking a multi-colored piñata suspended from a tree. In no time, they blossomed into extravagant catered affairs that often included professional magicians, several clowns stepping out of tiny cars, pony rides or the installation of a small train to carry little guests from the front door to the site of the party. The appearance of the cast of Cirque du Soleil to perform became a favorite and a party not to be missed. In place of the customary cellophane goodie bags full of Reese's pieces and gummy bears, handed out at the end of the party, I once received a beautiful Prada pocketbook, tied with a co-coordinating Hermes scarf and holding a one hundred dollar gift certificate for a manicure, pedicure and full body massage at a day Spa in San Francisco. I was nine years old! My mother immediately took away the scarf and the bag, leaving me the gift certificate, explaining as she did so, that when I was older and could appreciated the value of both the scarf and the bag, I could have them back. Not long after, my younger brother attended a large birthday party and was thrilled to receive a signed, first edition of the most recent Harry Potter book.

The father of one birthday girl purchased 101 stuffed Dalmatians of every size and shape and discreetly scattered them all over the lawn; hiding them in the bushes and trees and huge glazed ceramic pots. After seeking them out, we spent the remainder of the afternoon trading back and forth until we were each satisfied with our choice

At another party, as an acknowledgement to The Little Mermaid, the guests were each handed a large, clear glass bowl bearing our names and a small mesh scoop. Several hundred goldfish had been dumped into the pool the night before and any fish we managed to catch with our little nets, were ours, for the keeping. Unfortunately goldfish are not salt water fish and every one of them died within minutes of sliding into the water. Our hosts, visibly rattled by this disastrous turn of events could offer no remedy other than an emergency call to their pool service company. Disappointed, we all sat at the edge of the pool, our feet dangling in the water as the dead fish were sucked off the bottom of the pool before their little carcasses could clog the delicate filtration system. To carry the theme further, lunch consisted of small watercress and cucumber sandwiches with a slice of black olive for an eye, skillfully cut into the shape of fish and served with our lemonade. Given the days events, most of us chose to forego the tuna fish sandwiches in favor of the watercress. As a consolation, our empty, little, glass fishbowls bowls were filled to the brim with orange goldfish crackers. The birthday girl herself remained inconsolable; convinced her carefully planned party had been a disaster.

Children were now chauffeured to school in ominous black Hummers with dark tinted windows by small, menacing - looking Asian men wearing soft black slippers, black jeans, black t-shirts, black aviator sunglasses and a Blue Tooth protruding from one ear. They were allowed to assemble and spend the day waiting in the designated section of the school parking lot usually reserved for nannies. But many had been directed to maintain their posts outside each classroom, waiting to escort their little charges from one class to another and after school, to the playground, the soccer field or the restroom.

We attended a lavish wedding at the home of a neighbor and danced until dawn to Huey Lewis and the News and Sir Elton John clandestinely appeared on a regular basis to provide the evenings entertainment at more than one charity function. Twenty-five thousand dollars would buy you not only a fabulous dinner complete with wine and champagne, at a political fundraiser, but the dubious opportunity to have your picture taken with President Obama. Months later that photo would arrive in everyone's mailbox, carefully crafted into a festive Christmas card.

The Headmaster, a recognized pillar of the community, and not one to let an opportunity slip through his fingers, had finally found his true calling. Confronted with what he considered a frivolous misuse of considerable wealth he embraced his new role as a fund raiser with renewed enthusiasm and set out to separate the newly made millionaires from their newly made millions; and channel those millions into the coffers of his school.

He would often forego his black robe and instead don khaki pants, a white, monogrammed oxford shirt and with a pastel sweater casually draped over his shoulders, and could be found on any given Thursday night standing in the bar of our local Grille. With a glass of Scotch in one hand, he slowly worked the room; begging for donations, not alms; extolling the virtues of his institution versus any other private school in the area. He appeared to be on a first name basis with the bar tender and more often than not, a little the worse after several glasses of Scotch. Projecting what many parents, there to enjoy an evening out, considered an inappropriate example for their children. But by this time, his greed had far outweighed his sense of discretion. He was determined to fund the growth and development of his school and promised unsuspecting donors they would reap the benefits of a sizeable tax deduction. It was unsaid but generally acknowledged, that any large donation on their part would expedite their child's admission to his school when they came of age and ultimately, with a quiet word from him, guarantee their college placement.

As the community adjusted to the influx and influence of the nouveau riche, so too did the school. Latin, traditionally a long established course to be merely tolerated, was dropped from the rigorous academic curriculum. Computer science, Web design, graphics and robotics filled the void as the school attempted to compete with the fast paced and ever changing high tech world that they themselves had created and hoped their children would carry on into the future.

As the school changed to meet the growing demands, so too did the student body. The children of the wealthy were in possession of inexhaustible spending funds and spend it they did. The spread of drugs, the easy accessibility and the quality improved almost overnight as the demand increased. The son of one of the school's most respected and tenured faulty members, himself a recent graduate and something of an entrepreneur, recognized an opportunity and immediately established himself as the primary and only discreet dealer to every private school within the surrounding three counties. His father, a pompous, tall, lanky, chinless man who bore an uncanny resemblance to a ferret complete with wire rim glasses, clearly had no idea that his son was so firmly ensconced in the drug trade and that the school, so long recognized for its academic successes was now considered his son's undisputed territory.

The Headmaster, if he knew of the existence of drugs on his campus typically chose to ignore it and quietly prayed it would go away without any effort on his part let alone recognition. It only became worse and I left for boarding school.

We didn't need the New York Times, the Wall Street Journal, or the CBS Evening News to tell us our once sleepy, little community now housed the greatest concentration of wealth on the planet.

When Nat stepped off the plane in San Francisco for the first of only three visits in six years to my parent's home, he unknowingly stepped into a world he never knew existed and one far beyond his comprehension. My world. A world as foreign to him as his was to me.

Chapter Twenty Three

Four college coeds, dressed to kill, entering the Sundance Steakhouse and Saloon on the outskirts of Fort Collins, Colorado on any given Tuesday night is not unusual nor is it likely to go unnoticed by the regular crowd. Tuesdays were well known and advertised as College Night; whiskey shots were twenty-five cents, beer was $2.00 a bottle, the live band played non-stop until 12 am. and the jello shots were plentiful. The back of one hand, after checking numerous forms of I.D was unceremoniously stamped, verifying that the patron wishing to enter was over the age of eighteen but under the legal drinking age of twenty-one. Word of mouth, not withstanding on a college campus, we learned very quickly that copious amounts of hand lotion lavishly applied caused the black stamp to slip easily down the drain after one quick wash in the ladies room. Without the stamp, we were all free to participate fully and without restraint.

That particular Tuesday, the second semester of my freshman year at Colorado State happened to be Valentines Day; the biggest date night of the year! It is "the" designated night for those who are in love, those half-way there and those newly enamored. It is not a night to hook-up with a perfect stranger. Admittedly, if you are single or otherwise committed but still find yourself alone, for whatever reason, its an occasion better spent washing your hair, rinsing out your panty hose or curled up with last years best selling novel buried somewhere under a pile of textbooks scattered, helter-skelter across the floor.

By the time the four of us arrived, the festivities were in full swing. Red, white and pink crepe paper streamers tied to thousands of balloons filled the ceiling of the bar and given the heat generated from the crowd and the dance floor, finally fell to bounce on the floor. The five poker tables near the back were already filled and Texas Hold-em was the accepted game of the evening. All the regulation sized pool tables were completely occupied with several anxious players waiting their turn. Country music blasted and an announcement promised the first of several line dancing contests. The D.J. played Le Doux at a deafening level and non-stop; the pounding, ceaseless rhythm of the music causing glasses on the tables to nearly tip over and the heat level of so many bodies crammed into the bar was quickly rising to claustrophobic.

My best friend and my classmate, Sybil, was never one to miss an occasion or a good party. She had been insisting for days that I accompany her and three other girlfriends for a quick glass of wine and, what I hoped to be an even quicker perusal of the local talent. I really didn't want to be there but I had promised, days before, to be their designated driver for the evening. I was patiently waiting for my sniper to return from his latest deployment in Iraq and had no interest in whoever might be supporting the bar especially on that particular night. To be in a bar with three other women and obviously unaccompanied on Valentines Day, of all days, screams desperation. And we assumed any young man in the room worthy our attention had to be equally desperate. Why else would he be there? Valentines Day is not generally accepted as the ideal day to meet someone new or begin a relationship. Any self- respecting woman should and usually does know better and avoid the day altogether or wait for it to pass – unnoticed.

I saw Nat across the room the minute we walked into the bar. He was hard not to miss. Our eyes did not meet across that crowed room or in haze of cigarette smoke but I was acutely aware of his presence and his eyes on me. A presence that had I paid attention to the warning signs, cried danger. But Valentines Day is not generally recognized as a day to consider the possibilities of danger.

He sat, relaxed and familiar with the surroundings at a table with three friends. As often as I had been in that bar, I had never seen him before. He had to be new to the local scene. His long legs were casually splayed under a table on the edge of the dance floor, a Bud-Lite in front of him. He was attractive; there was no question of that, in a coarse, down-home sort of way. Either he wasn't aware of just how attractive he was and the effect he had or he took it for granted. I couldn't be sure. At first glance, he seemed a little rough around the edges but he had well developed muscles in all the right places, six-pack abs and a tight bum; well defined in jeans just a bit too tight but tight in all the right places. No doubt a runner. And from what I could see, a dazzling smile that reached everyone in the room. He and his friends, none of whom I recognized, were all in black jeans and well worn, scruffy cowboy boots, with regulation military haircuts. Nat wore a white T-shirt tightly stretched across his chest that left little to the imagination. At some point during his military career, he had his last name translated into a single Japanese Kanji character and tattooed on his right bicep that was now partially obscured by the short sleeves of his t-shirt. The four must have had a few days leave and wandered as far as Fort Collins from Fort Warren Air Force base in Cheyenne. That would explain why I had never seen any of them before tonight. Military personnel seldom wandered as far as Fort Collins especially in the dead of winter. Tonight had to be the exception.

Turning back toward the bar, I ordered a glass of white wine and as I reached in my bag for my credit card, I felt a warm hand in the small of my back and a jolt of electricity race up my spine. I spun around and came face to face with Nat. His face not two inches from mine, our noses almost touching. His even, teeth were blindingly white against a very dark complexion, a reflection, no doubt, of his Great-grandmothers Cherokee Indian blood. His short black hair, and deep, unusual grey-green eyes with that unmistakable 'come hither look', focused only on mine, never wavering. His smile was slow and deliberate in a lean, sculptured face with at least two days of black 5 o'clock shadow. The smell of pine and chocolate and something else, strawberries or raspberries; something sweet, no - B.B.Q. sauce; came off him and wafted into my face. I could easily loose myself in those eyes that seemed to hold so much promise. He was, without a doubt, the most attractive man in the bar and he knew it. He was also somewhat intimidating. How had he crossed the room so quickly?

How had he managed to navigate the dance floor and the crowd so easily? My mouth had gone too dry to protest his hand on my back when he said, very slowly, and barely above a whisper, "Let me get that for y'all, darlin.'"

Sybil, standing next to me at the bar, turned and seemed to be equally breathless at the sight of him; her mouth hanging open, threatening to drool on the bar surface at any moment. As memorized as I was by his presence; his eyes and his smile; I struggled, to come to grips with 'darlin'. No one had ever before called me "darlin'" with that look or that sultry tone of voice. If he asked my name, I realized I would be at a total, mumbling loss. I was reasonably sure I had a name but as long as his hand rested on my back, I was unable to recall what it might be. I was trying, desperately to protect myself from whatever this was coming at me so unexpectedly. Having completely lost my train of thought, I chose instead to make a mental note to call my brother in Washington DC. as soon as possible. It suddenly occurred to me he might want to consider adding 'darlin' to his somewhat limited repertoire of pick-up lines and try it out on the co-eds he was so enthusiastically pursuing in Georgetown. 'Darlin' could very well replace his "do you have a cell phone' line – learned so long ago at the kitchen table and no doubt overused at this point, if - he could pull it off as effectively as Nat and that was a big if.

I was stunned and more than a little confused. This was possibly the right guy but definitely the wrong situation. The timing couldn't have been worse! But I was also curious. He was smooth! It occurred to me that he wasn't addressing me at all, perhaps someone else beyond my limited field of vision, my eyes glued to his, until he picked up my glass of wine and with his other hand, still warm on my back, and holding my eyes, said, "Follow me darlin." I knew at that very moment that I wanted to be with him.

Given my current state of confusion, I would have followed him to the ends of the earth were it not for the sudden realization that my legs had turned to noodles and my feet appeared to be encased in concrete, impossible to move and completely unresponsive. After a few, very tentative steps, we started to weave our way back across the dance floor to his table. He was exactly my height. If I wore heels, I would tower over him. Nat didn't just walk; he sauntered, with a cocky, arrogant Top Gun swagger; confident that every pair of eyes in the room were appraising him from head to toe. He was, without a doubt, the walking, talking definition of charisma. It may have been the result of hours of practice or perhaps his jeans were too tight or the heels of his boots too high. I couldn't be sure but it was impressive nevertheless. Every woman in the bar, with longing in their eyes, followed him across the room. With the occasional, snarky arched eyebrow thrown in my direction, I concentrated on putting one foot in front of the other, struggling not to stumble and land on my face.

At one point, in what seemed to be our long journey across the crowded room, I noticed his three friends seemed to have disappeared, no longer occupying the table he had left just minutes ago. Were they playing pool, dancing or at the poker tables? With no warning that little drawer, safely closed in the back of my mind, flew open and the experience with Billy Andrews and the Headmaster so long ago came spilling out. The hair on the back of my neck immediately rose and I felt a sudden chill as goose bumps appeared unexpectedly on my arms. I had been down this road before. But this time I would heed the warning of the past. I was prepared. As my mother had suggested so long ago, I had studied diligently and learned the rules. Their rules and my rules. I was more than aware of the double standard. If I was the object of another dare, I wouldn't be caught unaware. Not this time. I was confident I could anticipate any miss-step and with my armor firmly in place, head it off. Any woman in the bar would have gladly welcomed his attention while I had appeared indifferent. Was that what had attracted him to me. Was I more of a challenge? Of all the women in the bar, he had chosen me. Why? It wasn't until years later, that he slipped, just once, in conversation and admitted I had indeed been the object of a bet. If he could successfully pick me up in just ten minutes, they in turn, would stand him to a round of beer. A round he never collected.

It was not love at first sight by any means but it was lust at first touch. There was a charge of something, some undeniable electricity between us that was impossible to ignore. He was so rash and utterly unpredictable, unlike anyone

I had ever met and so appealing. Even with my long established Type A personality and my OCD firmly in place, this was all new to me. In spite of the differences in our backgrounds or perhaps because of those differences, we were invariably drawn to each other and my curiosity quickly turned to obsession. He was, without a doubt, charming and full of promises and a scoundrel but I didn't care. I had never before known a scoundrel! From that moment on things started to move very quickly but neither one of us wanted to stop the momentum. As fascinated as I was, I was determined not to be drawn into his schemes or his dreams no matter how exciting they promised to be.

He was a tempest, threatening to boil over at any minute, constantly swirling in the middle of a storm of his own making and constantly in motion. I would never know from one minute to the next what to expect from him, where he was going or what he would say. When we were apart, which after that first night, was not often, all I could think about was being with him. Waiting for a phone call, waiting for him to pound on my apartment door, and waiting to be once again in his arms. I was always waiting. The ups and downs of our relationship would be completely unpredictable over the next six years; constant and never ending. It would prove to be a long, difficult but exciting ride. A zigzag through rough terrain, and seldom smooth. An emotional roller coaster that never seemed to slow or stop; at once exhilarating, terrifying and exhausting at the same time.

Chapter Twenty Four

The barn had long since grown quiet. All the horses had been fed, blanketed and were, for the most part, sound asleep, snoring peacefully and undisturbed. Everyone had left for the day, all except Odie and I. Only the single bulb suspended from the ceiling of his stall would give anyone any indication that I alone, remained at this hour. I didn't want to leave but Odie but he appeared to be content and dozing, unaware of my presence. The security guard strolled by on his hourly rounds with only a slight nod of recognition in my direction to assure me all was well.

Knowing Odie was asleep, I quietly tip-toed to my car. I was looking forward to the drive down the coast and the opportunity to stop the incessant chatter and the endless stream of questions that bounced around in my head, unable to connect to answers. They had become jagged and sharp, blistering my brain as they continued to swirl. The long drive would offer some much needed time alone and hopefully some peace.

I had spent far too much time on this scratchy bale of hay, in my corner, safely ensconced in Odie's stall and still my phone had not rung. I had dozed on and off for hours but it wasn't until Odie softly nudged me awake with his warm, velvet nose that I realized it was well past midnight. He was noticeably concerned, shifting from one hoof to the other and swinging his head from side to side, confusion clearly visible on his face. He was right, it was time to go. My phone informed me it was twelve-thirty and there had been no calls or messages.

As I drove up and over the hill to Highway 1, a distance of less than ten miles toward San Gregorio, the full moon, directly in front of me created a blinding beacon turning the ocean a dark, slate grey and lighting my way. Not another soul passed; no visible pairs of headlights either coming at me or following behind me. I was as alone as I ever would be and I embraced the feeling, buffered by the quiet. I wasn't so preoccupied with my own thoughts not to be aware of the beauty of the coast as I sped by. The soulful quiet of the sea that that hour, devoid of the crashing waves was reassuring and the beaches were deserted except for the lumbering, elephant seals who dozed loudly in the sand dunes.

Traffic at this hour, passing through Santa Cruz which is normally heavily congested, would be non-existent. The idea of a quiet drive along the coast was very appealing. I could put the top down on my car and let the wind blow all thoughts from my mind. If Nat didn't call in the morning, I would call him, regardless of our agreement. This week of silence that we had both agreed to had gone on for more than the agreed amount of time and I was tired of the waiting. I wanted to speak to him and I wanted answers – now. There were too many decisions that required our collective attention and too many questions to address. I was exhausted both mentally and physically and more than a little confused. This current game, whatever it was, had to end one way or the other. I couldn't do this anymore, for my own sanity. I had had enough of his games; the numerous, unresolved questions whirling around in my head and this ridiculous, forced silence. We had too much to talk about, too many decisions to make and no time for this game or any other.

The next morning at 5:45, with less than three hours of sleep, my cell phone finally started chirping. Caller ID told me it was Nat- finally! Bleary –eyed, and not quite remembering exactly where I was, or how I had gotten here, I found my cell phone buried somewhere in the folds of the duvet. The minute I picked it up I had a feeling that something was terribly, terribly wrong; goose bumps rose on my arms, my mouth was full of cotton wool and my stomach started churning. I was determined to get through this conversation, whatever it was, with some degree of dignity. He'd have to go a long way to provoke me this time and I silently and quickly swore to myself I wouldn't raise my voice in direct response to his. I would get through this with as much dignity as I could possibly muster.

"Hey." I said.

"Y'all up yet? Y'alls wastin' daylight thar', darlin'." He said in what appeared to be a normal tone of voice without a hint of anger. But why should there be any anger? We hadn't spoken to each other in over ten days. There was nothing to be angry about as far as I could see. I just needed a minute to gage his mood before continuing and a chance to completely open my eyes. Given the tone of his voice, I was encouraged. And then suddenly, I sensed a change and his anger once again quickly took over. I had a definite feeling this conversation was not going to end well.

"I was going to call you this morning. I have so much to tell you. So much has happened since we last spoke. Are you okay?" I asked.

"Shit naw. I'm as good as the hair on a frog. I'm jus' pissed as hell! I gots major shit rainin' down on my ass from every damn direction 'an it ain't likely to change none til I gets a grip on all this. This here is the first real chance I've had to give y'all a holler. Companies been runnin' my ass' round in circles fur the last week or more. But y'all gotta listen up cuz I'm only gonna say this once an' I ain't gonna sugar-coat it for y'all. So hush up, now 'an give a listen fur once. I know ya want me more'n y'all let on but that there ain't gonna happen. Fact is, Jory, I don wantcha y'all no more. You 'an me – we're done! We're over!"

"Excuse me" I said.

"Y'all heard me loud 'n clear. We're done! I don' love y'all no more and I don' wantcha in my life. There's jus' been too much hurt on both sides an' I'm done wit it – all of it. Can't take it no more. Best we jus' forget about it. There's too much history and too damn much heartache 'tween me 'an you, an' we ain't ever gonna be able to find our way back to where we once was. There's been a shitload of water under the bridge, too many bridges cross't 'an too damn many bridges we somehow managed ta burn behind us 'long the way. There's been too many battles fought 'tween us 'an too much shit gone down ta forget 'bout. God knows, you 'an me kept our fights purty darn clean fur the most part and the sex, good 'n dirty but it jus' ain't gonna be a enough ta see us through fur the haul."

"What are you saying? We are engaged! You have no idea what I've been through since Sybil's wedding or what I've put my parents through. My mother has told everyone she knows that I'm engaged and has started making some serious wedding plans. She's just been waiting for us to set the date. She has put together a preliminary invitation list of no less than two hundred people not counting your family and was just about to call your mother to ask her to go to work on her list! My father has had my Mustang completely rebuilt so it is road-ready and paid for a one-way ticket to Savannah. Which is not refundable! Both of my horses have been vaccinated so they can be transported across the country and I've given a commercial hauler a deposit to transport both of them as far as Savannah. The deposit, I might add, is nonrefundable! The puppy has had his last round of puppy shots and I have a certified health certificate from the vet so he can fly with me. I have given my notice at work and told most of my clients that I'm leaving at the end of the summer. What do you mean – we're over! This is crazy! Without intending to, or realizing it, my voice had noticeably risen. This was a complete surprise, and nearly took my breath away. My worst fear had suddenly been realized? Except this hadn't been one of my many fears. This hadn't been even a remote possibility. And yet, here it was staring me in the face. Once again, he had managed to catch me off guard. Of all the scenarios I had envisioned and played over and over in my mind the last few days, this hadn't been one of them. I flinched, but I was determined to maintain some degree of calm. I wouldn't give him the satisfaction of knowing he was capable of causing so much turmoil in my mind. What exactly was the name of this game?"

"You an' me ain't engaged – never was, not fur real. That there's a big step – huge - 'an I ain't takin' it wit y'all. I ain't gonna marry y'all. It ain't gonna happen – not now, not never. Y'all jus' got to let go'a that idea! We's done! I done tole y'all years ago that I'd marry ya when ya'll agreed to have my babies an' not before. That ain't news to ya'll. Seems to me now that ya don' want the job. I want a house fulla kids 'an I want it now! When we was in Denver a few weeks back, we was all tangled up in them bed sheets every minute when wasn't supposed to be some where's else. We was all hot an' sweaty an' rootin aroun' like two hogs in a slop sty. Y'all can't put no stock in what all I said in the heat of the moment. Y'all know ya can't believe a word I say when I get my blood up, that 'an other things, if y'all get my meanin'. We both said a lot of shit maybe we shouldna. Y'all got a ring on your finger? F… no! Ya got no such claim on me now do ya? An' ya never did –not really. Not like y'all think ya did. An' ya can forget 'bout that 2 carat sapphire an' diamond ring y'all got your heart set on. You're folks may have some stupid ole family rule 'bout a ring bein' two carats or more ta seal the deal 'an make it real but that's jus'plan bullshit. That there jus' ain't gonna happen!"

"I don't understand! Where is this coming from? You know I want a family some day but not anytime soon. My mother was thirty-seven when I was born and nearly forty when my brother came along. This isn't the time to think about babies! Two weeks ago you agreed with me. You know I want to finish my Masters Degree and then, go on to law school. That shouldn't be news to you. We've talked about all of this over and over again. What's changed in the last ten days?"

"Shit darlin' how much schoolin' y'all need? This here life's gonna pass y'all by iffen ya got your nose stuck in a book most of the time. Y'all gotta get yurself out inta the work force! 'Bout time ya started earnin' yur keep!" He said.

"I am in the work force; I'm a licensed trainer with 23 years of experience!"

"Teachin' them bratty, little rich kids an' their snooty, rich, bitch mommas the ass end of a horse don' 'xactly qualify as work."

"I have several clients who would disagree with you." I said.

I felt as though I had been kicked in the stomach. He had caught me completely unaware. Once more, I found myself reeling at this entirely unanticipated turn off events.

"Where are you? Are you driving?" I asked.

"I'm on the damn interstate, jus' leavin' 'Lanta 'an headin' back ta Savannah." He answered.

"What are you doing in Atlanta?" I asked as calmly as I could though my heart was racing. By this time, barely five minutes into this much anticipated conversation, I was becoming concerned. I could hear his fist pounding the dashboard and his hands slapping the steering wheel. As he continued, it occurred to me to scribble a note to my mother, asking her to get in touch with the Georgia State Highway Patrol by whatever means possible. I knew the make and model of his silver, Ford 150 as well as the Wyoming State license plate number. His truck couldn't be that hard to track; and easily distinguished by the Confederate flag hung in the rear window behind his gun rack. I couldn't be sure, but from my end of the conversation, I was convinced he was totally out of control. His temper had once again taken over and he was suffering from either complete mental exhaustion, a nervous breakdown or a cardiac episode of some sort. There was a history of heart problems in his family and even though he was just a few months shy of turning thirty, it didn't seem to be beyond the realm of possibility. I was terrified he would injure himself or someone else if he wasn't pulled over and given the opportunity to calm down and cool off.

"Company sent me on up this way on business 'an I had to be in the office first thin' Monday morning. Now I'm headin' back. Left my folks in Savannah late Sunday - ta get on up here in time. They sure as hell weren't happy 'bout me leavin 'em high n' dry like that, I don' mind telling ya'll."

"Your parents flew to Savannah?" I asked.

"Shit naw. Y'all know my folkes ain't never been in no air plane. They's scared shitless to fly. 'Don really get how that works. They drove over for the weekend in my ole man's truck. My guess is they jus' felt inclined ta come visit fur a spell. Scared the shit outta of me cuz I had no idea they was 'acomin'. Jus' sorta showed up outta no wheres. Found em' squattin' on my stoop Friday after work when I come home. I sure wish them folks would get themselves a cell phone. It would save a whole hell of a lotta of goin' back 'an forth 'an give me a heads up as to what the hell they's all doin'."

"What made them decide to visit now? I thought they never left Castlehill." I responded. "

"Appears they'all had a lot ta say, mostly 'bout you n' me n' they was of a mind ta say it all in person. Kinda up close n' personal, in my face, guess you'd say. Ever since I tol'em I had it in my mind ta marry' y'all they been on me like a duck on a June bug. Plumb wore me down wit all their jawin."

"Don't you think that's a bit of a coincidence? No sooner do you tell them we're engaged than they suddenly feel the urge to come visit you in Savannah?" I said.

"Never really gave it no thought. Takes one hell of a lotta some kinda shit ta get them ta leave home tho - 'specially for overnight. My ole man don' take too kindly to strange beds."

"What did you do?"

"Seeing as it was late 'n all, when they come over, we went on out ta the Cracker Barrel, out there on the Interstate, an' had us some supper. My ole man sure does go for them sausages n' gravy with biscuits n' corn bread. They gots the best corn bread this side of the Mississippi. I got 'em a room outta the Motel 6 there by the airport. Ain't no room for' em in my apartment. Saturday mornin' I picked 'em back up an' we jus' walked aroun' Savannah lookin' at the sights. They ain't never been thar afore this. They was jus' underfoot the whole F-ing weekend, yakkin away 'bout one thin' or 'nother. They'all got mightily pissed of when I had to take off 'an leave em standin' there so's I could drive on up here."

"What did they have to say?"

"It don' matter a whole heck of a lot what they had ta say. Y'all don' need ta know. It all made a whole hell of a lotta sense ta me tho. Really ain't none of ya'lls business. Bottom line – we's over! I done made up my mind 'bout what I want outta this here life an' y'all ain't it!. I want the real deal an' I want it now! Seems to me now you ain't the real deal. Ain't gonna happen wit ya'll. Don'tcha ya fight it now. That ain't gonna do no good either way."

With that I felt as though I had been slapped across the face – again. Where was this coming from? What had started out as a reasonably civilized conversation, though not the one I had anticipated was once again deteriorating as his voice continued to rise. His anger grew with each question I asked as I tried to determine what exactly had transpired between him and his parents. Our conversation was competing with his Cross Canadian Ragweed CD blaring loudly in the truck as he tried to shout over it and I tried to listen because of it.

"Of course it's my business! Since I'm the one getting dumped, I think I have a right to know what was said!" So many thoughts were buzzing around in my head, my pulse was pounding in my ears and my heart was racing.

"Shit naw, lets jus' leave it be. If y'all gotta know I'll tell ya but I gots a feelin' y'all ain't gonna like it none. 'An it sure as shit ain't gonna make no difference either way."

"Why don't you let me be the judge of that? Did they have anything to do with your sudden change of heart?" I answered.

"This ain't no change a heart on my part. I jus' been thinkin' over all this fur the last week, ten days an' I done made up my own mind. Done me some of that soul searchin'. Ain't nothing y'all can say gonna change it back to where it was. Iff'n y'all gots to know then I'll tell ya. 'Spose, when ya think about it, I owe y'all that much. Thin' is this, I want it all now not later an' y'all ain't inclined to give it ta me. That thar's the biggest problem much as I can see. It don' hep none that my momma jus' thinks y'all are one hoity-toity, spoiled, rich bitch. 'Ccordin' to her, y'all jus' don't suit."

"Suit what? I don't understand what that means."

"Y'all don't suit me or my family – ya ain't like us, y'all aint one of us an' it appears y'all don' wannabe or ya don' love me enough ta make the effort or make what changes in yur ways y'all gotta make ta make us work.- is what it means".

"I was under the impression I was going to marry you not your parents! We were going to start a life of our own in a new place; just the two of us! A fresh start together!

What happened to the adventure we were planning and all the hopes and dreams we had for our future?" I said. My God! Even I could hear the sudden whine in my voice.

"All them plans you 'an yur momma been makin'; them dreams was yours, not mine. Y'all got a head full of dirt road dreams that ain't never gonna 'mount ta nothin' but a crap-ton of dry dust. Don' y'all think fur a minute ya can shine me inta believin' ya was ever serious 'bout any of that ther. That's all on you , darlin' not me."

"Is it really this easy for you to just walk away from our relationship after six years?"

"My momma's of a mind y'all ain't never really gonna fit in. When ya was livin' in Bristol an' goin' ta school or when y'all came callin', ya never really tried ta make friends or reach out an' all when ya was at that fancy-ass, private college. She don' understand who gets a college degree in horse ridin anyways? Way she see it, y'all been ridin' horses all yur life. Why do ya gots ta go ta school ta learn somethin' y'all already knows? That there don' make no sense. Shit, ya could teach that course! She's of a mind that's sendin' good money after bad an' she don' think too highly of yur folks for payin' for all that nonsense. She's thinkin' they jus' always musta give inta whatever y'all wants. Yur jus' that spoiled. She thinks maybe yur folks was of a mind ta get rid of y'all or getcha otta town for some reason when they'all sent ya off ta that boardin' school back East 'an so far away from y'all's home. She jus' don't know what kinda reason they coulda had fur doin' that. It all kinda gives her pause."

"She actually said that! It was my idea in to go to boarding school near Baltimore. It was the only way I could compete in the Eastern Division. You know that! I've explained it to you several hundred times! What part of that don't you or your mother understand? It's not really that complicated."

"Seems to me, y'all are beyond hope – leastways in my mind. 'An y'all ain't no longer part of my dreams. There ain't no room for ya in my future. I'm movin' on. I jus' want outta of this here mess we's gotten ourselves inta. Can't say it no straighter 'an that. Way my momma tells it, y'all had yur nose in the air the whole time ya was down here. Never let yourself warm up ta the rest of the family. Always givin' off airs, thinkin' ya'll was better then most folks hereabouts. Talkin 'bout California all the time 'an womens rights as y'all see it. Kinda makes folks uneasy but y'all never cared 'bout that now didcha?. Ya didn't even try ta fit in down here an' that ain't gonna change. Ya'll are jus' gonna be too different for folks ta figure. Makes most folks mighty uncomfortable, is what it does. An' my momma, she don' want her granbabies getting' passin' back an' forth acrost the country from Virginia to California an' back, two three times a year."

"Again with the babies!" It was all I could do not to scream. "Seriously! Your mother doesn't want a daughter-in-law, she wants a brood mare! We agreed, years ago that we need to spend time together, just the two of us, in the same place at the same time. There is plenty of time to think about babies and who will be spending the holidays where! What possible relevance does that have now?" I could feel the anger building in me as confusion led to disbelief. I was finding it difficult to follow his line of thinking. It was too scattered. But, maybe that was the point. Considering the source, I couldn't be sure he was telling me the truth or making this all up for his own purposes. Had he thought this through or was he making it up as he went along? Was his desire to be rid of me and out of this relationship so urgent that he'd stoop so low as to lay blame on his own mother? Or was he just looking for an easy way out? Not this time! I decided I was going to make this as difficult for him as I possibly could. I wanted to lash out at him, wound him if I could and make him feel as small and humiliated as I felt at that moment.

As calmly as I could, I said, "Nat, I don't really care what people 'down there' think. Furthermore, I don't feel I have to explain myself or my parents to anyone, much less you or your parents! I don't owe anyone an explanation! I answer only to myself!" It was all dissolving now and so quickly, picking up momentum, and there didn't seem to be any way to stop it.

"Point is, iff'n y'all marry me, ya gets my family. It's a package deal. Jus' like I gots ta put up wit yur folks."

"At least my parents are fairly normal people and not seriously dysfunctional! There are no drug addicts, convicted felons or long lost relatives on parole pounding on the door demanding money, food or a convenient place to hide for a night or two. Neither do I have an eighteen year old cousin who swings by and callously drops her three illegitimate children on the front porch in the middle of the night just because she lost her job as a pole-dancer at some titty bar at Banners Corner. I'm sure her out of control cocaine habit had something to do with that! And, as a rule, my parents don't spend their weekends visiting other family members in prison, or bailing out wayward nieces and nephews for the occasional DUI. And, to the best of my knowledge, my parents do not have a close, working relationship with the local bail bondsman." I screamed.

"Hey, shit happens! That all's purty darn normal in these parts. Folks have a tendency to stray is all, kinda lose their way now 'an again. Family is family – no matter how F---ked up they is. My Momma don' get why all yur luggage gots to match. Ya know ya'll gots that brown luggage wit little; yellow L's an V's all over it. What's up with that?"

"Seriously! I can't believe we're talking about this! My parents gave me that luggage! I've taken it everywhere with me for years including boarding school and Europe."

"Ccordin' ta my momma, everythin' y'all wears gots somebody else's name on it. She swears up 'an down none of that there fancy shit is sold at WalMart 'an she outta know, seeing as how she's been workin' for'em since she was sixteen! Y'all aint got no clothes that's been made in Amurica. They's all foreign, for shits sake! My folks set a lot of store in Amurican made shit. An' that's another thin'. My Momma done tole me she offered ta speak ta her manager ta see iff'n they all had any openin's. See if she could get y'all a job; maybe as a cashier since y'all gots yourself a college degree 'an all. Or maybe in the stock room after ya graduated an' y'all jus' blew her off witout so much as a thank you! She done put herself out there ona' line ta speak up fur ya! She done tole me ya tole her y'all believed ya was over qualified! Makes her nervous is all I'm sayin'. Y'all left her feelin' like a busted 'mater on the side of the road when ya did that. Thinks y'all jus' got some pretty fancy ideas 'bout stuff an' workin at WalMart jus' ain't good enough fur ya. There's folks hereabouts that would run a plow through a mile high pile of shit fur jus' a chance ta work there what wit this lousy economy an' all. They pay real good wages after awhile. Long as y'all stick it out fur a spell. 'An ya jus' put yur nose in the air like y'all jus' run over a possum 'an messed yourself!"

"I am over qualified! Can you seriously blame me for wanting more out of life than working retail at Walmart? And that's not true! I did thank her for her offer! I can't help what she thinks. Maybe that's fine for her but I want to do something just a little more meaningful with my life! Let me get this straight, you call to tell me you're breaking up with me because your mother has a problem with my luggage and my wardrobe! Are you listening to yourself? It probably doesn't make any difference now but I know for a fact that your mother has gone through my luggage whenever I left it unattended at their house, and on more than one occasion. Who does that! Has she no respect for privacy? Don't you remember when she found a handful of condoms in my bag, and immediately onfronted you and convinced you that I was leading you morally astray! And what about all those so - called love letters she discovered in my backpack and actually sat down and read – word for word – and then ran to you. I put those old letters and postcards deep in the bottom of my bag, purposely for her to find when I realized what she was doing behind my back! If she had looked a little more closely, dug a little deeper, she would have noticed that most of those letters were at least five years old, if not older. But she didn't disappoint! Do you people really think I'm that stupid? Where did your mother ever get the idea it was okay to go pawing through other people's things because it's not okay! It's not only an invasion of privacy it's just plain rude! Speaking of your morality or the lack of it, did you ever tell your dear momma about the girl you got pregnant in Cheyenne? The same girl you refused to marry? Was she the Miss Maryland First Runner-Up or the Baltimore Bruins cheerleader who somehow ended up tending Bar in Cheyenne? Does your mother know about all the others? There have been so many it's hard for even me to keep track!

Here's a random thought. That's the perfect subject for your father's next sermon! Imagine his pseudo, righteous indignation, when his trusting, devout, unsuspecting followers, discover their beloved preacher's youngest son has the morals of a junk yard dog! That would certainly blow the hell out of his credibility, and give them pause, wouldn't it? How well would that "suit?" On the other hand, they are probably so accustomed to their teenage daughters getting knocked - up by some pimply, high school boy or a long distance trucker passing through town on his way to Kingsport that they wouldn't bother to bat an eye! And, your father is upset because he thinks my shorts are too short! I think he has much bigger problems to address; starting with his own family. Maybe he should worry a little less about the prying eyes and the opinions of his neighbors and concentrate on getting his own house in order!"

Suddenly there was complete silence. The quiet made my head hurt and my eyes burn. At some point, during this heated conversation, he had changed the CD to Chris LeDeoux and it was now the only thing I could hear, blasting in the background. I wasn't sure he was still on the line. Had he rung off? Had he dared to hang up on me? Or had I finally hit a nerve? If nothing else, I knew I had his full attention. But I was thinking much too slowly, my mind muddled and my brain completely confused as though the synapse had somehow slowed causing a temporary breakdown of connective thought. If my brain was slow, my thoughts and my ability to respond were even more sluggish. My thoughts felt thick and dull and not quickly forthcoming as though I had suddenly slipped into heavy, deep mud. While I struggled to follow his line of thinking, I only seemed to descend deeper and deeper, unable to lift myself out of the quagmire.

Very quietly and struggling with some degree of restraint he said, "Now y'all is jus' bein' plain ugly 'an I was hopin' ta avoid ugly. Sometimes y'all can be uglier than a wet cat in a wash tub! I shoulda never tole y'all 'bout that. That there's more'n ya needs to know. That ain't none of y'alls business anyways. All that shit went down long'afore I met y'all. Was no way in hell she could prove that kid was mine. Talk about bein' rode hard an' put away wet! That gal was slipperier than snot on a door knob! Any one of a hundred guys in Cheyenne coulda been that kid's daddy. She jus' got it inta her head she'd drop that load on me cuz I was the last guy she screwed afore she found out she was knocked up. That sure as shit don' make that kid mine!"

"And yet you dated her for over a year! In fact, you were seeing her when we first met in Fort Collins and you continued to see her while we were together. Is that why you refused to take a paternity test?"

"Don' matter none now. That's all over an' done wit. Done put that all behind me. My momma's worried cuz y'all seem prone to speakin' yur mind. That don't sit well wit her. She don' trust ya'll further'n she can spit! Talkin' politics, watchin' football an' drinkin' beer with the men folk jus' ain't natural. Always talkin' 'bout women's rights an' all. Thinks ya would do best ta keep your damn mouth shut an' stay in the kitchen where y'all belongs or tendin' ta my little ones. She ain't convinced ya knows your place an' y'all ain't likely to stay in it even if ya'll knew where it was ta begin wit. She don' hold wit pool playin' or poker playin' neither. Ain't fittin for a cultured Southern lady to gamble. Y'all embarrass me an' my folks. Makes me look like a fool in front of folks hereabouts. Like I ain't able ta control my woman."

"I embarrass you! Control me! You're woman! You've got to be kidding! What is this, the eighteenth century? Are you listening to yourself? No one will ever, as long as I breathe, control me. Certainly not you! Better men than you have tried and failed! I have never in my life been dependent on any man and I'm sure as hell not going to start with you! If that was your plan all along then I agree with you – we're done! I'm not a Southern lady, cultured or otherwise, though I'd be very interested to hear your mother's definition of "cultured"! And I have no intention of becoming one just to appease your momma and her warped idea of a women's place. I will not become something I am not for her or for you! Are we clear on that?"

"See. That there's jus' my point. Y'all don't fit in an' ya jus plain don' want ta. Y'all won't even try. I cen see that now. I thought once we got back home here y'alled be inclined ta try ta make it work for my sake, if nothin' else. But there ain't no way can ya find it in yourself to be jus' a little it more accommodatin'. That's why you n' me aint gonna work. We're jus' way too different. We don' want the same thins' outta life cuz y'all ain't willin'ta bend. Dang nabbit 'an Christ almighty! I gave up the Air Force for y'all! Whatcha givin' up for me? I like ta think ya could at least try ta fit in down in these parts for me. That ain't too much ta ask y'all for is it? But I guess maybe it is cuz I know ya aint gonna do that. Y'all are jus' too F… selfish!"

"I'm selfish! What am I going to give up? How dare you ask me that! Let's start with my family, the only home I've ever known, my friends, my job, my clients and my horses! I've done everything you've asked me to do. I have practically turned my self inside out and my life upside down for you! How much more ' accommodating' do I have to be? I'm prepared to give up everything I know and move 3000 miles across the country to start a new life with you and all you can talk about is babies, luggage and the clothes I chose to wear. There's something definitely wrong with you! I'm seriously beginning to believe you were dropped on your head as an infant! That's everything, that's all I have to give. Isn't that enough? I could ask you the same thing. What exactly are you prepared to give up?

Don't you dare say you give up the Air Force for me? That was your decision and yours alone. At the time, you were terrified you'd be reassigned to Minot, North Dakota if you decided to re-enlist. And the idea of living and working in North Dakota scared you senseless! I had nothing to do with that decision and you know it. Don't even try to put that on me! I suppose you also blame me for your knee injury that occurred at least six years before I even met you! While you're at it, why not blame me for losing your scholarship at nineteen as well! Before you made the decision to leave the Air Force, you couldn't even decide what you were going to wear on any given day or what to order in a restaurant let alone what you were going to do with the rest of your life, unless someone higher – up gave you a direct order! I had nothing to do with your decision to opt out of the Air Force and you know it! You certainly have acquired a somewhat selective memory in the last ten days or are you just trying to convince yourself of something else. What is really going on here? Tell me!"

Somewhere during this conversation, I had started to pace the floor in my bedroom, walking from one end to the other and back again. I stopped at one point to watch the sun rise slowly over the hills from my bedroom window. But I was outraged! Too upset and unbelieving to enjoy it. I couldn't remember ever having been so angry at anyone in my life. Of course, with all the shouting I was doing, I was acutely aware that my parents, fully awake by now, couldn't help but hear at least my end of this conversation. I could hear the juicer running in the kitchen as my mother squeezed oranges and the coffee pot bubbling as the smell of fresh coffee rose to meet me. What had precipitated his mood? Glancing at myself in a mirror as I passed, I realized I had fallen asleep wearing one of Nat's University of Tennessee t-shirts and suddenly I couldn't breathe. The room was too hot, and I wanted his t-shirt off me before I suffocated. This was too much.

"Y'all jus' bout' done wit yur little hissy-fit cuz I'm gettin' dern tired of listen' ta ya an' I done tole y'all it don' matter much ta me what all ya gots ta say right now. Y'all gots a mighty big a knot in your tail doncha? I really don' give a rats ass whatcha think cuz we're done – over. What part of that don'cha get? Ain't no amount of talkin' gonna change my mind ' bout this. No point goin over it all again an' again. Ain't gonna rehash the whole damn thing. It is what it is 'an that's over! There ain't no fixin' this, not this time cuz I'm 'bout as done wit y'all as I cen be."

Ignoring this latest outburst, my curiosity was starting to get the better of me. Now I wanted to know what exactly was behind his sudden decision. I knew him well enough to know that given time, he'd come back to me. He always did and this time wouldn't be any different. But considering everything he had said in the last few hours, did I seriously want him back! His insecurities seemed too deeply rooted. "Since you've told me everything your mother had to say, tell me what your father thinks. I would like to hear what he had to say."

"F... no! Y'all don' really wanna know. My aim ain't ta hurt ya. That's not why I give y'all holler. Can' y'all see that? Dern it! I'm trying my damnest ta be mannerly 'bout this 'an be a gentleman, an' ya'll seem determined ta just talk it all to death, aren'tcha. Why can'cha jus' let it all go? An me wit it!"

"You are a lot of things, Nat, but you could never, under any circumstances be considered a gentleman! Any gentleman would have the decency to have this conversation in person, not at six-thirty in the morning from three thousand miles away and while driving. At the risk of repeating myself, I think I have the right to know what your father said and I'm curious. You've come this far. Please, go on. What harm can it do now?"

"Okay, but 'member, y'all asked fur it. My ole man is kinda conflicted when it comes ta y'all. He don' mind ya sittin' on the couch watchin' football wit the guys 'an drinkin' beer. But he draws the line at a women gamblin'. 'Ccordin' to him, no lady ever needs be seen in no pool hall 'specially if she be kin. 'An since y'all have turned your back on Our Lord and Savior, Jesus Christ, he's mighty worried y'all be surely damned 'an on the road ta ruination; most likely on accountta' your loose upbringin' 'an all in California. He prays for ya day 'n night hopin' y'all will see the Light sooner or later an' come ta grips wit the error of yur ways. But he don' wantcha takin' me 'an his granbabies down that road witcha! That bein' said, be thinks y'all are one uppity, 'an high maintenance broad. He's of a mind, y'all are after my money."

"What money? Neither you nor your parents have any money! And you won't be salaried until you complete this phase of your internship with the railroad! Assuming you make it all the way through this process. Right now, you are the lowest man on the totem pole – the newest hire and even that position is tenuous. I seriously doubt you are even making the minimum wage."

"Everybody knows, money handlin' ain't none of y'alls business. My daddy always tole me ta never talk politics or money in mixed company. Women ain't got no head for dollars 'an cents. So y'all would take what I give ya 'an be damned glad ya got that! Iff'n y'all was ta needs more, fur whatever, like female stuff 'an all, ya let me know 'an I'll be the one ta decide whether or not ta give it. Finances is men's work! Y'all don' need to fill your head wit it. 'An my ole man surely is dead set against me signin' one of them pre-weddin' papers that yur folks got in mind. He says that's all bullshit goin' in, 'an y'all got it rigged against me. He don' believe y'all trust me ta manage our affairs an' your folks sure as hell don' trust me neither wit whatever in the hell they gots goin' on."

"It's called a prenuptial agreement! It has nothing to do with you and me. It's just good, sound, business sense. It's between my parents and their lawyers not us. We've had this conversation before and I thought, by now, you understood. But obviously you still don't get it! When my mother first mentioned the possibility of a per-nuptial agreement to you, jokingly, as I recall, you refused to consider it. As a result, my parents changed their will and their trust. It's a moot point. No one is asking you to sign anything! Why should my parents, who have worked hard all their life for what they have, suddenly agree to sign half of it over to you? They don't even know you! They have only met you two or three times! You haven't actually spent any time with them. Think about it! It doesn't make any sense! You know absolutely nothing about investments and even less about real estate or business. The Air Force has paid your bills for you, for God's ake, since you were nineteen! My parents are involved in so many different things, you are absolutely the last person on this earth qualified to manage all of their interests! You are in way over your head on that score and it will never happen. You can get that idea out of your head! It has nothing whatsoever to do with whether or not they trust you!"

"Thar! – that's what I'm takin' 'bout! It don' surprise me one bit that y'all agree wit'em an' not me! Iff'n we was ever ta get married, y'all gotta get yursef accustomed ta seein' thins' my way. I knew from the get go, y'all would take yur folkes side 'an not mine. If I was of a mind ta go through wit this, which I ain't, my folks come up wit a plan fur us, jus' ta give us a leg up, but I knows y'all ain't inclined ta agree anyways so thar ain't no point in tellin' ya 'bout their plan."

"No – please – continue - this is fascinating! Tell me. What was their plan for our future? I'm dying to know."

"Well, y'all know my Meemaw is getting' up there in years. She's doin' damn poorly 'an getting' a bit addled 'an …"

"What's a meemaw?" I don't know what that means." I interjected.

"Meemaw is my momma's momma. Mamaw is my Daddy's momma! Why the hell can'thca get at least that much straight in yur head! Anyways, she ain't feelin' up ta snuff these days cuz she's jus' plain as old as the hills. Shit, that woman moves slower than a slow movin' turtle 'ttemptin' ta cross a road! She sure has seen a lotta shit in her day, that's for sure. My folks went ahead 'an put her inta one of them homes fur ole folks but they can't afford ta keep her in there no more. So they up an' moved her inta that little house kinda back yonder on their property. Y'all know the one I mean? Ya seen it when y'all was up ta the house once."

"That's a house! I thought it was an abandoned duck blind!"

"Shit naw! My ole man got it all fixed up real nice fur her. He put in some insulation 'an even a winda. There's a little room in the back for MeeMaw cuz she don' need much now adays, 'an my momma picked up one of them pull out beds, coupla years back that theys' agreed give us. Got it fur next ta nothin' a somebodies yardsale. Even got's a turlet in there now. It's darn small but it'll do us fur the time bein'. Least til we figure out what's what. My ole man even got MeeMaw a hot plate 'an one of them little iceboxes fur her medication 'an all. Point is, they moved her inta there 'an she's as happy now as a huckleberry up a hog's ass. She's jus' pleased as plump ta be back wit her kin. Then my ole man, outta the kindness of his heart, give her a few yardbirds of her own. She swears up 'an down them birds give her some kind'a comfort, watchin' 'em 'an all. She sets out there on the porch in that ole rocker of her's all damn day jus' watchin' them birds pickin' 'an peckin 'round in the dirt."

"Yardbirds! Your father stuck pink, plastic flamingoes in the dirt for her to look at all day!"

"Flamingoes! Who said anythin' 'bout flamingoes! I'm talkin' yardbirds, darlin'! Yardbirds - them is chickens!"

"Oh, no. I draw the line at chickens! When we lived in San Francisco our neighbors kept chickens in their backyard and I can still smell that horrible chicken smell and hear all that noise. If your Meemaw is so enamored with her yardbirds, she can take care of them herself!"

"Y'all ain't makin' this easy are ya? My folkes been makin' her walk across't the pasture every evening ta take her meals wit 'em 'an that's gettin her out 'an doin' her a world of good getting' a little bit of exercise most evenings. She's sure as shit got a shitload of gumption for such an ole broad! She may be older 'an God but she's sprightly as hell. They was thinkin' you 'an me could move in there wit her 'an y'all could take care of her til she passes. See ta her needs, give her her pills 'an medicine 'an such when it's time 'an every once in a while, see she gets a bath. Once she's gone on to the Lord you 'an me could have the house free of charge. My folkes don' even want no rent from us. They swear up 'an down they won't charge us nothin'. "

"Are you out of your mind? First your mother wanted a brood mare and now she wants a care giver! I thought we were going to live in Savannah! I don't believe this! You haven't spent any time looking for a larger apartment for us in Savannah, have you? And, you haven't looked into any of the stables or boarding facilities in the area either. Lies, lies and more lies. Don't you ever get tired of it all?"

"Hell no, darlin'! That ain't gonna happen. I'm shit outta Savannah soon as I finish wit this here internship wit the company. ! Ain't'got no call stayin' there no more. That's jus' too big a city fur the likes of me. Too many folks jus' wonderin' 'round, too many damn cars 'an too damn much noise. I'm a country boy, born 'an raised, so I put in fur a transfer soon as I can to somewhere's closer ta my folkes home. Companies got itself a major hub the next town over from my folks. Sounds like I'm gonna travelin' a lot my first year or so 'an I don' want y'all stayin' by yurself. It would be better all 'round if I knew y'all was safe 'an had someone close by ta look after ya. 'An once my babies start acomin' my momma'll be close by ta help y'all. Sounds like a hell of a sweet deal to me. They's being mighty generous jus' offerin. Never offered the like to my brother. My folks are getting up there in years too so y'all can tend ta them when their time comes."

"You do have an older brother, how does he fit into this plan of theirs? And please don't tell me that since he found Jesus in the dark recesses of a coal mine his devotion now is to God above all else and not his family!"

"My folks are of a mind he ain't too dependable. They don' trust they can count on him none. He ain't up for the job anyways. He's got his band he's tryin' ta get offa the ground, playin' in some local bars 'an such 'an he's takin' to preachin' some hereabouts like my ole man. He's of a mind ta spread the Gospel where he can. Lots of Godless folks in these parts he feels sure as hell need savin'. 'An another thin', my uncle – he's got himself a farm of sorts not too fur a piece from my folks. It ain't' fancy a'tall, not what ya'll are used to, but he's got himself an empty stall an' a coupla of fenced acres. Outta nowheres, he up 'an offered ta letcha put Odie up in there, if y'all are of a mind ta. He ain't got no help so's y'all are gonna have ta get yurself over there ta feed him 'an all. The boy he had fur a bit, helpin' him out jus' up an' left him high an' dry few weeks back. But leastwise Odie'd have a place ta run – stretch his legs 'an all. The bad news is, he ain't got no room for two horses so we would have ta sell Sunny, 'an see jus' how much we could get fur her, cuz there ain't no place for her 'an we could sure use the money"

Where to begin? I was seething, almost too angry to speak! I suddenly couldn't get the words out of my mouth. Telling me what he thought I should or should not do with my horses were fighting words as far as I was concerned. Would he stoop so low as to actually hold my horses' ransom? He had finally hit a nerve. I was, at one point, during this conversation as mad as hell, now, listening to him; this entire conversation changed course and became laughable, almost comical. Had he always felt this way? We had talked about all this over the years and none of this had ever come up before now or to this extent. Why now?

"Let me perfectly clear. First of all, I have no intention of living in a rickety lean-to covered with a piece of rusty, corrugated tin, salvaged from the local dump on your parent's property or anywhere else within a one hundred mile radius of your parents in Castlehill. It's just a sleepy little town where nothing happens and nothing ever changes. It's nothing more than an obscure little dot on the map either lost or hiding somewhere in the late nineteenth century. The biggest thing to happen in that town in the last one hundred years was the installation of a single stop light across the street from the high school! Nor will I ever agree to live in a house on wheels that can be conveniently hauled further up the riverbank on the off-chance that the creak may rise. Frankly, I don't want your parents anywhere near my children! Yes, someday I want a husband, and a home of my own. And off course, I want children. Right now, I am more convinced than ever that I don't want yours! I am deeply concerned about the current, somewhat sorry state of your gene pool and, to be perfectly honest, it scares me to death. I have nightmares. I'm terrified any child of ours may be born with webbed feet and hands, a lazy eye or a cavernous void where its brain should be. You forget I've met your brothers spawn! I will never agree to look after your ailing, aged, grandmother or her yardbirds until she dies nor will I care for your parents as they age. And, I refuse to pop out a baby every year just to satisfy your mother! If you are traveling – so be it. I am perfectly capable of taking care of myself – I've been on my own since I was fifteen! I don't need to live next door to your parents for my own protection much less your peace of mind. How many times have I told you, I have a trust fund? I don't need your money and I certainly don't want theirs! Furthermore, and please listen carefully, because this is important. I will never put Odie out to pasture or in some rundown stall, in the middle of God knows where! He is a highly competitive dressage horse that I have spent years training and I would never do that to him. He is nationally ranked in his own right and far too valuable to me. You don't do that to an animal of his caliber! What are you thinking? And Sundae is not for sale nor will she ever be! Are you hearing me on this? I can care for both of my horses without any help from you or your family!"

"That thar ain't no surprise ta me. Y'all be singin' ta the choir on that one. I knew ya wouldn't go fur it. That thar's another reason we's finished. 'Ccordin to my ole man, them two horses of yurs are mighty costly ta keep up. Jus' a money pit – what wit feed 'an the vet 'an their care an' all. Plus they gots to have shoes put on kinda regular or leastways every now an' again. Don't believe we gots a soul 'round these parts knows how ta do that! Don' matter much cuz me 'n you ain't got that kinda money. Y'all ain't gonna be competin' much anymore anyways. Time to hang up them fancy-ass spurs of yours, darlin'. No more of them classy horseshows or hightailing' it all over the country an' on up ta Canada fur one horse show after t'other. Nobody gots that kinda money, leastwise me. Y'all gots to find yurself another hobby of some sort. Somethin' else ta occupy yur time like raising my babies 'an tendin' my home. An' y'all gots to 'member, iff'n we was ta get married, what all is yurs is mine 'an I cen do whatever in the freakin' hell I want wit them two critters of yurs 'an whatever else y'all gots comin' yur way. Them two horses are jus' as spoiled as y'all are ta my way of thinking."

Now he had gone too far! Would he seriously threaten me with my horses? I had been in the stall at 3 o'clock in the morning the night Sundae was born and I had bottle fed her for days when her mare had colicked. Selling her was out of the question. She was mine and she always would be. This was a deal breaker as far as I was concerned. Had he always felt this way? So he so desperate to be rid of me that he had decided to throw all this out now? Then it dawned on me. The proverbial light bulb snapped on. Of course. It was suddenly so clear. Why hadn't I seen it earlier? His parents had finally gotten to him. It was that simple. They had had an entire weekend to convince him not to marry me and they had succeeded. They had mutually agreed I didn't "suit." I wasn't marriage material. No wonder they had driven all the way to Savannah from Castlehill. They were terrified! I was the enemy in their camp. Too different and horror of horrors, a Yankee! They knew I would never fit in and the differences I brought to their community could very well ostracize them. How would they ever explain me? They would never tolerate a Yankee in their midst! They, like him, were too insecure to take that risk. They had spent the weekend twisting my words and his mind and I hadn't been there to defend myself. That was obviously their intention; isolate him, get him alone and then break him down. And he had fallen for it! I'm sure he didn't even see it coming. According to him, it was nothing more than an opportunity for a casual visit. What a pitiful excuse for a man he was. How pathetic and weak can one man be? Insecurity and control are one thing but continuing to let someone else do your thinking for you was beyond pitiful. Was his instinct to run, to escape any responsibility, that strong? They knew me well enough to know that I would never agree to their so-called plan for our future. They had forced my hand. They knew I would never willingly agree to move to Castlehill, live in a house of their choosing, and care for his aging grandmother while working the floor at WalMart. Nor would I ever agree give up my horses or make even the slightest concession as to their care. That was their ace in the hole. Given the choice of their son or my horses, my horses would win hands down every time. I had to give them credit; at least they knew that much about me. They were good! They knew their son far better than I and they knew exactly which buttons to push and how hard to push them. They had gotten to him and they had shamelessly and purposely set me up. I had talked Nat into going to college against their wishes years ago and in their minds, that would be the full extent of my influence and the last. I had picked up on the fact, years ago, that his mother, as quiet as she was, was controlling but I clearly had no idea of the full extent of her influence. How could I have been so blind? Not only blind but a fool! What surprised me more than anything was how easily he had given into their pressure. Could he really be that easily manipulated? What else did they have on him? Why did he acquiesce so willingly and so completely? Something still wasn't right. All of this, coming up now just didn't add up. There had to be more. We'd come this far, why not finish it? A suspicion was forming in the back of my mind and the seed of an idea seemed to take root and grow ever so slowly. The more I listened to him, the faster it grew until I couldn't ignore it. It was incomplete and ambiguous, making it difficult to grasp but I couldn't brush it aside. I had to confront it the minute it was fully formed; I knew instinctively it was the truth. Of course! At this point, what did I have to lose?

"Who is she Nat? Who is it this time? You lie to your parents and you lie to mine. You lie to me and most importantly, you lie to yourself. It's pathological! I have never understood how you do it – how you keep all those lies straight in your head! Now you suddenly realize all those lies have finally caught up with you and you are tangled in a vicious web of your own making with no way out. Struggle all you want but for once in your sorry, pathetic, dysfunctional life, tell me the God's honest truth. The deception stops now! Who is she? I demanded.

His hesitation told me I was right. He paused, vacillating once again between a lie and the truth, unsure how to proceed. Trying to decide which way to go – would I believe the truth, now, if I heard it or would another lie suffice? Which would I be most likely believe? And more importantly, which would be the easiest for him? He never could think very fast on his feet and I had finally managed to catch him off guard. The tables had finally turned in my favor.

"Why should y'all give a damn who she is. I ain't piddlin' 'round wit y'all no more. Ain't none of yur business what I do from now on. It ain't no longer any concern of y'alls far as I can see. All's ya gotta know is I done found somebody else 'an I'm in love wit her – not you! Whatcha gotta torment yurself fur? Why y'all makin' this all so damn hard on yurself 'an me. Y'all don' really wanna know anyways." He said, barely above a whisper. His tone of voice may have become quiet and somewhat conciliatory but his confession hung heavily between us.

"I'm sorry, I disagree. I would like to hear what you have to say. I really want to know. I'm curious to know just how far you'll go with this particular lie. Since we're over, what possible difference could it make? Is she that pear-shaped brunette that was sitting on your lap in the photo posted on Facebook a few months ago? The woman you swore up and down you didn't know and then finally, when you realized you had been caught, and I had seen the picture of the two of you, reluctantly admitted to knowing? Caught - dead to rights, weren't you?"

There was unmistakable panic in his voice when he finally spoke and I could sense his desire to flee, if he could, but to where? He was confined to his truck. I was suddenly so grateful I was safely ensconced in my room three thousand miles away and not in his truck with him because I knew I might find myself on the receiving end of his anger. He was out of control; and I knew first hand, that he was more than capable of physical violence. Perhaps he was having a nervous breakdown or some sort of mental meltdown. Given the extent of his anxiety, he shouldn't be driving. He'd kill himself or someone else if he wasn't stopped and soon. The fear of finally being caught in a lie and the shame in admitting it, as difficult as that was for him had finally overwhelmed him. I wasn't surprised when he said, "That thar would be her. I ain't gonna deny it. Not now leastways. It don' matter who in the hell she is. You 'an me is over, done wit, the end."

"Tell me, how long have you been seeing her? How long has this been going on behind my back?"

Again hesitation, a lengthy pause, the CD playing loudly in the background and then finally, 'bout eighteen months or more. So what? We ain't ever in the same place, you 'an me! What the hell y'all 'xpect me ta do? A mans got needs, ya know. It don' matter now anyways!"

I had anticipated another short-lived infatuation or a weekend indiscretion but eighteen months! That was an affair! On some level, I realized this was inevitable.

Why hadn't I seen it coming? I had always gone along, ready to concede or at the very least, look the other way and believe anything and everything he said. Not this time and not today. Today was the day to stop deluding myself and stop making excuses for him. Reality, no matter how harsh, has to be better than false hope or delusions. My shoulders were tense, my jaw was involuntarily clenching and looking down, I realized my hand had formed a fist threatening to crush my phone.

"If that's true, why did you even bother to come to Sybil's wedding in Denver?"

"I wanted ta see y'all one more time is all. You 'an me gots a lot of history between us. We'alls been through a whole hell of a lot together over the las' coupla years. I figure leastways I owned ya that much. I was gonna tell y'all when we was there but it jus' never come up. Never seemed ta be the right time. We was always so damn busy wit one thin' or 'nother when we was there or we was rollin' in the hay which don' 'xactly leave much room fur talkin'. Y'all looked so damn fine. Near took my breath away. Time was when me 'an you was good together. But not now. Thin's jus' up 'an changed, is all, 'an for no good reason that I can figure."

"For no good reason! Seriously! – let's start with your on-going affair with another woman for over a year! How's that for a reason? So, instead of telling me, when we were together in Denver, you decide to propose! Are you listening to yourself? Do you actually think I would believe anything you have to say at this point? Why can't you admit it! You wanted to sleep together one more time. You wanted to get laid! What was that? Break up sex? One last roll in the hay for ole time's sake only you neglected to tell me it was the last time! Who does that? You knew when you arrived in Denver you were going to break it off but once there you couldn't do it! When I left you at the Airport two and a half weeks ago, I would never have imagined, even in my wildest dreams, that it would be the last time I would ever see you. You knew and you just smiled that wicked smile of yours because you had a secret that had nothing to do with keeping our engagement quiet. You pulled it off. You came for a good party, all the free food, and drinks you could consume and a woman in your bed. You got it all! It really doesn't matter to you what woman is in your bed as long as she's willing. You're not that particular! And, if she's not willing, you have every confidence you can slap her into submission. Am I right? You're parents must be so proud! I should have known. In fact, I think I did know, on some level. I felt a shadow pass over me in the Denver Airport and with it, goose-bumps that I blamed on the air-conditioning. It was one of the few occasions that I did not listen to my instincts. I felt this coming; I just didn't want to believe it. You're good; I have to give you credit for that. You had me fooled and at the same time, you made a fool out of me; me and how many others? This has to be their idea. Your mother and this woman are behind this aren't they? You don't have the cajones to come up with this on your own. I'm just surprised it took you this long to succumb to their pressure - again. You really are an unscrupulous bastard and an unprincipled son-of-a bitch. Two weeks ago I would never have believed you were capable of such blatant depravity. "

"No point resortin' ta name callin,' darlin'. Not real sure what y'all jus' said there but that alls jus' water offen a ducks back, far as I cen see. Truth is, I wanted ta see y'all one more time, is all. Hey, cen y'all blame me? Besides I had me a ticket all paid fur; bought it some months back. Figured I might as well go after all an' get this squared away once 'an fur all. Ya'll gotta admit we was always damn good together in the sack or anywhere's else - truth be told. Besides, I had a blast with y'all at the weddin. Kinda like ole times. Me 'an you, dancing, drinkin','carin' on 'an all. Don' know 'bout y'all but I had one hell of a good time. I jus' tole ya what y'all what wanted ta hear, is all. It all jus' come pourin' outta my mouth afore I could stop it. How was I 'sposed ta know y'all was gonna run with it? Next thin' I knows, y'all are tellin me yur shoppin' fur a weddin' dress an' ya gots a gaggle of bridesmaids all lined up choppin' at the bit. I purely hate it when ya'll jus run off in another direction all by yourself.! I don' want a big, fancy shin-dig like that. That ain't me! When I get married, ta whoever, the two of us is jus' gonna go on down ta the county courthouse. Then maybe swing by the Cracker Barrel, in next town over, fur sumthin' like supper. Me being a veteran 'an all, chances are I cen get us a free meal. 'An then y'all start goin' on askin" me 'bout bread baskets 'an tablecloth colors 'an all that kinda shit. I don' give a God damn an' I ain't doin' it fur y'all or any body else. That ain't nothin' but a bad waste of hard earned money an' fur what?""

"Your arrogance has no limit! It's boundless! And is only matched by the extent of your insecurities. Your desire to escape this situation or lie your way out of it without blame is despicable. I don't know how you do it! Somehow you always manage to lay blame at my feet and come out completely unscathed. The truth, the real truth, not just your version, is either so far behind you or so far ahead of you, you wouldn't recognize it if it ever did catch up with you. It's never actually with you because you're out of synch with reality! But not this time!"

"Shit, darlin', now that all ain't fair ! I'm jus' a simple country boy, born an' bred in the South an' I do believe I been called a whole lot worser 'n pathetic. Y'all gots to go a ways further than that iff'n ya wanna get ta me."

"Let's be perfectly candid, here for once. I have no intention of going any further. I'm done! For once, I agree with you. You get a big atta-boy for this! Keep going, you're obviously on a roll! Now that I have had a thorough dressing down is there anything you may have left out? If so, now is the time. By all means, continue. You are unquestionably simple and you could be the poster boy for redneck country! Does this woman know you couldn't go through with our break up and instead proposed marriage? Does she know we slept together in Denver? No wonder your parents drove all the way to Savannah! You obviously deviated from their plan, again, and they will not tolerate that! You've gone against their wishes in the past and look what happened. You enlisted in the Air Force, finished your tour of duty with a marketable skill and completed you education! Quelle horreur! Both of which they would consider two strikes against you – don't push it to a third! But tell me, I'm curious, why did it take you this long to find the courage to make this call? And why bother to call at all? It would have been so much easier to just send a text. Simple, clean and to the point with as little actual interaction as necessary – no confrontation and no drama. You have always been more comfortable with the distance a phone call provides. That's more your style. You certainly can't be having a problem with your conscience because you clearly don't have one!"

"She ain't behind this. Wouldn't never occur ta her ta tell me what ta do or say. She knows jus' what all I wants her to know 'an this ain't none a her business. She 'don ask lot of dumb questions 'an she don' make lots of demands. She takes me as I am. An' right now she's as happy to have me as a fat hound with two peters. Her 'an me is two of a kind. Kinda like pie 'an ice cream. Me 'an you was more 'n like two cats in a bag most of the time. What went on 'tween you 'an me in Denver ain't none of her business, is all. Y'all may as well know, my folks brung her along wit 'em ta Savannah. That was the plan. That's why they come on over when they did. She's been fixin' ta move in wit me fur over a year now so's we all spent most the weekend gettin' her situated in my apartment. My roommate done lit out a few months back so's she's movin' in. It's over 'tween you 'an me ! How many times I gots to tell ya? What part of this ain't ya'll getting'?

"Finally – we agree on something! You can bet your sainted Meemaw we're over! There is nothing left between us. Your arrogance has seen to that!" I was exhausted from the lack of sleep and emotionally drained. We had been on the phone for nearly three hours and I wanted this conversation to end, the sooner the better. I couldn't do this any longer. He had clearly made up his mind and I had finally, at long last, made up mine. This was undoubtedly one of the few occasions and the last that we would be in complete agreement. .

"Listen up, now. I care fur y'all. I really do! But carin' 'an lovin' ain't one 'an the same thin'. Carin' ain't gonna hold fur a lifetime! So, if it's cool wit ya'll, I want us ta part friends. I wanna be able ta give y'all a holler every now 'an again ta check up on ya. See how y'all are getting' on. Ya gotta know, I'll love y'all the rest of my life. I'll love ya till my dyin day, 'an that's the God's honest truth. Hand ta God, on that one. I jus' can't live wit y'all. You 'an me ain't likely to make it in long run anyways cuz love's so damn complicated. It ain't gonna work for us. Love'll never be enough for me an' you. I know this all most probably comes as a shock to y'all; but I gotta sense fur these things. It's gonna be mighty hard on ya not havin' me in yur life. I get that! But y'all gots move on. Someday, give it acoupla years, yur gonna meet somebody better suited, is all. Life goes on, darlin'. This ain't the end of the world. Y'all gots alotta good thins' workin' for ya. Shit, y'all gotta lotta good years ahead, I betcha find some guy in no time even though the guy, whoever in the hell the dumb bastard is, ain't gonna measure up ta me 'tall. I knows deep down it ain't gonna be easy on ya. Truth is, 'an I'm sure y'all would agree, I was the best damn thin' that ever happened ta ya. I know y'all are disappointed but, hey, y'aller gonna land on yur feet. It's kinda like losing a shiny new penny, losing me 'an all, but I promise I'll be there fur ya' whatever y'all need. Ya ain't that old , ya'll gots time for Christ sake! Best we part friends. Y'all gots ta let me go. Me 'an you are jus' way too different. 'An like I said, ya'll 'us' don' suit no more."

"We are indeed different people! I don't know who you are anymore! And I'm beginning to think I never really knew you. You're sick, Nat. You're a very sad, sick person and you don't even know it. How do you convince yourself you are blameless? You have cheated on me and yet somehow you've managed to make this all my fault! I don't know how or when you became so twisted but you desperately need help. You should seriously consider checking yourself into the VA Hospital for a psychiatric analysis. It may very well be that you are hopeless and beyond any sort of help at this point. Unfortunately, you will not be getting what help you need from me because I'm done. I feel sorry for you, I really do. But right now, that's all I feel. But rest assured that won't last long. So, do not, under any circumstances call me again or attempt to communicate with me in any way and that includes texts and emails. We will never, never be friends or anything close to it. I never want to hear from you again for any reason! Are you clear?"

"Y'all make me so damn mad sometimes I could jus' spit in the wind! Y'all gots to ask yur questions 'an I answered 'em plain 'an honest. I got me one last question 'an it's damn important so I gotta know once 'an fur all. So here it is. Are y'all pregnant?"

"Seriously, what does that have to do with anything? Why would you ask that? What possible difference could that make – now?" I was shocked! "You used something in Denver. I know that for a fact because for some reason, your choice of birth control seems to be my responsibility to provide. Whether your mother chooses to believe it or not."

"Think again, darlin'. Think long 'an hard. Do y'all ever recollect me askin' fur it? Ya always manage ta get yourself so darned hot 'n bothered an' all worked up y'all woulda not a noticed.! "Specially after the weddin'. Maybe I used somethin' an' then again maybe I didn't. Don' reckon ya'll will ever really know fur sure till some times passes. Ya gotta admit darlin' I'm good – probably the best y'all ever had or ever will have anytime soon, truth be told!"

"For the love of God! Spare me your self-serving accolades! Why don't you take a victory lap around the state of Wyoming or give yourself a parade and see how many women show up to shout your praises. You may not realize it but you have left an impressive trail of broken hearts and angry women in your wake. What exactly are you implying?"

"All's I'm sayin is, if y'all are pregnant 'an iffen the kids mine, I'll marry ya tomorrow. I'll sign up for the long haul 'an even go through wit whatever rodeo you're momma's been planning. Tell ya what, I'll forget everythin' I jus' said 'an it'll be me 'an you an' the kid."

"Gosh! There's an offer worthy of consideration! Let me think about that for a minute. Are you out of your mind? Let me get make sure I completely understand because this is the last conversation we will ever have, and I want to make sure I'm clear on exactly what's going on here.

Don't bother to correct me if I'm wrong. We haven't spoken to each other for over ten days, at your insistence. After which, you finally bring yourself to call at five-thirty in the morning, from your truck, to break up with me. You propose marriage to me in Denver even though you are obviously involved in a relationship with a woman you have been seeing behind my back for the last eighteen months. Your parents believe I'm an over-educated, selfish, money-grubbing, overdressed, self-centered, feminist, Yankee bitch with what they can only describe as an unhealthy obsession with horses and a desire to corrupt you – morally. As if that's even possible!

Southern Discomfort

I have absolutely no intention of spending the rest of my life in a run-down shack or a double-wide mobile home. I refuse to live in a house on wheels in your parent's backyard, and in the middle of Cabbageville. I am not a care-giver for the elderly, or a baby-machine and I do not tend yardbirds or livestock. Which is, no doubt, is a constant source of disappointment and not exactly what your parents had planned for you or me or us. To add insult to injury, your parents have obviously taken it upon themselves to provide you with a more suitable mate to whom you are, no doubt related, and who just happens to be everything I am not. Not only is she infinity more qualified as a homemaker but most likely a mindless twit without an original thought of her own. And you – as charming as you believe you are, go along with your parents because you are incapable of putting two coherent sentences together without a great deal of difficulty and obviously lack, among other things, a spine, which would allow you to, once in your life, stand on your own two feet. You have absolutely no integrity, no soul and no heart! And you don't even have the decency to break up with me face to face after all the years we've been together! Nothing means anything to you! You want me to park Odie in some broken down stall somewhere in the middle of nowhere to save money and then turn around and sell Sundae to make money. You will graciously assume the responsibility for my finances as well as my parents interests because that's the way your patents do things and that's all you know. If it works for them, it has to work for us. What's wrong with that! Your mother wants me to have a baby, of your blood, which in itself, is terrifying, sooner rather than later while tending her aged, ailing mother on my days off from working in the stockroom at WalMart. Your father intends to control how much leg I may or may not show on any given occasion, when wearing shorts while encouraging me to convert to whatever religion he is advocating this week. Perhaps he should get his own house in order and stop trying to please your prying neighbors! And, if it isn't too much to ask, could I quietly change my current political affiliation and become a card carrying Democrat just to appease the neighbors and keep the gossip in the neighborhood to a minimum thereby eliminating any further embarrassment to your parents. How am I doing so far? I'm to give up poker, pool, all competitions and horse shows and don a straw sunhat and start growing vegetables, preferably 'maters or beans. And, in my spare time, I can help your mother turn her cucumbers into quarts and quarts of pickles, in anticipation of the annual year end Church Bizarre and then fry globs of dough in pork fat. If I truly apply myself, I may even learn the technique required to properly de-bone a catfish prior to frying in lard because that makes for mighty fine eatin'. Now, stay with me because this is the best part. If I am pregnant, you will forget everything you have just said over the last three hours and, as delusional as you are, agree to abandon this woman, who just moved in with you, and marry me anyway! And, if, for some reason, I am not pregnant, you would like some sort of guarantee that we will remain 'friends' because you will love me for the rest of your life and until your dying day. You're just that kind of a stand-up guy. That about sum it up? Are you out of your mind? I screamed.

"Since we're doin' this, goin' down this here road 'an all, may as well get it all out in the open 'an get it done wit one way or 'thuther. My folks wanna know whacha y'all wanna do with all that crap ya been storin' in their garage. When ya graduated from Virginia Intermount, 'an high tailed it back home ta California from Bristol, ya left purty near yur whole damn apartment wit them 'an now they want all yur shit otta their garage. They knows some folks in their church thats been burned outta their house 'an now they ain't got nothin'. My momma thinks it would be the Christian thing ta do 'an more 'an fittin' if ya was ta give them yur stuff, them bein' so needy 'an all. Y'all ain't usin' it. That shits been sittin' in there this long, jus' getting' dusty 'an all, 'an ya ain't likely ta come back for it, 'specially now. Y'all good wit that?"

"If those people are truly in need, your parents can give them everything I left behind. There's nothing I need or I can't replace but somewhere, in one of those boxes, there is a little black, mink teddy bear on wheels. It's a small child's pull toy with a string. It was a baby shower gift to my mother just before I was born and I've always taken it with me, wherever I go. I'd like it returned to me."

"Shit! That there ain't gonna happen, darlin'. When my ole man was goin' through all them boxes a yurs he found that stupid toy y'all are so fond of, even fixed one of them little wooden wheels that was broke 'an then he give it to some little kid here 'bouts he figured could get some fun otta it." He said.

"And just when exactly, did your father take it upon himself to go pawing through my things; things that obviously don't belong to him and without asking my permission? Or was it your mother? What is it with you people! She has a history of rummaging around in my bags when she thinks I'm not looking. Hardly a Christian thing to do! I can only imagine what she found this time and what she intends to do with whatever she discovered. That toy does not belong to your father! It was not his to give away!"

"Hey, what cen I tell ya? Shit happens. It's over 'an done – gone. Happened a long time go. I'm thinkin' that 'bout covers it. Ya know, y'all shoulda never given up on the law. Ya got a real flare fur it - a real good way with words. Y'all sure cen string 'em along. As long as ya are clear where we stand, then I'm good. Meanwhile, it goes without sayin', y'all are startin' ta sound jus' like yur momma. Half the time, I gots no idea what in the hell she's sayin' 'an most the time I don't get her meanin'. An' whys she all the time droppin' in all them foreign words like I'm 'sposed to know what in the hell shit she's talkin'! Makes me wonder if she's doin' that on purpose, jus' makin' a fool outta me. Seems to me y'all are startin' ta take after yur momma in a mighty big way."

"I wouldn't have it any other way! I'm actually very flattered to be so favorably compared to my mother. I'll take that as a compliment. The fact remains, you have finally broken us! I can see now that the damage you have done over the last six years to our relationship with your deceit and lies and cheating is irreparable. I know, that word has five syllables which is probably more than you can handle. Take your time, sound it out and if all else fails, Google it! You lie as easily as you breathe! You coast through life on your looks and your perceived sexuality with absolutely no regard for anyone but yourself. You have no honor and no integrity! If you woke up this morning determined to break up with me, consider it done. I have successfully been dumped. I go willingly with a clear conscience and only one regret. And that is, the day I ever laid eyes on you. As tempted as I am right now, I was raised to believe it was extremely rude to hang up on anyone regardless of the circumstances – even you – even now. So, if you will excuse me, I have heard all I care to hear. This conversation and this relationship are over! This entire conversation has made me feel dirty and I suddenly feel the need for a long, hot bath, preferably with bubbles. As far as I'm concerned, you and the horse you rode in on can ride straight to hell!"

One last thing and listen very carefully because this is important. What I do or do not do from this day forward is no longer any of your business. You have just forfeited that right. Whether I'm pregnant or not, is no longer any concern of yours. While you're thinking about that, see if you can process this. If I'm pregnant through your own vanity and neglect what I chose do about it is no longer any concern of yours. Just as what you do from now on is no concern of mine. As you know or maybe you don't know, I am Pro-Choice and a staunch advocate of Roe vs. Wade and abortion, like my grandmother and my mother before me. I also support adoption and foster-parenting. There are far too many children in this country who need loving parents. Why in the world would I risk having yours? Think about it, darlin'. You - think long and hard! Rest assured, if I am pregnant, you will never know. Live with that!"

Chapter Twenty Five

Before I slipped into my mother's Jacuzzi tub, nearly overflowing with steaming hot water and the welcoming scent of lavender oil, I tore Nat's t-shirt off and threw it across the stone floor. It was no longer a treasure; it was offensive. The smell of B.B.Q. sauce, pine needles and chocolate that lingered now made me nauseous.

My father, had hastily retreated to the sanctity of his library seeking quiet among his journals and books and solace from the hysterics and loud voices emanating from my bedroom. My mother, as usual, was probably seated at the table in the breakfast room with her tea, perusing the Arts & Leisure section of the New York Times and trying very hard not to listen to the earsplitting, window -rattling noise coming from my room just above her.

I slid into the tub, welcoming the warmth of the hot water rushing over me; giving all eighteen jets the opportunity to sooth my cramped muscles and relax my frayed nerves from eighteen different angles. I was determined to steam, boil and pommel every toxic remnant of him out of every pore in my body, to be rid of him – forever. All the pressurized jets had been strategically aimed at specific muscle groups. I glanced again in the direction of his t-shirt, crumpled in a pile across the floor. Suddenly nothing else seemed quite as important as what to do with it. How to be rid of that too? That was all that remained. All that was left of him, with the exception of my memories – such as they were and collectively there weren't that many. I didn't have any Valentines, or birthday cards or Christmas cards and even fewer photographs of the two of us together. No theatre Playbills, probably because had never attended the theatre together and no concert stubs or tattered souvenir programs from Frontier Days in Cheyenne. Six years and so little to show for it. Rather than go over everything that had been said between us during the previous three hours, it seemed crucial to come to some decision as to how to dispose of anything that held any association with him. How to physically rid myself of him completely and then set about erasing the memory of him from my mind. He had forced my hand. I knew, without question that I had made the right decision, under the circumstances and given everything he had just said. He hadn't left me much choice. I was finished with self-analysis and hindsight, there was no point. I wasn't going to waste another minute on either. What could have been will never be. I had come so close – to what, exactly? But it no longer mattered to me or, apparently to him. He had once again, successfully pushed me into a corner but this time, much to his surprise, I had come out swinging. This endless revisiting of the past wasn't about to change the outcome. I had loved him beyond all reason and now, lying in the tub, I couldn't, for the life of me, recall what that reason had been. I was emotionally shattered, reeling from everything that had been said by both of us; visibly shaken and a little bruised here and there but I had survived his final verbal onslaught.

Suddenly, I started to shake uncontrollably and I was cold. So very cold! My teeth were chattering and I was covered with goose-bumps. Yet I was submerged in hot water. Then, the tears started. Not a single tear or a dribble and a drip falling unnoticed on the bubbles but a torrential out-pouring that I couldn't stop much less control. It was a release and it felt so good just to let go. I cried desperately not at his loss but at my own stupidly and the sheer relief that it was over – finally. I had spent six years obsessing over someone I now realized I never wanted. Not really. I have no idea how long I sat in that tub but at some point, I quietly crawled back into my bed, pulled the comforter up over my head and fell into a deep, untroubled, sleep for the first time in a very long time.

Chapter Twenty Six

I have no idea how long I slept but when I final woke it was again dark. What happened to the day? Where had it gone? A soft knock at my bedroom door brought me completely awake and back to reality. I wasn't too sure where I was or how I'd gotten here until I remembered my moonlight drive down the coast. My mother entered softly, almost on tip-toe, carrying a tray of something steaming hot and smelling warmly of toast. I realized I was suddenly ravenous and couldn't remember the last time I had actually eaten.

"That was quite a phone call! I'm sorry but given the volume level, Daddy and I couldn't help but overhear. How are you feeling? I thought you might like to eat something." She asked quietly.

"How am I feeling? Good question, Mom. The truth is, I'm relieved. I never thought I'd say this but I'm glad this endless nightmare is finally over. Everything feels different somehow but it feels right. I have to admit, though, I never saw this coming. It's amazing how easy and uncomplicated decisions can be when they are forced. What was once so clear to me, no longer is. What I thought we wanted or at least, what I wanted, seemed so real, but not really. How quickly things can change. One minute you're in love and the next minute – nothing. Whether it seeps out of you or is forced out – it just goes and I have no idea where! But now that it's over, I'm fine, Mom. I really am. As I said, all I feel is an enormous sense of relief. There's no need to go back over the past, looking for answers to questions that no longer matter and no need to consider what might have been. It's taken me this long to finally realize how wrong the entire relationship really was – from the beginning. But there it is! This morning, he threw back the drapes, opened the shutters and exposed himself, warts and all, to exactly who and what he is. He can no longer hide in the shadows and neither can I. I realized, not only how little I actually knew him, but now selfish and cruel he really is. He has a cruel heart, Mom! He's a very mean person underneath all that carefully contrived country charm! And he covers it so well! But no more and not to me! I can't decide if all this is funny or tragic because, right now, I feel absolutely nothing. Nothing good, nothing bad, just nothing. Losing him made me suddenly realize, in no uncertain terms, that I never really wanted him in the first place. He was never meant to be my destiny. If anything, I know now, in the end, he would have been my downfall. This entire relationship was tragic and more or less doomed from the very beginning but I have to tell you, this breakup that he and his parents orchestrated, is nothing short of comical. We're finished! And I'm overjoyed! That's how I'm feeling. I'm not about to puddle up, sorry for what I've lost because I'm not sorry and I haven't lost anything! " I explained.

"Good! Finally! That's over! You're well out of it. It's his loss not yours.

"Seriously, Mom! There's another woman that he's been seeing for over a year. I had my suspicions but this morning he confirmed what I have suspected for a long time. At least I wasn't completely blindsided this time. He played me and he believes I fell for it! But not this time! "

"Of course there's another woman. That shouldn't come as a surprise to you! There always will be another woman lurking around in the shadows. You would do well to remember, that at one point, not so very long ago, YOU were the other woman. From everything you've told me, you have lasted far longer than most. Don't be so on hard on yourself! It's a very sad realization. You are no longer his first priority! Like a feral cat, he's moved on. But sooner or later the same old tired cycle will start up again. It's really all he knows. He'll start playing the same old games with this woman and then the lies and the affairs will follow.

He lives for the chase, not the conquest. To him, the conquest is always a fore gone conclusion."

"How did you know? Mom. How could you have been so sure about him from the very beginning? Why didn't you tell me how you felt and what you thought?"

"I did try to tell you, more than once, but you didn't want to hear it! As I recall, just a few weeks ago, I gave you my opinion on this very subject when we were in Denver. I've seen it before. It's not that difficult to recognize! You choose to ignore what was in front of you from the very beginning. You were blind and incredibly foolish! It happens to all of us sooner or later. You were in love! But you're no different than the rest of us. We have all known someone like him at some point. He's a pathological liar and a sociopath. His arrogance and vanity and self-loathing will eventually destroy you if you let it. Just be glad all this has happened while you are relatively young. It gives you a definite advantage. Sometimes you give your heart away, your whole heart, only to discover you've given it to the wrong person and they turn around and dig it out with a spoon. It happens! Don't beat yourself up. Learn from it and let it go. And, in this instance, just be damn glad you got away so easily! I was forced to stand by and either watch you make a terrific fool out of yourself or let you stumble and fall on your own, even through I could see what was coming while you couldn't or wouldn't. You can be very stubborn and determined when you decide you want something! You honestly believed you were in love with him and you couldn't see what the rest of us saw. You have to get past this idea that you can save every abandoned mouse, rescue every bird with a broken wing or pick up every stray and unstable guy that you meet. He can't be saved! He's damaged goods and the damage is irreparable. I don't know how or why he is damaged but it seems to me, that is no longer any or your concern. He's given you a way out. Take it! And put as much distance between the two of you as you can and don't look back! I know your heart was in the right place and I applaud your good intentions, but sometimes it just can't be done.

"It still hurts, Mom."

"Of course it hurts! Everything he said this morning was said specifically to hurt. But it won't hurt for long because you know it wasn't right from the beginning. The truth may sting a bit initially, but at least it's palatable. Lies have a tendency to last forever and do far more damage in the long run. In a day or two this will all be forgotten. It took this long for your head to catch up with your heart that's all. And thank goodness it finally did! But you'll survive. You'll see, this too shall pass and you will be a lot wiser for the whole unfortunate experience."

"What time is it? How long have I been asleep?

"Almost twelve hours. You were absolutely exhausted so I let you sleep in. Is there a reason why he had to call so early in the morning?"

"There's a three hour time difference, Mom!"

"I am aware of that! The question is – is he? That's just rude!"

"Oh. My god! I had clients and students scheduled all day and the vet was coming out today to remove Sundae's wolf teeth! I promised him I would meet him at the barn to assist with the surgery."

"Calm down. Since Nat's call at that ungodly hour, we were all up. I called down to the barn and asked them to reschedule all of your classes and clients for the day. I told them you weren't feeling well. The vet has come and gone and Sundae is fine. A little bit sore and groggy from the anesthetic, which is to be expected, but she was eating by this evening and is now resting quietly. I called a few times to check on her and spoke to the vet who reassured me her surgery went very smoothly. Her teeth just popped out so he didn't need you after all. He would like to see you first thing tomorrow morning though to go over her recovery care and he left a tube of antibiotic paste in your office to give her in the event she spikes a fever. He also said to keep her off the bit until those sockets have a chance to heal properly and make sure her feed has a lot of water in it so it's mushy and doesn't require a lot of chewing."

"You wouldn't believe some of the things Nat said to me."

"Oh, under the circumstances, I think I would. He's confused and desperate and someone else is obviously in control so I imagine he'd say just about anything. It really doesn't matter now though, does it?"

"He doesn't think very highly of you or daddy. Neither do his parents." I said.

Laughing, she said, "I don't give a damn what he thinks of me. I never have. I don't think very highly of him either so I think we're even on that score. And, I know Daddy isn't going to lose any sleep over what Nat may or may not think of him. Daddy could care less. He's just very concerned about you right now. He hates to see you hurt or upset. When you're hurting, so is he."

"What does Daddy think about all of this? He has gone to so much trouble for me. He had my car practically rebuilt and he paid for an airline ticket!"

"I'm not sure what your father thinks. His first reaction, not surprisingly, was to call Ron to ask for his Uncle Vito's number in Detroit. He wanted to get some idea of what it would take to put out a contract on Nat. What with travel costs, per diem and meals, it is not as easy as you may think. Daddy decided it would be very tragic and unfortunate if Nat accidentally, of course, happened to slip and fall off a very fast moving train, into a ditch, in the middle of the night, somewhere between Savannah and Castlehill. He was very pleased with himself for coming up with that particular scenario. He got quite a chuckle at the irony. He has never understood what you saw in Nat, any more than I have. You and Daddy have always been exceptionally close and Nat just never measured up. In fact, he never came close to meeting Daddy's expectations. I know you think no one will ever meet daddy's approval and you're probably right but Nat was too far off the mark to even be considered. Daddy always thought Nat was just another poor little mouse that you were batting around for your own amusement – like a bored cat with no heart for the kill. He never thought you were serious and the possibility of marriage was completely out of the question, in his mind. Not to be undone, your brother called this morning from DC. He had a few ideas of his own to contribute but most of them involved the use of rather harsh, caustic and disfiguring chemicals or a non-sterile, non-surgical procedure to separate Nat from his nether parts. He couldn't quite decide which method he preferred. But he was very supportive of Daddy's idea and sorry he didn't think of it himself. I thought it was very thoughtful of him to offer to help."

"Mom! Daddy can't do that!"

"Let him plot and scheme. It's his way of dealing with all this drama. It will take his mind off your troubles and keep him entertained. If all else fails, Daddy's fairly confident he "knows a guy." The thought kept him amused for awhile and the whole idea managed to put a smile to your face, didn't it? Actually, he took a glass of bourbon up to the garage and spent the evening cleaning his shot gun. He wants to be prepared in the event Nat changes his mind or just happens to show up on the doorstep."

"I wish he would." I replied.

"What? Show up or change his mind? You can't be serous!'

"I wish he would show up. I'd like to see Daddy blow his balls to Glory!"

"Believe me, Nat won't do either. His mind was made up for him a long time ago. His parents saw to that. You know as well as I do that independent thought has never been his strong suit. Besides, he doesn't have the cajones! Remember, this is the guy who couldn't, or wouldn't, for whatever reason, make the effort to ask your father for your hand in marriage. What do you suppose that tells Daddy? Nat wouldn't dare show up to try to fix this. Your father will shoot him where he stands on principle alone. In your fathers mind, this is a perfect example of what happens when he is denied the opportunity to go over the ground rules with any beaux who comes calling.

"They all had a plan; both he and his parents that I knew nothing about."

Before I could go any further, she crossed the room to put the breakfast tray down on my desk. Settling on my bed, next to me, she said, "A plan! Well, there's a shocking revelation! Did you know anything about a plan before this morning? I can't wait to hear it. Go on. This should be good!"

"First of all, he isn't staying in Savannah. He has already requested a transfer to a company hub somewhere closer to Castlehill and his family as soon as he has completed this internship."

"Of course he has! His first paycheck will go directly toward a down payment on a double-wide mobile home that can be wheeled into his parent's back yard. That shouldn't come as a surprise to you!"

"Nat firmly believes, what's mine is his! That would include everything that is mine now or ever will be mine in the future, including my paycheck as well as Odie and Sundae. That's the way his parents handle their finances and because it works for them, it stands to reason it should work for us. Right? Money, bills and any and all financial matters are strictly a man's domain. I have been informed that I don't need to fill my empty head with such matters. I'm sure his father has him convinced that too much thinking on my part would divert precious energy away from my uterus thereby rendering me barren and we certainly can't have that! It says so in the Bible."

"It does! Where? I must have skipped that chapter! Your uterus! Seriously! Has it occurred to you that these people seem to have a somewhat abnormal preoccupation with the current state of your uterus?"

"Nat's mother wants grandchildren." I replied.

"Didn't you tell me he has a brother, nine years older, who has two or three children? So they already have grandchildren. They can wait for yours! What's the hurry?"

"Those children are not of his brother's blood and therefore do not count! His brother married a woman who had those children from at least one previous relationship, if not three. I think the youngest one may be his brother's but I'm not sure. As far as I now, she never married until she met Nat's brother so they really aren't his kids."

"And this matters, why? I should think his parents they would welcome an infusion of fresh blood. It seems to me their existing pool may be somewhat overused, if not exhausted. You can only dip into it so many times over several generations before the blood runs a little thin and bizarre things start happening to your children. They often become weak by nature. I site Nat as the obvious example. "

"Nat wants me to keep yardbirds!"

"Those horribly garish, pink, plastic flamingoes that people stick in their flowerbeds? Why? What's the upkeep on lawn ornaments? Would you be required to hose them off periodically?"

"No, that's what I thought too. But I have been informed that yardbirds are actually chickens!"

"Chickens! You haven't been anywhere near a live chicken since we moved from the City, years ago! What are you supposed to do with chickens? Pluck them and fry them in lard or put a basket over your arm, collect the eggs and sell them door to door? They don't raise fighting cocks, do they? I believe that is illegal, even in rural Virginia. Then again, maybe not. It might depend on just how rural, rural is."

"I'm told chickens can be very comforting." "

"Comforting! To whom?"

"His MeeMaw."

"Whats a MeeMaw?"

"His maternal grandmother as opposed to Mamaw who is his paternal grandmother. Get it?"

"MeeMaw! What does MeeMaw have to do with any of this?"

"Oh, Mom! You would be surprised. It would seem MeeMaw is in need of long-term, live -in, around the clock care and I was expected to fill the position. Stop laughing. Mom! They were serious!"

"Well, unless they intend to put MeeMaw in a box stall on a bed of hay and cover her with a horse blanket, I'm afraid her Golden Years may prove to be somewhat of a disappointment. You don't know the first thing about caring for the elderly! Why would they ask such a thing? No – wait – they expect you to work for free. Am I right? No doubt a consideration when appraising the suitability of a future daughter-in-law. This just keeps getting better. What else did they have in store for you?"

"They want me to give up playing poker as well as pool."

"Why? Who said that!"

"His father would insist! Any Southern woman worth her weight in biscuits and gravy wouldn't dare be seen gambling. Apparently 'it ain't fittin! Again, I site the Bible."

"Damn! I had my money on MeeMaw! What's wrong with pool and poker? You're an exceptional poker player; Daddy frequently asks you to sit in if one of his regulars cancels at the last minute and you manage to do more than hold your own. And you're an even better pool player. You've competed in several charity benefits! Can you give me an example of a suitable pastime that they would consider appropriate? Perhaps you could churn butter and make your own clothes."

"That would be gardening."

"I see. And what does he expect you to grow in this garden of yours? 'Maters or 'taters or both? What about beans? A bean patch might be nice! What is the objective with this garden? Is it purely recreational or are you going for complete sustainability by 2024? Do they expect you to bring in a crop? Maybe if you ask nicely, you could have a cow to go with the yardbirds. I think a cow would be nice. You're going to need a hat! A big floopy, straw hat with a ribbon around it.:

"Mom! Get serious! Nat would also be in control my income and trust fund, my horses and finally my portion of your estate, in the event of your deaths, of course. He would give me an allowance every month. As I understand it, I would have to go to him to beg for my own money and then explain what exactly I intended to do with it! It gets better, Mom. Stop laughing! I would no longer be allowed to compete in any horse shows; locally, regionally, nationally or internationally. And that would, of course, include the Canadian Nationals. I would have to give up any and all competitions!"

"Wow, those are fighting words! How bold of him to make such a demand! But why? It's what you do? What about you're national ranking? You have to compete to maintain that! You can't just walk away!"

"I'm told competing is much too expensive and we can't afford it!"

"What We! There is no "We" as far as your horses are concerned! It's your life and your livelihood and you're damn good at it. You don't just turn your back on all those years of hard work and all you've accomplished on his say so! What is he thinking?"

"He would insist that I retire Odie and put him out to pasture! His uncle has a few fenced acres of pasture land close by that Nat thinks would do. And I am to sell Sundae – for money!"

"Well, that in itself is a deal breaker! Odie is much too young to retire! He hasn't even reached his peak yet! He is just now beginning to come into his own! If you put him out to pasture, it will kill him! He won't understand! And, selling Sundae is absolutely out of the question especially now! She is finally starting to show some promise as a hunter jumper."

"Apparently my going off to horse shows would take me away from him, most importantly, then his parents, his MeeMaw and finally their grandchildren. They are afraid I would fall behind on my daily household chores, which probably includes a lot of vacuuming and ironing. as well as my outdoor duties which obviously includes the upkeep and maintenance of the yardbirds and my agricultural pursuits. The garden would inevitably go to seed in my absence!"

"Oh dear! You're going to be a very busy girl! Nat should learn to quit while he's ahead! It sounds to me like they have covered just about everything. So – what exactly are you left with?"

"A life of mindless servitude - at their beck and call! Mom! Stop laughing! This isn't funny! You keep it up and your going to wet your pants!" I said, laughing along with her.

"I'm sorry. I can't help it. Of course it's funny! Daddy's going to be sorry he missed all of this! You can't make his stuff up! This is a comedy of the absurd! Nat obviously doesn't know you at all."

She was laughing so hard; she rolled over and bit the corner of my pillow.

"Now I feel badly. Is it possible I have misjudged him? He has some cajones after all! First of all, he should do his homework. Our financial situation is none of his business and never will be. You are far more capable of taking care of your own trust fund and your own horses than he ever will be. Nothing he has done or said to date, leads me to believe he has the wherewithal to handle our portfolio let alone yours! Quite the opposite. Our will and your trust fund is irrevocable. Our attorney, who, as you well know, is your Uncle and a Federal Judge, will bury Nat in paper for the rest of his life if he tries to get his hands on either. He's way out of his league on that one! But it would be fun to watch him try. As for your horses, he should take a moment to peruse the California State Statutes regarding the proprietorship of livestock, specifically horses. We take that sort of thing very seriously in this state! Both of those horses are registered in your name not his. He can't touch them and he could never sell them without your consent."

"There's more, Mom"

"I don't know how much more I can take! If I had known his call this morning was going to be so much fun. I would have insisted you put it on speaker! It gets better every minute!"

"Mom! I'm a Republican!"

"Of course you are! Your grandfather was Head of the State Republican Party for over forty years! We've always been Republicans! So what? Is that a problem?"

"They're all Democrats! In fact, according to Nat, in 2008, during the Democratic Convention to nominate a candidate for President, people in his part of the South refused to vote for either a woman or an African American if they were the party's candidate."

"There's a statistic I'm sure the Democratic Committee for Election would like to have known. I really don't know what to say to that! It boggles the mind! Why? – Because Hilary Clinton is a woman and Obama is African American and as such, both are unsuitable candidates? If they refused to vote for either one of their parties nominees, who, then did they intend to vote for?"

"They didn't intend to vote at all!" She gasped.

"I see. That's a somewhat irresponsible reaction to the entire electoral process. Don't you think?"

"I'm also an atheist.! Mom. I'm damned and on the road to ruination!"

"Ruination! Oh dear! Was that an observation or a threat? You've made an intelligent and educated decision concerning your own faith – in whatever - and your beliefs. Religion is a very personal matter. You are, of course, aware of my position on any organized religion. Especially one whose core of belief is centered on an execution. So, no need to go there now. In my opinion, there has been too much death and destruction in this world, all in the name of God and it continues to this day! We see it everyday; we're bombarded with the legacy of a man-made God or Gods that even man can't seem to define to his own satisfaction. I think we can safely thank God for man's inhumanity to man and very little else! Pick a God – any God – they are all the same, it really doesn't matter. What matters is man's self indulgent interpretation. One that serves his own needs, first and foremost. "

"They're not – atheists!"

"What exactly are they? Conservative Evangelicals? I've never been completely clear on that subject. It seems to me, for people who profess to be so God-fearing, they clearly lack any tolerance for diversity. I'm sure there is a passage somewhere in the Bible referring to tolerance. Perhaps if his father checked under the heading of "Love Thy Neighbor." You have told me his father preaches the gospel in some local church but he did not graduate from any college let alone seminary school nor has he been ordained! Which makes him, more or less, a self-taught, self-professed, roaming evangelist on par with Elmer Gantry with a penchant for pointing out the error of other people's ways. Or is his proselytizing simply a hobby?"

"He has an avid interest in the Bible and it is sort of a hobby. He has several hundred spiral, school notebooks filled with his own interpretations and musings. Chapter and verse. He frequently stands up on Sunday and shares his ideas and opinions on anything and everything with the members of their church. He's very well liked and somewhat respected for his insight. It's hard to say what they are exactly but somewhere to the far right of Southern Baptist, I think. It's a little bit hit and miss as far as I can tell. They seem to pick and choose whatever suits them. I answered.

"Tell me, in his diligent study of the Bible, has he yet come across the chapter and verse that clearly states, "Judge not, least ye be judged? It seems to me that particular verse is pretty straight forward. Apparently his father sees room for interpretation."

"Nat firmly believes that absolutely nothing happened on this planet until the birth if Christ. And don't get me started on Adam's rib!" I said.

"Excuse me! Run that past me one more time! This is no longer funny! Who created the Cave paintings in Lascaux, France? Who built Stonehenge on the Salisbury Plain in England not to mention the Pyramids and The Sphinx in Egypt! Where did they come from if not primitive Man? All of which pre-date Christianity! Never mind the art, architecture and cultures of Ancient Greece, Rome, and Mesopotamia. Etruscan art, Byzantine sculpture, the contribution of China and most importantly, Louis Leakey's excavation of Lucy at Oldavai Gorge in Tanzania which has been proven, beyond a doubt, to be over two million years old! The discovery of that skull is the very basis of human evolution and origin! I could go on for hours but I can see it's futile. How on earth did you ever get involved with these people? Surely you know better! These are facts and facts do not cease to exist because his parents chose to ignore them. You can't just erase them! Shall we have a debate - Creation versus Evolution? Are they aware the Scopes Trial took place practically in their own backyard? As you are now aware, false knowledge is far more dangerous than ignorance, yet they do not hesitate to proudly, almost arrogantly, flaunt both! They just call it something else and cloak it in religion. Are they at all familiar with Charles Darwin's "Origins of the Species? There's a page turner that might open their eyes and give them pause for reflection!"

"They can deny all that and they do!"

"Honey, you're getting out just in time! This is absurd, to say the least. It's a good thing you're not a lacto-ova pescatarian! Imagine what they would do with that, assuming they could figure it out? They would probably bolt the front door, draw the drapes and hunker down, pretending they weren't home, until the threat passed or scurry deep into the woods of the Appalachian hills!"

"We're not done, Mom! Nat would want me to get what he refers to as a "real" job and join the work force to contribute to the household expenses as a responsible wage earner."

"Dear God! Where does this nonsense stop! You have a job! Which he does not, I might point out! You're a professional trainer with twenty three years of riding experience. You have a growing client list of your own and national recognition! I would venture to say; you earn a great deal more than he does! What kind of a job did he have in mind? A waitress at the local Squat and Gobble? Though between your scheduled household chores, all those soon-to-be children, your garden and tending to the yardbirds, I don't see how you will have the time to actually hold down a full-time job!"

"I'm also a Yankee!"

"Please tell me he didn't bring that up again! Their hypocrisy is as transparent as their religion and it never seems to end! This is all part of the ripple effect of their intolerance! All they have accomplished since the end of the Civil War is to create a culture of despair and prejudice. A society with an underbelly of hatred, anger and fear that they insist on perpetuating; perhaps because it's all they know or care to know. There is a great deal of security in ignorance. And yet they wonder at the cause of the long-standing tradition of dismissal by outsiders? Just be glad you are a Yankee! I certainly hope this woman they have found for him, whoever she may be, meets all their criteria because this is all a rather tall order. No wonder they are so anxious to be rid of you! It would take too much work on their part to bring you into the fold! And you wouldn't go quietly! Why didn't you tell me you were under this much pressure to conform to their ideal of the perfect wife for their not-so-perfect son?"

"Wait, Mom. It gets better! If I'm pregnant; if I got pregnant in Denver at Sybil's wedding, he'll forget everything he said this morning and agree to marry me anyway. Apparently I'm in a competition that I had no idea I had entered. For the last ten days, he hasn't been thinking about us at all. He hasn't looked for a larger apartment or researched boarding facilities for me as he promised. He's been waiting all this time for the results of a pregnancy test, hoping I'd call him hysterically and beg him to make an honest woman of me. The first one of us to get pregnant, by him, of course, wins the prize."

"I'm almost afraid to ask. What's the prize?"

"He is!"

"Of course, he is! Why didn't I see that coming? Tell me, is there a consolation prize? What does the first runner-up win?"

"Yes! As it happens, there is a consolation prize! The first runner up has the dubious honor of retaining his undying friendship forever."

"And here you thought you were the one that got away when you are actually his back-up plan! He's holding you in reserve just in case it doesn't work out with this other woman. That's not someplace you want to be! But either way, he's got himself covered. This is a practice that has worked for him several times in the past. So why not this time? If you are pregnant, and that's a big if and if you decide to keep the baby, I will see to it that he never finds out. Fortunately in this day and age, you have options. It must be obvious, even to someone with his limited intelligence, that I have more time, more money and better lawyers than he does. We'll cross that bridge when we come to it."

"Mom, There's something else I've never told you."

"Well, now is as good a time as any. Let's hear it."

"Do you remember, a few years ago, after Nat's first visit, he asked if he could call every now and then to get to know you and daddy?"

"Yes. I do and I remember, at the time, being very surprised that he would take the initiative. Why?"

"He wasn't anxious to get to know you at all! That was a lie! He was pumping you for information! Everything you told him, during those conversations, was eventually thrown back in my face!"

"Why? To what end? What did he hope to accomplish? I related childhood stories and amusing family antidotes, nothing more. Certainly nothing he could use against you."

"Oh! He found a way to twist and turn everything you said to his own advantage in an attempt to humiliate me and alienate me from you and Daddy. He was slowly trying to drive a wedge between me, you and daddy, by using whatever you told him. I'm sure he thought that by eliminating everything I love, everything that was important to me; my family, my friends and even my horses, I'd have nothing left but him and I could devote every waking moment to loving him and him alone without any other distractions. "

"Why didn't you tell me this at the time? I would have found some reason not to take his calls if I had known that was what he was up to. Nobody is that insecure!"

"It doesn't matter now, Mom. I never told you because I didn't want to hurt you or Daddy. And I believed, in the beginning, he was actually making the effort to get to know you both. It was only later that I realized what he was doing and by then it was too late. In fact, it slowly developed into a game for me; trying to thwart his obvious attempts at control."

"In the future, could you please give me a heads-up so I don't make that mistake again?

Listen to me for a minute. I'm beginning to think this breakup is really very simple and painfully clear. It's a little too coincidental and far too obvious. You're telling me his parents suddenly and unexpectedly show up in Savannah, for a surprise visit, and spend the entire weekend picking away at him. Which, truth be told, shouldn't have taken quite that long. They covered pretty much everything they believe is wrong with your relationship; and then threw out a plan they knew you would never tolerate much less agree to.

In the event he put up a fight, and fought for you, which we know from past experience, he does not have the strength to do, they brought along this other woman. By doing so, they effectively covered all their bases. If they couldn't convince him to break up with you, they needed her there, with them, to finish the job, so to speak. They were counting on her support and, if all else failed; she could simply screw him into submission. She was their ace in the hole! She obviously has a bag of tricks, overflowing with feminine wiles and has used every one of them to her advantage for the last year and a half. She could get to him in a way that they could not. He was probably so busy drooling all over himself; he didn't give you a second thought. The bottom line is – you both got screwed! They won! So what? Let them at least believe they did. Let them enjoy their hollow victory. But at what cost remains to be seen. I'm sure they are very proud of themselves and think they are very clever. They were more than willing to sacrifice you, him and your happiness to get what they wanted. That end justifies their means. That, in itself, is a fine example of Christian doctrine in practice! It would seem their hypocrisy extends at least that far! I suppose we could all take lessons in hypocrisy from them if we were so inclined. You've always known that what he actually wants out of life has no nothing to do with what they want for him. He has always feared their disapproval. Why, I don't know, but it is obvious.

We saw it when we were in Lexington at the horse show. Let them think whatever they want to think! Do you really care? Now at least you know exactly who and what they are, all of them. And you are right to be relieved! I'm sure by the time they finished picking away at him, he would have agreed to anything and everything, and, in the end, that's exactly what he did. He caved! All they required of him was a phone call to you ending it and even then it took him over a week to come up with the courage necessary to pull that off! I'm surprised they didn't make that call for him!

He has no integrity and even less strength. If he cared for you at all, if he ever had any feelings for you, or any respect, he would have made the effort to tell you to your face that he had met someone else. But he didn't. What does that tell you? Instead he came up with a string of pitiful excuses as to why your relationship would never work. It's really very sad, when you think about it. He is without a doubt, a coward and that whole exercise this morning on the phone is all the proof you should need. Did he ever apologize for anything – for any of this - ever? No! And why? Because in his shallow, little mind, he honestly believes he has done no wrong."

"Do you remember, while you were at Colorado State, a few months after you first met Nat, you were approached by a college recruiter to ride for St. Andrews in Glasgow, Scotland. They offered you a full, four year scholarship and a position on the Varsity team; which you turned down because you didn't want to leave him. I remember you telling me that you regretted that decision the minute you made it! But you can't dwell in the past or think about what could have been. Turning down that scholarship will most likely remain the biggest regret of your life! Then you decided to drop out of school, move to Cheyenne and play house with him! You cooked and cleaned and were there to make sure he and his two, rather unsavory, slovenly roommates had clean boxer shorts until you couldn't stand it any longer – about three months, as I recall. I don't care how good he is in bed; nothing can replace what you gave up for him. And, if that wasn't enough, he now wants your freedom and practically everything you own or ever will own. This is all nothing but an attempt at control. It's obvious his parents control him and it follows that he wants to control you. I don't even think he knows what's going on. Anyway, by the time you came to your senses, that scholarship offer was off the table. Don't make the same mistake twice! This is his dream, not yours! Can you imagine what your life would be today had you not wasted six whole years – good years, practically you're youth- on someone so undeserving! Imagine how different your life would be! What a different path your life may have taken!

Daddy and I didn't intervene because it was your decision; your life and only you could decide. You did what you thought was right. You've devoted several years to this relationship but now that its over, its time to take back your life. You have very little to show for those years except a great deal of experience and mild case of heartbreak. Live and learn, as they say. You've lived! You've had a good long run – now you are learning. Don't you see, what happened this morning is a good thing! You may have lost him but you now have your freedom. Grab it with both hands and don't look back!

This new love of his may have won what you lost but what exactly is that? A loosely woven relationship based on distrust and suspicion! You cannot lose what you don't have and you never had him, not really. I doubt anyone ever truly will. You know as well as I do that you would never have been happy in his world; anymore than be would be in yours. You come from two very different worlds and unfortunately there is no bridge between them, least of all love. Like Odie put out to pasture, you would never survive in that environment. You are nothing more than a threat to their way of life and rather than embrace you, they have chosen to push you away until you succumb to their way of thinking

. No doubt leaving your children; their grandchildren behind, to be raised by them. Which, from everything you've told me, is a terrifying thought in its self! They fear what they don't know or understand! Even if you did agree to all of their demands, they clearly would not have made it easy for you. The social pressure and the pressure his family brought to bear on him to break up with you had to have been over-powering! It would take a great deal of strength to resist that kind of pressure. The kind of strength he does not have nor will he ever have. He is putty in their hands, soft and malleable. He is also afraid. There is nothing you could have done or can do except hold your head up high and walk away with grace and dignity."

"You saw this day coming, Mom. Didn't you? You saw it in him years ago. "Why didn't you tell me?"

"My telling you would not have changed today's outcome even though I did try, more than once. I admit I had my suspicions. I spent several hours with him in the hotel in Denver when you went off to the dress rehearsal and I remember feeling very uncomfortable. He always says one thing but means quite another, whether he does that intentionally or not, I have no idea. His thoughts, such as they are, seem to run on and on and they are not particularly deep. They're chaotic, confusing and almost purposely vague. It's exhausting just listening to him let alone trying to decipher what he means. His mind is so scattered, as though he has some inability to focus. He had quite a bit to say about this other woman but he kept it somewhat abstract, as though he was baiting me, trying to illicit a reaction. I suppose that is why I was watching both of you so closely at the wedding. I thought he might see Sybil's wedding as an opportunity to make a scene. When you told me he had proposed, I put all those thoughts out of my head. You seemed to be so happy! However, in the overall scheme of things, this is nothing more than a hiccough. This time, next year, you will have forgotten all about him and finished your Masters Degree. By then, you'll have the results of all those law school applications you submitted months ago. You never told him you have applied to law school did you? Did you ever intend to tell him?"

"He has his secrets and I have mine. There was no reason to tell him – now or ever!" I said.

"In the meantime, you have five or six horseshows left in this season, including the Canadian Nationals and if you continue doing as well as you have been so far this summer, you will be in a very good position to try out for the Olympic Team in Palm Beach. That has always been your dream; ever since you were two and a half years old. Don't let go of that dream because of him! If you do, he wins! Odie has never been in better form than he is now and he's raring to go. And Sunny is finally showing some potential."

"It wasn't always bad, Mom – our relationship." I said.

"Really! When was it ever good?"

"I'm thinking. I'm trying to remember."

"If you have to think about it that long – you have your answer." She replied.

"Just to recap so that we're all clear. Basically, she, or any woman for that matter, who could feasibly meet with his parent's approval, must be born and raised in the South and embrace all that that represents. In other words, it would be a distinct advantage if she hailed from the same town or at the very least, the same county. And it probably would be ideal if they were somehow related. Proximity goes to shared culture."

"She must agree to either live with his parents in their home, in a hovel or something comparable, on the immediate grounds of the family homestead and within shouting distance. Right?"

"She should be of child-bearing age with an intact, fully functioning, viable uterus and willing to bear his children and only his children. Previous existing children, while proof of her fertility, are unacceptable. And they are intent upon perpetuating their bloodline regardless of the long-term consequences."

"It goes without saying that she does not drink, smoke, swear or participate in games of chance even though Nat engages in all of the them on a regular basis and with a great deal of enthusiasm. It follows that she has on overwhelming fear of God and his thunderous wrath in the event she dares to misstep! If she has any snap at all, she should fear Nat's temper in this world far more than God's anger in the next!"

"She is unfamiliar with her basic rights as a woman in today's world which leads to her confusion regarding women in the political arena and she is deeply suspicious of African-Americans as a whole."

"She is, for the most part, largely uneducated but the proud recipient of a high school diploma which, in itself, was difficult to obtain. She has no intention of continuing her education beyond that point because she obviously has her limits and that does not include an active curiosity. Reading, for her, is difficult at best and restricted primarily to the Bible. Anything else is heresy! Neither does she speak a foreign language because there is no immediate need, it would tax her mental capacity and, like him, she has enough trouble with English. This is, after all – America!"

"She is a Democrat, but only on paper because she doesn't have the wherewithal to support any parties' ideology or its chosen candidate. If she votes at all, she will vote the way she is told to vote – if not by her father than by her husband. She is, at least until the babies start popping out, gainfully employed and not at all opposed to handing over her hard earned paycheck to any male who may or may not reward her with a bit of spending money of her own. That would be entirely up to his discretion."

"She is equally familiar with the care and feeding of poultry as well as the care and feeding of MeeMaw or his parents, when their time comes. She will look the other way whenever she is confronted with his numerous affairs and indiscretions, tolerate his lies, and at the same time, share his delusions. By doing so, she will stand by her man or behind him, depending upon the circumstances, without a thought in her head, especially one that may run contrary to his. Above all, she will keep her mouth shut and her opinions, if she dares to have any, to herself. Nothing she has to say matters anyway! To her advantage, she is a consummate gardener who knows instinctively what to grow where and what to plant when. Legumes are unquestionably her forte."

"And finally, it would definitely be in her best interests if she came with a deep fat fryer! I get the distinct impression the women in his family don't readily share their small electric appliances! That's a tall order! I understand now why you just don't measure up, considering the rather warped measuring stick they are using against you! No wonder they want to be rid of you!"

"Up until this minute, I didn't understand where all of this was coming from or why now, but after everything you've told me it is beginning to make sense. This has nothing whatsoever to do with your luggage or the designer labels in your clothes! When the two of you were dating, that was harmless enough. You posed no threat to their way of life. But the minute he took it a step further and proposed marriage you became far more problematic for his family. You represent an entirely different way of life than the one they know and they feel threatened not only by you but by the fact that they have no guarantee they could or would ever be able to control you. If they can't control you, it stands to reason; they will loose control of him. And they have no intention of surrendering what control they have over him to you! Which brings us to chaos and you know where that leads! These ideas you are talking about; of family, politics and religion are fundamental values that are impossible to change and even more difficult to compromise. They are also very personal decisions, some based on your upbringing and others on your experience. Recognizing all these differences for what they are, they felt compelled to jump in and remind him. I'm not saying you should marry the boy next door but they definitely want him to marry the girl next door! In the long run, it's safer and easier for everyone concerned, especially those who live in fear. Rather than embrace what they perceive to be the differences between the two of you, they have chose to define you through them. They purposely made it impossible for you to agree to whatever they had planned, knowing full well that would be the end of you. They prefer, all of them, Nat included, to go through life wearing blinkers which is their prerogative, but its not you and it never will be no matter how hard you try or how much you may think you love him. They can see only what is directly in front of them. Their convictions are shrouded by ignorance. They have no peripheral vision because they know where they have come from and as long as they stay on the straight and narrow, they know where they re going. Anything broader than that and they are lost. You can't change who you are anymore than he can and you can not ask him to be someone he is not. Nor should they ask you! Face it! He's been hobbled! He can't stand on his own! Your grandfather's question is just as relevant today as it was nearly forty years ago, if a bird marries a fish, where are they going to live? In retrospect all this now makes perfect sense." She said.

"How's that for a closing argument? I think I hit all the high points, didn't I?"

So – now, you've had a long hot bath and a good cry but its time to put all of this behind you and move on."

"No wonder you're in such a state. Wow! I'm exhausted and I can't remember the last time I laughed so hard. My sides hurt."

"Please eat something while it's still hot."

"I've made all your favorites. Classic Midwestern comfort food; just what this situation calls for. A big mug of Campbell's Cream of Tomato soup, made with milk, not water, and a little pat of butter, unsalted, of course, melting on top. A croque monsieur on a fresh sourdough baguette with grilled chicken instead of ham, because I know you are watching your salt in-take, covered with melted gruyere and fontina cheese, and toasted until it's crunchy and a pickle."

"Mom! What about you? What about all the wedding plans you've made? You've gone to so much trouble and now, for nothing." I asked.

"For starters, just let me have five minutes alone in a room with Nat. It wouldn't take me much longer than that to straighten him out in no uncertain terms. Don't worry! All the plans we talked about can be cancelled very easily. We'll do it all again someday and the next time, we'll do the way it should be done."

"As she turned to leave my room, she asked, "What do you want me to do with that University of Tennessee t-shirt lying on my bathroom floor?"

"Burn it." I said.

"I can do that."

"Oh, Mom. What did you ever do with that brown suede jacket Nat forgot in the hotel room in Denver? Did you ever send it to him in Savannah?"

"I gave it to Alejandro this morning."

"Mom! That jacket wasn't your to give away!"

"Neither was that teddy bear on wheels that his father gave away. So, I think we're even."

"I feel sorry for her, Mom, whoever she is. I really do."

"All things considered, so do I! But she'll soon find out. Let her clean his mobile home and cook his grits and collard greens and everything else in grease. Let her tend the yardbirds and grow 'maters, 'taters and beans or whatever. She obviously wants the job and she's gone to a great deal of trouble to make sure she got it. Who's to say? Desperate people do desperate things. It's possible she wants a man who won't abuse her but abuse comes in many forms and he wants a family at any cost. Either way, it's no longer any of your concern."

"Mom, do you think he'll marry her?" I asked.

"Maybe. Probably. He is clearly very anxious to marry somebody! Since you ask, I think it will depend upon just how quickly she gets pregnant. But even then, he'll find some reason to stall and wait until she is well into her third trimester. Then and only then, will he commit to marriage – not before."

"Mom, I feel like such a fool! I think I'll swear off men for awhile. They are too much work and nothing good ever seems to come from all that effort. I never seem to be able to anticipate what they are thinking. The only male, outside of the family, I can trust, completely and unconditionally, is Odie. At least he accepts me for exactly who I am and doesn't make any unreasonable demands or try to change and humiliate me! I can be myself and he's fine with that! That's all he really wants or expects of me."

"I agree with you completely! But one last thing, you are in unfamiliar territory here. Until this particular incident, you have usually been the dump-or not the dump-ee. Am I right? You're shocked and frustrated right now because you didn't see this coming. This is your first major heartbreak! You have been out-maneuvered because they had the advantage. You're here and he's there! Distance gave them an opportunity. Their surprise weekend to Savannah wasn't a particularly sophisticated move on their part but it was effective in its own rather crude way. No one, as far as I know, has ever broken up with you before! It's always been mutual or you're doing. From everything you've just told me, he knew in Denver he was going to end it, and in all honesty, he should have but instead he proposed and let you go on and on; making plans for the wedding of your dreams, moving across the country, and hauling those two horses to a new place . That's just plain cruel! The bottom line – he stood by and let this all happen. I seriously doubt he said anything in his own defense let alone yours to his parents. Right now you are nothing more than collateral damage! Damage that doesn't really concern them. You have to understand, this wasn't his decision. Other forces have been at work that did not have your best interests at heart and he's too weak to resist. There's really nothing you could have done to stop this. It was inevitable. It's been out of your hands for quite some time. You just didn't know it. Don't build a wall around your heart! Remember, it's not always a matter of what you want but what is right. And this wasn't right from the very beginning. You know that now and I suspect you knew it years ago! Don't mistake passion for love! Passion will inevitably fade but love will and should, last.

"You've been fighting a losing battle because of the distance between you. Had it been me, I would have walked away from him years ago. He's one horse you don't want to ride! You've been unseated before. Stand up, brush yourself off and get back in the saddle. Now you know what to look for and what to avoid.

But it's not a total loss, no matter what you may think right now. You may not believe it but what happened this morning this is actually a blessing. You have all those years of valuable experience - hold onto that. Learn from this and, if you do, I seriously doubt you will ever let it happen again. I'm very proud of you. Keep in mind; independence and freedom are not at all the same thing. You now have both! He gave you no choice but he did give you an opportunity. Everything you once saw in him, including his spirit, is gone! He's been broken and there's nothing left. And, his parents will not hesitate to do the same to you. Let her have whatever is left of him – the dregs. He may have been shallow before but, he's empty now. Do you seriously want to be a part of that? There are no excuses for his behavior this morning and even less accountability, so just walk away and don't look back. By the way, you haven't told me, what did you say to him when he laid out this plan of theirs?"

"I told him, in his own vernacular, so there would be no misunderstanding, that he, his parents and his MeeMaw could, "put their plan where the sun don't shine!"

"Good for you! That's my girl! Somewhere along the way, you lost yourself in this struggle. You haven't failed! He failed you and it wasn't the first time. He let you down – again. Sooner or later, we all have to make difficult decisions. But, you know now you have made the right decision! Sometimes, no matter how hard you try or how much you may want it, you cannot hold onto something that doesn't want to be held. Sometimes, like a bird or a fish, you have to let go."

"Mom, you're getting an awful lot of mileage out of that metaphor!"

"Maybe so – but think about it! It's true!"

"You don't get it do you? Mom."

"Get what? What are you talking about?"

"He has played me more often than I care to admit over the last few years." I said. "This morning, I played him. He pushed and pushed and pushed and I finally pushed back! It's really that simple. Do I have to walk you through this?"

"Perhaps you should because if I was confused before I'm completely at a loss now. I was under the impression you were in love with him!"

"Seriously, Mom! Maybe at some point I was in love with him or at least I convinced myself that I was. Deep down – somewhere – it never felt right! I don't think I should have to try that hard; it shouldn't be so much of a struggle! Since when is being in love that much work? Do you honestly think I would give up everything I know and love for him! Do you think that by now, I don't know exactly what and who he is and more importantly what and who he is not? Give me a little credit!"

"I don't understand!"

"After listening to him this morning for over three hours, I decided to take the moral high ground." I said.

"Always a wise choice! I wouldn't expect anything less of you."

"I made my decision about him and us and our relationship, if you could call it that, several weeks before we went to Sybil's wedding. I was determined to break up with him, in Denver, when we were together. I intended to use that opportunity to tell him face-to-face. I'd like to think, unlike him, I have at least that much dignity! What makes it all so funny is the fact that the two of us were, apparently, working at cross purposes. We didn't know what the other intended. And for whatever reason, neither one of us went through with it?"

"I still don't understand."

"Mom! Listen to me! He's a – he's a, well, if I tell you what he is, you will probably drag me into the bathroom and wash my mouth out with soap! He's a douche! There – I've told you. Now you figure it out. If it walks like a duck and quacks like a duck, it must be a duck! My god! Listen to me! I sound like Nat with his stupid, non-stop barnyard analogies! He's all that and more and he isn't going to change anytime soon for me or anyone. And I'm not going to sit around and hope or wait for him to change. I admit, at first he was so different and amusing, and then he was fun. But somewhere along the way, he became predictable and frankly, very tiresome. He was too much work; too insecure and too needy, and I was the only one working at it. It didn't take long for the whole relationship to turn into nothing more than convenient.

He's cruel! When I was at school in Bristol and he was in Knoxville at UT, we had a raging argument about something that I can't even remember. Whatever it was, it wasn't important but at one point during that particular row, he actually threatened to put his dog "down" if I ever left him or broke up with him. And he was serious! Who thinks like that? Unfortunately Duke died of natural causes before Nat could make good on his threat. But why purposely kill a defenseless dog just to get back at me? That's just sick! In fact, it goes beyond sick – it's twisted and it scared the hell out of me. That's only one of many reasons why he scares me to death on so many levels. I shudder to think what he would do if he ever got his hands on my horses! This morning, I wanted to see just how far he would go with this charade. His long overdue phone call confirmed what I have suspected for a very long time. I've known about this other woman for months. There are photos of the two of them posted all over his FaceBook page. It's difficult to imagine anyone could actually be that stupid unless it was intentional and solely for my benefit.. And I knew he wouldn't stay long in Savannah because big cities terrify him. Any burp, town or city with a population over 2500 people, scares him senseless! And his definition of diversity is anyone he isn't directly related to. It doesn't matter because I stopped caring ages ago! I knew he'd run and he did. I wanted to see just how tangled he would get in his own web and what lengths he would go to to extricate himself. Once again, he didn't disappoint. He has cheated and I have been deceived! I can not forgive either and I'm going to savor this for a very long time! This morning I gave him just enough rope to hang himself. Do you honestly believe I would ever agree to his outrageous demands or his parent's plans for us? If you do, then you don't know me as well as you think you do. I'm not stupid, Mom!"

"Of course, you're not stupid! I thought you were being somewhat cavalier about all of this and I wasn't sure why? It's not unusual for people in love to do stupid things!"

"If that's true, Mom, then I have had enough stupid to last the rest of my life!"

"Well, you certainly fooled me!"

"It wasn't you I was trying to fool, Mom."

"You're an extraordinary young woman, Jory – do you know that?"

"I'd like to think I'm getting there, Mom. Contrary to what Nat may think, his absence in my life doesn't make me feel lost or empty. Quite the opposite. All of a sudden, I can breath again."

Chapter Twenty Seven

Overnight the news of our break up burst into cyberspace via the Internet. I have no idea who posted it or why. Many took it upon themselves with malicious glee and seized the opportunity to join in the fun and exacerbate my misery by creating what they considered amusing hash tags, Twitters or blatant, outspoken opinions on their Facebook pages, all at my expense without a care in the world for my feelings. Few took responsibility let alone accountability for their musings. Some people thrive on other people's misfortune and others can't seem to resist the opportunity to exploit it or at least enjoy it from a safe distance in complete anonymity. Hoping against hope that an unexplainable complication might arise to add a dash of unsavory flavor to the current controversy. The resulting social fervor continued for days but I didn't care. Friends of mine as well as Nat's; acquaintances and even complete strangers on both sides, inevitably took sides. The line had been drawn. It seemed anyone and everyone had an opinion on the present state of my love life and didn't hesitate to express it. Whether I wanted to hear it or not didn't seem to be at issue. I could ignore the gossip swirling around me and I refused to respond. My life was suddenly under glass, rudely exposed for all to see and comment upon. I chose to ignore the hysteria and took a great deal of comfort in my indifference.

Some were sympathetic; tip-toeing around me and speaking in whispers as though I was in mourning and numb to their mumblings. Others were outraged;

not quite believing I had let him go. Was I out of my mind? One or two quietly suggested I slink off to Europe for an extended tour until the current tempest blew over. I had it on good authority from my former roommate at boarding school, who happened to be passing through San Francisco on her way home to Dubai, that the best way to get Nat out of my system and put my life back into perspective was to have a brief, transient dalliance with a young Frenchman or an Italian or both. I could spend time in Paris or Rome, enjoy his company completely unencumbered, without attachment, and as an added advantage, brush up on my French or learn Italian or both. She also didn't hesitate to remind me that she had an older brother, who was currently at Oxford in London and unattached. Of all the remedies thrown out for my consideration, her suggestion held the most immediate appeal.

Another old friend, a trainer herself outside of Chicago, invited me to join her on a three week ride through Ireland, stopping at one rustic, country inn after another along the route. It was a trip that we had often dreamed of taking together one day when we were at school together. What better time to go than now? The only snag in that plan was shipping Odie overseas and the mandatory month long quarantine for animals entering Ireland which was entirely out of the question for so many reasons.

A few were quick to recommend I crawl into a deep hole somewhere to lick my wounds. Little did they know, I had no wounds to lick. Many had thought we were the perfect couple and our love would endure. If we couldn't make it, who, amongst them, could? Everyone seemed to have an opinion on our relationship and where it had gone wrong. I had somehow managed to make a complete muddle of my life but they had the answers and unsolicited solutions.

Still others begged me to reconsider and ask his forgiveness; agree to anything and everything, whatever it took to get him back. But I had no intention of groveling. A few suggested I fly immediately to Savannah, find him, confront him and talk him off this latest ledge. One was bold enough to ask for his phone number, which I gladly surrendered. If we were truly over and he was back on the market, she hoped to be the first in line either for his affections or pick up the pieces I had left behind. If I was devastated then it stands to reason, he must be vulnerable. I wasn't devastated, I was relieved and he was anything but vulnerable. He had simply switched horses. Even our two former roommates in Cheyenne agreed that his leaving the Air Force had been the beginning of his downward spiral. To them, there could be no other explanation for his behavior. His Commanding officer at Fort Warren, who I had come to know, also felt obliged to weigh in on the subject of our break-up. He called me to personally apologize for Nat's recent behavior, calling it reprehensible and assuring me that he was embarrassed to admit that Nat had ever served under his Command. Nat's actions were, in his opinion, well below Air Force standards and certainly not those of a gentleman.

For the most part, all were confused by my reluctance to either confirm or deny the rumors that were swirling around me. The overall consensus seemed to be that I was in denial or suffering a delayed reaction. The repercussions of which would eventually catch up with me. Perhaps I was in shock. Given time, I would understand just what a prize I had forfeited and find my way back into his good graces. I was beginning to feel as though I was going though a very public divorce rather than a mutual breakup.

Sympathy in my court was in short supply as rumor and innuendo spread and drama grew exponentially with the following days and weeks. Sybil alone understood my aloofness and my need to distance myself from the fray, by reminding me, "I never understood what you saw in him in the first place, except of course, his obvious good looks. He isn't your type! And, he never was! I didn't think the two of you would last through that first summer until you told me had he shown up at your parent's house stone cold drunk! I've known your parents since I was four years old and I think they showed remarkable restraint under the circumstances. I'm still surprised your father didn't punt his bony, white ass off the terrace and into the pool! I don't remember where you were at the time, maybe a horse show somewhere but Nat once actually tried to seduce my mother when she was visiting in Fort Collins? That's creepy! She's my mother! Who does that? He's supposed to be with you and yet he's hitting on my mother in front of me! That's just sick! There is something definitely wrong with him!"

As the days passed, I continued my silence, which did nothing more than incite speculation and fan the flames of public opinion, often against me, rarely for me. It was my business and mine alone and I didn't feel I owed anyone an explanation for my behavior nor could I begin to explain Nat's. It was between the two of us. No one need ever know exactly what had transpired or why. I could barely understand it all myself let alone explain it to any one else. My indifference was infuriating to many yet I continued to feel only relief and an overwhelming sense of freedom. And I caught myself smiling more than once. The balancing act was over and I was back where I belonged and on a level playing field. A field I knew so well; my own familiar turf. My only confidante throughout it all reminded Odie. He alone knew my innermost thoughts and once again he didn't judge me, he just listened. To him my current situation was no different than any other that had occurred over the years. How many other tales had I told him? I may not have been able to tell anyone else the truth but Odie would at least hear me out with his usual bias toward me. His life made far more sense in the long run. Greed, arrogance, self-pity and an indefinable God did not have an influence on his trust or devotion. He took it all in stride. I could be full of hate, but I wasn't. Any love or feelings I had ever had for Nat were gone, evaporated; while I chose the security of indifference.

I have no desire for revenge. Revenge requires a certain degree of disgust which I had, and a desire to hurt, which I did not have. I had no intention of allowing myself to be swallowed up by pity; mine or anyone else's. I don't want Justice. Justice is blind to everything including revenge and the scales are never truly balanced. I am finally free to live my life on my own terms, to pursue my dreams, not someone else's, within the limits of my own conscience. I have no intention of going backwards or standing still. I am not about to wither on the vine of Nat's disapproval and betrayal. It had been a long, hard ride on a horse that couldn't be ridden; and I had finally been forced to realize the futility in trying. I'd been thrown in the past with considerably less dignity, but I hadn't hit the dirt and nothing was broken, especially my heart. Not this time. I may be a little bruised but I would survive. It would take a great deal more than Nat's blistering words to unseat me or bring me to my knees.

Stella Benson

Chapter Twenty Eight

I spent the following weeks of summer, as a permanent resident at the barn; riding from the first light of dawn well into the dark of night, forcing the grounds keeper to turn on the floodlights in the main covered arena for Odie and me every evening. I taught my regular clients and gained several new ones during the day and Odie and I worked tirelessly as soon as the sun set; hour after hour, day after day. I began to sleep on a cot in my office or on a bale of hay in Odies stall. We had less than seven weeks to prepare for the Canadian Nationals. Odie seemed to sense my need for urgency as well as perfection. My position on this year's pedestal and my standing was shaky at best and I couldn't afford to let myself crumble or fall. But, before I could begin to anticipate the long haul and the international competition in Canada, I had scheduled three more regional horse shows for myself and my clients. I pushed Odie as hard as I dared and myself even harder, leaving little or no time for thoughts of Nat. He had made his choice and I had made my decision. It was finally behind me.

Odie and I practiced the fourth level dressage patterns tediously, day after day, until we had mastered the required movements and appeared to be flawless. True to his nature, Odie grew bored with the ceaseless repetition, often refusing to acknowledge the reins or the commands communicated through my legs. But I continued to push him on regardless of his occasional refusal and his attitude of indifference. We had to present ourselves as a perfectly synchronized and balanced team to the judges. Collected and cadenced to perfection. There was no room for error. Every movement would be carefully scrutinized; each and every step in our performance was crucial, one step leading to the next all the while maintaining our rhythm. Odie had to know exactly where to put each hoof, because every step he took counted, each one perfectly metered and timed. He couldn't tire or drag a hoof. The energy we showed and our consistency were just as important to the judges as our accuracy. If either one of us faltered, there would be no second chances. With the rare exception of Odie throwing a shoe in the ring, it was start to finish – one chance, and one chance only, to be absolutely flawless with no hesitation.

My job was to concentrate for both of us and stay one step ahead of him, pushing him forward to the next move. He relied on me just as much as I depended on him to keep us balanced, giving the judges the overall appearance of confidence. We both had to feel it, at exactly the same moment if we were going to be successful. Neither one of us could allow ourselves to be distracted by the cheering crowds, a loose dog running across the dressage court or an uninitiated spectator suddenly popping a large colorful golf umbrella. The judges were unforgiving, focusing their complete attention on just the two of us when our turn came to perform for them. Every detail would be monitored. Coming in second or third was not an option. Anything less than a first in every class I had entered would cause us both to slip and possibly loose our current standing. The slightest misstep or deviation and we could both be disqualified.

Slowly, as the days and weeks went by, the interest in my love life began to lose momentum. The gossip and rumors gradually died down as the outspoken participants on both sides of the line lost interest and moved onto the next, most recent tragedy; feeding on the scraps of someone else's misfortune and I was all but forgotten. With the drama of my downfall and the sudden, renewed interest in my availability, I felt I could easily have been back on that merry –go-round. But not this time! Knowing what I now knew, there was no chance of me stepping back on. Gradually, day by day, it became more difficult to imagine Nat's face. The edges were becoming more and more vague until it all but disappeared in a gauzy haze. His words seemed to have obliterated his image and pushed his face out of my memory. Any memories I may have, either good or bad, became obscured, elusive and finally, faded completely. I was now old news, which was exactly where I wanted to be. My refusal to participate in any way to the feeding frenzy swirling around me, continued to meet with a great deal of disapproval but I was determined to ignore the furor and concentrate on the weeks ahead.

I willingly rejoined my Tuesday night poker game, usually held in an empty stall at the barn with the guys from the Feed & Seed, the vet, several other trainers and a handful of grooms, all of whom could care less about my love life. As long as I had the ante, I was welcome. I also accepted an invitation to compete in a local charity pool tournament to raise funds for Breast Cancer Awareness and another for the Wounded Warriors Project. When I wasn't spending time at the barn, I was home, wedged between my parents in my old spot on the sofa holding a bowl of popcorn as they caught up on the most recent Scandinavian noir.

As the drama surrounding me died down, and everyone moved on to the next tragedy, I was surprised to find my popularity on the rise. Word had spread. I was a novelty and curiosity had piqued. After six years and being so dramatically thrown over, I was suddenly available. One after another, invitations started to flow and were too many to even begin to consider, even if I felt inclined. Most I declined with deep, albeit feigned regret. I wasn't ready for any degree of social interaction with the exception of an invitation to participate once again in the annual Fall Fox Hunt.

My sudden increase in popularity was quite a heady feeling and very flattering but I had been out of the dating scene far too long. I was reluctant to jump back in at this point and I needed more time. I wanted to remain focused on the rest of the summer and what lay ahead. Odie was my first and all consuming priority. The last thing I wanted was another demanding, all consuming relationship. I had too much on my mind and too little time. After what they deemed a reasonable amount of time for me to mourn my loss, friends, meaning well, began to call, offering to fix me up with this friend or that. The very idea of spending an entire evening on a blind date terrified me. I wouldn't know where to begin and I wouldn't be very good company under the best of circumstances. Socializing over drinks seemed a dreadful prospect, one I hoped to avoid at any cost. And my conversational skills, for now, were limited to nothing more than barn gossip or instructions directed at children in the simplest of terms. I refused to allow myself to be caught up in cocktail party banter or snappy dinner repartee! And I had absolutely no interest in trying. I had never learned the complicated games involved or the insincere, forced flattery and meaningless conversation that were required on a first date. I had no intention of learning the rules at this point, and even less desire. I had had my fill of games that I didn't understand; games devised by someone else for their own gratification, not mine. If I learned anything from my relationship with Nat it was simply; take me as I am or not at all because I will never change who I am or become someone I am not – for anyone. The few skills, the so-called feminine wiles I may have had acquired over the years were either long gone or obsolete, probably from lack of use, either way, they were forgotten. I turned down each and every attempt at a fix-up or a casual foursome with one exception.

He called one afternoon as I stood in the searing hot arena trying to teach several equally hot and uncooperative little charges. He very boldly reminded me that we had met once ten years ago. We had been introduced by a mutual friend just a few days before my birthday in July. Searching my memory, I vaguely remembered spending an afternoon with a girlfriend who had insisted we go to Baskin Robbins for an ice cream. Giggling, she proudly introduced the two of us, very satisfied with herself that she had been able to pull this meeting off. The stop for ice cream had been prearranged by the two of them, at his request – leaving me completely in the dark and unsuspecting. I'm not a fan of surprises! He had insisted she introduce the two of us before he missed his chance. He was working and saving for college in the fall, one scoop at a time. This unscheduled stop had been entirely his idea. During that first call, he reminded me, of that day, so long ago, when he had given me a one scoop Chocolate-chip Cooke Dough ice cream cone – on the house. It was not a very subtle set up! That was ten years ago! I found his memory and attention to detail a little unnerving as I tried, with little success, to recall anything memorable about the entire incident.

Apparently I had made quite an impression on him but it was so long ago! So much had happened in that span of ten years and while I may have made a lasting impression on him, I was at a loss now to put a face to his name. Too much time had passed. And yet he continued to call. Who was this guy? And, what was his problem? Over the next few days and several of his unwarranted calls, my excuses became increasingly more vague and it wasn't long before I felt I was pushing the limits of rudeness; slowly running out of polite ways to discourage him. Eventually I came to the conclusion he had to be one of those men who would not or could not take no for an answer. Another control freak, no doubt! Do I unwittingly give the impression that I am a doormat? I decided it would be better, in the long run, to meet him, face to face, whoever he was and put an end to his constant attention before this went too far. I didn't want or need a new friend, a buddy or a relationship. I had sworn off men for the time being! And I was quite content with my decision. With his last call, I reluctantly gave in and agreed to meet him in three days. And then I forgot all about it and turned my phone off.

With the unseasonable summer heat and the constant work, overnight Odie began to show all the classic signs of colic. It couldn't come at a worse time! We couldn't afford several weeks of forced stall rest! He began to pace, back and forth, twisting and turning in obvious discomfort, banging his hooves incessantly into the stall boards, wall-eyed with fear, his nostrils flaring as he gasped for air. Had he drunk too much water or not enough? Had he eaten too little or too much? Either way this was not the time to make a change in his diet. Had someone unknowingly dropped something on the aisle floor that he had swallowed? A paper wrapper, a potatoe chip bag or a bottle cap? Could that be what was causing a blockage in his belly or torsion in his lower intestine? Fortunately, the vet happened to be on the grounds when Odie was at his worst, saving me an emergency farm call.

Together we tried everything at our disposal to alleviate Odie's abdominal pain. We both knew, all too well, if Odie went down on all fours in the stall, he may never get up again. The risk was too great. It was imperative that we keep him constantly moving; endlessly round and round the outdoor pen, up and down the aisle; Odies first instinct to ease his own intestinal discomfort was to lie down and roll. Then get up and roll again. We couldn't let that happen. The timing for his recovery was crucial if he was going to survive this bout. He had to keep moving regardless of the pain he was showing. I was beyond myself with worry and exhausted from the constant exercise. When he spiked a fever, I moved into his stall to be with him even though he continued to swing his head from side to side, thrashing and snorting; his eyes rolling and his nostrils flaring, continually curling his upper lip. Alternating between the shivers and shakes of cold and the sweat pouring off him, I stayed with him, trying in vain to do what I could to at least make him comfortable. Had I pushed him too far? Or too hard? The loud, audible burbling in his gut told me it was possible I had. Our only option at this point was wait and watch and hope it passed and soon.

Finally, after three days, he rallied without any outward signs of long term injury. The danger had finally passed and he was slowly showing clear signs of recovering. With Canada less than a month away, I was going to have to scale back our training or risk a reoccurrence.

I hadn't had the opportunity much less the time to shower or wash my hair in over three days and I was covered in dust and dirt, straw, cedar shavings and sweat. I ate whatever my mother put together and ferried down to the barn for me; dropping off paper cartons of carry-out food and flats of bottled water. I was exhausted and coughing as I stood in Odie's stall late one afternoon; bent over with Odie's rear hoof between my legs and held on my knees. A most unladylike position. I was picking clods of dirt and straw out of his hooves with a hoof pick and quietly talking to him; trying to reassure him he was on the mend when suddenly he shifted his weight unexpectedly, and reared, nearly knocking me to the concrete floor.

Dropping his hoof with a thud, I looked up and over Odie's rump to see what or who had caused Odie's sudden movement, a curse already forming on my lips. There he stood, at ease, my persistent caller, I assumed, who wouldn't take no for an answer, his arms casually outstretched on either side of the stall door.

"Hey! What is wrong with you? Never – ever sneak up behind a horse! Especially one confined to a stall! You could have gotten me killed! I shouted."

"That would be my loss." He quietly answered.

"You obviously don't know the first thing about horses!"

"You're right. This is the closest I've ever been to a horse."

"The office is closed for the day. What do you want?"

"Jory – we had a date, remember? Your cell is either off or dead. When you didn't show up, I called the house and your mother told me I would find you here."

He was very tall; well over six feet and strikingly handsome with blond hair, intense, ice blue eyes; eyes bluer than mine, and a pixie smile that would rival Pucks with a deep dimple in his right cheek.

"I don't mean to criticize this early in our relationship but you look like...?" He started.

"What relationship?" I said, as I rolled my eyes.

"The relationship I'd like to have – starting now. The relationship we should have had over six years ago. I've waited this long for you. I don't intend to wait any longer. I've heard what you've been through and I can tell you, if I ever run into that bastard, I'll shoot him where he stands."

"That's very gallante . I appreciate your concern and I support your intentions wholeheartedly. I'm very flattered but I'm afraid you'll have to get in line behind my father and my brother. My father is wielding a shot gun these days and my brother is currently researching caustic chemical combinations. If there's anything left when they finish with him, you'll welcome to it." I said. Now very curious about this stranger who was beginning to look vaguely familiar. Who are you?

Looking at me, still with a smile on his face, he said, "If your horse is feeling better, maybe we could get away for awhile. Is chocolate chip cookie dough still your favorite? As it happens, I know just the place." He replied.

I stood there, and just starred at him, completely unaware of just how disheveled I must be. Then I felt my heart start and jump and slowly sputter back to life as he stood in the stall doorway, ram-rod straight and in full, dress Army uniform. I smiled at him and he smiled at me and we stood there smiling at each other.

Be still my heart.

Epilogue

I never spoke to Nat again. Within the next few weeks, he sent me two texts. The first to ask if I found life worth living without him and the last to pledge his eternal friendship. I deleted both without responding. If he thought he had destroyed me, he was wrong. If he hoped to hope to break my spirit or my heart, he was wrong again. If anything, I am stronger.

Less than six months later, he sent a FaceBook photo. They had been married on 11.12.13 in a civil ceremony in the old, whitewashed, clapboard, Russell County Courthouse in Southern Virginia. There she stood, radiant and triumphant in a faded, dime-store gingham dress, scruffy cowboy boots and her ponytail swinging. The not-so blushing bride, a very seven months pregnant, holding his hand and clutching a handful of daisies in the other.

She had won the first prize through guile and deceit. Betrayal and justice now hand in hand.

About The Author

Stella Benson currently resides in Carmel-by-the-Sea, California with her family, her horses and her dogs.

Printed in the USA
CPSIA information can be obtained
at www.ICGtesting.com
LVHW051137041023
760081LV00014B/285/J